SECRETS & CURSES OF FATE

Shay Taylor

Westwind Publishing LLC

CONTENTS

For those who love what others fear—because sometimes the soul longs for the monster who sees us, not the hero who saves us.

<u>***Hierarchy Of Elloryon***</u>

The Heavens

Old Gods & Goddesses

The Stars

Gods & Goddesses

Elite Magic Fae; Witches

Fae with magic

Mundane or Magicless beings

Please be advised that this story contains heavy themes that may be triggering for some readers, including but not limited to:

Violence, cursing, physical and mental abuse, treason, torture, killing, gore, death, religious context (sin, rebirth, gods & goddesses), kidnapping, blood, manipulation, betrayal, mental health issues (depression, suicidal thoughts and behaviors, anxiety, trauma), fighting, lying, sacrifice, and explicit sexual content.

SEA OF VOID
AKECIA
KIZAR
FALGON
BLOOD WITCH
COVEN
EXILE
CRIMSON
FORBIDDEN
WOOD
ELLORYON
SEA OF VOID
ISLANDS OF
DEATH

CHAPTER 1

DELLA; 293 YEARS AGO

I tilted my head, as if a different angle might change what I was seeing. My mate was kissing a pretty, blonde-haired woman—the same one he'd been with every day I came to see him. I took in everything about how his eyes softened when he looked at her and how his hands lingered when he touched her. I'd been coming to Kizar every day for two weeks, ever since I stumbled upon him by accident. His dark blonde hair was chaotic as she ran her hands through it. She deepened the kiss, and a small sliver of confusion passed through me.

I wanted to know what that was like. He pulled back and smiled, tucking her hair behind her ear. He was in love with this woman. The love for her was undeniable in his stormy blue eyes. My mate already belonged to another. I was too late.

This should hurt my feelings. I should want to kill this woman. But I was more confused about how little it upset me. He was supposed to be mine. I did not want to share him. So why wasn't I more upset seeing him kiss someone else?

"I love you," he said softly.

The woman stilled at his confession. I knew that if she said it back, I wouldn't ruin his happiness. My heart pounded as I waited for her answer. She touched his cheek, her finger tracing over the curve of his jaw.

"I love you, too."

My mating bond burned at her words. I waited my entire existence for him. My eyes stung as tears spilled out. My sudden grief had the sky ripping open, making rain pour down onto the two of them as they started to kiss. Lightning scattered across the sky as rage filled my chest. My mate and the woman began laughing at the sudden change of weather, unaware it was my heartbreak.

He stood, pulling her with him, and twirled as they began dancing. I was unable to turn away, as this sick display of love exploited my pain. I did not understand why the heavens made my mate love another. Was it because he hasn't seen me yet? Maybe that is why he thinks he loves her instead of me. Hope slowly crept into my chest as I watched them dance.

The sun began to set, and he would be heading home soon. I would find a way for our paths to cross so that he could see that I was his, not this woman. I smiled to myself as I vanished and reappeared closer to his home. His family home was quaint—not oversized, but not small either. I had seen his parents once. Both of them seemed so kind that I hoped my mate would be just as nice. I scanned the street, searching for the perfect excuse to cross his path.

Maybe I would pose as a seller or fall—so he would stop to help me. My mind raced with ideas as I muttered to myself. I began pacing back and forth, my heart pounding, my thoughts scattering. I had to do this perfectly so he would feel our connection immediately.

I wanted my mate, even if the connection was not snapping into place like it should. His stormy eyes and dark blonde hair filled my thoughts. He was handsome, and hope filled my chest that he would find me pretty. But first, I needed to kickstart this damn bond inside of me to wake its ass up and claim him from the woman he thought he loved.

I would show him what love actually was. I stopped pacing and began practicing falling so it looked natural—not desperate. I pretended to trip over my feet, but what if he thought I was clumsy? So, I practiced tripping over a rock

I tossed on the ground. After a few attempts, I felt dumb, so I stopped.

"This is so damn stupid. Why is this so fucking difficult?" I asked no one in particular. I shook my arms, trying to loosen the tension in my body. I could do this. My mate would love me. I had not waited an eternity for him to belong to someone else. He belonged to me.

I would fight her if I needed to.

"Get a grip on yourself," I said out loud. "You can do this. It's simple. You've done harder things than talking to a man before."

But none of them had to do with my mate. I should not have to convince him to pick me over another woman. He was only supposed to be attracted to me, unless everything we knew about mates was wrong.

"That's ridiculous," I scoffed. I turned to take my place—only to find him already there, smiling softly. His hand was resting on the gate to his family's yard. Gods, I hadn't even heard him come up. I stilled. He could see me.

"Are you alright?" he said with amusement. His stormy blue eyes met mine, and I swallowed hard. Fuck, how much did he see?

"Umm." I glanced down at my dress, which was covered in dust from my fake falling. When I looked up, he had a full smile. Fuck, he was more handsome this close.

"Is there a reason you kept falling for no reason? Do you need a healer?" His deep voice wrapped around me like a hug.

"I... really don't know how to answer that." My cheeks heated. His eyes drifted over my face like he was admiring what he was seeing. My heart pounded, hoping he liked what he saw.

"You seem very familiar." He tilted his head to the side. "What's your name?"

His hand dropped from the gate as he took a step toward me. I smiled at the gesture; maybe his mating bond was telling him to come near me. I didn't understand how he saw me right now when he hadn't noticed me once in the past two weeks.

"Ardella," I said with a nervous smile.

I glanced over his tall frame; his dark blonde hair was shorter than I realized earlier and messy, like he'd been running his fingers through it.

"Are you lost?" he asked.

"I think I'm exactly where I should be."

He stepped closer and glanced around, checking if anyone else was nearby. He stopped a few feet in front of me. He smelled good, like a frosty morning in winter. Gods, he was taller than he looked from a distance, too. I craned my neck back and looked up at him.

"Tell me why you're out here tripping and talking to yourself."

I blushed at his question. Gods, this was fucking embarrassing. His eyes stared intently at me as if he already knew this was a ploy to talk to him.

"I was trying to find an excuse to get you to notice me." I decided to be honest. He cocked his head to the side, watching me.

"You've seen me before?" he asked.

"Yes, but you haven't noticed me." My voice was barely audible.

He frowned slightly.

"I don't know how I could have missed you."

His words hit low in my gut—warm and sharp. He was flirting with me. Gods, I didn't know what to say to him. He glanced at his home before looking back at me, hesitating for a moment.

"I was going to grab something up the street. Do you want to come?"

I looked around us before staring at him.

"Unless you actually hurt yourself falling like that," he said with a grin.

I narrowed my eyes at him.

"Let's go." I turned and started walking but stopped when I didn't hear him following behind me. He was bit-ing his lip to stop smiling. I swallowed hard at how cute he looked.

"This way." He tilted his head in the opposite direction I was going. Heat crept up my neck again. But I lifted my chin in defiance and walked past him. He was quick to move next to me.

"This was a pleasant surprise," he said with a smile. "I thought today was going to be boring."

I chuckled softly.

"Well, it certainly took me by surprise." I looked over at him as he stared at me intently. I thought today was going to be a regular day. I didn't expect that my mate and I would finally talk. We walked in silence for a moment, and there was nothing awkward about it.

"Are you always so quiet?" he asked.

"Only when I am nervous."

"Do I make you nervous?"

"Yes." I peeked up at him, then quickly looked away toward the vendors lining the path. We walked past quite a few of them, and he hadn't even glanced in their direction. Maybe he was looking for something specific.

"So, what are you looking for?" I asked as the end of the vendor carts drew closer. He glanced over at the carts before looking back at me, rubbing the back of his neck and chuckling softly.

"I didn't actually need anything. I just wanted an excuse for you to stay a little longer."

"Oh." My face was on fire. I did not know how to respond to him.

We awkwardly turned back around and started for his home. He kept looking at me—watching me like he was trying to figure me out. When our eyes met, I gave him a small, shy smile.

"I was just about to eat dinner; do you want to join me?"

"Really?" I gawked. "You don't know me."

He paused for a moment as if he were thinking of something.

"I don't understand why that phrase seems so wrong, but I feel like I've known you for my entire life." Gods, I was not expecting him to be so forward with me. He always seemed so timid when I watched him from afar. Maybe his mating bond was making him brave. "You don't have to stay if it makes you uncomfortable."

"No, I would love to," I said too quickly.

He chuckled softly as he nodded for me to follow him. He pushed open the wooden gate, holding it open for me. I slipped past him, brushing dust from my black dress. He walked next to me, and I could feel his gaze, but I was too nervous to look up.

I didn't realize the mating bond would snap so suddenly, that he would want to spend time with me immediately. Not that I was complaining. I was desperate to learn everything I could about him.

When we walked into the house, I was pleasantly surprised by how bright and homey the space was. It was bigger on the inside than it appeared from the street. The comforting feeling of this home was unlike anything I had experienced before. Mine and Mikel's home was nice and large but not comforting in the same way this was.

I followed along as he walked through a sitting room and toward the sound of clanking dishes. I froze. This was his parents' home. We weren't going to be alone. He stopped and looked back at me.

"What's wrong?"

"I just realized that there will be others."

"There is no reason to be worried. My parents are the nicest fae you will ever meet."

It wasn't them being mean I was worried about—it was me embarrassing myself.

"Won't they think it's odd that you're bringing home a stranger?"

"Yes, but not for the reason you think," he said with a chuckle.

He reached for my hand, causing a warmth to spread through me. I glanced up at him.

"It'll be alright," he said, smiling gently.

I nodded, and he didn't drop my hand; he only squeezed it tightly in his and tugged me along with him. When we entered the next room, there was a mid-sized dining table next to a spacious kitchen. His parents had their backs toward us.

They were talking softly before they both laughed loudly at whatever joke they shared between themselves. His father was tall like him, and his mother was small and petite beside him. Her dark hair tumbled down her back in tight curls. His father must have heard us because he turned, and I could not believe how much they looked alike. His dark blonde hair matched my mate's, but he had dark brown eyes. He looked between the two of us, and then our hands connected. His wife seemed to notice his silence and turned to see what he was staring at. Her pretty, stormy blue eyes stared at both of us. Her mouth fell open before shutting quickly, like this was the last thing she expected.

Gods, did they know he was seeing that blonde woman? I dropped my hand quickly from his. I didn't want them to think I was a mistress or something. My face was burning with worry. Did they like his girlfriend? I had not seen her come here, but that didn't mean they didn't know about her.

"Haden, you brought a guest." His mom smiled brightly.

Haden. I had not heard his name yet. Him and the blonde woman just called each other baby or sweetheart. Shit, I was jealous now that I talked with him. I was upset that he had kissed that woman and told her he loved her. Betrayal was pumping through me. He shouldn't have desired anyone else but me. I wasn't getting any of his firsts, and he would get all of mine.

"This is Ardella. Can she join us tonight?"

His parents practically ran over to us and smiled brightly.

"Of course," his mom gushed. "I am Penelope, and this is my husband, Henry." She hesitated when I put out my hand to shake hers, instead stepping forward and pulling me to her for a tight hug. "We are a hugging family." She smiled, and Henry laughed when I looked terrified.

"Gosh, you are so pretty," she cooed, and I felt my face heat even more.

"Mother, you're scaring her," Haden said.

"I'm sorry, we just thought you would never bring someone home to meet us." She beamed, and Henry pulled her away from us and back to the kitchen with an apologetic look. I looked at Haden, and he smiled. His hand came to rest on my lower back as he led me to the dining table. He pulled out the chair for me, and I sat down. Haden slid into the seat next to me, and his eyes softened at my terrified expression. Is this how all families are?

"You look like you might bolt," he laughed. "My mother has waited for this moment since I was old enough to date. Let's not disappoint her," he challenged me.

My throat tightened.

"Maybe you shouldn't have brought me then. Shouldn't you want to save this for someone special? You don't know me at all."

"Something tells me that you will be very special, Ardella," he said as he picked up his drink and sipped it. Gods, his mating bond must be going crazy to want me this close already.

"Your parents seem wonderful." I changed the topic. "You are lucky."

He glanced over at me and grinned before looking into the kitchen to see his parents spying on us. They quickly pretended to be busy so it wasn't obvious they were watching. I looked back at Haden.

"So, you've never brought a girl home? What about girl-friends?" I wondered if he would tell me about the blonde woman he said he loved only an hour ago.

"I've not dated anyone. No one ever really caught my eye."

I wanted to press the issue because he was lying, but his parents set down the food, which smelled so good. I glanced over the roast, bread, and vegetables. Haden helped me get a plate before his parents both bowed their heads.

"Thanks to the gods for a wonderful life full of health and love," they said in unison. I stared at them because I did not know that the fae expressed gratitude in this way. My chest was tight with emotion as I watched them. Haden was observing me closely as I took my first bite. Shit, this was good.

"So where did you two meet?" Penelope asked.

Haden looked at me with amusement when I froze.

"Ardella fell, and I helped her." He had a mischievous glint in his eye. I relaxed slightly when I met his gaze.

"I'm pretty clumsy." I smiled at Haden. "Haden was very nice."

He watched me as his parents beamed. Why was he staring so much? I raised my eyebrow at him, and he seemed to snap out of whatever trance he was in.

"What do you two do for a living?" I asked as I took a bite of everything on the plate. Gods, they were wonderful cooks.

"I'm a healer in the village, and Henry is an artist." Penelope looked behind me. "All the artwork in here is his."

I glanced behind me at the paintings of nature and animals. They were so well done that you could hardly tell that it was a painting. I had always wished I was artistic, but I could not do anything of the sort.

"They are beautiful."

"Thank you. What do you do?" Henry asked.

Shit.

I couldn't tell them I was a goddess. I hesitated for a moment before the lie blurted from me.

"I am a maid." I glanced at my plate, feeling guilty for the lie. They didn't say anything for a moment before Haden filled the silence.

"I am a builder," he said. "I build houses."

"You didn't tell her about your job before?" Henry asked. His friendly eyes filled with confusion as he looked between the two of us.

"No, we just met outside before dinner," Haden admitted as he took a bite of his food.

My eyes widened. His parents were silent, and I glanced up at them. Haden was grinning at me.

"Don't worry, Ardella. My parents aren't judging us. They got married after knowing each other for two days." He looked at his parents. "Right?"

"When you know, you know." Penelope smiled as she glanced between the two of us. I relaxed when Haden's hand rested next to mine on the table.

"We always told our children that sometimes the right thing happens at the exact right moment, and time does not matter." Henry looked at his wife and gave her a kiss.

I looked at Haden as he studied me closely. I did not know our mating bond would make us feel this way so quickly. I suppose it made sense. The heavens knew we were meant for each other. His eyes drifted over my face and down to my mouth before meeting my eyes again. Something in his eyes made my insides melt with anticipation.

"Everyone told us that we didn't know each other well enough to get married. They said we would regret it. Now look at us." Henry glanced at each one of us. "Although Haden has always been the skeptical one about finding true love."

My gaze snapped to Haden.

"Really?" I asked.

"Yes." His eyes filled with a look I didn't know how to decipher. "Don't worry, I think I am changing my mind on the matter."

My eyes widened with how forward he was being. But gods, I liked how confident he was. I turned back to my plate of food and finished. Mikel and I really needed to figure out how to cook better.

As soon as we were done eating, they began clearing the table, and I stood to help.

"We've got it," Henry insisted. "Haden, you should show her the plans you're making for the house you want to build." Henry looked at me. "Haden is only living here until he can get his house built."

"I would love to see it." I smiled at him.

He looked at his parents and gave them a look like he knew they were up to something. He stood and held his hand out for me. I took it, and Haden led me up the stairs to a small bedroom. I knew it was his immediately—it smelled like him. There was a desk overfilled with plans and paper, and his walls had sketches pinned on them. But the rest of the room was tidy.

He just stood at the doorway with me, holding my hand and letting me take in everything. I stepped toward the desk, eager to learn about this home he had envisioned for himself. Honestly, I was just so nervous that I needed to do something with my hands so I didn't stand awkwardly. Haden walked with me, not letting go of my hand. I reached out with my free hand and started to trace my finger over the plans for the house sitting on top. It was a large home with open living spaces and a second story. I looked at the picture of the outside he had drawn and colored. It was dark wood, with lovely stone accents and big windows.

"It's a large home." I glanced over my shoulder at him.

"I plan on having a big family." He smiled.

I averted my gaze from him as I bit my lip nervously. A big family. I never gave much thought to my life after I met my mate. I didn't think about children or the type of home we would share. But now that I had seen a glimpse of what he pictured, I realized how badly I wanted all of that. Haden squeezed my hand softly until I looked at him.

"Why did you come here today?" he asked.

"What do you mean?"

"You said you have seen me before and wanted to speak with me. Why did you decide that today was the day to approach to me?"

I would rather not tell him that I heard him and that woman exchanging heartfelt words or that he was my mate.

"It just felt like it was time. I just wondered if you would feel the same about me."

He moved slightly forward, easing the embarrassment of my oversharing.

"And what do you feel?"

"A strong connection to you," I said honestly.

He smiled softly.

"Me too. But I have to come clean about something." He looked over at me. "I have seen you around for two weeks, Ardella. I told myself this morning that if I saw you again, I would talk to you. Imagine my surprise when I find you standing outside of my family's home. It's like our paths were meant to cross today."

He had seen me before and was drawn to me. My heart was racing. His gaze dropped to my mouth. This was overwhelming. I was feeling all sorts of things toward him that I didn't understand. Where were all of these feelings these past two weeks? Being this close to him was... different.

"You can kiss me if you like," I said, feeling confident in the way he was watching me.

Haden dropped my hand and pulled me to him; his fingers slowly moved the hair from my face and skimmed over my cheek before grabbing my face on both sides and leaning in closer. Our lips met softly, but it ignited a fire inside of me. Haden pulled back and stared at me like he didn't know why a simple kiss felt like that.

We both rushed toward each other at the same time. Our mouths clashed as we deepened the kiss. Haden held me against him with one hand on my lower back and the other on the back of my neck. I ran my fingers through his hair as his tongue swept across my lips, and I parted them to let him in. He hummed as our kiss quickly became desperate.

A sudden loud crashing downstairs made us pull apart and look at the bedroom door.

"What was that?" I asked, out of breath.

"I have no idea." He looked back at me and gave me one last lingering kiss. "Let's go." He grabbed my hand and dragged me downstairs with him.

CHAPTER 2

DELLA

When we entered the kitchen, his parents looked at us.

"Sorry, your brother dropped his cup," Penelope said as she narrowed her eyes on someone to my right.

I glanced at Haden's brother before dropping his hand immediately as if it burned me. There was another Haden sitting at the table. He looked up, and I froze, blinking as if that might clear the confusion blurring everything. I scanned his face—same mouth, same jawline—but not the same. This version of him was a little different. His eyes were lighter. Still stormy, but not *Haden's* storm.

My *mate* was sitting at the table with the blonde woman.

I turned to look at Haden beside me, taking in his face like I'd never really seen it. He was taller, and his hair was shorter. His face had harsher features than his brother's did. His expression… concerned.

"Ardella, this is my twin brother, Holden, and his girlfriend, Sara." Haden smiled, but when I just stared at him, his smile faded. "You look like you've seen a ghost."

I was trying to find a response, but I couldn't. My gaze bounced between the two of them as my pulse pounded in my ears. Haden's eyebrows pinched together, growing more concerned by the second.

"I didn't know you had a twin," I barely whispered as my focus went to Holden.

Holden's eyes met mine. I held my breath.

Please don't let it be him.

A faint tug stirred in my chest—barely there, like a thread pulling at the edge of a seam. It wasn't like what I felt with Haden. It wasn't even close. Holden stood and offered a polite smile. His girlfriend, Sara, stepped forward and hugged me—warm, sweet, undeserved.

My world had just imploded, and everyone else was acting like nothing had changed.

"I didn't know Haden was dating anyone. It's so nice to meet you." Gods, she was friendly. I should want to punch her or something for having my mate. Holden tugged me into an embrace, and I stiffened uncomfortably. My mating bond hummed at his touch, but I recoiled from it. I didn't like this. Confusion slammed into me. This wasn't normal.

"It's nice to meet you, Ardella." Holden smiled. There was no flicker of emotion or mating bond reaction from him. Relief spread through me as he didn't seem to feel anything toward me. But it was short-lived when I realized how wrong it was. Holden was my mate and should feel drawn to me. But it wasn't him I was fucking kissing minutes ago; it was his twin brother, who was not my mate.

I glanced at Haden to make sure I wasn't mistaken. Maybe I had been following the wrong brother around. But my heart sank slowly because I knew without a doubt that Haden was not who I shared a mating bond with. When I glanced at Holden, I could see the soft golden bond between us. It was like a small string, glowing brightly. It stretched from his chest all the way to mine. My gaze assessed it to see if there was a crack or tear within it that was making it not work properly.

Nothing—there was absolutely nothing wrong with it.

My hands were trembling as a cold sweat broke across my skin. I couldn't breathe—or think. My thoughts shattered into millions of tiny shards of glass, impossible to piece back together where this made any logical sense. Haden knew something was wrong with me as his hand came forward and gripped mine. Terror coiled inside of me as I yanked my hand from his.

I needed to leave.

"It's nice to meet you, Sara and Holden," I said softly. The heavens had to have made a mistake. I turned to Haden. "I have to go. Thank you all for such a lovely night." My voice cracked with my panic.

"What? But..." he started to say, but I practically ran from him. I could hear him following me, but I didn't slow down.

"Ardella," Haden called out. I was losing my fucking mind. "Ardella, please stop." The desperation in his voice made me stop and turn to him. His face fell when he saw I was upset. The light that had been in his eyes earlier had dimmed. I felt bad that I was the cause, but my world felt shattered. My shoulders sagged with disappointment because he wasn't mine. He was the one I wanted.

"What's wrong?"

"Nothing."

"Liar." He frowned. "Something freaked you out in there, and now you're running."

I closed my eyes tightly because I couldn't wrap my mind around what was happening. I did not have a mating bond with Haden, but I felt more connected to him than his damn brother. I opened my eyes, and Haden was begging me with his eyes to stay.

"I forgot I have to do something," I said lamely, my words failing to do my emotions justice.

Haden slowly moved toward me. His eyes glanced around frantically, like he would find something to make me stay.

"Is it because I kissed you?" he asked. "I'm sorry, but don't you feel it too? This connection we have."

"No, it's not because you kissed me," I said softly.

His eyes took in whatever emotion was on my face and looked disappointed. I'm sure he could see that I wanted out of there. I wanted to run away and hide from whatever this was.

"You'll come back to see me?" He asked, hopeful.

His words made my chest squeeze. He wasn't supposed to be mine. According to my mating bond, the heavens had made me for his brother. What if the bond just hadn't snapped completely into place? I didn't want to lead Haden on. His shoulders slumped in defeat when I didn't answer.

"I hope you will come back to see me," he tried again. His sad voice tugged at my heart. There was a tension in the air that made it hard to concentrate on my bond issue.

I wanted to make Haden feel better because I did not like the look he was giving me right now.

"Maybe."

I stepped forward and hugged him to me. His arms wrapped around me, holding me tightly like I would float away if he loosened his grip. This felt right. I had not felt like this when Holden hugged me. I closed my eyes and buried my face into him, wanting to sear this moment into my memory forever. When I pulled back, Haden's eyes seemed impossibly dark.

"Is it because we don't know each other, but this already feels so right?" he asked.

Without knowing what else to say, I simply whispered, "Yes."

He smiled and kissed my forehead.

"No reason to be scared, Ardella. Maybe this is our destiny. Maybe our fate was to meet."

His words crushed me. I leaned forward and kissed him softly before I stepped back. My eyes did not leave his as I summoned my star mist, and it twisted its way around me. The silvery glow lit up the street where Haden and I stood.

"Please, come back," he begged softly as I disappeared.

When my magic moved away from me, I was standing in my bedroom. My throat was tight with emotion. This was never supposed to happen. Immediately, I went to find my brother, Mikel. I walked through our home that now felt cold and sterile since being at Haden's welcoming house. Mikel was in the sitting room with one of the books he was always reading. He glanced up at me, his matching star-colored eyes widening with concern at the sight of me.

"Ardella, what is wrong?" He stood up. My brother towered over me. His black hair was perfectly styled, and his clothes were way too fancy for a man who never left this house. I walked to him and pulled him to me for a hug. He immediately wrapped his arms around me for comfort. I didn't know what to say to him. It felt wrong to tell him that I didn't *want* my mate. Mikel wouldn't understand; he wouldn't know how to help me.

"I had a terrible dream." I lied.

He frowned as we both sat down on the couch. Mikel looked more worried when he saw tears falling down my cheeks.

"Fuck, Ardella, was it that bad?" He wiped my tears from me.

"What if we get a mate and we do not want them?" I asked.

Mikel stared at me oddly, then he began laughing. My jaw clenched tightly at his reaction.

"You don't need to worry about that. The heavens make sure we get someone best suited for us. Is that what your nightmare was?"

"Yes," I whispered. "What happens if we find our mate and they are already in love with someone or have a family? Are we supposed to expect them to destroy their lives for us?"

Mikel's eyes roamed over me. There was a flicker of suspicion in them.

"That is impossible. Our mates are made for us, and us for them. Why is this worrying you?"

I glanced at my hands in my lap. Holden should want me and only me. I should not want Haden. Something was wrong with us. This did not feel like fate. It felt like hell.

"I don't know. We just wait so damn long that I worry something will go wrong. What if that did happen; could we choose someone else? Can the bond transfer? Do we not get a mate if they reject us? Can we reject them?"

Mikel's hand squeezed mine until I looked up at him. Shit, there was definitely concern in his eyes.

"Did you meet your mate?"

"No," I lied without thought, which was strange. I had never lied to my brother before. He was my best friend; he would help me. But part of me felt guilty for not wanti-ng Holden. My brother had always talked about what he wanted in a mate. He always sounded so excited about it. I, on the other hand, hardly thought about it because I didn't want to drive myself crazy wondering how long it would be until I met him.

Mikel always had his whole life figured out. He couldn't wait to find his mate, get married, and have children. Mikel was made to be a husband and father. He said it was his purpose. How could I tell him that not only had I found my mate first but that I did not want him? What if he became worried that his mate would do the same thing that mine did? There was no way I could put that stress on him. I didn't want to crush his dreams. So, I kept my secret to myself.

"The heavens will take care of us, Ardella. Our mates will be everything we want and more."

I nodded as he hugged me. I only needed to spend a few hours with Haden to know that he was what I wanted, what I needed. I had followed Holden around for weeks and seen him with Sara, but it did not elicit anything significant within me. Haden made me feel things I did not know were possible in such a short time. The thought of Haden with another female, though, instantly pissed me off. I pulled away from Mikel and gave him a soft smile, doing my best to mask my emotions.

"You're right. It was just a terrible nightmare," I said, hoping to drop this uncomfortable topic.

He stared at me for a long moment. "Do you want me to read to you?"

I nodded and settled on the couch as Mikel's soft voice drifted into the silence of our home. I closed my eyes and tried to relax, but all I could think of was Haden kissing me. I shoved the thoughts of him away, determined to focus on my mate. Holden was obviously picked by the heavens for me for a reason. I would find a way for my bond with Holden to snap into place. For that to work, though, I needed to avoid Haden.

CHAPTER 3

HADEN

I stared at the spot where Ardella disappeared from after using her odd magic, waiting for longer than necessary to see if she was going to come back. Gods, I desperately wished she would have stayed longer. Something had scared her away. Maybe it was too fast for her—meeting me and my entire family. But she was fine until she saw my brother and Sara. Why would that have made her so tense?

Taking a deep breath, I got ready for the onslaught of questions that would be coming. I stepped inside, and my entire family was waiting in the sitting room. My mother's eyes glanced behind me with a frown. My father's friendly eyes were gleaming with excitement at meeting Ardella.

"Did she leave?" Her shoulders slumped.

"Yes," I said with a sigh.

"Do you think we scared her off?" Holden asked.

I shrugged and stared at my loving, overbearing family and grinned. She would fit in well with us. They all stared at me, wanting me to say something, but I didn't know where to start. I didn't think I would meet her today; my vision showed her coming in a few weeks. The details surrounding her were still fuzzy at best. I also couldn't see everything that would happen between us, but I saw enough to know she was for me. Ardella was the one I had been waiting for—the heart that beat in rhythm with mine, the soul that filled the missing pieces of mine.

"Gods, Haden," my mother sighed. "She is the woman from your vision, isn't it? The one you ask to marry you?"

I smiled brightly.

"Yes."

"Well, she was great." My father smiled. "She's going to fit in well with us."

My family began talking about her, and it made my longing for her more intense. Growing up, I hardly had any visions, and if I did, they were insignificant. But all of my visions of Ardella had shown me a future that I was desperate for.

I don't know if it was because I prayed to the stars to show me what woman I was supposed to end up with, but the vision came to me in a dream that very night. She didn't know it yet, but we were about to fall madly in love with one another. But I could feel her hesitation tonight after the kiss. Maybe she thought it was too soon to feel things so quickly. How did I explain to her that I saw where we were headed and it was beautiful?

"Are you going to tell her about your visions?" Sara asked.

"Maybe." My family all looked so happy for me.

"Well, she seemed to be completely taken with you," my mother said.

I hoped so. She had finally sought me out today, after I had seen her sneaking around the village for weeks. I still had no idea what she was doing, but she had acted as if no one could see her. But I could.

"Are you going to tell her that you know she is a goddess? The poor girl looked terrified when we asked her what she did," my father said with a worried look.

I hadn't thought about how difficult it would be for her to answer basic questions. Ardella was trying to blend in with the fae in the village, but she never could. I would have known she was heaven-sent even if I hadn't seen her confess to me in a vision that she is a goddess. She was too pretty to be anything other than a woman that others bowed to.

I knew that she wouldn't be back for a few days. She was running from this feeling.

"No, I will get her to confess it to me so she doesn't feel like she has to be dishonest. She will tell me when she is ready."

"I can't believe the stars thought my little brother should be destined for a goddess," Holden joked. Younger by minutes, but he never let me forget it.

"Jealous?" I smiled.

He grabbed onto Sara and gave her a kiss on the cheek.

"I've got my own goddess right here."

Sara rolled her eyes. "Please, don't say strange shit like that." Her cheeks heated as my brother smiled at her. "It's so corny."

"I'm sorry," he chuckled.

"Well, I'm going to go to bed. Thanks for not scaring her too much. Now let's hope she comes back soon." I smiled as I headed up the stairs to my bedroom. I couldn't wait until the home I was building was done and I could move there—we moved there. I had seen Della and me together, living in that house. It was ours.

I walked over to the drawing of the house Ardella traced earlier. My heart had nearly fallen out of my chest when I thought she was going to pick it up. Slowly, I lifted the picture, and my drawing of Della from my vision lay under it. Gods, I could not stop smiling. Della was finally here, and I couldn't wait to see my visions come to life.

☽★★★☽★★★☽

I was walking home from work when I spotted Della sneaking around the street like a thief. She didn't see me, as she seemed engrossed with something else. Glancing around to make sure no one else noticed her, I decided to follow her. Gods, she seemed focused on something, but I couldn't see what it was. I moved quicker so I could see who she was stalking. A frown tilted my lips when I realized it was Holden she was watching. Why was she following him? Was that why she became strange after he showed up? She wanted Holden and not me. A pang of jealousy spiked in my chest before I thought about it rationally.

She probably thought it was me. Holden and I were fairly similar, but I thought she would be able to tell the difference. I walked up to her slowly so she wouldn't hear me and watched her for a moment before her body stiffened. I smiled because I knew she sensed me behind her. She turned quickly, and her pretty, star-colored eyes widened, and her pouty mouth fell open. Inappropriate thoughts flashed in my mind, showing me how pretty she would look when she came. My jaw clenched as I exhaled through my nose, hoping to tame those images.

Fuck.

I looked away from her so that I could control the vision of her being a pleading mess below me. Shit. Fuck. There was a heat creeping up my neck as visions of Della begging me to make her cum started taking over my mind. Fucking hell. My hands fisted at my sides as I tried to not have a physical reaction to the vision.

"Haden," she breathed, and it did not help my desire coiling within me. Slowly, I opened my eyes and stared at her. I could not help admiring how damn pretty she was with flushed cheeks and wide, innocent eyes—but I knew better. Della was nowhere near innocent. The woman could bring me to my knees with the filthy things that fell from that perfect mouth of hers. She may be a goddess, but there was nothing holy about what she did and said to me in my visions. That mouth and body were made for sin.

"Haden?" She tried again, and I snapped out of my intense thoughts.

"So, you do know it's me." I raised my brow at her.

"What do you mean?"

I looked behind her to where Holden was talking to a street vendor. She didn't even turn to see who I was looking at. Her bronze skin flushed red, and I had to look away from her again.

"I was spying," she said.

"Why on Holden?" My tone was clearly not amused.

Ardella looked up at me with wide eyes as I crossed my arms over my chest.

"I thought it was you at first, but then I realized it was Holden. Then I started wondering if you two were similar to one another."

"And what did you find out?"

"You two are nothing alike," she huffed. "Aren't twins supposed to be similar to one another? You two don't look the same, and your personalities are different."

"You don't know me," I challenged, and something about that made defiance flare in her eyes.

"I know enough." Her snarky attitude made me smile. Oh, I liked her sassiness. "Quit looking at me like that."

"Like what?"

"I don't know, whatever that look means." She swallowed hard.

I didn't stop because she liked it. Her pupils dilated as she watched me. I don't think she realized she took a step toward me.

"Are you grumpy today?" I asked.

She frowned slightly as she thought of her response. "Yes."

"So, Della, are you going to share with me how Holden and I are different and why you care?"

She scoffed like it was a stupid idea. I couldn't help but smile. Della crossed her arms over her chest and stared at me with stubbornness.

"I'm waiting." My tone was demanding.

Her defiance melted away as she watched me. Did she prefer the way Holden looked? We were similar but definitely different. Is that why she was refusing to answer me? She didn't want to hurt my feelings. Too bad for her that Holden would never leave Sara, and I would never allow it. She was mine.

"You are taller than him. Your chin is at the perfect height to rest on the top of my head if I am not wearing heels. His eyes are a lighter blue, but yours are a captivating, stormy color. Holden has talked to every street vendor and their mother, so I'm assuming it's safe to say he enjoys others' company. You strike me as the type that doesn't mind being alone. Especially after you said you never dated before."

I opened my mouth to say something, but she cut me off.

"I'm not finished." Her eyes narrowed on me, and I shut the hell up. "Holden is more outgoing, but he also seems more timid. You are confident, but it is not a typical confidence. You are comfortable with who you are, and you like things a certain way. But with me, you seem to be *very* confident. It makes me wonder if you are like that with all women. Holden is more timid with Sara—gentle in a way where you are...rough, or maybe rugged is the right word."

For fuck's sake, how long had she been stalking around the village today to learn all of that?

I saw the way her eyes flared when she mentioned me being confident around other women. "I'm not, like, that with other women. I know you didn't like thinking that maybe I do this with everyone. You have all my attention, Della."

She stared at me oddly.

"You're very observant."

"Only when something interests me." She smiled.

"I really hope you are referring to me and not my brother."

Her eyes widened.

"He has a girlfriend, and I kissed you."

My gaze dropped to her mouth, and she let out a long exhale. Gods, she was so damn pretty that my chest ached when I looked at her.

"Have you thought about the kiss?"

Immediately her gaze was moving away from mine. She had.

"Have you?" she asked timidly. Oh, she didn't want to seem too eager.

"Every day for the past three days," I confessed, hoping she would do the same. She met my gaze, and her eyes flashed pure white for only a fraction of a second. Fuck.

"I've thought about it a little bit."

Liar.

"I was thinking we should kiss again."

"Why?" She tried to sound appalled, but her eyes were giving her away. They dropped to my mouth and did not look away.

"Well, for one, you want to, and I want to. Secondly, I think you are downplaying how good that kiss was."

"I never said it was bad," she said weakly.

"Okay, fine. Then let's kiss because I really want to again."

She looked around as if someone were watching us. I stepped forward slowly, giving her time to tell me to stop. But she froze in her spot when I was finally flush against her. I lifted both of my hands to her face and tilted her head up, her dark hair falling behind her shoulders. My thumb ran over her bottom lip, and she closed her eyes.

I smiled as I leaned down and pressed my lips to hers; Della melted against me as soon as our lips met. She was the first to move her mouth as one of her hands snaked up to the back of my head, dragging her fingers through my hair and pulling me closer to her. I moved us backward two steps so her back was against the wall of the inn, then tilted her head to the side, deepening the kiss. Gods, there was no way this woman was not made for me. She sighed, and I pushed my tongue against hers. Della pulled me to her feverishly. We could not get closer unless I was buried inside of her.

Della's tongue tangled with mine, and I couldn't help the moan that escaped me. She was going to be the death of me. I pulled back, and she tried to follow my mouth with hers as her lust-filled eyes opened.

"More," she demanded as she pulled me to her again; this time she was the one to deepen the kiss, like she needed my mouth to breathe.

"Hey."

We were both startled as we ripped apart from one another when Holden appeared next to us. Della's face was full of panic as she shoved me back. I smiled at her as she tried to pretend like she hadn't just been rubbing herself against me.

I glared at Holden. If he weren't my brother, I might have punched him for ruining this moment with her. Della's eyes flickered to Holden, then to his chest, like there was something on it. I didn't see anything when I looked, though. Her swollen lips were red as her gaze went to me and then to my mouth before she smirked in a satisfied way.

"Hey, Holden," she said in a friendly tone.

"Well, you two are looking cozy over here in the dark alleyway." He was a dead man walking. I glared at him. "I just wanted to say hi. I'm on my way to Sara's house. Della, you should come by for dinner again. Our parents won't stop talking about you." He grinned.

"Really?" She looked at me with her eyebrows raised and a pleased smile on her face.

"Yes, you made a good impression." I looked at Holden. "Goodbye."

He tossed his hands up before smiling and leaving. I turned to Della, hoping she would kiss me, but she had that same terrified look on her face that had appeared the other day.

"Please don't run."

"I'm not running. I'm using magic."

"Stay," I pleaded.

"I can't." Something like sadness flickered in her eyes. She stepped forward and gave me a chaste kiss before her magic swirled around her, and once again, she was gone.

I leaned back on the wall and ran my hands down my face. I was fucked. I already missed her, and I hardly knew her. I smiled at the memory of her mouth on mine. Then I tilted my head to the heavens and thanked them for letting her be mine. Della was everything. A noise somewhere close to me had me looking around. Someone was close by—I could feel their eyes on me. At first, I thought it might be Della, but I dismissed that thought when the air became heavy with darkness.

Something evil was near me. I stood up straight and listened closely for the danger. There was an odd sensation as if my body was reacting to this evil presence.

As the thought crossed my mind, I felt that familiar shiver run up my spine, letting me know the void was coming forward whether I wanted it to or not. I didn't understand why this other personality inside of me felt the need to come out right now. I tried to hang on to consciousness and not let him surface. He was being persistent, and I knew I would not win this struggle over who would be the presenting personality. He must think he can handle the danger better, and he was probably right, so I released my control.

My eyes closed tightly as the void swam through my veins and took control of everything, forcing me down into the deep depths of my chest so I wouldn't know what he was doing. The void side of me raced through every fiber of our body, pushing out anything nice about us to make way for his bad attitude. It seeped into my mind, shutting down my emotions and any logical reasoning. My body tensed almost to the point of pain as I switched personalities.

I shook my head as I surfaced. My gaze looked around for a moment because I could feel *them* lurking close by. It was why I needed to be present right now because the nice side of me did not know they were here. He didn't even know who they were. They stepped into the dark alleyway I was in. All six of them wore cloaks with the hoods up like I didn't know who the fuck they were.

"Take the hoods off." I rolled my eyes.

"How odd," Elra said as she lowered her hood. She didn't look away from me. "I don't think I will ever get used to seeing your *nice* side."

I ignored her, mostly because she pissed me off every single time she showed her face to me. The others lowered their hoods too, but I didn't move my glare from Elra.

"Is the other side of you going to be a problem?"

"No, he doesn't know what I do or say unless I let him. What the fuck do you want?"

"Why do you need the other side of you? Get rid of him; he is a weakness." She was an idiot.

"You realize he and I are the same? We are one man; there is no getting rid of one another. And no part of us is weak, so don't piss me off. One man, two personalities—it really isn't that hard to comprehend."

Her eyes flashed red with her anger. It was too easy to annoy her. I crossed my arms over my chest and gave her a look that said she should start talking or I was fucking leaving.

"Did you meet Ardella yet?"

"Yes." I did not give them any other details.

"And?" Mateo stepped forward.

"And nothing."

"Did she realize who you are?" he asked.

"No." Relief filled their faces. I was also relieved, but it was more because I wanted to kiss her some more before she realized who and what I was. Della did not seem to remember when we first met, thank fuck. It meant my magic worked on her.

"So this will work?" Daya asked eagerly.

"Yes. But do not get comfortable coming here to babysit me. I have this under control and do not need you fucks breathing down my neck. Have some patience; I literally just met her."

"Fine, but you need to make this as quick as possible. Did you have any more visions of the future?" Elra asked.

Yes, I did, but most of them revolved around Della moaning my name.

"No," I lied.

"Well, let us know if you need any help." Mateo offered with a smug smile, like I couldn't handle this.

"I'll be fine; now fuck off." I didn't wait for them to disappear before I turned away and headed in the direction of a bigger problem I had. I glanced over my shoulder to make sure they left and weren't following me. Once I was sure I was safe, I hurried up the street, following the golden mating bond in my chest.

When I came up to her house, I hesitated. I had been to this house a dozen times, and it never elicited any sort of emotion within me. My mate was on the other side of this wall, and it did nothing but enrage me because it was not Della. Falling in love with Della was not part of the plan, but I did not care. I tilted my gaze to the stars and flipped them off with both hands.

"Fuck you for not letting me have Della as a mate." She was supposed to be mine. I was supposed to belong to her. Fates be damned, I was not keeping this bond with...

"Haden?" I looked at the door of the small home and saw Holden staring at me. He looked up in the sky before looking at me. "Is there a reason you are flipping off the sky—outside of Sara's home?"

Sara walked up next to him, and my eyes immediately fell to the bond between us. Disgust filled me. I didn't find anything about her appealing. The stars did this to me because of who I am. They did not think I was worthy of a goddess as a mate. When I fucked with fate all those years ago, I did not think the stars would intervene so drastically. They could have let me have Della. I would make her happy. But my bond was with my brother's girlfriend.

Sara's friendly face did not show any recognition that I was supposed to be the one she loved, and thank the stars for that.

"Oh, I was just getting out some frustrations." It was technically the truth.

Holden's gaze looked over me before he frowned.

"You're void; are you upset about something?" he asked.

"No, I am just feeling overwhelmed about Della." Also, not a complete lie. "I didn't even realize I walked here; I was just trying to clear my mind with a walk."

Holden stepped forward and watched me closely.

"Are you sure? I am here if you need to talk. You haven't been void for quite a while."

"Yes. Don't worry about me. I promise I am fine. You two enjoy your night together; I'm headed home."

They both stared at me with concern, but I took off before they could ask me any more questions. I need to figure out how to sever this mating bond with Sara. She was not the woman I wanted, and the fates can fuck off if they think a bond will keep me from Della. Della was mine, and not even divine intervention would keep us apart.

CHAPTER 4

DELLA

Holden and Sara walked hand in hand down the busy street of their village as I watched unseen by anyone. I waited for jealousy and anger to take over, but nothing even remotely close to that happened. Sighing heavily, I tried to force an emotion out. They walked right past me without noticing. How could Haden see me when I was supposed to be invisible but my mate couldn't? This was stupid. I had been following him for a week, and being around him was doing nothing. If anything, it made me think about Haden more. I huffed out an irritated breath because I had no desire for this bond to snap into place with Holden.

Haden and Holden may be twins, but they were not the same. I liked how tall Haden was, and his hands were rough from working hard labor. Gods, and the way he smelled was heavenly. Fuck, I didn't even care to learn anything about Holden as I watched him all week. I buried my face in my hands and groaned loudly.

"Why must I be so fucked in the head?" I snapped.

Soft laughter behind me startled me. I knew it was Haden before looking.

"What are you doing?" I turned quickly, and Haden was smiling at me. My eyes traveled over his dirty clothing. He was sweating slightly, as if he had been in the sun working all day. I swallowed hard at how perfect he looked before having to look away so I wasn't gawking inappropriately. He had seen me again when I should have been invisible. Shit, I was buzzing with excitement that he had found me. No, I needed to not let those thoughts happen. He was not my mate. But that kiss in the alleyway had felt so... right.

"Nothing." I narrowed my eyes on Haden.

"I was worried you were going to disappear for good." He frowned as he looked over at me. "It's been a week."

"I was busy." Guilt clawed at me when I saw just how disappointed he was.

He glanced over at me like he had missed me, then ran his hand through his sweaty hair.

"You look upset that I am here." His brows furrowed. Instantly my fake anger dissipated. I really didn't like him looking at me like that.

"Sorry, it's been a strange week." That was the truth. "I'm happy to see you."

Haden smiled as he stepped closer, his scent hitting me.

"Oh yeah? Then why didn't you come back sooner?"

"Like I said, I was busy."

"Liar." He called me out immediately. "Tell me the truth."

I sighed and put my hands on my hips.

"Are you always so damn difficult?" I asked. Haden nodded, but I did not back down with his intense gaze. "You scare me."

He looked at me, surprised, then stepped backward to give me space.

"I don't think you will harm me, Haden," I said quickly. "I am scared about this whole thing happening between us. Don't you think it's odd?"

"Not at all." He shook his head.

"Well, maybe that is part of the problem. You are just letting us be reckless." I accused him purely because I needed someone to blame.

"There is nothing reckless about this, Ardella. Why are you really trying to downplay this?" He smiled brightly, his feelings almost radiating from him, and my stomach fluttered at how perfect he was. "You told me I could kiss you, so technically you are the reckless one."

I felt my cheeks heat immediately as he laughed. Gods, I liked that noise. Was there anything about him that I didn't like? My gaze traced over him, looking for anything.

"You like what you see?" He stepped forward. "Do you think of me like I think of you?"

I swallowed hard and nodded.

"I do, and that is the problem," I said in a defeated tone. His eyebrows shot up into his dark blonde hair.

"Why do you look so surprised by that?" he asked.

"Because we don't know each other at all. This is moving too fast."

Haden stepped closer to me, so we were a foot apart. "Do you always lie this much?" he asked in a breathy tone.

He called my bluff. His head tilted to the side, amused by my sudden flustered state. "Something that feels like this can't be... rushed, especially if it feels like fate. It will happen as it is meant to happen."

His words made me pause. Gods, he sounded as if he thought I was his mate. But fae didn't get fated mates often. It usually only happened for gods and very powerful elite fae or witches.

"Fine," I sighed. "I am scared by how much I feel for you, and it scares me that I do not think it is happening too quickly."

Haden reached out for me, his hand rubbing the side of my face. How did he do this, act like we had been doing this for years? His thumb rubbed back and forth on my cheek.

"You're so pretty when you're flustered." His words immediately made my eyes close so I could soak it in. "I will keep in mind that you like me telling you how pretty you are."

I opened my eyes, and they flashed white with overwhelming emotions. Haden bit his lip to stifle back a smile. He was a damn tease.

"Do you flirt with everyone?" I asked. Instantly jealousy bloomed in my chest at the thought of him flirting with another woman. Fuck, this is how my mating bond was supposed to work with Holden.

"No." He smiled. "Only you get my flirting, Ardella."

"Good," I said before I shut my mouth. I was worried that I was going to say things that were too personal. Haden's eyes practically shined with his happiness. My chest ached with longing for him. I liked that I made him happy. Haden ran his hand through his hair before glancing over his shoulder like someone would be standing there. His smile was contagious when he turned back to me.

"Are you busy right now?"

"No." I was desperate to spend time with him. His eyes softened as he held out his hand, and I took it immediately. He walked up the path of the village. The fae in town stared at us, probably wondering who the hell I was. Haden stopped at a small vendor that was selling some sort of pastry. It smelled delicious. The two women behind the stand smiled at him, but when they saw him holding onto my hand, both of their smiles fell. I squeezed his hand tighter, and he looked over his shoulder, smiling at me.

"Haden," one of them purred, completely ignoring me. "We've missed you. It's been weeks."

He gave her a tight smile.

"I've been busy. I'll take two of my regular." He looked over at me. "Do you prefer strawberry or blueberry?"

"Either is fine."

"I'll take two of each flavor then." He pulled out money and set it down on the wooden table. The women glared at me, but I ignored them. Haden grabbed the pastries and thanked them before dragging me up the street again. I couldn't help but smile. I'm sure Haden had his fair share of women chasing after him, but I liked that he didn't pay any attention to it.

Haden cut across a tall field of dead grass. Gods, I needed to stop wearing dresses and heels. He looked back to see why I was slowing down, glancing down at my feet and back up to me. He handed me the pastries before he scooped me up and started walking again.

"You don't have to carry me," I said quickly.

"Trust me, I do. We have to make it through the woods, and you're in heels and a dress."

A smirk tugged at his lips as he glanced down at me. I gripped our pastries in one hand and wrapped my arm around his neck. Haden's arms tightened on me, holding me as close to him as he could.

"Noted." I chuckled. "I will stop wearing dresses and heels when I come."

Haden looked at me oddly.

"If you want to keep wearing them, then I will carry you whenever you need me to." His gaze lingered on mine.

I leaned up and kissed his cheek. Haden stopped walking and pressed his lips to mine. Then, he pulled away and started walking through the forest of birch trees like he hadn't just left me breathless. The leaves were starting to change orange and yellow with the season. It was so pretty. I lifted my head toward the sky and watched the canopy of leaves pass by us, content to be in his arms.

After a minute, we broke through the tree line and made it to a half-built house. I recognized it instantly as his house. He set me on my feet and turned around with his arms spread out.

"What do you think?"

"I didn't realize you had already started building it." I stepped toward it. The property it was on was stunning. It was a large, grassy field surrounded by large birch trees. To the left of the house was a large pond with birds floating on the surface. I inched forward as my gaze tried to take in everything at once.

"I was going to work on it a little bit. Do you want to hang out with me while I do?"

"Yes." I nodded.

He grabbed my hand and pulled me toward the steps that led to the doorway. Haden had the floor down, and the frames for the walls were up. The roof was on, and he had some walls on the outside finished.

"So, when you walk in, there will be a pretty foyer with lots of windows so the sun can filter in. To the left will be a big sitting room." He pulled me to the right. "This will be the dining area and a huge kitchen that has a view of the pond."

Haden turned to me to see my reaction. His eyes gleaming with excitement.

"This is going to be such a beautiful home, Haden." I smiled at him before dropping his hand and walking in a small circle, admiring the work he had done already. I ran my hand over the cabinets he was making in the kitchen.

He was talented. Haden moved a makeshift stool over to me so I could sit. He reached in the bag of pastries and handed me one of them. I grabbed it and took a bite.

"Gods, that's fucking good." I groaned and took another bite.

Haden laughed softly as he ate one too. He kept glancing at me without saying anything. His eyes drifted over my outfit, and I shrank back slightly. Did he like the way I looked?

"What?"

"I like the dresses you wear," he said softly. "Even though they are far fancier than any maid I know could afford."

I stilled at his accusation. He started working on the cabinets, but he kept looking at me, waiting for me to say something. Great, he knew I was lying about my job.

"I'm not a maid."

"I know, Ardella." He laughed. "Why'd you lie?"

"Because I didn't know what to say." That was the truth of it all. I had no idea how to tell someone I was a goddess. Would they even believe me if I said that to them?

"How about the truth?"

"The truth feels complicated, and I worry that you won't believe me."

Haden stopped whatever he was doing to the cabinet and looked at me. He frowned slightly before continuing.

"I promise I'll believe you. I just don't want you to feel like you have to lie to me. Honesty is the best foundation of a relationship."

"Is this a relationship?" I asked.

Haden nodded once, confirming what I already knew. I liked him way more than I should have so quickly, but he was just as fucked in the head because he felt the same. I nodded as I nibbled on the second pastry. My chest tightened with worry as I stood up and set the food on the small bag. I squared my shoulders as if that would make me feel more confident. But as soon as I met Haden's stormy eyes, I deflated.

"I don't have a typical job." I started, and he nodded as if to encourage me. "I'm... gods, this is going to sound crazy."

Haden watched me without his face changing.

"My name is Ardella, and I am the Goddess of Life." I stared at Haden, looking for any indication that he thought I was a lunatic.

His eyebrows pinched together, but apart from that, nothing changed. After a moment, his eyes traveled over me—assessing me. Gods, he thought I had lost my fucking mind. I tried not to show how anxious I was, but he still hadn't said anything. My body was tense as the silence stretched between us.

"I can go." I turned.

"No, stop." Haden's voice echoed around me, and I turned to him, but he wasn't looking at me like I was crazy.

"That is why you have that odd magic," he said. "The starlight."

"Yes. Do you believe me?" I asked.

"You are far too pretty to be anything but a goddess." He smiled. Something about him believing me made me rush forward to hug him. Haden wrapped his arms around me, and everything felt like it would be alright. How could the heavens not see that he was the one for me? He rubbed his hands down my back, making my worries seem to disappear.

"Do you want to see my other magic?" I asked. "Then you can show me yours."

I pulled back and smiled. Something like worry flashed in his stormy eyes.

"How did you know I have magic?"

"I'm a goddess; I can feel it when you are close to me." I grabbed his hand. "Come on."

I led us outside and closer to the pond so rain would not get into his house. I dropped his hand and moved a little bit farther from him. Haden's eyes watched me closely as

I lifted my hands out to my sides. Dark clouds rolled over us, and Haden's handsome face tilted toward the heavens to see what it was.

Then lightning split and scattered across the sky above us. Haden looked at me, and his mouth fell open. My eyes had turned pure white as I summoned energy from around me to form a small tornado on top of the pond. Thunder echoed in the sky, and rain began to fall around us. Haden gawked at me as I lifted my hand, and a ball of lightning appeared in my upturned palm. I pointed at a small tree on the other side of the pond, and it shot from my hand, striking into the tree with a small explosion.

I stopped my magic immediately, and the dark clouds moved away. The rain dried up instantly as I looked at Haden.

"My storm," he muttered.

I smirked at him.

"Your turn."

Haden nodded as he looked into my eyes. His eyes went from dark blue to sky blue as the temperature around us dropped significantly enough that I could see our breath. Haden's fists were covered in a frost that seemed to radiate out and cover his entire body. I gasped when the ground around his feet became frosted as well. The layer of ice quickly shot out from him and covered the entire field.

Even the pond froze, the strange noise from the ice form-ing sounding strangely like music.

A cold gust of wind knocked into me, and I turned back to Haden, smiling as my hair whipped around my face. Then he lifted his hands, and snow burst from them. I turned my face to the sky, where the tiny white flakes fell in what felt like a winter blizzard, but the sun was shining brightly. The snow fell on my hot skin, melting instantly. I was so distracted by the beauty of Haden's magic that I didn't hear him approach me.

His cold fingers gripped my chin, pulling my face down so I could see him. He leaned forward and softly pressed his lips to mine. His mouth was cold as his tongue swept past my lips and tangled with my own. I pulled him toward me and deepened the kiss. Haden's snow began whipping around us in a flurry as he tangled his hands in my hair.

Suddenly, I was knocked to the ground by a forceful wind. I stared at the snow falling from the sky as I lay on my back.

"Shit," Haden muttered as he leaned over me. "Are you alright? My magic got out of control..."

Sitting up, I grabbed my arm as an odd tingling sensa-tion ran through it. Haden kneeled and moved my hand, exposing my skin as a silver shape began appearing, ex-panding quickly in lines and whirls that seemed to glow with an eerily beautiful light. When the magic finally stilled, a glittering array of snowflake tattoos was left behind, so bright that it reminded me of the way that the snow shines when the sun hits it just right. Haden's fingers traced the pale lines of the snowflakes that started at my shoulder and moved down my arm.

"Gods, I didn't mean to do that. I didn't even know I could," he said frantically. I glanced up at him as he panicked and laughed. Haden stilled as I laughed louder.

"Why are you laughing?"

"It must have been overwhelming emotions that made your magic act out," I answered softly. "Mine acts out too when I feel things deeply."

He swallowed hard.

"I was feeling deeply about that kiss you just gave me." His eyes flashed icy blue again, but only for a moment, and I became silent.

"Me too," I confessed.

"Are you sure you're not hurt? I don't want to go to hell for injuring a goddess."

Amusement flashed in his eyes as he gave me a boyish grin. I scoffed as I chuckled and stood up.

"Why did you believe that I was a goddess so quickly? Did it not cross your mind that I was a lunatic?"

Haden's shoulders shook with silent laughter.

"There are a few reasons. One, your starlight magic is not regular. Two, I've seen you sneaking around as if no one can see you, and I realized at some point they couldn't, but I could." I stood still at his confession. "I saw you crying one night when you didn't know I was there, and your tears glowed like the stars. And like I said, you are too pretty to fit in with us regular fae. Which brings me to my next point: you don't have pointed ears."

"I didn't realize you were so observant," I said because I couldn't think of anything else to say. "Not having pointed ears could just be because I am a vampire or something."

"You don't have fangs. And Elloryon does not have vampires. They live in another realm." His eyes traveled over me slowly again. "Plus, your eyes shine like the heavens."

Haden stared at me and waited for me to say something to refute his claims. I didn't know what to say, though. Haden ran his hand through his hair like he wanted to say something else to me.

"Why is a goddess mingling with fae?" he asked.

"That is a secret, and I would rather not tell you." I frowned.

"Alright. Do you believe in fate?" he asked instead.

I jerked back as if he had slapped me. Where was this going? Did he know that I was here to find my mate and his brother was supposed to be it? I needed to calm the hell down; there was no way he knew that. My anxiety was going to make my thoughts spiral.

"Yes, I believe in it."

"I didn't, until recently." He looked away from me and started pacing around. "Growing up, Holden and I were the same in every way. We liked the same foods, we hated broccoli, and we enjoyed the same hobbies."

Where was he going with this?

"Until we were old enough to start noticing women. Holden immediately began dating and talking to them." I waited for his words to make me enraged with jealousy, but they didn't. "He kissed girls, and I had absolutely no interest in them."

Good.

"I knew my parents were worried about it. They always tried to set me up with friends' daughters." My fists clenched tightly. "But I never responded the way that they wanted me to. It didn't bother me; I just figured I would be alone and do my own thing. Until Holden told me he was going to ask Sara to marry him. I don't understand why him getting married triggered this panicked feeling within me. I suddenly felt like I needed to find someone. I went on a date..."

Lightning cracked into the sky above us as I tried desperately to rein myself in. Haden glanced up before looking at me. A slow smile spread across his face as he saw my eyes flashing white.

"I went on one date, and it was awful. It ended very early." His words had my jealousy calming down slightly. "That night, I went home, and I did something I have never done in my life." He looked up at me. "I prayed to the stars to show me who I was supposed to be with. I wanted any kind of sign to know what woman, if any, was meant for me."

I stepped forward, watching him closely.

"Did they give you a sign?"

He nodded, and my heart pounded so violently that I could feel it throbbing in my neck.

"I had the strangest dream that night. One that, at first, made no sense to me. But then I started to see you lurking around the village. It wasn't until the day we actually met that I understood my dream."

I was so confused. Why would the heavens show him a sign that led to me? Haden started laughing softly.

"My dream was just a woman falling over and over." He looked at me oddly. "When I saw you practicing falling in the street, it all clicked into place. I think maybe the stars were trying to tell me that you are everything I need, and even though we have not spent much time together, I can't help but think they were right."

Guilt clawed at my insides. Why were the heavens being cruel to me? Haden must have seen the guilt on my face because he stepped closer.

"I know that you are a goddess, and I am... just a mortal fae, but I just want a chance to show you that maybe this is written in the stars. My parents talked all the time about how they just knew after two days, Ardella. I used to think they were just lucky that they fell in love with each other, but now I understand what they were talking about. It was more than just luck. You have taken over my mind, whether I am awake or sleeping. It acts like it has never seen anything else but you.

"Your voice fills the empty space in my mind when you aren't near me. And I cannot stop thinking about how fucking right every kiss has felt. It is as if I was sleeping through life until I saw you, and my heart and mind started working only to obsess over you. You are all I think about, and I'm worried that you do not feel the same. I'm worried you will leave today and never return to me." He paused and stared at me. "I just had to tell you how I feel. Just in case you leave, but more importantly... just in case you might feel the same about me."

His chest was moving in quick breaths as I watched him closely. Did he really think I didn't like him?

"I hope I didn't scare you, but my mother said I should just tell you."

"You told your mother about your feelings for me?"

He nodded.

"And my father." He hesitated. "And Holden and Sara."

That warm feeling began spreading through me. Maybe the heavens knew they made a mistake, and this was their way of telling me that it was okay to pick Haden.

"Did your family think it was crazy for you to feel this way?"

"No, they are happy for us." Haden hesitated for a moment, and I knew his next words were going to be difficult for him, whatever they were. "There is something else." He took a deep breath and then said, "I have visions."

"Visions?"

He nodded. "When I was younger, I would get them sporadically about trivial things—the weather or someone getting hurt. Then the visions died down and became almost non-existent, until recently. After I prayed to the stars to show me who I would end up with, and it showed you, I began having more visions of us. It was like my prayer awakened a magic inside of me that I had lost."

My heart was pounding violently in my chest as Haden watched me closely. He looked worried that I would bolt.

"I have seen parts of our future, and it is beautiful, Della. I know this is overwhelming because it hasn't been long, but..." He trailed off and watched me. "You are it for me. And not to spoil anything for you, but we are going to fall in love, and we are going to have a wonderful life together."

I swallowed as my throat became itchy with my unshed tears. Somehow, I knew his words were true. I was already feeling deep emotions for him. I didn't understand why, but maybe I wasn't supposed to. Haden had seen our life, and he was ready for it. The heavens wouldn't send him visions of me if I were supposed to stay away.

"You are killing me with your silence," Haden sighed. His pretty eyes were wide as he waited for a response. I looked around, not sure what to do. Was this my decision to make, or were the heavens testing me? When I looked back at Haden, I realized that I didn't care about the consequences if I kept Haden instead of Holden.

"I do feel the same," I whispered. Haden was moving toward me before the whole sentence fell from me. He wrapped his arms around me and gripped me tightly, lifting me off the ground. "Everything about you feels right, like I was always supposed to belong to you."

He pulled back so he could see my face. His eyes seemed to darken.

"You are all for me, Storm, and I won't ever let go."

He kissed me, and it seared into me, claiming me as his. I did not need a mating bond to tell me who to love.

CHAPTER 5

DELLA

I looked up from my book and smiled at Haden when he came inside. My smile dropped, though, as I looked over his sweaty, bare chest. Fuck. I tried to look away, but Haden grinned at my gawking. He set the wood down and came over to me, giving me a hard, lingering kiss. I moved so he could deepen the kiss, but like always, he stopped.

I frowned as he walked back into the kitchen. I didn't know when I became so desperate for the touch of a man, but I was. Haden never made a move on me, even though I had been coming to the house every day for two weeks. He would always have some delicious food waiting for me. He just seemed to be happy that I was keeping him company. Which I was thankful for, but I would also be thankful for an orgasm or something. Maybe he didn't find me attractive in *that* way.

I swallowed hard as I watched him over the top of my book. He lifted a giant piece of wood over his head, making the muscles on his back flex. Heavens, forgive me and my dirty thoughts, but I could not stop them. I wanted to feel him under my fingertips. I closed my eyes tightly. For fuck's sake, Haden was working innocently, and I was looking at him like a piece of fucking meat.

"So, do you have parents? How does a god come to exist?" Haden asked as he kept maneuvering the wood. I closed my book.

"No, I don't have parents. Gods are created from a star. When they settle down, they can have children, but most children will not go on to be gods."

Haden gave me an odd look.

"What determines if they will or not?"

"How powerful the god and their partner are," I said. "It's almost like a tiered system. On the top are the heavens, then the old gods, then the stars, then gods like me, the elite magic, regular magic, and no magic."

"Old gods?" he asked.

"The first gods that were created. They hold the most power." I wasn't sure I should have told him about that. Something flickered in his eyes, and I wondered if he knew about any of this before. "But they hide from everyone."

"So, you don't have a family?" He changed the subject.

"I have a twin brother, but that is all there is to my family." I smiled. I loved Mikel; he had always been good to me.

"We're both twins." A small smirk played across his lips. "When we have kids, then we have a high chance of twins."

I dropped my book. When, not if, we have kids. Haden laughed at the look on my face.

"Is that too forward of a thought?" he asked. His eyes traced over me as he tried to hold his smile back.

"No." I blushed. "How many children are you picturing?"

"As many as you are willing to give me," he said casually.

"Gods, Haden," I breathed. For a man that never made a move on me, he had me blushing. So he had thought of me in an intimate way.

"Sorry, I just like seeing you flustered for me, Storm."

That wasn't helping. He was such a tease. I grabbed my book off the floor and opened it again, pretending to read it. Haden worked like he was doing the easiest job in the world, and I admired that about him. He was a hard worker and creative.

"Are you artistic like your father?" I asked.

Haden didn't look away from what he was doing.

"Yes, but I prefer drawing houses, but every now and again I get inspired to draw something else."

"What was the last thing you drew that wasn't a house?"

"You." He turned quickly to see my reaction. "It was after the second or third time I saw you. I was worried you would disappear, and I would forget how pretty you are."

I smiled to myself.

"Well, I hope our children inherit your artistic abilities, because I have none," I said just to tease him, but Haden lost grip of the wood he was holding, and it hit him in the head.

"Fuck." He held his head as I rushed to him.

"I'm sorry. I was just trying to tease you like you were to me." I panicked when I saw blood on his hand. Haden watched me as I grabbed him and shoved him onto the stool. "Lean down so I can see how bad it is."

Haden listened, and I noticed that the gash started dripping blood. Immediately, I used my magic and sealed his wound.

"There, all fixed."

Haden lifted his gaze to mine. His hands wrapped around the back of my thighs and pulled me forward, so I was standing between his legs.

"Kiss me, Storm."

He didn't need to tell me twice. I pressed my lips to his, and he kissed me softly. Then he tugged me into him for a hug.

"I'm sorry I made you get hurt."

"I started it with the teasing; you don't have to apologize."

Haden just held me, and I couldn't help but think how perfect this was. I thought of him when I woke up in the morning, and he was the last thing I thought of when I went to bed. Even my dreams were of him, and still it did not feel like we saw each other enough.

"I'm glad it was you," he whispered. "I'm glad the stars decided that you were the one for me. I don't think I could have picked anyone better."

That damn guilt pierced into my heart.

"You are everything," I answered back.

I pulled back and kissed him again before moving so he could get back to work. Haden hesitated for only a moment before he stood up and went outside for more wood. I read my book in silence for a while before I noticed that Haden hadn't come inside for a long time. I stood up and went looking for him, finding him at the tree line, bent over doing something. I waited for him to turn around.

When he did, he held up a giant bundle of flowers and began running over to me. I smiled at him as he got closer.

"I thought you might want some of these." He handed them to me.

"I love wildflowers." I smelled them.

Haden watched me for a moment before looking around.

"I'm done working for the day. Do you want to go somewhere with me?"

I nodded eagerly. He grabbed my hand and led us into the house to grab the food he had brought with him, smiling at me as I followed him closely with the food in one hand and my hand in the other; we took off into the woods.

☽★★★☽★★★☽

We walked for a long while before the sound of rushing water faintly reached my ears. It grew louder as we gradually got closer to the source. I was so excited to just spend the day with Haden that I didn't even wonder what we could be doing. I looked around and noticed that the familiar birch trees were mixed with a different type of leafy tree here.

"There is a town in that direction." Haden nodded to the right. "Raynor, I think. I'm not sure; I haven't been there before. But I stumbled upon this one day."

We broke through the tree line and stepped into what felt like another world. A babbling stream ran through the trees and fell over the nearby rock wall as a small waterfall, emptying the mountain water into a large lake below. A hazy mist filled the air around us, causing rainbows to form when the midday sunlight tried to shine through it. Near us, the edges of the stream were covered with wildflowers, displaying varying colors to mix with the rainbows from around us in an overload of color and sweet perfume. My mouth fell open at how beautiful it was. I dropped Haden's hand so I could run toward the water's edge for a better view. The waterfall was not very large, but it fell from such a distance that it created the loud roaring noise we had been hearing.

"You like it, Storm?"

I turned toward him and nodded.

"This is the most beautiful thing I've ever seen." I smiled.

"I can think of something a bit prettier." Haden gave me a flirty grin when I looked at him. "But it's up there."

My cheeks flushed with heat as he watched me closely. After a moment, he grabbed the blanket he brought and laid it on the ground before slipping off his boots and tunic.

"What are you doing?" I asked.

"Swimming."

I glanced at the water for a moment in disbelief before looking back at him.

"It's going to be freezing."

Another smile overtook his face. "Go feel it," he said mischievously.

I hesitated for only a moment before leaning down and gliding my fingers through the water, pleasantly surprised by its warmth. What the hell? I dipped my hand in again and smiled at the temperature of the water. It was almost... soothing. I turned back toward Haden and gasped to see that he was practically naked. My eyes dragged down his body slowly before coming back up and meeting his.

Heat crept up my neck when I saw him watching me stare. "Why is it warm?" I asked, looking for a reason to change the subject.

He shrugged.

"I have no idea. But it makes for the perfect temperature to swim. Are you coming in? I will turn so you can get undressed."

I glanced at the water before swallowing hard.

"I don't know how to swim."

Haden stepped forward with an odd look.

"Gods don't know how to do everything?" he asked seriously.

I gave him a pointed look.

"Of course not. We have to learn how to do pretty much everything you do. We are just older when we learn it because we are never children."

"Never children?"

"When we are created, we are formed mentally and physically around the age you are now, between two hundred and fifty and three hundred years old. I was never a child."

Haden glanced at the water before looking back at me.

"So, I can teach you things?"

"Yes."

"Storm, this is exciting." He smiled as he walked closer to me. "I'm going to teach you so many things." His eyes seemed to darken for a moment, and my stomach clenched when I realized what he was thinking about. I licked my lips as I tried to get my brain to start working and not think of how good Haden's skin would feel under my hands.

"Do you want to touch?"

My gaze snapped up to his eyes, not realizing that I was staring so aggressively at his bare chest.

"Yes."

Surprise flashed in his eyes before he smiled.

"Then you need to take your clothes off and meet me in the water so I can teach you how to swim."

I didn't realize that the idea of swimming would make me so anxious. What was under the surface of the water?

"It's alright. I won't let anything happen to you. Do you trust me?"

I nodded. "Yes."

"Good. I am going to get in the water, and I'll keep my back toward you until you tell me to turn."

"Alright."

Haden kissed my forehead on the way by. I watched him walk out into the water until everything but his head was covered. Slowly, I started undressing. I kept my camisole and underwear on, though, so I wasn't completely naked. I took a step into the water and sighed at how good it felt on my feet.

"You can turn," I said with a pounding heart. I was not in the water yet, but I wanted him to see me. Haden turned, and his eyes widened as he stood up, the water rolling off his chest. Gods, he was a fucking sight. I smiled as I walked toward him. Once I was close enough, he grabbed me, and I wrapped my legs around him as he kissed me.

The feelings I had for him were overwhelming, and I could feel the tears burning in my eyes. Gods, this was stupid. I released my legs from around him and turned away so he wouldn't see that I was getting emotional. He wouldn't allow it, though, and paddled around me in the water so that I was once again facing him.

"Are you crying?" he asked suspiciously.

"No," I lied as glowing tears fell down my cheeks.

He sighed. "You know that your tears are literally impossible to hide. What's wrong?"

I stared at him for a moment and felt everything bubbling up again. I tried to shove it back down so I didn't embarrass myself, but I couldn't help it.

"Sometimes, I feel overwhelmed when I see you."

He frowned.

"No, not like that," I said quickly. "I mean, I do feel overwhelmed, but in a good way. It is like all these feelings start swarming in my chest when I look at you. I am overwhelmed with how much I like you." I was babbling, and I knew it. I stopped talking, and Haden stared at me with a bemused expression on his face. I panicked. "And we've only known each other for a short time. Can you imagine how much more I will love you in a month? A year? Hundreds of years from now? It's going to swallow me whole. It is swallowing me whole already, Haden. I think of you when I wake up in the morning; I spend all day with you, and then I think of you as I fall asleep, and it still feels like I am not with you enough. I did not expect you to be so... perfect for me."

Haden was smiling at me, and it knocked some sense into me. I stopped talking and tried to dash for the shore-line, wanting to run away from my embarrassment. But Haden easily grabbed me and pulled me back.

"Are you falling in love with me, Storm?"

"Yes," I whispered.

"Good," he whispered back. "You're finally catching up to me."

Letting all of my anxieties go, I leaned forward and kissed Haden. He kissed me back while slowly pulling me farther into the water. Realizing I could no longer touch the ground, I gripped onto him as he tried to pull me off of him. He laughed softly.

"One day you may need to know how to swim, and you'll be glad I'm teaching you."

I took a deep breath to fortify myself and let my legs fall away. Haden took a few steps back until his arm was the only thing keeping me up.

"Kick your legs like I showed you." I did what he asked. "Good girl, now move your arms like I showed you."

Haden had to repeat himself because I was stuck on the praise. For some reason, hearing him call me a 'good girl' sent shivers through me. I started doing what he had showed me, wanting to hear him say it again. I felt ridiculous, though. Until Haden smiled at me, that is, and then I felt a little less ridiculous.

"You're doing such a good job."

Gods, if he kept praising me, I was going to jump him. I looked over at him, and I realized that his arms were both out in front of him, empty. He wasn't holding me. I panicked and slipped under the water. Haden's arm wrapped around me and dragged me back up.

"Fuck, Storm, you don't need to panic; you were doing great."

"Sorry," I coughed up water and laughed. "I won't drown though; my magic would save me."

"I'll save you if you need saving."

My laughter died out because Haden's words made me realize that he had already saved me. He gave me a purpose, a new meaning to life, and saved me from a meaningless existence.

"Careful, Storm, you look like you might be falling more in love with me." He half-joked. I nodded and leaned my head against his shoulder as he carried me out of the water. He set us on the blanket, and we both lay together in the sun. Once we were dry, Haden started getting our food ready. I just sat and admired him, wondering how I had lived so many lifetimes before knowing him. It seemed wrong to exist in a reality without him for so long.

Fear trickled into my mind at the thought that Haden would grow old. He would leave me one day, and I would be shoved back into the lonely life I had before him. My mating bond would not grant him the immortal life that I possess to let him live an existence with me, and that thought terrified me. How could I exist if he did not? Haden glanced up at me and paused.

"Why do you look like you are going to cry again?"

"I don't want you to ever leave me. I do not want to exist unless you are next to me."

He looked at me with understanding.

"One day, I'm going to die, but it will be so far from now that you will have a lifetime of memories to comfort you. But I won't be gone forever, Ardella. I believe with everything in me that I will belong to you in every life I live. The stars can't keep two halves of the same soul apart for long. I vow I will always find you. You own me now, and in every reality in the future."

I lunged at him, hugging him to me, desperate for the bond to magically transfer to him so I did not have to live any amount of time without him. I wanted him exactly how he was now. I pleaded silently that the heavens would make him my mate in this life and the next.

CHAPTER 6

DELLA

"Where are you sneaking off to?" Mikel asked as I got dressed for dinner with Haden and his parents tonight.

"I met a friend," I lied.

Mikel seemed surprised.

"That's great." He smiled and stepped into the room where I was trying to fix my hair. "What's her name?"

I stilled as I raked my fingers through my curls. I couldn't tell Mikel that it was a man. He would tell me that men had ill intentions. But Mikel shouldn't worry about Haden's intentions; he should worry about mine. I had been going to see Haden every day for two months. Usually at his house while he worked on building it. Haden was nothing short of a gentleman, only giving me a few lingering kisses but never going for more. I was hoping he would tonight, and if he didn't, maybe I would be brave enough to move it to the next level.

"Penelope," I said quickly when I realized my mind had wandered for longer than necessary.

"What are your plans? You look pretty." Mikel smiled at me.

"Dinner with her parents, nothing too crazy." I felt bad about lying, but there was no way that I could tell him I was trying to seduce a man who was not my mate.

"I wanted to talk to you yesterday, but you were gone. I just wanted to say that you seem so happy lately, and it makes me so happy to see, Dells. Being a god can sometimes feel suffocating and lonely. And I am thankful that the stars made us together, but I know that you have craved a friendship besides me. I am happy for you."

Tears filled my eyes.

"I love you, Mikel. You will always be my best friend." I reached out and squeezed his cheek playfully.

"I love you too. Have fun tonight."

"I plan on it."

I watched Mikel walk out of my room and felt like an asshole for lying. I would have to tell him eventually. I shoved away those impending thoughts and glanced over at the mirror, checking over the simple dress I wore tonight. Excitement coursed through me as I thought about Haden. I would be a bit early, but because I hadn't seen him yet today, I couldn't wait any longer. I summoned my star mist. When my magic fell away, I was outside of Haden's family home. I smiled when Haden stood up from the front steps eagerly.

"Did you hear me praying that you would show up early?" he asked.

"No. But I couldn't wait to come see you. I missed you so much."

"Today was terrible." He leaned in and kissed me. "I know you have to work, but let's not spend an entire day apart again."

I chuckled softly as I gave him one more kiss. Haden led me inside, and his entire family stood to give me a hug. The food smelled so good. My greedy eyes looked over the steaks and large array of side dishes I had never seen before. I sat down eagerly. I was starving. Haden plated food for me when he saw how impatiently I was waiting. His family started talking about wedding plans.

"You are engaged?" I asked Holden and Sara.

"Yes, sorry, we assumed Haden told you." Sara gave him a pointed look. Then she lifted her hand, showing me the pretty golden band with stones around the entirety of it. At first, I wasn't sure what to think about being friends with them, but when I saw Holden and Sara together, I could not help but wonder if they were supposed to be written in the stars. There was nothing remotely romantic that stirred in my chest for Holden. But each time I looked at him, I could see our bond floating between us, reminding me that I was supposed to be his.

"When is the wedding?" I asked.

"Soon, we don't want to wait too long, but we haven't picked an exact date." Holden grabbed Sara's hand on the table and squeezed it. They started going into detail about the food and flowers. I had never been to a wedding. They weren't custom for gods; we just completed the mating bond and were married. Would Haden want a wedding?

Haden was already staring at me when I looked at him. His hand came under the table and rested on my thigh, and he began rubbing his thumb back and forth on my bare skin. The simple touch was igniting a frenzy inside of me. I glanced at him out of the corner of my eye and saw he was staring at me—admiring me as if I couldn't see him.

"Ardella, you need to come to dinner more often." Henry smiled. "This has been such a great night. Watching our two boys with two incredible women has been the highlight of our parenting life thus far."

I smiled at them.

"I think our parents might like the girls more than us," Holden said to Haden.

"Do you blame them?" Haden smiled.

Penelope stood up and pinched Holden's cheeks.

"My boys will always be irreplaceable." She smiled. "But it is nice not being the only woman." She started grabbing dishes and smiled. "Ardella, do you mind grabbing those?" She nodded to the dishes in front of me.

"Of course not." I stood up quickly and grabbed the plates, then followed her into the kitchen to set the dishes down. Penelope was watching me closely, so I looked at her, and she smiled softly. She glanced at the other room to make sure everyone at the table was in conversation, then leaned over and said, "Haden told us who you are."

My smile fell, and I glanced down at the counter.

"I always knew that Haden was different," she started. "He was always so much more guarded with his feelings and wants than Holden was. We were so worried he would never settle down because no one ever caught his attention. I should have known that he would not settle for just anyone, but I was surprised when he told us who you are."

I looked up at her and smiled, relieved at her reaction.

"Holden is my free-spirited child, but Haden, he is not a risk taker. He will not go all in with something unless he is certain that it is exactly what he wants. I don't think I could have picked a better fit for him." She smiled at me. "I just wanted to tell you that we are so happy for you two, and one day, maybe we will all be one big family. Is a goddess allowed to get married?"

I smiled softly at her question.

"We do get married," I said. "Thank you for making me feel welcome. I did not grow up or have parents, so all of this is new to me. But I can't imagine a greater family to show me what it is like."

Penelope hugged me tightly. I hugged her back, and I wondered if this is what it would have been like to have a mother. After a long moment, she pulled away.

"Take care of him; he's all in on you."

"I promise."

Haden walked up, and his mother let us have space. He smiled down at me and saw the tears welling in my eyes.

"What's wrong, Storm?" His thumb brushed against my cheek.

"I'm thankful that the heavens brought you to me."

Something flickered through his eyes as he leaned down and kissed me softly.

"I want to take you somewhere," he whispered. "Can you take us to the house with your star mist?"

"Yes." I smiled.

"Ardella and I will see you guys later." He called out without looking away from me. My star mist circled around us, and when it disappeared, we were standing next to Haden's house. I glanced at it and stilled. It had the outside walls up. I looked at Haden, and he smiled brightly.

"My dad and Holden helped me get them up today."

He grabbed my hand, led me up to the door, and pushed it open. He fumbled around for a minute before a lantern lit up the space. There were no internal walls finished, but it looked like a home.

"Haden, this is so exciting. It's looking so good." I turned and looked at the progress he made since I left a day ago. I froze when I saw the bed he had set up and looked at him.

"I was thinking about staying here some nights."

I nodded, and Haden stared at me. I could feel the tension between us. *Please come over here and kiss me*, I begged silently. Haden swallowed hard as he looked over at me. His eyes lingered on my exposed skin. When his eyes met mine, I held my breath and waited for him to finally make a move. He cleared his throat lightly and ran his hand through his hair. When he turned away from me, disappointment coursed through me.

I looked at the bed and sighed softly. Did he not want to do anything? Was it not customary to do anything like this before marriage?

"Is there a reason you never touch me more than kiss-ing?" I asked, sounding far braver than I felt.

Haden turned to face me quickly. He stared at me, frozen to his spot, like maybe he hadn't heard me correctly.

"Do you want me to?" His voice was shaky.

"Are you kidding me?" I asked, smiling at him.

He exhaled loudly, his nostrils flaring as he looked at me. "I just assumed that you didn't do that until marriage."

My brows pinched together with confusion. "Why would you think that?" I asked.

"The whole being-a-goddess thing? I don't know; I just figured it was like a spiritual thing." He fumbled his words in such an adorable way.

I laughed softly, and he finally relaxed as well.

"Hell, no, Haden. I have been impatiently waiting for you to make a move. I thought that you didn't want to for some reason."

Haden's eyes traced all over me. "Fuck no, I have been holding myself back."

"Well, stop holding back."

That was all he needed to hear. Before I could react, Haden was pulling me to him, his mouth crushing mine. His hands gripped my hips and tugged me against his body. Haden backed us up, so the backs of my knees hit the bed, and we fell on the bed together. He stared down at me, his eyes drinking in my face. His fingers gripped my jaw before his thumb rubbed against my mouth roughly.

"So pretty, Storm," he whispered.

His words shot straight through me, making my stomach clench tightly.

"I've not done anything before," he confessed as he stood up. I smiled because I was happy that I would be his first and his only.

"Me neither."

His frost magic filled his eyes, and a possessiveness came over them. Sitting up, I lifted his tunic, kissing his toned stomach. He let out a soft sigh as my mouth trailed over his muscles. He grabbed his tunic and ripped it off of himself. I looked up at him and admired how fit he was from working hard.

I lifted my hand and ran it down the length of his torso. Haden watched silently as I got to the band of his trousers. I untied them as I stared him in the eyes. Haden snagged his bottom lip with his teeth as he watched me push them down. I shot my star mist out, and his boots were gone as well. He smirked at me, now standing completely naked for my appreciation.

"So eager for me, Storm?"

"You have no idea," I sighed.

"You've thought about this?" he asked. I nodded as I grabbed his hard length and moved my hand down it. Haden moaned loudly, and his eyes fluttered shut. Note to self: Haden likes this a lot. I did it again, and his hips surged forward involuntarily. He grabbed my wrist and pulled me up so I was standing flush against him, giving me a fleeting kiss before turning me around. His hands made quick work of my dress, letting it pool at my feet.

He then gently traced my silver tattoos before turning me back around. His eyes slowly fell down my body, and he bit that lip again and looked like he was memorizing everything about me.

"Fuck," he said softly. "I've thought about this a lot, and my mind did not do you justice."

His hand lifted hesitantly, and he wrapped it around my neck softly before slowly dragging it down my chest, down my stomach, and then, so slowly, he touched me where I wanted him to the most. I sighed when his fingers dragged through my arousal. Haden's eyes took in everything about my face as my mouth fell open.

"Fuck," I moaned softly. His eyes moved down, and he stepped back slightly so he could watch his fingers push into me. I reached out and grabbed his shoulders. Haden's mouth fell open as he pulled his fingers out and slowly sank back into me. I grabbed his hand and moved his thumb, circling my clit. I dropped my hand away, and Haden was touching me perfectly. Heavens above, I wanted him to feel good too. I reached down and stroked his hard length. Haden gripped my hand and tightened my grip, pumping my hand faster.

"Just like that, Storm."

I kept doing it, and Haden's eyes closed tightly before he withdrew his fingers and lifted me up. He laid me on the bed and crawled over me. His mouth crashed into mine, and I kissed him feverishly. I was desperate to feel him inside of me. I wrapped my legs around him and rubbed him against me. Haden rocked his hips forward and through my wetness.

"Fuck, Storm, are you sure?"

"I have never been more sure about anything in my life," I said breathlessly.

Haden pulled back and lined our hips together before slowly pushing inside of me. Gods, I felt impossibly full as he moved forward. I clenched my eyes tightly at the small pain. Haden began to pull away, but I tightened my legs around him and thrust my hips forward, taking him in as far as I could.

Haden moaned, and we both didn't move for a moment. No thoughts came to me as we both waited for the other. Fuck, this was better than I imagined. The pain subsided, and I slowly loosened my thighs on him.

"You feel like fucking heaven," Haden breathed. He pulled out and pushed back in slowly, glancing at my face to make sure I was doing alright. I moaned at the pure ecstasy of this. I did not know this would feel so euphoric.

"Faster, Haden," I begged.

He listened and moved his hips faster.

"Oh, gods," I muttered softly. "Just like that."

Haden was staring down at me. His eyes were turning icy blue, and I smiled at him. My fingers pushed through his damp hair and yanked him down to me. My mouth was demanding, making him move faster.

"You look so pretty under me, Storm," He ground out. His hips surged forward hard and circled again and again. Haden's skin glistened with sweat as he moved against me quickly.

"You feel so good. I did not know it would feel this good."

Haden sighed before he leaned down and kissed me roughly. My fingers dug into the flesh of his back as a sensation started building deep in my stomach. Haden's hands came up and gripped my jaw tightly as his mouth devoured mine. He pulled back and knelt so he could grab my hips, then he yanked me against him roughly. His gaze fell to where he filled me.

"Fucking hell," he muttered. "I'm close."

"Me too."

"Tell me what you need to cum around me as I bury myself inside of you."

Shit.

I grabbed his hand and showed him how to rub my clit as he drove into me.

"Yes, do not stop doing that."

Haden was getting more and more frantic with his thrusts. I stared at his face, but the feeling of tipping over the edge made me close my eyes tightly.

"Eyes on me; watch me when you cum."

My eyes fluttered open as my orgasm tore through me. "Haden." I moaned out as he slammed into me, desperate to cum with me. He buried himself deep inside of me with a final moan. He panted as he collapsed on top of me, and we both lay there tangled in each other's bodies, our breathing filling the space. After a minute, Haden looked up at me and gave me a grin so big that my heart squeezed.

"How does anyone get things done when they can feel like that all the time?"

I laughed, and he leaned up to give me a chaste kiss.

"You own me, Ardella. I am yours for my entire existence."

Tears stung my eyes as I pulled him down and hugged him to me tightly, once again begging the heavens to let me keep him as my mate.

"Will you stay the night with me?"

"Yes." I smiled as we both wiggled our way under his blankets. Then he pulled me back against him, his arm wrapping around me like I would disappear if he let me go.

CHAPTER 7

DELLA

Haden handed me a plate of food and kissed the top of my head as he sat down next to me. We had been holed up in the house for three days now, eating, sleeping, and making love. This was everything I wanted.

"What are you thinking about?" he asked.

"How lucky I am to have you." I smiled when he snapped his gaze up to mine, and I could see a war waging in his eyes.

"I'm in love with you," he suddenly blurted out.

I wondered when he was actually going to say it to me. He had told me in every way possible without using the words, but I still wanted to hear them.

"I love you, Haden," I said without thought. He sighed with relief. "Did you think I didn't?"

"No, I knew you did, but hearing it just does something to me." He took a bite of his food and looked at me. He was thinking of something again. "I'm confused about something. If a god gets married, shouldn't their mate become immortal? How fair is it for you to marry someone and outlive them, just to do it all over again?"

My chest immediately felt like it was being stabbed. Gods, I was going to have to tell him about my mating bond. I set the plate of food down and already felt the tears stinging my eyes. Haden set his plate down and went to grab me, but I stood up out of his way.

"Storm..."

My gaze traced over his face like it was the last time I would see it. Haden was going to be devastated, and there was nothing I could do to fix the pain this would cause him. I just hoped that he loved me enough to believe that I wanted him.

"You asked me why a goddess was hanging around mortal fae, and I told you I didn't want to tell you, but I know I need to be honest with you. I just don't want you to be upset with me when I tell you."

Haden looked at me with fear in his eyes. I waited to gather my courage, but deep down I knew this was going to upset him. How could it not?

"Gods get a fated mate," I said.

Haden's reaction made me pause. His fear disappeared, and a big smile took over his face. Guilt slammed into my chest.

"You are not mine." I shook my head. His smile fell instantly. Haden stood and began pacing back and forth in the bedroom.

"How is that possible?" he asked. "But you can reject him and pick me?" he asked with way too much hope. His big, stormy eyes looked at me, pleading with me to lie to him and tell him that I could.

"No, gods don't get to reject their mates, but I already picked you."

His eyes filled with unshed tears as he glanced around frantically. Haden's anger and hurt filled the air, making it tense and hard to breathe.

"I don't know much about fated mates, but isn't there a bond or something? You can't choose me if you haven't met him. What if we start a life and he comes along, and you leave me? That will kill me."

Haden started pacing around again.

"I have met him." I frowned because this was the part I didn't want him to know. "You saw me sneaking around the village for weeks because I was following him. I didn't feel any sort of connection to him at all, though. I was trying to figure out why I had a bond to someone I did not feel anything toward. I thought I needed to be near him longer, but the more I was near him, the more I realized I did not want him. But the first time I saw you, I felt what I should have for him."

"Who is it?"

"Haden..." I begged.

"Tell me now."

"It's Holden."

Haden froze in shock. His entire body went rigid as icy blue took over his features. His magic suddenly exploded out of him, knocking me into the wall. Snow flurried around us as I stood up.

"Please, the heavens made a mistake because the moment I saw you, I finally felt something. You are mine, Haden. I do not want him."

"Get out," he said softly.

"Please, I don't want to lose you."

"Get out!" he yelled with so much hurt and anger that the walls shook. "Please, I need you to leave."

I didn't move, so he walked over to me and grabbed me by the upper arm. Haden pulled me to the front door and gently shoved me out before slamming it behind me. I pounded on the door, begging him not to leave me. Then I heard it, his soft crying coming from inside the home, and my chest felt as if it were caving in. I did that to him.

Haden was hurting because of me, and I didn't know how to fix it. How was I supposed to reassure him that I chose him and always would?

I sat on the stairs of his home, waiting for him to come out. I physically felt ill that I hurt him. It felt like hours before the door finally opened. Quickly, I stood up, but he didn't look at me. He slammed his door shut and began walking through the field. I followed desperately, just to be close to him.

"Can we please talk?" I asked, but he ignored me. Silently, I walked behind him because of his ridiculous pace. Haden didn't look back at me once as he twisted and turned through the village. I made myself invisible so that no one would see me crying and following him like a crazy lady. Haden stopped at the pastry stand, and the two women smiled at him.

"No girlfriend today?" The dark-haired one smiled.

"No," Haden said quickly. He was going to leave me, and I couldn't stop it. There was no bond between us; he didn't need to reject me. He could just walk away from me, and I would have to let him.

"Well, in that case, do you want to get a drink at the tavern tonight?" she purred.

Jealousy instantly filled my chest. Haden glanced at me, and I saw the devastation in his eyes. If he said yes to her, he might as well carve my heart out with a knife. I gasped when he closed his eyes, a shiver seeming to run through him. His breath hitched. For a heartbeat, he didn't move. Then the color bled from his eyes, icy blue giving way to black. The air dropped several degrees around me, and a pressure coiled in my chest like a storm waiting to break. Gods, there was something different about him. It wasn't Haden staring back at me; it was a different version of him.

"Never in a million years," he said angrily.

"You are such an asshole." She glared.

He shrugged, and he turned to look right at me. I saw the devastation in his eyes, but there was a harsh anger in them too. Fuck, the darkness of his eyes would haunt me.

"Please, don't do this," I whispered. "You are mine."

Haden grabbed his pastry and left, but as soon as he was out of hearing range of the woman, he stopped with his back to me.

"Apparently, I am not yours, Ardella; I never was." His shoulders rose and fell quickly. "You should have told me it was Holden."

"Does it matter who it is?"

This pissed him off as he turned toward me.

"Yes, because they gave the bond to the one man I would never hurt. If it had been anyone else, I would have..."

He sighed heavily. "It doesn't matter because it wasn't someone else; it was *him*. Holden is a good man; he would make you happy."

"You make me happy." My voice cracked as emotions tightened my throat.

"Stop following me. I need time to process what is happening. I will call to you if I want to see you."

Haden's eyes flashed red, but he quickly blinked it away. What the fuck? I wanted to ask him why they did that, but he walked away from me. When he walked away this time, I did not follow. Devastation and hurt warred inside of me as I watched him practically run from me. I swallowed the lump in my throat. I felt like I was going to pass out. If gods could die, I would think I was at this very moment from a broken heart. I stumbled forward and braced myself on the shed.

Anger filled me as I thought of how cruel the heavens were being to me.

"What did I ever do to deserve this? You gave me the wrong fucking mate, and now he doesn't want me. I will never forgive you for this, do you hear me? I will never forgive you for not making Haden mine." Angry tears streamed down my face. "I'm going to be alone for my entire existence." I cried into my hands. The one thing I had to look forward to was taken from me before I ever knew I had it.

My star mist circled around me, and when it disappeared, I was back at Haden's home. I sat on the steps and waited for him. I would waste away on the stairs if I had to. This is not what was supposed to happen.

I pushed my palms into my eyes and knew this was my fault. Glancing around, I knew I should feel guilty about what I did. It made sense why Holden and I didn't have a true bond. I stood up and began pacing around, knowing that I messed with fate. The fucking heavens or stars did this as a punishment when they were the ones who forced my hand.

Haden was mine, and I knew that from the moment I met him hundreds of years ago. Gods, did he remember anything from before? Of course he didn't. His eyes turned red, and he seemed to know that he should hide that from me.

"You will not take him from me. I will always be two steps ahead of you." I warned the sky. "I will find a way to fix fate because he was supposed to be my mate—you know it. You may have given the bond to his brother, but I will never choose anyone but him. I do not care who or what he is; he is worthy of me."

It was getting dark out, and Haden never came home. I was pacing around his porch, trying not to lose my mind over the thought of him with someone else, even though he wasn't mine. The thought instantly pissed me off. He was mine.

I used my star mist to go to the village. The tavern loomed in front of me with big windows, and so many fae crowded in the place that I could hardly see through them. I watched carefully, looking for any sign of Haden. After a few minutes of staring through the window, I saw him sitting at the counter with a drink.

A woman perched a stool away, laughing too loudly, trying too hard. She leaned in, speaking with animated hands. I watched every movement, bile rising with each second. Then she scooted closer. Gods, it was worse than torture. But I couldn't look away. I needed to be near him, even if he didn't know.

She reached out, fingers brushing his shoulder. He flinched, then shrugged her off. A growl of thunder rolled overhead, deep and angry, rattling the windows as if the sky mirrored my mood. Lightning tore across the clouds—and then came the downpour. Haden looked outside. His gaze immediately finding mine. His eyes turned to the woman before he shook his head and stood up. My heart felt like it was being carved out of me with a rusty knife. My chest was caving in on itself.

I turned away from the tavern. My gaze darted around quickly, as if an answer to my problem would appear. But I already knew there wasn't an answer.

"Storm." He gripped my shoulder, turning me toward him. "That is not what you think."

"I have been waiting for you at home," I said softly. "So we could talk. And you... avoided me."

His expression faltered. Shame clouded his eyes. I saw the truth there, plain as daylight. He *had* been avoiding me. And suddenly, I felt stupid.

If he wanted to see me, he would have come. He would have called for me, like he promised.

I swallowed the words rising in my throat—the desperate, aching ones. *Please do not leave me.*

"I told you to stop following me," he said.

A final blow.

Maybe he didn't love me like he claimed he did. I let this truth sink into me and take root deep in my bones. I glanced over his face once more. I wanted him to be happy, and if that was without me, then I had to be fine with that.

Maybe he wasn't supposed to be mine.

Maybe it was a test from the heavens, and I had failed miserably. I looked away from him but hesitated. I did not want to leave him. I waited for a moment longer just in case he told me to stay. But he didn't. I stepped back from him.

"Okay, I'll leave you alone," I whispered, and it made my chest ache painfully. Defeat coursed through me as I used my star mist to go home before I fell apart.

CHAPTER 8
DELLA

My brother was blabbering about something I was not listening to. There were three other gods in the room with us, discussing issues in the realm of Ellory-on, but I did not care. I had left the tavern a week ago, and I still felt like I was dying without Haden. He didn't call to me, and I wondered if he ever would. I was falling apart.

"Ardella?" Mikel asked.

"What?" I jumped, startled in my seat, and looked over at them.

"What is the population doing? Do we need war or disease to wipe out some of it to keep the balance?"

The God of War, Admes, looked at me oddly. His red hair looked like flames, and his eyes were dark like the night. He looked terrifying.

"The population is not a threat at this time. Birthing has declined in the past hundred years."

Mikel frowned at whatever he saw on my face.

"Well, there hasn't been a war in hundreds of years. I would like to have one." Admes glared. Mikel looked at him with disappointment.

"We aren't going to approve a war for fun, Admes."

"Okay, how about a small battle?" he asked. "A tiny one."

Mikel looked at me for help. I sighed heavily in annoyance before looking at Admes.

"We aren't going to create problems for the realm because you are restless. You know war comes when it is needed, not when we create the need."

Admes glared at me.

"Do you have something to say, Admes?" I snapped. "I'm in the mood to fight, so please, go ahead." My eyes flashed white, and he backed off.

"Kaios would agree with me if he showed up today." Admes pouted. I glanced at Admes, confused.

"Kaios, God of the Sea, was supposed to come today. Why didn't he show up?" Mikel asked.

Admes shrugged his shoulders. "I have no idea. He was supposed to meet me last week for a meeting, and he didn't show. When I went to his home, he didn't seem to be there."

Mikel stared at me with concern.

"He must be visiting someone," Mikel suggested.

"Kaios would have said something about leaving. He is not a man that just leaves without a word."

"So, what are you suggesting? That he is missing?" I asked.

"I don't know, but I'm giving him a week or two to get back home. If he isn't there, then something is wrong." Admes sighed as he looked at me. That is odd. Kaios isn't the type of man to not say anything about missing a meeting.

Mikel stared at me with concern. The other two gods, Lara, Goddess of Peace, and Dramis, God of Health, both gave me a concerning look.

"A small battle, I beg of you," Admes pleaded.

"The meeting is over; get out," I snapped. All three gods looked at me before standing up and leaving without arguing. I pinched the bridge of my nose, feeling pissed beyond reason. I was having a hard time controlling myself this past week. I went from bouts of anger to grief and back to being irate. Several times I told myself I would check on Haden, but then I decided against it.

It was hard to respect what he asked me to do when the right thing felt like going to him and begging him to not leave me. I was terrified that he would find a different woman. But I also knew that if he didn't want me, then

I needed to stay away. Going to see him would only start this process over.

"Are you going to be alright with the next meeting, or will you scare her away too?" Mikel asked. "You have never been so irritable before; what's wrong?"

I looked at him and hated that I couldn't tell him what I did.

"I got in a fight with Penelope," I lied. "She doesn't want to be friends anymore."

"Oh, Dells, I'm sorry." Mikel frowned. "Maybe she just needs time to cool off. Everyone fights; no relationship is perfect. I'm sure you can figure out the differences and make them up in no time. Just give her a little space and then try again if you really want to work it out."

I sat up a little straighter. There was a need to go to Haden and let him know that I was not giving up on us. I wanted it to work, and if Haden loved me like he said, then he would want to fix things as well. My patience was running out.

"You're right." I smiled softly. "I'll give her some time, and maybe she will come around."

Mikel gave me a big smile.

"Alright, Brim sent this next woman to us, saying it was very important and to please consider what she is saying. Her name is Bayla, Queen of the Blood Witches."

I hesitated at hearing Brim's name. I needed to go check on him and make sure he was doing alright. It had been a little too long since I had seen him.

I nodded as Mikel went out of the room and came back in with her. She was beautiful. Her dark hair fell down over her shoulders; her pale skin was dusted in light freckles. Her pink lips pulled into a genuine smile as her red eyes met mine. Her dark red dress looked like blood, which seemed fitting. We had not met before, but she looked at me as if we were long-lost friends, and I smiled at the thought.

"Ardella and Mikel, thank you for seeing me on such short notice." Her voice carried a confidence in it that told me she had some serious power. A red stone hung around her neck, and it pulsed with magic.

"Please, have a seat. Brim said it was urgent." Mikel gestured for her to sit. Bayla sat down and looked at us nervously. She glanced around the sterile white office that Mikel had not decorated at all. He had said something about it causing distraction during important meetings.

"I'm not sure how much Brim told you, so I will start from the beginning." Bayla took a deep breath. "I have been having visions of Elloryon being ripped apart and destroyed by a great war in the future."

Mikel and I looked at each other.

"I do not have the power of seeing the future," she hesitated. "The visions only started recently after my mate, Killian, was murdered. He had this gift, and he has been visiting me, warning me of what is to come."

I stilled.

"If he is dead, then how is he still in contact with you?" I asked.

"He is waiting for me to move on to the next life." Bayla's eyes became wet with tears. "I know that gods' laws prevent you from meddling in our lives too much, but this war will destroy everything. Something needs to happen."

How did she know of the gods' laws? Something about this made me feel frantic. I could not explain the sudden overwhelming feeling that her visions would impact me in some way. Was it because so many lives would be lost? Even as the thought slammed into my mind, I knew that wasn't it. I sat up a bit straighter in the chair and watched this woman closely.

There was something about her, but I could not put my finger on it. My gaze stayed on her, worried I would miss some sort of clue as to why I felt drawn to her.

"Well, when is it supposed to happen?" Mikel asked.

"I'm not sure. Maybe 300 years from now? It changes timelines in my visions every time I see it. I do not have a definite answer."

"Is Admes going to defy what we said?" Mikel looked at me. "We won't be able to stop it until it is happening, and that might be too late."

"The god is not responsible for it," Bayla said quickly before hesitating. "Did Brim not tell you of the prophecy?" Bayla asked. We both turned to her quickly. Damn it, Brim. Now I definitely needed to go talk with him. "There is an answer to the problem."

"Do you want to help?" I guessed.

She shook her head and swallowed hard.

"I will not survive that long. I have seen my daughter grow up without me in my visions." She rubbed her belly instinctively. "These visions started when I became pregnant with her. Her name will be Thea, and she will save the realm. I have seen her prophecy, and she is so powerful that no one will compare to her. She is the key to saving the realm."

"How can you be so sure?" Mikel asked.

"Because Brim saw her prophecy as well." She frowned. "I want to make a bargain with you."

I watched the grief on her face. I couldn't imagine being a mother and grieving the thought that I would die before I saw my daughter grow older.

"You and Thea are going to be great friends." Bayla stared me straight in the eyes.

"Me?"

She nodded, and somehow, I felt the truth of her statement. Was that what was drawing me to her, her daughter's soul already forming in her stomach?

"You'll become family," she smiled.

I didn't know how to respond to her words, but Mikel ignored her confession completely.

"What bargain?" Mikel asked.

"Thea needs to be star-blessed for the prophecy to happen."

Mikel looked at me. I was the one who got to decide if her child would be blessed by the stars. It would make Thea a god, but to what extent? Mikel was watching me closely, but I was focused on Bayla. Something about her pulsed with familiarity. I could see the soft glow within her, Thea's soul forming within her stomach. It glowed a pretty shade of dark green.

"I have never star-blessed a creature before. We do not know what will happen. Perhaps nothing happens; maybe she becomes a goddess herself, or maybe she will only receive elite magic. How can we be sure that this is what is needed?" I asked.

Bayla smiled softly at me.

"I would choose a different option if I could. Do you know how terrible it is to see your child's future being one where the weight of the realm depends on her? Thea will not have an easy life, and I hate myself for being here and telling you of my visions because it sets into motion her difficult fate. But you know it is the right choice. You can tell just by looking at me that I am not lying. This is the only way. Whatever happens after she is star-blessed will be exactly what is needed."

I glanced at Mikel, who was watching silently. I waited for doubt or reason to pop up in my mind, but it didn't. My mind was blank—quiet. I stood up and moved closer to Bayla. She suddenly looked at Mikel with a menacing glare for some reason unknown to me.

"Is this your coven's stone?" I asked.

She nodded as she gripped the pulsing red crescent moon around her neck. I reached forward and picked it up. I hesitated for a brief moment before my star mist circled around it, and when it moved away, the color had faded to purple. Bayla looked at me oddly.

"If she is a goddess, then she will need her own star for her powers—for her mate. This will be passed down to her and her alone." Bayla shook her head in disbelief. "Now, I can see her soul forming within you, and I can already feel her power."

I looked over Bayla, and she looked terrified.

"The bargain is as follows: I will star-bless her, but I do not know if it will be painful, and in exchange, Thea's prophecy will be to save the realm, and this stone will be passed to her."

Bayla nodded, "I agree."

"Alright, give me your arm."

Bayla stuck her arm out, and I gripped her wrist, preparing to sear a star bargain into the both of us. It could not be fulfilled until both of us kept our part. Four glowing orange stars appeared in a line across both of our wrists.

Bayla's silent tears fell from her eyes as I reached forward slowly, resting both of my palms on her stomach. My magic seeped from me, pouring into her slowly as I recited a prayer to the heavens to bless Thea. We would not know if it worked until she was older, but I could feel it. I could feel her power already pulsing from her soul. Thea would change the realm, and I hoped to witness it. I pulled my hands back, and Bayla jumped up, gripping me tightly.

Relief flooded her as she held my wrists.

"Thank you, Della. Not only for this, but for taking care of Thea later when I am no longer here," Bayla whispered. "You will take care of each other. Tell her I wished there was another way, and I am so proud of her."

"I will."

I pulled back and looked over her face and stilled. Her tears that fell were lit with the soft glow of the stars. Mikel stood up and looked at Bayla closely.

"Fucking hell, it's going to work," he said.

Bayla smiled at me, and I knew that this moment had just changed my entire life. That frantic feeling subsided slightly, but it was there in the back of my mind, like an itch.

"You are not allowed to speak of this to anyone but Brim," I decreed.

"I promise." She smiled. "Thank you both."

Bayla bowed her head down, and when she lifted her gaze to me, there were so many emotions floating in her red eyes that I didn't know how to decipher any of them. Bayla left, and I turned to Mikel.

"You believed her."

"Yes." I nodded. "Something about her made me feel like I was meant to star-bless her daughter."

"You may have just created a goddess," Mikel said with wonderment.

I smiled at him.

"I guess we will see if Thea makes a name for herself in the future," I nodded.

Mikel stared at me like he was lost in thought. His eyes traced over me like he could see something different about me.

"I am going to go have a drink after the day we just had," he sighed.

"I'm going to check on Penelope."

Mikel nodded and gave me a hug.

☾★★★☽★★★☾

Haden was working on his house when I showed up. He didn't know I was standing in the birch trees close by. I sat on a downed log and watched him work without a shirt on. I waited for the woman to come out of the house or show up, but she hadn't so far. Fuck, I wanted to go speak to him, but my aching chest and heart felt better just from being close to him. So, I stayed and watched for hours. This was the best I could do to respect that he wanted space. So, I would watch from a distance.

Haden didn't stop his ridiculous pace of working. He was making quick progress on the house, and I wished I could see it. The sun began setting, and the sky turned pretty shades of pink and orange. Haden glanced up at the sky and admired the beauty for a moment before looking around.

"I know you are here," he called out. "You've been here all afternoon."

Shit. I stepped forward, and his gaze immediately found mine. He didn't say anything as I walked closer.

"You're just sitting in the woods?" He raised his eyebrow.

"It just feels nice to be close to you," I whispered. "You never called for me. I was hoping you'd be ready to talk now so we can work through this."

He shook his head. His eyes were cold—hidden behind a wall that let no emotion in. I rubbed my chest as the dull ache shot through me painfully.

"There isn't anything to talk about," he said, his voice flat and unreadable. He looked down at the log he was cutting and began working again. That was it? He was just fine with ending things like this? "You have a mate, and it will never be me."

I could hear the pain in his voice even as he tried to hide it. But his words ignited a wrath within me that I could not control.

"There is so much more to talk about. You are acting as though I went to the heavens and told them to make Holden my mate instead of you. This was out of my control."

"Listen, Ardella, I don't know what you want me to say. Do you want me to be fine with the fact that you were made for my brother?" The sadness in his voice made me pause. "I do not understand why the heavens did not think I was worthy of you."

The heartbreak and confusion in his trembling voice made my anger subside. He was better than any mate ever could have been.

"You are. You are the only one who can love me in the way I need. Please, I am begging you to hear me when I say that there is no one more worthy of me."

"I'm not, and you need to leave. This will be easier if we stay away from each other. If you and Holden become a couple, I will not hold animosity toward either of you." His voice was untouched by emotion.

His words enraged me.

"You really think I am going to pursue your brother?" I snapped. "And I don't believe you for a second that you would just step aside and let another man have me."

"What choice would I have?" he yelled. "Holden and I are twins; it would be easy to fall for him instead of me."

I scoffed.

"You have lost your fucking mind." I glared at him. "You and Holden could not be more different. You do not even look similar to me."

His chest was heaving as he stared at me as if I was a pain in his ass. He looked away from me, not even giving me the respect of a response, as he began working again on his damn piece of wood. I used my magic and threw it across the field.

"What the hell?"

"Stop trying to act like this isn't hurting you, and fight with me if you need to. Tell me how I can make you realize that I meant it when I said I love you."

Haden looked me in the eyes and sighed. "You won't convince me. Just let me go so I can forget about you."

My anger immediately formed into grief.

"You won't ever forget about me because I am not letting you do this. I chose you. I want you. I will choose you every single fucking time you are an option, and if you aren't, then I will change fate to have you. I am in love with you, Haden."

He frowned as he looked away.

"Why do you not love me enough to hear me?" I cried.

"Loving you is not the issue here." He looked at me again. "You should have told me immediately that Holden was your mate."

"I didn't want to lose you."

"You lost me anyway, but at least that way I wouldn't have fallen in love with you first," he snapped and went into his house, slamming his door.

I stood there hoping he would change his mind and come back out. He didn't, but I was not backing off. When my legs became tired, I sat down. And when hours of sitting in the grass hurt my back, I lay down. I would sleep out here if I needed to. I stared at the stars twinkling above me, and I prayed to them.

I prayed that they would correct this mistake because that was exactly what this was, a huge fucking mistake. I curled into a ball and closed my eyes.

CHAPTER 9

HADEN

I was standing at the window watching Della sit in the damn yard of my home, waiting for me to come out. The fucking stars had done this to us because of what I am. Della didn't know that this was my fault, and if she did, she would understand that she had no business loving me.

Her having a bond with Holden was the awakening I needed. Holden could treat her well. He was a good man, and I was not. Della was talking to herself as she watched the house, not knowing I was watching her. Gods, she was just as pretty as she was all those years ago when I met her. I told myself that when I found her again, I would make her mine. My anger began seething inside of me. If it had been anyone but Holden, I would have ripped their goddamn heart out. There was no man that was going to have her, but I could not kill my brother.

The void told me she was not our mate, but I didn't realize how pissed off I would become when I let that realization soak into me. The void wanted her too. Our personalities agreed on something for once—and she should be off limits.

"What the fuck am I supposed to do?" I asked the void, but he didn't answer me. I looked around the house and frowned. This was supposed to be our home.

Della was now lying on the ground, and I sighed heavily because she was so damn persistent. I wanted to go out there. I wanted to scoop her up and never let her go, but that small sliver of doubt trickled into my mind. What if she ended up loving Holden? It would kill me. I began pacing around the foyer trying to let fate have her, but stars above, I was losing it. There was a reason the stars and heavens had fucked with fate, and the reason was I was not a good man. Desperately I was trying to hold onto the sliver of good inside of me and let her be happy with another man.

I felt the void pulsing deep inside of me. No, no, no, I tried to shove it down because when the void came out, I did not think about anything. I closed my eyes as I rested my forehead against the front door. My fingertips digging into the door as I tried to make him stay buried inside of me.

Stop it and let me out. He demanded.

"You are going to keep her if I do. She is Holden's, and we can't have her." I argued with myself like a lunatic.

Storm is ours, and you will never let her belong to another man. Go out there and get her.

"No. Even you said she had a mate. Why would you let me get attached to her knowing this?"

Ardella was always going to be ours, fates be damned. She doesn't want Holden, so quit being a pussy and go get her. She is stubborn; she will never allow you to leave her.

"I'm trying to do the right thing."

The fuck you are. The right thing is to go out there and get our woman.

"I did not let you be present with me at the same time to argue with you over this. I thought you would be helpful. But I should have known better; you are a greedy bastard."

His laughter echoed in my mind.

You realize that I know when you are lying? You called to me because you knew I would do what we both want and not give a fuck about the consequences. So let me out so I can fix the damage you are inflicting on the woman we love.

"But—"

Fucking hell. Stop it. Please, go get her; she is in distress. Stop being so damn nice and do what you actually want.

"This is a terrible idea. What if she falls in love with Holden? I will die."

Is that what has you acting like this? He sighed heavily. *Della will never love Holden. She has loved us for a very long time, and I am not going to explain to you what that means. There are things that you do not understand or know about us, and that is for your own good.*

"Tell me, or I will refuse to let you surface."

I warned you. She is ours and has been forever. Della will never choose another man over us, so you are doing this for no reason. You will not keep her from me.

Then the void burst out of the depths of my soul and dug his claws into every fiber of my body. I felt the shiver run up my spine and groaned as the void seeped into my mind, not letting me make decisions anymore. I opened my eyes and sighed heavily. He would thank me later when he realized how stupid he had been to push her away.

"Much better." I smiled.

My vision pulsed black in my wrath. What the fuck was the *nice* part of me thinking? We had no choice in this. Della was ours, bond or not; it did not fucking matter. I looked up at the ceiling and smiled, hoping the stars and heavens saw me.

"You stupid fucks. Do you really think a bond will keep us apart? When she is calling my name to the heavens as I am buried inside of her, then maybe you'll understand she is mine. I will mark her in every way imaginable. I don't need your permission to have her."

I could feel the tugging of my other side of me trying to get out, but he wouldn't. He would stay inside until he stopped being so damn noble and trying to give my woman to someone that she didn't want.

I looked out of the window and instantly shoved the door open when I saw her lying on the ground. *What the fuck is wrong with you?* I asked myself. He didn't answer me, and that was probably for the best. I was going to lose my fucking mind. When I got to her, she was curled into a ball. Anger simmered under my skin as I looked around. She should know better than to sleep out here. There are monsters.

"Oh, Storm," I whispered and scooped her up in my arms. She seemed to be too tired to process that she was moving. Her scent filled my lungs, and I inhaled deeply. She smelled like heaven and flowers. She curled into me as I walked us up the stairs. The boards creaked under us as I moved her into the warm house. She was cold. I laid her down just as her eyes fluttered like she might be waking up.

"Why the hell are you sleeping outside?" I snapped softly. "You could've been killed by a monster."

She opened her eyes and stared at me, her mind finally registering the fact that she was in our house.

"Gods can't die," was all she could say. That wasn't true.

"Well, they can get hurt. I can only imagine being mauled by a monster would not be a great time, especially if you can't die."

"Careful, Haden, you sound like you care." Her attitude was deserved.

My eyes narrowed on her. "I do fucking care."

She sat up and looked at me. "Then please stop pushing me away. I feel so lost without you."

"The heavens say I am not yours," I started to say, but she cut me off in her rage. And I shut my mouth because Storm's anger was one of my favorite things to admire. Her pretty face instantly became hard-pressed as she glared at me.

"Will you stop saying that?" She stood up, irritated, thinking that I was not understanding that she was mine even if the heavens told her she wasn't supposed to want me. I had no choice in this because I was in love with her.

"You know that is not true," she hissed. "You are mine. I do not want Holden. If I wanted him, I would have taken him from Sara, but I didn't. I do not care that my supposed mate loves another woman, Haden. But what I do care about is that you are shutting me out. I am terrified that you will disappear. I am terrified that you do not think I am worthy enough for you to love me back. You are my mate in every sense of the fucking word. So, what if we don't have a bond? I don't need some stupid bond to tell me you are everything I have waited my entire existence for."

She couldn't stop herself as more words poured from her mouth in a rage.

"I slept with you! Do you understand the importance of that? Gods are not supposed to feel any desire for anyone but our mate. We do not sleep with anyone unless they are our mate. I chose you, and isn't that better than some stupid bond? I looked at you and *knew* you were mine. No one will ever be you, Haden.

"If you tell me to leave, then I will. I will leave you alone so that you can enjoy your life without me. But don't think that I will move on. I can't. I would walk out those doors knowing that I will never have a mate after you. I would not get married. I would not have a family of my own. I would not love another male. But if you truly do not want me, then I love you enough to let you be happy without me. I will give up everything about my happiness if it will make *you* happy. I am so in love with you, Haden. And I am destroyed by the thought that you hate me for a mistake the heavens made. I have cursed them. I have demanded that they fix this. Because I know in my heart, my soul, that you are the one meant for me."

I stared at her as she fell apart in front of me. Tears streamed down her face as she stared at me. Honestly, I was at a loss for words.

"Please say something," she begged. "Tell me to leave, or tell me to stay."

I took a deep breath, trying to form a thought about how I felt about her. She exhaled deeply, and her shoulders deflated. Devastation slammed into her eyes. She hurried around me. Just as her star mist was wrapping around her, I reached forward and grabbed her arm, turning her around. My mouth crushed into hers as I yanked her flush against me.

I pulled her to me with desperate hands. My arms circled around her in a death grip as she deepened the kiss. Slowly, the passion fizzled into tenderness. I pulled back and traced over her with my eyes.

"I'm sorry. I thought the right thing was to let fate have you," I said quickly. "I'm so fucking sorry. Please don't leave. Forgive me for trying to make you want Holden instead of me. Forgive me for trying to push you away. The heavens and hell both know I was lying when I said you weren't mine. I love you, Storm. I do not know how to stop."

"Then don't," she whispered. "Please do not ever leave me again. I will not survive it."

"I'm all in if you're all in." I smiled softly.

She kissed me. "I'm all in."

"I will never let you go. I'm serious; you are mine. I want this life with you. I want to marry you and build a life together."

I stared at her intently.

"I was yours from the first moment I looked into your stormy eyes. You are stuck with me, Haden. I will never leave you."

I sighed heavily and held her to me. This was it. This was the beginning of forever. Now I just needed to figure out how I could keep her safe from Elra and Mateo. I knew what my duty was, but I couldn't do that and have her. But it wasn't even a hard decision. Della would always be my first pick.

☽★★★☽★★★☽

The next morning, I woke up to Della sleeping in our bed. Smiling at her, I gave her a soft kiss on the cheek before going to the kitchen to fix us something to eat. Before I could start seeing what I had for food, I spotted them outside of the kitchen window.

"Fucking great," I whispered.

I glanced around, making sure Della was still sound asleep on the bed in the living space. I slipped out the door and headed to the tree line, where they stood in their cloaks. Della couldn't see them; she would start asking who they were, and if she did that, then she would figure out who I was. I was avoiding that at all costs. Walking past them without a word, I knew they'd follow me deeper into the trees.

Once I was satisfied that we were out of sight from Della, I turned to them, my eyes flashing red. I knew Elra was in the middle as she stepped forward.

"Take that ridiculous hood off," I snapped. "Who are you hiding from? I know who you are, idiots."

Elra slipped her hood off and glared at me.

"You are always so pleasant to see, Haden." She glared.

"What do you want?" I asked.

Her eyes narrowed on me as I crossed my arms and stared at her with hatred. I didn't move away as she acted like I would back down.

"What the fuck are you doing?" she asked. I knew what she was asking, but I played dumb.

"What do you mean?"

"You know what I am saying; do I really need to say it out loud?" Her voice was full of irritation.

"I think I'm going to need you to say it because I don't know what you are talking about," I lied.

She pointed to the house.

"You are playing house with your whore."

I clenched my jaw tightly but didn't give her the reaction she wanted.

"Della is not yours to keep. She is the key to ending the curse, so quit planning a life with her, or I will fucking kill you myself."

I glanced at the five others standing behind her and sighed heavily.

"That's it? That is all you came here for?"

"You son of a bitch!" Elra stepped forward, and I gave her a look, letting her know I was not above punching her in the face.

"I dare you to touch me, Elra, and I will rip you to shreds and send you straight to hell."

She hesitated, which was the smartest thing she had ever done. Her eyes flickered over me and then to the house. Elra was thinking hard about something. I didn't like that she knew Della was this close.

"You are actually in love with her." She accused. "Are you insane? She will never love you back."

"She already does."

My chest was filling with anxiety. I should not have said that. Elra's eyes gleamed with her evil fucking soul.

"Do you really think she would love you if she knew who you are?" She laughed, and so did the rest of them.

I would like to say that she would love me no matter what, but I wasn't sure about that. Della loved me, but it was because I manipulated her into loving me, kind of.

"You better remember why you are here." Elra stepped toward me. "To break our curse, not to crawl into that goddess' bed and pretend like you have a real future with her."

"I know what I am doing."

"You better, or I will kill you, and one of us will take your place. This curse is ending, and you don't even know what will happen to Ardella when that happens. She might not survive this." Elra stepped forward. "She will end you when she knows why you are here. That you are using her to break a fucking curse. She will rip your soul out without another thought. She is the heavens' favorite goddess, for fuck's sake."

"Are we done with this conversation? I have shit to do," I sighed in a bored tone to hide that a cold sweat formed on my skin. My heart was beating like crazy because I knew Elra's words were true, but I truly loved Della and did not know how to let her go. Maybe she would understand why I did what I did.

"Haden?" I heard Della yell, and I instantly froze, watching each of these pricks to see if they would do something. I would skin them alive.

"Speak of the whore," Mateo said with a smile. My attention turned toward him when Della began walking toward the woods. She was in my tunic and showing way too much skin to these pricks. "Gods be damned, Haden, I see why you follow her around like a little bitch. She is fucking stunning. Maybe I should see if she'll suck my co—" I punched Mateo in the face. He looked at me, his nose bleeding black blood. His eyes widened before smiling.

"Well, it looks like we found the first thing that Haden has ever given a shit about in his pathetic life." Mateo chuckled but flinched when I went to punch him again.

"Haden?" Della's voice was getting closer.

"Fuck off, all of you," I hissed.

"Count your fucking days, Haden. You have clearly lost sight of what you are supposed to be doing." Elra smiled before they disappeared.

Shit. I stepped forward, and Della came from around the tree.

"Storm?" I smiled to throw her off of what I was doing.

"What are you doing out here?" She looked around like she expected to see someone pop out.

"I thought I saw someone in the trees, but I must have been seeing things." I lied and hated it. She nodded and held out her hand for me to take. I slid my hand into hers and walked her out of the woods. Della glanced at my face like she could see I was struggling with something.

"I did not like waking up to you missing from bed." She smiled when I looked at her.

"My mistake, Storm; I will not do it again."

I tugged her to me and kissed her.

"What are your plans for today?" I asked. As much as I wanted to spend the day with her, I needed to go see Brim. My visions of the future were changing, and not for the good of Della and I.

"I have some meetings, but I should be back within a few hours."

"I have some things I need to get from town, but I should be back before you."

"Will you pick up some pastries? They are so good." Her eyes gleamed with excitement.

"Yes, I will get anything you wish."

She looked at me with such love in her eyes that I felt like a piece of shit. I did love her, but that was a problem. I knew that.

"I love you." I smiled.

"I love you more." She kissed me before her magic wrapped around her and she disappeared.

As soon as she left, I felt the small pulsing in my mind. I knew what it meant: a vision was coming, but this one felt more intense than the others I had before. Shooting pain coursed through my mind, making me fall to my knees, groaning as visions plagued me.

Della was yelling. Why was she crying so violently, like she was dying? I looked around, but the vision did not let me see what was happening around her. But what Della did next made my mouth fall open in shock. Della became so enraged that she grabbed her mating bond with Holden and severed it with her magic. Gods cannot reject mates.

"Haden!" She screamed so loud that it ripped me from the vision.

I opened my eyes and glanced around confused before another vision came barreling into my mind, making me fall over onto the ground. My head was pounding violently as bits and pieces came to me.

"I know how to change fate," I said to Brim. I was desperate for Della. I would do anything.

"You can't change fate, Haden," Brim said with conviction.

"Yes, I can."

Brim stood up, his eyes filled with concern.

"Haden, don't do this."

"It's too late; I have no say in the matter anymore. It will happen."

My eyes fluttered open as I tried to make sense of what was happening, but as I tried to stand, I collapsed back to the ground.

"Storm," I whispered when I heard someone, but it wasn't Storm.

Brim stood over me, his face full of concern. If Brim was here, it meant he had a vision, and it was not good. His friendly eyes were filled with concern for me.

"Haden, what have you done?" he asked. "I can't see Della's future anymore."

I tried to speak, but there was a heavy fog in my mind. Why couldn't he see her future? I shook my head, trying to concentrate. Show me her future, I demanded from my magic, but nothing came to me either. No. What did that mean?

"Brim... help her." I begged.

"She is not the one that needs help, Haden. You are going to die, but we can stop it." He frowned. "You had the vision too? There were cloaked figures, and they killed you. They are so angry with you. Who are they?"

I could not tell him. He would not be able to stop them if they wanted to kill me. How did I explain to Brim that I had been lying to everyone about who I was? My head was pounding as I tried to stay conscious. Della. She would be devastated. My eyes rolled back, not being able to fight it anymore as I passed out.

CHAPTER 10

DELLA

I frowned when I glanced at Haden. He had seemed so distant since I got home an hour ago. His eyes were dim, and his smiles did not reach his eyes. He looked lost in thought as I slid onto his lap as he sat in the chair at the table. His normally stormy blue eyes were replaced with dark black pools. This was the other side of Haden that came out sporadically. There was a subtle difference with him when he was like this.

"Please tell me what is wrong," I whispered. "You look so sad."

His eyes searched mine like he was looking for an answer to something. His arms wrapped around me and rubbed my back. He tried to give me a reassuring smile, but it didn't reach his eyes.

"I'm not sure; I just feel sad for some reason," he said with a tinge of pain in his voice. I rubbed his back as I held him tightly.

"Did I do something to make you feel this way?"

"No." He squeezed me tighter. "I just get like this sometimes. You always make me happy, Storm."

I pulled back and saw the sadness swirling in his pretty eyes. I cupped his cheek and wished I could make him feel better.

"I'm sorry I didn't get the pastries for you today. I didn't leave the house after I started feeling like this."

"It's all right." I leaned forward and kissed his forehead. He was keeping something from me. "We can get pastries a different day. We have a lifetime."

He swallowed hard and nodded.

"A lifetime with you sounds like heaven." He smiled, and this time it reached his eyes. "I had a dream about you last night," he whispered.

"You did?" I smiled. "Tell me."

"You and I were married. We lived in this house, and we had children running around us. Gods, we were so damn happy." Tears sprang to his eyes as he looked at me. "Just as in love as we are now."

"That sounds like a good life," I confessed as emotions filled him. "Why is that making you cry?"

"Because I love you so much. All I want is that life with you. Nothing else matters to me." His eyes lost all of their happiness again. Fear trickled into my mind as I watched him. My hand brushed against his cheek.

"Are you sure you don't want to tell me what else is bothering you? I will not be mad if that is why you are worried."

His eyes bounced between mine as he contemplated his response. His hands started rubbing up and down my back again as if I was the one who needed comforting.

"There is nothing else, Della. I am just feeling off today, but tomorrow will be a wonderful day. I promise."

I wished he'd tell me, but I didn't push it.

"Then let's go to bed so we can get to the wonderful day sooner." I smiled when he leaned forward and kissed me softly as he stood, holding me to him. I wrapped my arms and legs tightly around him. As he carried us to the bed in the living space. I hoped he felt better tomorrow because I did not like seeing him so sad.

☽★★★☽★★★☽

Haden was gone when I woke up. I felt his side of the bed, and it was cold. Frowning, I sat up, holding the blanket to my naked chest. Stars, I needed to go home today and get some new clothes. I had not been home in a week, except for a brief meeting with Mikel yesterday.

He just assumed I was hanging out with Penelope, and I didn't correct him. I could not leave Haden for a long time without missing him.

"Haden?" I called out. He didn't answer. I slipped out of bed and tugged on his tunic from last night. I went to the kitchen thinking he would be waiting for me, but he wasn't there either. Terror gripped me after I remembered how upset he had been last night. Did he leave without telling me? I was about to turn around when a note on the counter caught my attention. I smiled at the small bundle of wildflowers sitting next to it.

Storm,

Sorry to leave you waking up to an empty bed, but it's for a good reason. Come find me at the pond.

- Haden

I smiled and hurried out of the house. Haden's tall silhouette was standing at the water's edge. He must have heard me walking up because he turned and smiled at me. I paused when I saw how nice his outfit was. I glanced down at my bare legs, and Haden's gaze moved too. He smiled brightly.

"Should I change?" I asked before looking around. "Why are you dressed so nicely?"

Haden's eyes filled with amusement.

"Did you not notice?"

I turned and looked at everything around us. Nothing looked different. I glanced back at him and shook my head. Haden chuckled softly as he dragged his hands down his face.

"Come over here, Storm." He reached out to me. I walked up to him, and he brought up my hand and kissed the back of it. I didn't move. I stopped breathing. My eyes flickered up to his before moving back down to the ring on my finger. This has been on my finger this whole time?

"Haden..."

My heart was pounding as nervousness and excitement coursed through me. Tears pricked the backs of my eyes as I stared at him.

He fell to his knee in front of me.

"Ardella, you are the love of my life—no, the love of my existence. I meant it when I said I was all in. I do not want to wait for what others may deem as an appropriate time to start our beginning together. I know that if it is a day, a year, or a century, I will still be in love with you. I have pictured a future with you, and I am desperate to live in that reality. In you I have found love, but I also found the soul that completes mine, the voice that calms my heart, and a friend I used to dream about finding. You are everything.

"I promise to love you, to protect you, and to always comfort you. My heart, my soul, my everything is yours as long as you promise to marry me. I am desperate to be yours, to belong to you. My love for you knows no bounds. Please do me the honor of becoming my wife, Della."

I stared at the small silver band with the prettiest red stones and diamonds decorating it. It almost seemed to glow. Haden's nervous dark eyes watched me. I nodded as the words wouldn't come out yet.

"Yes, a million times yes. I will choose you in this lifetime and any that follow."

Haden sighed like he was worried I would say no. This was it. This was the happiest moment I had ever had in my existence. This was everything that I waited for. An overwhelming wave of love slammed into me as I stared at him. I leaned down and pressed my mouth to his.

Suddenly, Haden yanked me down and laid me beneath him. His movements were frantic as he tugged his tunic off and reached for mine. He moaned softly when he saw I was naked under it. His hand skimmed down my stomach, making me sigh with anticipation. He leaned down, trailing kisses from below my breasts, down my stomach, and the insides of my thighs. Haden grabbed my legs and spread them apart, wasting no time devouring me.

"Fuck," I moaned into the sky.

My hands dragged through his hair, pulling on it slightly. Haden's tongue circled my clit as he plunged two fingers deep within me. My hips rolled against him, and he sucked me into his mouth. Before I knew it, I was at the pinnacle of pleasure, ready to fall over the edge. Fuck, he knew how to use his mouth. My greedy hips rolled into his mouth.

"Haden, I'm going to cum."

He hummed against me before withdrawing his fingers and using his perfect fucking mouth to drive me crazy. I leaned up so I could see him. Haden's stormy eyes looked up at me as he consumed me. His eyes darkened as I watched him closely.

"Oh, my gods," I breathed. Haden's gaze did not leave mine as I came apart in his mouth. After a moment, my trembling passed, and he gave me one last, slow lick before he slowly crawled up my body, his mouth trailing kisses. He smiled when I reached down to his trousers and undid them, yanking them down just enough to free him.

"I need you inside of me now," I demanded.

Haden grabbed my wrists and pinned them to the ground above my head.

"I like it when you're bossy," he whispered softly. "But I also like it when you beg me."

"Please, Haden, I want you." I tried to roll my hips, but he pinned me below his large body. His gaze moved all over my face as I moaned softly.

"Look how pretty you are when you are a pleading mess below me, Storm," his voice was a confident whisper that made goosebumps spread across my skin.

"Please." I tried to move again, but he only held me in place with a smirk tugging his lips. My eyes flashed white at his teasing. Two could play this game. "Be a good boy and give me what I want."

His nostrils flared, and his eyes flashed red. Oh, he liked to be praised as much as I did.

"Do you like that, Haden?" I purred as his hips slowly moved, teasing me.

"Yes," he leaned down and kissed me. "Tell me exactly what you want from me."

He pulled back so he could stare at me. I yanked my hands free from his grip. My fingers traced up his neck and through his hair, tugging it roughly.

"You know what I want."

"I want to hear your pretty mouth say it, Storm."

Fuck, he was enjoying this too much.

"I want you to stop teasing me. You can do that for me, can't you?" I smiled. "You're going to make me cum so hard that I see the stars."

"Yes." He moved forward slightly, teasing me until neither of us could stand it anymore. His mouth fell open as he slowly pushed into me.

"Good boy, you listen so well."

Once inside me, he leaned forward and gave me a chaste kiss. "You feel good, Storm."

Without answering, I pushed my hips up, causing him to slam into me.

"So greedy for me," he muttered and refused to move his hips. "Beg me." He thought he was the one in control, but we both knew who actually was.

"Please, Haden. I need you to make me fall apart. Show me how eager you are to please me."

His long exhale let me know that he was having a hard time controlling himself. I yanked him down like I would kiss him but stopped. He tried to close the distance, but I yanked his hair back.

"Della..."

"You can kiss me after you've taken care of me. If you want my mouth, it will be after you make me cum with your cock buried inside of me."

His nostrils flared with his exhale, and I smiled because I knew he wouldn't deny me any longer. He rolled over, pulling me with him so I was straddling his hips as he sat up. Then his hands tangled in my hair, controlling the quick movements between us.

"You know how to drive me fucking crazy, Storm," he ground out.

"Haden," I cried. "That's fucking perfect. Do not stop."

"I like how perfectly you say my name when you are losing control."

I gripped his shoulders and helped him lift me up just to slam me back down on him roughly. His loud moan made me clench tightly around him.

"That's it, use me, ride me until you're calling out to the heavens who you belong to."

"Look at how good you take care of me." I demanded, and his movements became quicker. "This body, every inch of it, belongs to me."

"Fucking hell." He moaned.

My eyes squeezed tightly when Haden's tongue licked my nipple before sucking me into his mouth, teasing me. With that, I came hard and fast. It was so powerful that the ground shook beneath us, and thunder echoed all around us. Lightning even struck the pond behind me. I'm sure the heavens and the stars heard his name fall from my mouth.

"Good girl, Storm; now show me those pretty eyes. Watch me as I cum inside of you."

My eyes met his, and he slammed me down twice more before he finally came, his frost shooting out in all directions as he did. He called my name to the stars, and then he stilled against me. His chest was heaving so much that I could feel his heart beating against my chest.

"I love you." I grabbed his face and pulled it back. His lips parted as he tried to catch his breath. His eyes were hazy with his pleasure. "Kiss me," I said as I leaned forward and kissed him with every ounce of love I had for him.

"I love you more."

CHAPTER 11

DELLA

"**I** feel like I haven't seen you." Mikel looked at me skeptically when I came home to take a bath and grab some clothes. I grabbed a dress and held it so my ring was covered from him.

"I know, I have been hanging out with—"

"Penelope," he said in a way that made me look up at him. "Are you sure that is who you are going to see?"

I was going to have to tell my brother eventually, but I did not feel like having this conversation right now.

"Yes."

Mikel frowned. "You know you can talk to me about anything, right? If maybe you are seeing someone that isn't Penelope, I won't judge you."

I gave him a pointed look.

"You are literally the God of Judgment."

He waved his hand. "You know what I mean." He looked over at me like he could see I was different. "I won't press it because I know that you'd tell me if you wanted me to know. But just know that I am here for you—always. Nothing will ever change that."

"I know." I smiled. Mikel wandered out of the room, slow enough to give me a chance to tell him what he wanted to know, but eventually he was gone. I glanced around, realizing I would not be living here after I married Haden. Would Mikel be alright being alone? He was going to love Haden's family— soon to be my family. He might want to move to Elloryon to be close to us. Besides, if I met my mate, then Mikel should meet his soon, I would think.

I glanced in the mirror again to make sure I looked alright for Haden. I swallowed hard as that odd feeling overcame me again. For the past hour I had not been feeling well, like something was wrong. Something felt out of place. At first, I thought it was keeping this secret from Mikel, but something like dread filled me to the point that I knew it was something else. A sharp pain slammed into my chest so forcefully that I dropped the dress in my hands as I fell to the floor. Fuck. I rubbed my chest, hoping it would pass.

Ardella!

Standing up, I grabbed my head as Holden's voice pierced into my mind. What was happening?

Ardella!

I stumbled into the wall as the sound echoed around me. Fear froze me in place as I realized something was happening. I left everything as I summoned my star mist. When it moved away, I was in the field by Haden's house. I frantically began looking around for the source of Holden's panicked call. There was a faint sound of pain coming from somewhere in front of me, but I couldn't see in the dark. I shot my starlight out to help me find him. A gasp escaped me when I saw his boots sticking out of the tall grass.

"Holden?" I hurried over to him and saw how much blood he was losing. "Oh, my gods! Holden, hold on."

I fell to my knees and ripped open his tunic to see several stab wounds. Just as I was about to heal him, I heard another sound that sent a spike of fear straight to my core. It was Haden's soft whisper close by. Panic raced through my chest as I froze. Maybe I was hearing things.

"Storm." His pained sob made me realize I was not hearing things.

"No," I scrambled to find him in the tall grass. It was hard to see anything in the darkness even with my magic illuminating the area. "Haden, where are you?" I cried out.

Frantically, I started walking through the grass, begging the stars to help me find him.

I heard him let out a small whimper of pain somewhere close to me. Out of the corner of my eye, I saw his hand sticking out of the grass. Rushing to him, I fell on my knees.

"No, Haden, please stay with me," I begged. I ripped open his tunic and saw the same wounds as Holden. Who the fuck did this? I was sobbing as I tried to stop the blood. Haden was gasping for a breath. I could feel death lurking nearby. My head was shaking back and forth as I tried to comprehend what was happening.

I grabbed his face, and blood ran out of his mouth.

"Haden, please do not leave me. You promised you'd never leave."

"I—" He coughed up blood. I tried to use my magic on Haden, but nothing was happening. Why wasn't it healing him? Then I felt it, that tugging of my mating bond with Holden. No. I tried to heal Haden again, but nothing happened. The tugging on the mating bond was so forceful now that I knew it would not allow me to save him until I had saved Holden first.

"Haden, I will be right back. I have to save Holden first; my magic won't work on you until I do. I love you; hold on for me."

I laid his hand on the ground and rushed back to Holden. I could feel his soul slipping away. Tears blurred my vision as I realized how much magic it would take to save him. Quickly I released my power and slammed it into him. My starlight frantically raced through his veins, healing every wound it could find. After a minute, my magic slammed back into me, knocking me backward. I groaned as I tried to move toward Haden. My body and mind were exhausted from saving Holden.

"Haden!" I begged. With every ounce of energy I had left, I began crawling toward him. But I had only made it a foot before I noticed a soft orange glow next to me.

When I turned to look, a violent sob tore through me, and the entire realm shook with thunder at my grief. Haden's soul form was kneeling next to me, watching me desperately trying to get to him.

"No, no, no, no," I begged. "You can't die!" Finally, I reached his body and pulled him to me. I buried my face in his unmoving chest. I grabbed his arm and wrapped it around me, begging him to hold me. I could hear my pleading, but I felt as if I was not in my own body as I held Haden. The fates were being too cruel. He didn't deserve to die.

"I'm sorry, please don't take him," I called out. I'm sorry I changed fate. I'm sorry I loved him when I was never supposed to, but this was too much of a punishment. "I will never forgive you if you take him from me!" I yelled to the heavens.

My face fell back to his still chest, and I breathed in the smell of a frosty winter morning, but it was not bringing me comfort.

"Storm." Haden's soul spoke softly. When I glanced up at him, he was crying. "It's alright. You need to let me go."

I realized I was gripping his soul tightly in my hand. I shook my head. If I let him go, he wouldn't come back.

"Please don't leave me here alone," I cried. "What am I supposed to do without you?"

"You know I don't have a choice." He frowned as his head tilted to the side. "I can't stay now."

I stared at him and wondered how I could ever let go.

"I will not survive without you."

"You're wrong. You are so strong, Della."

"Fine, then I don't want to survive without you. If I didn't have this stupid bond, I would have been able to save you."

"I am glad you saved Holden. I am not upset with you." He was being too fucking understanding.

"I am upset with myself!"

Anger and grief created the perfect storm inside of me when I saw the stupid golden glow of the bond. I released

Haden's physical body and grabbed the bond, yanking on it. Haden looked at me sadly as I summoned lightning into my palm. I shaped it like a knife before picking it up and slicing through the bond connecting me to Holden.

It exploded in a shower of golden sparks, shockwaves radiating out from the cut. The ripples of power knocked down trees—it even collapsed Haden's home. All of his hard work was gone in an instant. Our home lay in a pile of rubble. A sharp, unforgiving pain stabbed into me as the severed ends of the bonds retreated in a snakelike fashion back into each of us. We were no longer connected.

Haden's soul was standing above me.

"Storm, I promise if I come back, the heavens and stars will not keep me from finding you." I reached out for him so that he couldn't leave. "I love you. I love you so much that I will recognize it in the next life. Death cannot take my love for you away from me. I'm sorry it had to be this way."

"Wait!" I yelled. The chunk of mating bond was still gripped in my fingers, and I cut off part of it. The small piece of it glowed brightly in the palm of my hand. This should have always been Haden's bond. I looked up at Haden's soul as he watched me curiously. His eyes traced over me before looking at the bond in my hand.

"Della?" He wanted to know what I was doing with that. I opened my mouth to tell him, but no words formed. My mind was not thinking clearly. Haden leaned down toward me to see what I was doing. The closer he got to me, the more my bond pulsed in my hand. It was like it knew that it belonged to him.

"I do not trust fate to not mess this up again," I finally whispered. "I will never leave this to chance."

Haden looked me in the eyes, confusion swarming in them. I knew I was changing fate. I knew the stars and heavens would be angry. I did not fucking care.

"I am all in," I said as I grabbed his soul, yanking him closer before I slammed the mating bond into him. He fell to his knees next to me, and I gripped his soul tighter.

"I'm sorry," I cried as I tore a piece away from him. Its orange glow burned brightly in my hand, pulsing with his power. I looked at Haden when he looked so confused about what I was doing. If I made him my mate, then he wouldn't die. But if I had a piece of his soul, then when he was reborn, he would be drawn to me because of it. Maybe it would lead him back to me.

I took a deep breath before slamming the piece of his soul into my chest.

Pain seared through me as his soul wrapped itself tightly within mine, like it knew that's where it belonged the entire time. Haden looked at me before the bond that snapped between us. It glowed bright gold and calmed my frantic heart. Relief filled me. The heavens would not take my mate. He would be alright. Haden sighed, relieved, as if he felt how euphoric our bond felt. The bond was glowing so brightly that it lit up the entire area around us.

"Haden," I breathed when his eyes met mine.

"Storm," Haden said, fear evident in his ghostly eyes. Suddenly, he burst into a million tiny specks of light. The mating bond severed, slamming into me again and dying as Haden's soul disappeared. The pain of losing Haden raced through my veins, scorching grief into my bones.

I yelled my pain into the stars and heavens. It didn't change anything, though. Haden was dead. Haden was gone. Tears poured from me as a sudden storm appeared over us. I curled against Haden's dead body, putting his arm around me again, burying my face into his chest, and inhaling the scent of home. And even though I knew he was dead, I couldn't help but worry that he would get cold in the storm, so I covered him as much as I could.

I could hear the movement of someone coming closer to me, and I opened my eyes thinking it was Haden. But disappointment coursed through me when I saw Holden. Tears streamed down my face as he watched me cling to Haden. My gaze shifted when I saw cloaked figures standing at the edge of the woods. They were gone in the blink of an eye, and I was too caught up in grief to care.

"Ardella?" I glanced up at Holden when he started crying uncontrollably at the sight of Haden's body. I rested my head on his chest, thinking that at any moment it would start moving again. He just left, and I already miss him so much. I felt hollow, like my heart and soul had been cut from me. There was a shuffle as Holden knelt on the other side of Haden, crying as he held his hand.

I stared at the side of Haden's face. He looked like he was sleeping. I reached up and touched his cheek, thinking maybe he would wake up and tell me I was in a terrible dream. When he didn't, I swallowed hard.

"Please open your eyes," I whispered. "I do not like this dream. Wake me up."

Holden perked up like he heard something. He was looking behind me, but I did not care who or what it was.

"Holden?" I heard Sara yell.

"Haden!" Penelope and Henry were calling out.

Holden stood up and raced to his family, but I didn't leave Haden.

"What happened? You guys were supposed to show up for dinner." Henry's voice sounded like Haden's, and it shot pain through me.

"We got attacked by these cloaked fae." Holden was struggling to speak. "Della saved me, but..." he started crying loudly.

"But what?" Penelope asked frantically. He couldn't compose himself enough to speak. "What happened?" she yelled, her voice full of fear.

"Where is Haden?" Henry asked frantically. "Haden!" He called out.

"Della!" Penelope called out to me, but I did not have the energy to call out to her. "Please, Holden, tell us!" She cried out. "Where is Haden!"

"Haden is dead," he said between sobs.

"No, he can't be," Henry said, his voice coming out angry from the fear. I heard them walking toward us frantically. Then their footsteps stopped, and I could hear one of them breathing heavily as they processed what they were seeing.

"What happened!" Penelope screamed, her shock not letting her process what was happening.

I closed my eyes tightly, knowing that their hearts were being ripped out of them too.

"No!" Penelope's scream tore from her as she and Henry fell to their knees next to us. They grabbed his hand and immediately realized that he had been gone for a while. Henry pulled Penelope into his chest as she cried out for

Haden to open his eyes. She looked down at me and cried, "What happened?"

"I tried to save them both, but I couldn't," I sobbed out. "I was too late to save him."

Penelope looked at me, holding onto Haden like a lifeboat in a stormy sea. She rubbed the wet hair from my face as I sobbed louder. Henry reached down and gripped my hand in his. Both of them watched Haden's face for a moment before looking at me.

"We should get you out of the rain," he said softly. But I shook my head. "Ardella, I know you don't want to let go of him, but you have to."

I knew I needed to. But this was the last time I would feel him against me. I wish I had the gift of time so I could go back and stop this. Sitting up, I looked at his handsome face. He looked as if he were sleeping. I leaned forward and pressed my lips to his forehead, recoiling from how cold his skin was. My fingers traced over his face, trying to remember the way he felt against my fingertips. I pushed his soft hair from his forehead, trying to memorize the way it slipped through my fingers.

My gaze drifted to the ring he gave me today, and I started crying again. Emotions crashed into me, suffocating the sobs that wanted to come up. He was alive this morning. He proposed this morning. I stared at him. How could he be dead? I could feel his family watching me. They could leave me out here until I rotted away.

"I love you," I whispered. My broken mind waited for a moment to make sure he wasn't going to say it back. Slowly, I released my grip on him, wanting to pull away from Henry and Penelope so I could curl back against him, missing the way he felt. I realized I would crave that feeling of him for the rest of my existence.

I noticed there were others in the field with us. I did not know when they arrived, but they all stared at me with pity. They moved toward Haden to retrieve his body. I took a step toward him, not wanting to let him go, but a hand reached out and gripped me. Holden was staring at me, and it was a gut punch. He looked so much like Haden but so different.

Holden was staring at me, and he was a reminder that Haden had to die because I had a stupid bond with him. "Let them take him," he said gently.

I nodded and watched the love of my life being hauled away. I didn't know what to do. It was as if time itself had frozen because it knew the realm should not move on without Haden in it. Holden gripped my hand in his to keep me from collapsing.

"Let's go to the house and get you warm," Sara said as she came up on the other side of me, wrapping her arm around my shoulders. I nodded, and together, we walked in silence to the house, like we all died with Haden. This was all wrong.

Everyone was crying, but somehow their focus was on me, like I was going to die next. Gods can't die, but right then, I wished I could.

I sat on the couch, not remembering anything about the walk there. Haden's perfect face plagued me. It was only this morning that he asked me to marry him. Why did that feel like a lifetime ago? I twisted the ring on my finger as our last morning together played out in my mind. Every kiss, every touch, and every word repeated like my own personal hell in my mind. He was sad yesterday. I should have stayed with him instead of going to work. Maybe that would have changed the outcome of today. I shouldn't have gone home to get clothes; I could have saved him from those cloaked fucks that attacked him.

I should have protected him. It was my fault he was dead. If I would've been with him, he'd be alive. Guilt was clawing its way through my mind and soul. The love of my life died, and I had to live an eternity without him. *Please take me with him. I do not want to live without Haden.*

I did not realize anyone was talking to me until Sara knelt in front of me, breaking my trance on the wall.

"Ardella, can I run you a bath? You are shaking." Her eyes were red from crying.

I was going to say no, but I was covered in blood—Haden's blood. I nodded, and she squeezed my hand tightly. She disappeared but came back a minute later, helping me off the couch and walking me to the washroom. Sara looked at me struggling to get the clothes off and cried silently as she helped me. My gaze immediately glanced in the mirror at the snowflakes marked into me. I had to look away from the sight because a memory of Haden's big grin made me want to cry. He would never smile again.

Sara helped me into the tub and didn't leave my side. She helped wash my hair and hands. Then she just sat with me as I stared at the water. I pulled my knees to my chest and rested my head against them.

"What am I supposed to do?" I asked Sara softly. "How can I exist without the other half of me?"

Her tears fell quicker at my question. "I don't know," she choked out. She tried desperately to hold in her sobs. "Thank you," she whispered.

I looked at her, confused.

"For saving Holden." Her eyes filled with guilt. "I will never take anything about him for granted again."

I nodded because I could see in her eyes that she wanted to say more, but she didn't need to.

Sara sat with me for a bit longer before she left to find me clothes. When she shut the door to the washroom, I heard a loud sob escape her. Once her footsteps disappeared, I stood up, wrapping a towel around me and slipping from the washroom. I hesitated when I got to Haden's bedroom door. Slowly, I pushed it open, and his scent hit me.

I walked to the drawer of clothing and pulled his clothes out, slipping on a tunic that covered all of me. Then I turned and slipped into his bed. I closed my eyes as I pulled his extra pillow against my chest, pretending that it was him lying next to me.

CHAPTER 12

DELLA

"**A**rdella?" I heard someone calling for me in the distance. I shook my head to stop zoning out on the wooden coffin in front of me. It had been Holden calling me. I had stopped walking with them without realizing it. Holden and Sara both looked back at me to see if I would start walking again. When I didn't move, they both moved toward me.

Haden's body was in the pine box in front of me, and it made me feel queasy.

"I don't know if I can do this," I whispered. I took a step backward, but Sara gripped my hand. She had helped me get ready this morning in a pretty black dress that Haden would've loved. I stared at the heels I wore. Haden wouldn't be here to carry me anymore when I needed him to. My eyes closed tightly as the memory of him carrying me to our home for the first time slipped through my mind. I was desperate to get swept away in the memory—the way he felt holding me, the way he kissed me. He had been so happy to show me the house.

"You can go as slow as you need to," Sara encouraged me, pulling me from the memory. I watched Penelope and Henry at his coffin, talking to him—saying goodbye. It had only been three days. Three. And I had an existence more to live without him. Penelope and Henry moved away from Haden, and I let Holden and Sara step up to say goodbye next. In all honesty, it was because I did not feel brave enough to do this. I wanted to run back to his room and fall asleep in his bed. I never wanted to wake up again if this was my new reality. Sara and Holden turned to me after a few minutes. I swallowed the lump in my throat.

It was my turn to say goodbye.

"I can go with you," Holden offered.

"No, I can do it." I tried to convince myself.

They nodded and stepped aside. My gaze immediately landed on Haden's face. He was too pale as I took a hesitant step toward him. I didn't know what to say or do. How did I say goodbye to the love of my life? So, I stared at him and how handsome he looked in the black outfit his mother picked. My gaze lingered on his hands, folded perfectly on his stomach. Memories of him holding my hand hit me. Those hands would never draw again. They would never work on a house. They would never trace over my skin. I almost burst out crying at the thought that I did not get to put a ring on his finger and claim him as my husband.

I would never get to marry him or have the big family he always talked about.

I thought we had a lifetime to make memories. Hesitantly, I laid my hand on his chest, where his heart used to beat for me. All of our dreams for the future would now just be fantasies. I closed my eyes and told the heavens if they gave him back to me, I would protect him at all costs. I would do better.

I stared where my hand rested, thinking that Haden's chest would magically start moving again. *Please, wake up.* But he didn't, and my heart and soul could not fully grasp that reality.

"You were everything, Haden," I whispered. "Please find me when you come back. Even if you do not look the same, I will recognize your soul."

This wasn't fair. I wanted him exactly as he was in this life; there was not a single thing I would change. For a moment longer, I admired his handsome face once again—his straight nose that led to kissable lips and a strong jaw with a slight stubble on it. I glanced at his family watching me, unsure how I was supposed to walk away from him.

"I do not think I will know what happiness feels like again until the day you find me. I don't understand how the realm continues to go forward when you are not in it. But maybe it is only my world that ended when you did."

I leaned down and kissed his forehead before touching his soft hair one last time.

"I love you more, and I am still all in. I am waiting for you."

I stepped backward, and it was the hardest thing I had ever done. Penelope grabbed my hand as a man in all black lifted the heavy wooden lid to Haden's coffin and set it in place with a final thud. He would never feel the sun again. The coffin was slowly lowered into the grave they had dug for him. I closed my eyes when they began shoveling the dirt in the hole. He would be in the dark, alone, and that made me feel terrible. Logically, I knew that he didn't know this. He was dead. But I still worried he would be scared. Everyone else turned to leave, but I didn't; I couldn't.

"Ardella, do you want us to stay?" Henry asked.

"No, I will see you guys later," I whispered. They hesitated, but I turned to them. "I'll be alright."

They nodded but did not seem convinced. I stood at his grave long after they finished burying him, not able to find the strength to walk away. Instead, I sat down and sighed heavily as I stared at the pile of dirt that stood between us. When night fell, I could not bring myself to leave him alone in the dark. I laid down next to him.

"It's alright, Haden. You aren't alone. I am here."

I rested my hand on the dirt and closed my eyes.

"Oh, Ardella," I heard Penelope whisper from nearby.

I turned to look at her from where I lay. She came and sat by me, her hand rubbing my back softly.

"I'm sorry," I told her as silent tears fell down my cheeks.

"What for?"

"You are grieving a son, but you keep trying to make me feel better. You should be at home with your family."

Penelope let out a soft sigh as she thought about my words.

"You are our family, and you don't have to apologize for grieving. We all are missing a brother, a friend, a son, but you are grieving the man you thought you had forever with. I can't imagine that kind of pain."

I sat up and moved next to her.

"We tried to give Haden and Holden good lives growing up, and I think we did that." Penelope smiled softly. "But I don't think Haden was truly living until you came along. He was so happy, Ardella. You made him so happy, and I know that no one else could have brought that out of him."

"He made me happy, too," I whispered. "So much that I do not know what I am supposed to do now. How can I just keep living like my heart and soul aren't buried under this pile of dirt?" I turned to her, and she wiped the tears from my cheeks. "I keep thinking that he will be alone if I leave. Or maybe it is that I will be alone if I leave him here."

"You will always have us."

But I won't have him.

"Thank you." I leaned my head on her shoulder, "for giving me Haden, even if it was not long enough."

Penelope wrapped her arm around my shoulder and held me tightly.

☽★★☽★★☽

"Dells, what is wrong?" Mikel asked as I lay in bed. "You haven't left your bed in months, and you haven't talked to me. Please, tell me how I can help you."

I stared at Mikel and knew I couldn't tell him the whole truth because he was the God of Judgment, and I broke the laws of the gods to try and save Haden. But I needed my brother—my best friend.

"I fell in love with a man who was not my mate," I confessed.

Mikel looked at me and frowned. "That's impossible."

"And then he was murdered," I said.

I tried to find those responsible for his death, but I couldn't find any trace of them.

"Did you fall ill with something? You are not making any sense." He frowned as he checked my temperature with the back of his hand. "Our new maid, Pia, can bring you some tea if you'd like."

"No."

"You may think that you loved him, but that is impossible, Dells. We only love our mates. I'm sorry that you lost him, but whatever it was, it wasn't love."

I finally felt something other than grief.

I instantly felt fucking enraged.

I jumped out of my bed and pointed forcefully at the door, lightning crackling from my fingertips. "Get the fuck out of my room!" I yelled. Mikel stood up quickly, confused about what he had said wrong. "You know nothing, Mikel. I loved him. I love him! I love him." I broke down in uncontrollable sobs.

"Ardella... I'm sorry."

"Get out! Leave me alone. Do not come back in here."

Tears filled Mikel's eyes when he saw how truly devastated I was. He didn't leave, though. Instead, he came over to me and pulled me into his chest, at which point I promptly fell apart. I gripped him to me, and he held me in his strong arms as I sobbed loudly.

"I loved him with everything, Mikel, and he is dead."

"Shh, it's okay." He rubbed my back.

"No, it's not. That isn't all of it. I met my mate and did not love him. I loved his brother."

Mikel stilled against me. "You met your mate?"

I nodded and pulled back. I couldn't tell Mikel any more about what I had done. We were not allowed to change fate or reject our mates. Both of which I had tried to do.

"I did not love him, and he didn't love me. He rejected me," I lied. "I fell in love with his brother."

Understanding flitted through his eyes. He knew what this meant for me. I was alone now, forever. Mikel's tears fell silently down his face as he pulled me back to him. "We'll figure it out together."

"Why did the heavens punish me?" I asked. "I do not know how I am supposed to live like this, like I did not experience true love. And then feel a grief so intense that I can't even think of anything but him. I can't picture one good thing about my future. I do not even want a future."

Mikel's hands were still on my back as the reality of my grief hit him. He squeezed me again, and I closed my eyes tightly. Haden's smiling face immediately filled the darkness in my mind. Mikel laid me down and covered me up. His tears glowed down his face as he watched me, rubbing my hair for comfort.

"I will bring in some hot tea; that will help your mind relax," he said with a frown. I could see that he did not know how to help me, and that hurt him. I nodded and wrapped my blanket tightly around me.

Mikel walked out of the room, but the door cracked open almost immediately, and a petite blonde woman walked in holding a cup of tea.

"I was already brewing you a cup of tea. I heard you crying all night and figured you'd be tired." She set the cup down, her friendly eyes taking in the mess I was. "I'm Pia. I am here for anything you might need."

I sat up and sipped the tea she made. Gods, that was good. Pia smiled softly before turning to leave.

"Thank you," I muttered.

"You're welcome." She paused. "I am sorry about your loss. If you need anything, a shoulder to cry on, or someone to talk with about him, my door is always open."

I nodded as I swallowed the lump in my throat. Pia left, and I sipped on my tea. My eyes ached with exhaustion, but I knew sleep would evade me. And if it didn't, Haden's memory would haunt me. I stood up and went to a small desk in the corner of my room, then grabbed a few sheets of paper and sat down.

I began writing all of the memories I could of Haden. I did not use his name, just in case Mikel found it. I didn't want him to go snooping around and figure out what I had done. When I couldn't remember anything else, I started writing him letters.

My emotions and thoughts about my days without him spilled from me, flowing from my quill and leaking across the page before me like tears made of ink—grief in every line. There was something freeing about writing to him, almost as if he could read my words. So, I decided that I would write to him as much as I could. And I would always end my letters the same way. *Always, your Storm.*

CHAPTER 13
DELLA-200 YEARS LATER

I laughed hysterically at Henry's terrible joke. Penelope slapped his shoulder, telling him that he wasn't funny, but I could not stop laughing. Sometimes it felt like I was the only one who understood his dry humor and appreciated it. Henry's eyes shined brightly.

"Della thinks I am funny."

"Yeah, well, she is the only one," Holden scoffed.

I turned to him and smiled. Sara was laughing behind her glass as I glared at Holden. Penelope stood up and clapped her hands together.

"I almost forgot!" She ran into the kitchen that looked exactly the same as it did when I first came to the house with Haden. "I made a new recipe," she called from the kitchen.

My eyes widened. Henry glanced at all of us with a look of terror.

"She spent all day on it," he warned us.

"Last time she spent that long on a dessert, I got food poisoning," Holden whispered harshly. His father gave him a look that he better lie to his sweet mother and tell her that her dessert was the best thing he had ever tasted. Sara was laughing softly to herself as she watched Holden and Henry bicker back and forth. I was smiling, and out of habit, I turned to the seat Haden used to sit in. It still took my breath away when I saw it was empty. The pain stabbed through me, but I tried not to let it show. I could practically see him sitting in the chair next to me, looking like he did when I first met him.

I pictured his stormy blue eyes watching me closely. His dark blonde hair is messy from working on his home. The mischievous glint in his eyes was like we shared secrets. I swallowed hard, and the image in my mind floated away. I rubbed the back of my neck as it stiffened with tension. Quickly, I blinked back the tears that stung my eyes. I looked forward and grabbed my drink. Henry gave me a small smile full of sadness. He knew what I was thinking. Penelope came out and set down some sort of pie.

"That smells wonderful." I inhaled the pleasant scent of the pie. "Lemon?"

"Lemon and blueberry." She moved it so we could see how well she had done. "Now I know my baking has been...rocky, but I promise this is delicious."

Henry served us each a piece, and we all stared at it, wondering who was going to be the bravest one to try it first.

"Oh, I forgot the silverware." Penelope stood, and Holden looked at me.

"Goddesses can't get sick; you test it first."

I threw my napkin at him. Penelope handed each of us a spoon and waited for us to dig in.

"Holden, you do the honors of the first bite." I smiled sweetly.

Henry's shoulders shook with silent laughter. Sara snorted softly when Holden's eyes narrowed on me. He lifted his spoon and took a bite, chewing hesitantly before swallowing.

"This is your best dessert so far." He smiled. Penelope beamed at Holden before turning back to the kitchen. Holden shook his head, warning us all that it was not good. But we all ate it without complaint. It was her best dessert, but I'm pretty sure she forgot sugar, so it was an odd flavor.

"That was great." I complimented when I finished first.

"Thank you, Della."

I sat there for a long moment before looking at Haden's empty chair again. Grief slammed into me. It had been two hundred years, but the grief never got easier—I just became used to it. Some days I still couldn't get out of bed. Mikel and Pia always came and sat with me on those extra hard days.

"Do you mind if I go to Haden's room?"

"No, of course not," Henry said.

I excused myself and headed up the staircase I had been up hundreds of times over the years. But each time it felt overwhelming. I opened the door to Haden's room and inhaled his scent that still lingered. My magic kept this room standing still in time. The effects of time could not get to it. It was exactly as Haden had left it, and it would be forever. I instantly relaxed. My gaze went to the desk that we had shared our first kiss in front of.

That kiss had changed everything. I could still feel the way he gripped me to him and picture his flirty eyes. I smiled softly. Part of me loved the memories, but another part of me recoiled from them. It was still painful to remember specific times with him. It made the longing for him swirl, and my grief seemed to triple. My gaze didn't move from the desk, enjoying this memory.

My chest tightened at the sight of the plans for his house sitting on top. I traced the lines he drew and felt tears prick my eyes.

I ran my hand along the desk and chair. Haden had touched all of these things, and it made me feel closer to him somehow. I turned and walked to the bed. Slowly, I sank down onto the edge and let the feeling of missing Haden consume me. I grabbed his pillow and inhaled deeply.

"I miss you," I whispered as if he could hear me.

A soft knock on the door startled me. Henry came in and sat next to me.

"I can't believe it's been so long since we've seen him." He sighed heavily as he glanced over Haden's room. His eyes paused on certain things longer, and I wondered what wonderful memories he had of Haden.

I nodded.

"Some days it feels like 200 years, and others it feels longer. On bad days it feels like it just happened days ago," I confessed.

"I feel that way, too."

We sat in silence for a long time, just sitting with our shared love and grief for Haden. I gripped his pillow tightly. Henry slung his arm around my shoulder and hugged me to his side once I couldn't keep the grief inside anymore. Tears fell down my face as my body racked with silent sobs.

"I still miss him so much that it is all-consuming," I cried.

"I know you do." Henry tightened his arm on me and held me as I fell apart. "It just means you loved him so much that no amount of time can take that from you."

I squeezed the pillow to me even tighter. I thought time was supposed to heal wounds. But it just felt like each year that passed made my wound deeper, steadily ripping me open and exposing my heart. Where would Haden and I be in life if he hadn't died? We would be married. We would have that family he dreamed about. We would be madly in love.

"Penelope and I would like you to take some of his things with you—for you to have when you are away."

I looked at him. "Really?"

"Yes, anything you want," he said with a smile. "As much as you want. I'll let you look around and pick some things." He stood up and left the room. I immediately went to his desk and grabbed the plans for the house he had been building. When I lifted the paper up, I paused at the sight of the picture of me that he had drawn. I lifted it and traced the lines of my face that he drew. My heart rate spiked. I had never seen his drawing of me, but it was so realistic.

He had told me once that he was scared I'd disappear and he'd forget what I looked like. That memory brought me comfort as my gaze stared at his artwork.

My eyes were closed, and my head was on a pillow. He had drawn me as I slept. I took that one too. Then I turned to where his clothes were. I grabbed a few tunics before looking around. Gods, I wish I could take his whole damn bed, but I only took his pillow. I grinned at the thought, glancing around once more before deciding that this would be enough. Tunics to smell him and pictures of his future plans he never got to achieve—me and our home.

"I love you." I paused for a moment as if I would hear his voice from where he was hiding in the room. Disappointment coursed through me when that didn't happen.

I walked out of the room and shut the door softly. When I came downstairs, his family was smiling at me and my items.

"Thank you." I smiled even though tears burned my eyes. "This means everything to me."

"Of course. We should have done it sooner." Penelope stood up and hugged me. "We love you."

"I love you guys too."

I was thankful that Haden gave me a family, even if I had to enjoy it without him.

CHAPTER 14

DELLA- PRESENT DAY

I wandered through the small village in Kizar, unde-tected by anyone—always unseen. I took in the sight of all the fae as they laughed, kissed, hugged, and smiled at one another. A deep sadness filled me. I miss that. Haden had been gone for 293 years, and I still felt dead inside.

There was nothing special about this place. It was one of the worst villages in Kizar; the poverty level was extreme-ly low, and most of the homes were falling apart. But I couldn't shake this feeling of urgency that filled me. I was meant to be here, but I found nothing that would make sense for me to be called back here every single day for a week straight. This was a feeling I had never experienced and therefore did not understand.

So, I walked around without purpose, jealous of the fae who lived, even in squalor, because they felt something. I only felt longing, longing for something else to fill my boring days, longing for Haden. I was so lonely that I wasn't sure if life would ever bring me any sense of joy again. I was losing hope with every year that passed by without him coming back to me. Maybe the heavens thought I wasn't worthy after what I did.

Pausing, I glanced around the street. The smiling faces around me felt like they were mocking me and my grief. I couldn't take this anymore. I summoned my star mist to take me to my home in the stars but stopped when I felt that tugging again; only this time, it was more urgent. Turning around, I saw nothing out of the ordinary, making me frown with disappointment. Something was wrong in this place, but I could not tell what it was.

I made it a few steps forward when suddenly, a man ahead of me caught my attention. I stopped dead in my tracks—just to stare at *him*.

This was some kind of fucked-up dream. I closed my eyes and shook my head to wake up. Please do not do this to me. I will fall apart. I counted to three and opened my eyes. I didn't dare move. I didn't blink, just in case he disappeared. Haden was walking up the dirt path in town. He was taller than I remembered, but just as fit, just as handsome. I held my breath like it would scare him away if I breathed wrong.

His dark blonde hair was chaotic as if he had been running his fingers through it. He was talking to a girl his age who had bright red hair. She looked at him in a way I didn't like—like he was hers. Gods, he was beautiful. Tears filled my eyes as I stared at him like he was a ghost. This couldn't be real. He couldn't be real. I shook my head as my chest ached and burned with grief and confusion.

Swallowing hard, I took a step toward him without thought. His pretty orange soul glowed inside of his chest.

"Haden," I whispered to myself.

My heart was beating so hard that I had to put my hand over it to make sure I wasn't actively dying. Haden was here. This is why I had been coming here for a week. For fuck's sake, he was a village away from his parents. Had he been this close the entire time?

He was getting closer to me, but his face was turned toward the girl as they talked heatedly about something. I couldn't stop staring at him. I couldn't believe my eyes. It was him. I had waited for this moment, and it felt like it would never come. His smooth skin, his straight nose, which led to kissable lips, and a perfect smile were the same as before.

I realized he was smiling, and I finally snapped out of my gawking. He was going to walk straight into me, but it didn't matter. He would not see or feel me. So, I stayed where I was because I wanted to admire him longer. The red-haired woman was talking his ear off when I glanced up into pretty, dark blue-grey eyes that reminded me of a violent storm in the sea.

Shit, he was perfect. He was just as he was all those years ago.

I admired everything about him, staring far more than what would be deemed appropriate if he could actually see me. His brows furrowed as he looked toward me. But I just kept staring. Amusement filled his eyes as he smiled slightly. I wondered what the woman was saying to him to make him look happy. Jealousy bloomed in my chest.

Was I too late? Was this his girlfriend? I swallowed hard as those memories of mine and Holden's bond hit me. Were the heavens this cruel that they would show him to me and not let me have him after I waited centuries for him? I would die. Even a god could not survive that type of damn torture. He stopped a foot in front of me, and that smell of a frosty winter morning slammed into me and made my grief swell.

"Excuse me," he smiled down at me. His head tilted slightly to the side as his curious eyes stared at me. His voice shot straight through me and gripped me in a welcoming hug. He sounded the same.

My eyes widened when I realized he was looking me directly in the eyes. I turned to see who he was talking to, but I was the only one standing there. I pointed to my chest, and his smile widened. For the love of the stars, he could fucking see me, and I was staring. My cheeks heated. He was going to think I was crazy.

"Who are you talking to?" The redhead raised her brow curiously.

He turned to her and back to me.

"To her." His pretty eyes drifted over my face slowly. Shit, did he like what he saw? Fuck, that would kill me if I waited all of this time for him to not want me. All these new fears were hitting me at once, making my chest tighten.

"Haden, there is no woman in front of you."

My heart slammed into my ribs as I heard his name. Haden. She called him fucking Haden. He looked at the redhead as my mouth fell open with excitement and fear.

"Kira, she's right here." He pointed at me. I could see her eyes searching for me, but she wouldn't find me, not unless I wanted her to. But he could. My heart felt like it was going to explode into a million pieces. I could not believe it was him. I had dreamed of this for hundreds of years, but I did not ever think it would happen like this—so casually.

Haden.

Mine.

I grinned at him when his stormy eyes met mine.

"You don't see her?" He asked as a smile tilted his lips.

"No, maybe your father hit you a little too hard in the head because there is no one in front of you, and others are starting to stare."

He didn't look away from me, like he couldn't.

"Her eyes look like the stars," he whispered to himself.

My breath caught when I felt the small feeling of being pulled toward him. Relief flooded me as a euphoric, warm sensation that began in my heart and raced to every part of me. The tugging in my chest became persistent before suddenly the golden string of our bond emerged from me and made its way to Haden. When it went into his heart, he showed a slight sign of discomfort as he rubbed his chest. I waited to see what would happen. After a moment, the bond snapped in place between us, its connection slamming into me like a breath of fresh air. Images of it doing the same thing the night Haden died before it failed to take root made me hold my breath.

It tugged and hummed strongly between us. I could feel the tears stinging the back of my eyes as I thanked the heavens for forgiving me, promising to protect him with everything I am. My gaze could not look away from the golden bond that swarmed between us. It was bright and glowed with flecks of gold and silver around it. It was very strong.

"Seriously, Haden, everyone is staring."

He looked away from me and looked at the fae watching him talk to someone who wasn't there, like he was a freak, and that pissed me off— a lot. He hesitated for a moment, like he didn't want to leave. He swallowed hard as he side-stepped around me and kept walking. I turned to watch him, feeling a deep sense of longing for him.

After a minute he turned to see if I was still there. His lips pulled into the most breathtaking smile when he saw I was still watching him. I waved at him awkwardly, thanking the heavens that they gave me Haden as a mate in this life. I could keep him forever, and I never had to lose him again. He turned and kept walking.

Desperately, I hurried to where he had disappeared and looked for him. There was no way I could leave. I made myself unseen even to him and scoured the streets to find him. After a few minutes, I located him at a street vendor trying to sell some sort of vegetables. The redheaded woman was still lurking close by. My gaze drifted over her. She was stunning with her copper-colored hair and bright blue eyes. Her clothes were far fancier than what Haden wore. They were definitely from different social classes.

Gods, what was his new family like? Obviously, they were poorer than before, but I bet they were kind. I couldn't wait to meet them. I couldn't wait to meet him and see how different and similar he was to the man I fell in love with. This was all so exciting and scary at the same time. What if he was exactly the same? I stared at the back of his head as he talked to the man who was looking at him with unkind eyes. He was talking poorly to Haden, and Haden wasn't saying anything back to the man. I frowned. Why did he think that was alright?

I looked at the woman to see if she would say something. But she didn't. She was staring at something behind me, and I glanced at a handsome nobleman smiling at her. I turned back to her, and she was looking at Haden again. My gaze didn't leave the redhead.

She watched Haden closely. Was this a girlfriend? Instantly, jealousy overtook me. My mate bond did not like that my mate may already be with someone else. This is what I should have felt with Holden—this wrath of a thousand suns. Haden turned and looked over his shoulder, staring directly at where I stood. His pretty eyes flickered around as if he could sense me close by, but he couldn't see me.

I froze in my spot and watched him looking around for me. Longing slammed into my chest again as I stared at him. I did not know I could long for someone so violently as they stood a few feet away. He rubbed his chest softly as his stormy eyes frantically looked for me. He glanced at the woman, and I didn't see a flicker of anything in his eyes for her.

"Fine." Haden frowned at the man with unkind eyes. I watched him slide a small pile of money to Haden, who immediately seemed disappointed by the amount. Haden and Kira began walking in the direction they had originally come from. I followed closely, hoping to learn anything about my mate that I could.

It was painfully silent between the two of them. I walked just a few feet behind them and watched closely for any indication that they were a couple. I wanted to respect his choices, but I would kill her if they were together. No one was taking him from me. He was mine.

"Did you really see a woman?"

Haden paused slightly before continuing to walk. I perked up at the topic of conversation.

"Yes." Fuck, I couldn't believe even his voice was the same. The heavens heard me and listened. My chest squeezed tightly with appreciation. I had missed that sound so damn much. Haden glanced over his shoulder and smirked slightly to himself.

He knew I was watching.

Kira crinkled her nose at him without him noticing. My anger surfaced. Why was she looking at him like he was crazy? When he glanced at her, she put a fake smile on her face.

"Something is wrong with me, isn't there?" he asked her. *No, you are perfect.* "As if I needed more of a reason to be an outcast."

His comment made me hesitate for a moment. Haden was an outcast, and I wanted to know why. How could *he* be an outcast? Fae here obviously had no taste or sensibility.

"Well, maybe your father hit you a little too hard." She shrugged. His father hit him. My eyes burned pure white at this news. It did not cross my mind that his new family would be cruel. Kira acted as if this was normal and completely fine, but I would rip his father's hands from him if he hurt Haden. I prayed to the stars that he did not have a cruel life this time.

"Yeah, maybe." He rubbed the back of his neck and glanced around. "I've never seen anyone before, so maybe it was just a one-time thing." I saw him frown as if the thought made him sad. How long would it take for the mate bond to snap into place for him? Was it instant, or would it take a while?

"Was she pretty?" Kira asked with an edge of jealousy.

"The woman in my mind?" Haden laughed. She nodded. He was oblivious that she liked him. "Very pretty."

"Hmmm." Kira crossed her arms over her chest and looked away. I was smiling brightly behind them because Haden said I was very pretty.

"You know, Liam asked for my hand in marriage." Kira glanced at him. Okay, I didn't like the way she was staring at him. It's obvious he didn't want her.

"Congratulations." Haden smiled genuinely.

"I told him no." Kira's shoulders were tense and uncomfortable as she watched Haden's reaction.

"Why would you do that?"

She swallowed hard.

"I don't know; I thought maybe someone better would come along and notice me."

"He is the highest nobility in the village." Haden looked completely oblivious that she was talking about him.

"Bloodlines and rank aren't the most important things."

"Yes, they are. You like fancy things, and you will want a mate who can provide everything for you. As someone who grew up with nothing, trust me when I tell you that you do not want to worry about where your next meal will come from. Love is not enough to survive that."

My gaze drifted over Haden. His clothing was ripped and torn. His boots were falling apart on his feet. Guilt clawed at me. My mate was not well taken care of. I would change that once I got the courage to talk to him. I would make sure he had everything and wanted for nothing.

"I was thinking that maybe *you* might be interested in me?" Kira spoke boldly to Haden. I was tense as I watched confusion, and something else, cross his features. If he admitted he wanted her, she was dying tonight.

"Me..." he said slowly. "Kira, I do not have feelings for you."

Instantly, Kira turned beet red as anger took over her pretty face. Her hands fisted at her sides. I let out a heavy breath filled with relief.

"Why not?" She demanded an answer. "I'm noble. I'm pretty. Any guy in the village would beg for my time."

Okay, conceited much? I scoffed as I watched Haden's reaction to see if he was lying about his feelings for her. A cold indifference flickered in his eyes for just a moment. Oh, that was new; he looked pissed. The flash of anger made a chill run down my spine.

"I don't know." Haden dismissed how angry she became. "I just don't."

"Fine, it's not like you could afford to keep someone like me anyways." She shook her head, making her copper hair sway behind her. Haden's face let me know that she had hit him with an insecurity. *This bitch.* I was not letting anyone treat him poorly.

I lifted my hands to my sides, and the sky suddenly went from bright and sunny to dark within a moment. Both of them looked up, concerned about the change of weather. I smiled as I focused on Kira, ready to evaporate her with lightning.

"What the—" Haden's sentence was cut off when lightning flashed between the two of them, making Kira fall to the ground. I readied my magic again to send a bolt of lightning directly into her cold fucking heart, but Haden stopped me when his eyes looked directly into mine, and he froze.

I swallowed hard as his eyes traced over me again. He seemed to realize that I was the cause of the weather change and lightning. *Okay, note to self: I can't lose control of my emotions around my mate because he can see me.* I lowered my hands and stared at him, unsure of what to say.

"Storm," he whispered, and it instantly shot through my mind, replaying a moment I did not want to remember. I shook my head and focused on him. Why did he call me that? Did he remember me? No, that was impossible.

"I don't like the way she is talking to you," I muttered.

Haden's mouth opened like he was going to answer me, but Kira stood and looked at him, then to where he was staring.

"Oh, my gods, you're seeing a woman again, aren't you?"

His eyes turned icy blue, surprising me. He had magic again. When he breathed out, his breath could be seen as if it were cold outside. Shit, he was feeling overwhelmed. Was it because he was seeing me or because Kira was questioning him?

"Sorry," I whispered before making myself disappear. Haden turned around quickly, looking for me, but frowned when the only woman he saw was Kira. Her anger at his rejection was clear on her face.

"You're a freak," Kira snapped.

I could feel the anger bubbling up, but Haden didn't say anything as he turned and practically ran away. I went to follow him, but Kira's comment made me stop.

"You'll fucking regret that," she said with a sneer in the direction where Haden disappeared. She turned quickly on her heel, and I followed to see what she was up to. Kira walked with confident strides through town before she came across a group of men that were Haden's age. She smiled and walked up to them.

"Kira." One of them smiled.

"Did you guys hear what happened with that freak, Haden Vale, today?"

Their eyes widened with excitement at the gossip. She told them all about how he was seeing a woman who wasn't there. They laughed and made jokes about Haden. Fury engulfed me at how cruel they were being. I wanted to kill them all. Would the heavens understand if I slaughtered the lot of them?

I was about to do just that but stopped. I was the Goddess of Life; I was not supposed to be killing the fae. So instead, I smiled and lifted my hands, causing a huge gust of wind to knock into Kira. She cried out in pain when her body fell awkwardly on a pile of wood, snapping her arm. I stood over her as she sobbed loudly. The men rushed to help her, and all I could think of was how good that made me feel. I could already tell she was going to be a fucking pain in my ass.

No one was going to treat Haden like that. He was to be a god, even if he didn't know it yet.

☽★★★☽★★★☽

When I arrived at Haden's old family home, which was only a few villages over, I felt overwhelmed. There was still the grief of losing Haden in my heart, but now it was colored with the new possibilities I would have with him. The home had not changed in the nearly 300 years I had been visiting. I paused at the gate and smiled as images of when Haden and I first met flashed in my mind. Grief flooded me at the memories playing out in front of me.

I knew a part of me would always grieve my first life with Haden. But I also knew that this was my chance at happiness, one where I did not need to worry about not having a bond or him dying. Haden was mine in every single way this time—for his entire existence.

I pushed the gate open with images of Haden and me playing on repeat, as if my mind and heart knew I could think about it without falling apart because he was back. His family knew about the bond to Holden. I had waited hundreds of years to bring it up, but it needed to be told. Holden did not understand why I wouldn't save Haden first, so I told them what happened. I did not tell them about giving the bond to Haden or taking a sliver of his soul.

And this was one secret I could not keep from them either. They had saved me from a path of destruction after Haden died. They were my family. They deserved to have a part of their heart healed too. My chest was tight with excitement and fear. I couldn't wait to tell them, to see their faces when they saw that he was exactly the same.

I didn't bother knocking; I hadn't knocked on this door for hundreds of years. Everyone would be here already. I was usually the last to show up for family dinner night. I breathed in the smell of delicious food, but my stomach was too queasy to eat. Haden's family had no idea that there was a possibility he would come back to me. I could never bring myself to tell them, just in case he didn't.

When I walked into the dining area, everyone turned to me as if they sensed me.

"Ardella!" Holden stepped forward, lifting me into a tight hug. Sara came over and smiled fondly before tugging me to her for the next hug.

"You two look well." I smiled.

"Sara has never felt better; thank you for healing her." Holden looked at his wife with nothing but love.

"Della." Henry smiled fondly at me as he gripped me and lifted me off the ground by a few inches.

"Henry, you're going to break my spine," I wheezed. He chuckled and set me down.

"Sorry, Della, it's just so good to see you."

"I was here last week and every single week for almost three hundred years," I laughed.

"It's not enough."

"Della, sweetheart, ignore Henry. I think he forgets that you are a goddess and have things to do, unlike him since he retired." Penelope rolled her eyes as she hugged me. "He is driving me up the wall," she whispered in my ear, making me laugh.

"Hi, Penelope. It smells so good in here."

"I made your favorite."

I smiled at the huge steaks on the table before I looked up at them. Gods, I had never been more excited about anything in my life.

"Actually, I would like to take all of you somewhere for just a few minutes. I promise it won't be long, and then we can come back and eat."

"A surprise?" Henry's eyes shined brightly, but he had no idea what I was about to show him.

"Yes, one that I think will make you all incredibly happy."

Holden's blonde brows pulled together. His hair was starting to turn white, and his youthful skin was now aging. It was odd to see him like this; he still looked so much like that boy I first met all those years ago. This is what Haden would look like if he hadn't died.

"Yes, let's go." Sara clapped her hands. Her blonde hair was starting to fade to white, but she was still so beautiful.

"I am so excited." Penelope reached forward and gripped my hand. I nodded and used my starlight to take us to the village in Kizar where Haden lived. When my magic disappeared, everyone was looking around confused.

"We are still in... Kizar?" Penelope asked, confused. I chuckled at her disappointment. "Is this Raynor?"

"Della, my dear, this is not what I thought you had in mind," Henry teased.

"No one can see us, but we can only stay for a few minutes." I glanced around and smiled. "He's coming."

"Who?" Holden asked.

"Him," I whispered when Haden appeared at the end of the path. His stormy blue eyes glanced around as if he could feel me close by. I heard Holden take in a shaky breath. But I watched Penelope's and Henry's faces as they recognized their son. They were in shock at first before they started smiling and crying.

"Haden," Penelope said with such love in her voice that it made my chest ache.

Holden shook his head and stared at Haden. I saw the devastation for only a moment before happiness took over. Haden walked past without seeing us, but he stopped and turned. His eyes seemed to glance to where I was standing before he smiled softly to himself. He knew I was watching.

"Storm," he whispered, like I would come out. He glanced around, only two feet from his parents. He knew I was close by, but I wouldn't show myself to him right now.

"Is it...*him*?" Holden asked me.

"Yes," I whispered. "It is."

"What is his name?" Holden asked.

I couldn't help the smile that spread across my face.

"It is Haden."

"Oh, gods," Penelope cried as she hugged Henry. "It's our baby."

"Has he seen you?" Henry asked.

"Yes," I nodded.

"Does he remember? He called you Storm." Henry looked at me for a brief moment.

"No, he doesn't remember, but I admit that it is odd he calls me that." I frowned. "Are you guys happy?"

They all turned to where Haden was walking away before turning to me. Then they rushed me, giving me a group hug, and I smiled.

"This was the best gift," Holden cried. "If you ever tell him the truth, will you introduce us?" Holden asked.

"Of course. You are my family." I smiled as Haden disappeared. "And his, he just won't know that."

"Is he your mate?" Sara asked, hope in her voice. My face broke out into a big smile. They all stared at me when they realized that was a possibility this time.

"Yes, he is."

They all hugged me again, and I used it as an opportunity to move us back to the family home. When they pulled back, I felt tears brimming in my eyes. This is what I had waited for, and it was finally here. I didn't know how to feel. But there was a fear present—fear that I would lose him again, fear that he would not love me like he did before.

Instinctively, I grabbed the ring on my right hand and twisted it. The ring that Haden proposed to me with had not left my finger since the day he gave it to me. I just hoped the heavens did not mess this up again because it might be enough to kill me if he was taken from me.

CHAPTER 15

HADEN

I knew I was being followed, but I wasn't sure why. Sure enough, when I looked behind me, I saw Kira's father, Barron, trying to sneak up on me. His burly form stood on the pathway with his two little henchmen. His eyes narrowed on me as if I had done something to offend him. Why was he watching me like that? I hurried to sell my handful of vegetables so I could buy my twin sister, Remy, new boots that would actually fit her.

My face was black and blue from the beating my father gave me last evening, and I knew I looked like shit, but my eyes narrowed on the old prick who was gawking at me. It was nothing new to see me beaten to a pulp. Everyone in the village of Raynor knew my father was abusive, and no one cared.

"What are you looking at?" I glared.

The whole village had been watching me a bit closer these last few weeks. They all stared at me like I was a fucking freak because of a woman I had seen twice. I knew Kira had told the entire village that I was crazy, but she didn't know the half of it. The old man bought my vegetables for half of what he normally did, but I did not have any power to bargain for more.

Asshole.

When I glanced around the street full of fae, I hoped to see her—the woman with star-like eyes that had smiled so freely at me. The only woman who made me wonder what it would be like to have their attention. But she had disappeared just as quickly as she had appeared. I could feel her close by, though. I didn't know how I knew it was her, but I did, and I wished she would stop hiding and show me her pretty face again.

As I glanced around, I noticed darkness falling and felt an urgency to get home before something bad happened. Bad things always happened at night. So, I looked at the ground and hurried up the path toward my home, hoping to make it there without any sort of confrontation. My feet slowed when I felt her presence again. Hope coiled inside of my chest, making a tugging sensation more noticeable. Turning around to see if she was watching, I was met with nothing.

"I know you're there," I said, hoping she would appear. "Are you ever going to show me your face again?"

Disappointment filled me when she didn't appear. I started moving up the dirt path again, only to be suddenly cut off by Kira's father.

He stood with two men, one flanking each side of him, wearing clothing that was worth more than my entire house. I went to walk around him, but he stopped me by grabbing my shoulder. I didn't like being touched, so I stepped away from him.

"Where's your father?" Barron asked.

"Did you check the tavern? He practically lives there," I said.

"It's the first place we checked. Galen has been giving us the runaround."

"Well, I don't know where he is."

I tried to get around him, but he stepped into my path again. Okay, I was getting fucking annoyed. Glaring up at his chubby face, his blue eyes narrowed on me.

"He owes me a lot of money."

"You and half the village. I don't know why you're talking to me about *his* business."

The men chuckled humorlessly. Barron grabbed me by the shirt collar, yanking me toward himself, ripping my small pocket open, and taking the money I earned for Remy's boots.

"This will buy him a few days, but you better tell him I expect a payment."

"That is my money."

He shrugged. His red hair swayed with the movement. I could feel my anger bubbling up. Remy needed new boots. Kira's father was making a very big mistake right now. He didn't know it, but his next words would determine if he lived or died tonight.

"You're his son; you can help pay it off."

"The fuck I will. That bastard can pay off his own shit; I will not be responsible for his stupid ideas. Give me my money back now, or you'll fucking regret it."

The two men with him looked at me like I was an idiot.

"You can either give us this money, or we will take payment a different way." The way he said it put me on high alert. What did he mean by that? Before I could ask, he smiled.

"Your sister is pretty. I'm sure we could work out an arrangement."

Disgust filled me. I guess he was dying tonight.

"Take the money," I demanded.

"That's what I thought. But maybe I will offer that deal to your father, since you pissed me off. Gods know, he would probably agree to it."

"If you even look at Remy, I will rip your eyes out and make you eat them."

Without warning, Barron punched me in the face, making me fall to the ground. I didn't fight back. It wasn't the right time, but soon he would feel my wrath. Barron and the two men with him laughed as they walked around me and headed up the street.

I watched them, imagining all the ways I would hurt them. Lightning scattered across the sky, and instinctively I looked for the woman. My violent storm. It had been a clear day, but this storm had come out of nowhere. I didn't see her, so I stood and headed home, no longer hurrying. I was late, and now I knew what would be waiting for me when I got there.

When I saw my shitty home, I glanced around, hoping that woman wasn't watching me from anywhere. I would die of embarrassment if she saw that our house was missing parts of the roof and the wood on the sides was crumbling away. One day, I would build myself a house that felt like a home.

Taking a deep breath, I headed inside only to be instantly met with a sucker punch to the stomach by my father. I fell to my knees and tried to take a breath in, but it was useless. I was on the ground gasping for air when he backhanded me. My head snapped to the side at the impact.

"Where the fuck have you been?" he sneered.

"Barron stopped me and demanded that you pay your debt."

My mother was in the kitchen, staring out the window. She didn't do or say anything to help me. She never did.

"Well, you're old enough to start helping with household bills."

I clenched my fists. My eyes were changing color as my frost magic desperately tried to explode from me.

"What's wrong, boy?" My father taunted me. "I can see it in your eyes; you have something to say, so say it."

I said nothing.

I never did.

"For once since you've been born, you'll be useful for something." He smiled. His eyes traveled over the frost clinging to my fists. "Disgusting elitist."

His words didn't hurt me as much as he had hoped. When you hear the same things your whole life, you start to see the truth of them, and I was under no impression that I was worth anything to anyone but Remy.

"Get out of my face," he spat at me.

I stood and went to my bedroom, which was basically a closet with a small window. Shutting the door, I moved my dresser in front of it so he couldn't get in later when he was drunk beyond reason. I began pacing back and forth in the small space. Rage was consuming me, and I tried with everything inside of me to control myself because I knew what would happen.

The village had practically shunned me when I developed my elite magic, but they didn't know that there was something much more sinister that lived inside of me. Another side of me that was pissed off all the time. The void loved to come out and take care of all of my problems. He would come out tonight and take care of Barron; I knew he would. The words of both Barron and my father were enough to make me lose control. Running my fingers through my hair, I knew I needed to get out of there before I did something I would regret.

Not even Remy knew what happened to me when I became this angry. She would think I was a monster. No one would love a monster like me.

I climbed out of my window and quickly ran to the woods. The shift was quick. I normally felt too much of everything, but when this...other side of my personality took over, I felt... void. It was like another person stepped into my mind and took over, someone more... deadly.

When I was him, I did not think about the consequences of my actions, I did not have a moral compass, and I did not fear anything. I was dangerous. The shiver that ran up my spine every time this void took over was the only indication that I was given of the coming change. And no matter how many times I tried, I couldn't control who I became. Because once he was in control, I was pushed deep in the depths of myself, unaware of what was happening.

It was like he was protecting me from remembering the horrible things he did. I didn't mind because he would share important things with me when needed.

In a flash, I was no longer running scared. My feet slowed, and the emotions that filled me disappeared and drifted away. My gaze lingered on the town and the firelight flickering in the windows as night fell completely. Glancing up at the moon, I smiled; tonight would be a good night to kill a man...or three. With that thought, I headed into town to find Barron and the two men who dared to threaten Remy. Kira's family owned one of the biggest homes in the village, which made it easy to find. My grin turned wicked as I quickly made my way there.

Barron answered the door at my banging and glared at me. I could see the confusion in his eyes as he looked me over, trying to figure out what was different about me. He wouldn't know until it was too late.

"I have the money my father owes you," I lied.

"Give it and go," he snapped.

"I'm not an idiot. I didn't bring it with me. I have a hiding spot. If you want it, you'll come get it."

His blue eyes lingered on my face. I bet his instincts were telling him not to come with me. They were trying to warn him that even though I looked like the innocent, push-over Haden, I was not him right then. I was a monster lurking in plain sight. If he looked into my eyes, he would no longer see stormy blue. Instead, he would see the black void of my soul staring back at him.

"Alright, but if this is a trick, I will gut your sister in front of you."

The nice side of me would have been paralyzed by fear at this statement, but this evil part didn't bat an eye. I welcomed him to keep talking. It only made the need to break every bone in his body worse.

"You might want your two friends from earlier to help carry the bags, because I won't."

He clenched his jaw as he stomped his way up the street. Barron kept looking over his shoulder at me as if he expected me to attack him out there, but I was a patient man. I wanted to hear him begging and pleading for me to show mercy—mercy I would not give him. We stopped at both men's homes, and they came willingly. One of the men stared at me for a long while, though. As if he knew there was something different about me, too.

"What's wrong with you?" he asked.

I gave him a smile void of any emotion, which seemed to scare him more.

"Nothing."

"Your eyes... It's like looking into the night sky."

I just watched him with a smile until he looked away. My fake smile immediately disappeared. I led them through the woods.

"There is a small shack just ahead of us that I kept the money in to hide it from my father," I said.

The idiots believed me. It was honestly too easy.

For just a moment, I stopped and glanced around me. My skin prickled, and I knew she was watching me from somewhere. But I was sure that after she saw what I was about to do, she would never show her pretty face to me again. Even as this empty shell of a man, I felt the disappointment of that realization. Did she wait for me all these years, or did she move on? Fuck, I was pissing myself off by thinking like that. My eyes darted around the woods, and I knew I would fucking gut any man that had touched her since me. I had missed those starlight eyes. I smiled to myself. How would my Storm react to seeing how different

I was now? The thought made me hesitate, but nothing would deter me from killing these three fucks.

"Where is this damn shack?" Barron turned and glared. I stared him down, not bothering with fake smiles or emotions anymore.

"Oh, shit, I forgot." I pretended to be remembering something as I leaned down and picked up a small round log that was perfect for beating someone to death with. "I lied." I smiled as Barron's tiny brain figured out this was a trick.

"Get him," he demanded from his stupid little henchmen. The first of the two came at me alone, his long braid trailing behind him. He was running at full speed toward me, but I didn't move. Instead, I lifted the log, drawing it back and then swinging it forward with all of my might. It cracked across the side of his skull with a wet, smacking sound. He dropped to the ground, eyes rolling back and blood spewing from him. I watched him suffer for a moment before leaning down and wrapping his long braid around his neck. My eyes never left Barron as I strangled the life from his friend.

I shoved his dead body away from me as I stood.

"Well, that was hardly a fight." I tisked and stood up. "Next."

The second man didn't move, but Barron did. He pulled out a knife and swung it at me. I dodged it easily and chuckled when Barron turned quickly. I cocked my head to the side to watch him. He was terrified of me, and I liked seeing it.

"I knew something was wrong with you when you looked at me with those soulless eyes. Are you possessed?"

This made me let out a genuine laugh. Barron was trying to distract me enough that I wouldn't notice his friend coming up behind me. I let them think they would win this fight.

"No, I'm not possessed." I glared at him. "Then again, maybe I am." I shrugged, not knowing for sure.

"What is wrong with you?"

I smiled.

"Let's just say that I have two sides to me. The nice, innocent man that everyone loves to torture, and this version." I waved my hands down the front of me. "A man no one will overpower; do you know why?"

He shook his head no.

"Because I do not *feel anything*, Barron. Emotions will not stop me from releasing this wrath I have inside of me. I will not feel guilty about taking your life. In fact, I think I will quite enjoy watching the light drain from your eyes.

Although, I do like the thought of ripping them from their sockets and forcing you to swallow them."

Barron's face paled. He knew I was not bluffing. He had sealed his fate the moment he thought he could hurt Remy.

His friend made his move, launching himself at my back with his knife in the air. But I turned and grabbed his wrist, twisting the blade in his hand before shoving it into his chest and yanking it up to his throat. His blood drenched my hands. It was warm on this cold, frigid night. Barron's heavy footsteps alerted me that he was running like a coward. I tossed the dead man to the ground.

"I don't think so, Barron." I shot my frost magic at his feet, which instantly froze him to the ground. The sudden stopping made his ankles snap. He wailed out in pain, and it sang to the void monster I was. I took my time getting to him, whistling a little tune on my way.

Barron looked at me, horrified.

I smiled as I said, "You're a coward, just as I thought you were. You should have never threatened Remy."

"I'm sorry. You have my word I will never do it again."

"I believe you, Barron." I smiled down at him, and he sighed, relieved. "Because you'll be dead."

He looked up at me in horror as I held out my palm, and a long icicle formed in my hand. He raised his arms up in defense, but it was no use. I stabbed the ice through his heart, smiling as the light slowly faded from his eyes. When his body sagged against my hand, I jerked it out, making him slump over dead.

I closed my eyes and took a deep breath. Gods, I felt fucking good. I cracked my neck and tried to stifle back my smile. I turned quickly when I heard her soft footsteps.

She smelled like night and heaven—the same. It made my chest ache with longing.

"I know you're watching me, Storm." I turned, expecting her not to show herself, but to my surprise, she stood only a few feet away. There was a sadness in her eyes when she stared at me. But then it left and was replaced by curiosity. "Fuck, you're even prettier than I remember."

As soon as my void eyes landed on her face, a flood of memories slammed into me. Flash after flash of mental images and the sound of overlapping voices assaulted my brain, and I had to close my eyes briefly. My head pounded as memories of Della and me from a different life assaulted me. I looked at her and had trouble breathing. My heart faltered for a moment. My Storm.

Gods, I had missed her.

Her cheeks flushed. She cocked her head to the side as she watched me. Could she tell I was not the same man she had smiled at in town?

"Haden," she purred.

She glanced at the dead bodies. My hands were still coated in blood as she looked back at me. I summoned snow to my hands and used it to wash the blood from me. I don't know what reaction I expected from her, but her smile was not it.

"You know my name, but I do not know yours." I lied.

"Ardella," she answered.

She didn't look like an Ardella.

"Can I call you Della?"

Her pretty eyes shined brightly.

"Yes."

"You watch me a lot. I don't always see you, but I can feel you." She smiled when I took a step toward her. She stepped toward me too, and something about it felt validating. Della should be scared of me, but there was not even a hint of fear from her. She never had been wary of me.

"You're different than when I first saw you."

I watched her as she seemed to be studying me. Her gaze drifted over my face before looking over my body. There was a familiarity in her eyes that I longed to see. Did she mean different from town or the life before this one?

"But you are the same, too," she finally said. "Is this some sort of magic?"

"No."

"Then what is it?"

"A way to survive," I answered. "I needed to become a monster to stay alive because the nice part of me would have been killed years ago if I didn't."

"So, you have two... personalities inside of you."

"A good one and an evil one." I took a step toward her. "Does this side of me scare you?"

Della gave me a big, genuine smile.

"No."

"It should." I stepped even closer to her, and she didn't flinch when I reached out and stroked her face. "Do you like what you see?" Fuck, I needed to rein it in. She couldn't know that I remembered her and our previous life together when I was like this. Damn it, I could hardly contain myself when she was close to me. My eyes dropped to the ring I slipped on her finger centuries ago, and damn, it made me happy to see.

"If I said yes, would that be too forward?" Her starry eyes stared directly into my void ones. I softly gripped her hair and yanked her head back slightly. She let out the prettiest moan. I was fucked.

"Answer me, Della."

"Yes," she whispered.

Her one-word answer made something in my cold heart warm up.

"Why?"

Something about my question made her tense. Oh, she wanted to keep secrets. I smiled when her eyes fell to my mouth. I had never kissed a woman, never had the desire to in this life, but I knew her mouth would fucking ruin any other kiss I ever had. My soul knew that she was the only one worthy of getting me intimately.

"You're more handsome up close," she confessed before her cheeks heated. I liked that a lot.

Her whole chest flushes like this when she cums.

"Yeah?" I whispered. Della nodded before she lifted her hand and touched my face. I was beaten to hell, and I'm sure I was covered in blood. I felt something warm pass over me, and the throbbing of my wounds disappeared. My voice softened a bit at her touch. "I feel like I've known you my whole life."

Her eyes flashed pure white when they met mine. I had missed her.

"Maybe we knew each other in a past life." My words made her frown for just a moment. I inched her closer to my mouth, and she didn't fight me. She was going to let me kiss her, and something about the submission made me feel... possessive over a woman I shouldn't get involved with again. Della still didn't know who I really was or that I was her enemy.

She studied me as if I were something precious that she had lost long ago. "I like this side of you," she whispered.

A noise behind me in the woods made me turn my gaze from her for a split second. But when I turned back, Della was gone. I was confused. Quickly, I turned and looked for her. She was standing in the woods nearby, smiling. How had she left my grip without me feeling it?

"I'll see you soon." She promised.

Then she was gone. I could feel the hold of the void letting me go as I smiled. She was going to be mine, and I didn't think I would ever let her go. The monster inside of me had already claimed her—again.

CHAPTER 16

HADEN

Everyone stared. I heard their whispers as they watched me walk down the path. I heard them call me a freak. I didn't need more of a reason to feel out of place in this village than I did growing up with the town drunk as a father. Smiling to myself, I walked with my back straight and my head held tall. I didn't care much about what they thought of me today.

My gaze scanned the crowd to see if she was close by, but I didn't see her, which made me frown. I hadn't seen her in a week. The village was bustling today because Barron and his two friends had been found dead in the woods. I smiled when they blamed monsters. They weren't wrong; a monster *had* killed them. The void had shared those memories with me. He also shared us flirting with Della.

I could only remember bits and pieces of when I was void. Most of it felt hazy and only came in flashes that didn't always make sense. But I remembered Della—how damn pretty she was with her big eyes and soft lips, the way she watched me carefully like I was the most interesting thing she had ever laid her eyes on. Gods, I didn't know her, but when I looked at her, I felt like I did. My chest ached with something furious as Della took up every thought.

I should've kissed her.

Something hitting my chest pulled me out of my daydreaming. I glanced down to see a giant tomato sitting at my feet. The rotten fruit left a huge stain on one of the only shirts I owned. Damn it, I couldn't afford another one. Fuck, I couldn't even afford this one—I stole it. When I turned to see who was laughing, I wasn't surprised to see it was the young noblemen of the village.

Little fucking pricks. Would the town notice if I started picking off all these noble bastards one at a time?

Kira was with them, laughing like it was the funniest thing she had ever seen. I was not about to give them a reaction. So, I didn't say anything as I kept walking toward the woods. There was only one thing on my mind, and that was seeing Della.

"Hey, Haden!" One of them called. "Did you make up an imaginary friend because no one here likes you?"

I ignored them. It shouldn't matter what they thought. My mind was already weighed down with everything that had happened at my house last night, and I needed to get out of there before I unleashed hell on the whole town.

"Freak!" one of them yelled as I made my way into the forest. I heard them all laughing, but I still didn't say anything back.

My face ached with pain from the beating I had received from my father the night before. I closed my eyes tightly as I tried to get rid of the sound of my sister, Remy, begging him to stop hurting her. My father had always been cruel, but it was usually toward me. When I went to see what was going on, I found my father pinning her to the wall by her throat. I don't know if I had ever felt anger like that before.

I saw red. Unfortunately for me, though, my void side did not come to my aid.

I had charged at him and did everything in my power to beat the shit out of him for hurting her. But in the end, my mother had helped him by distracting me, allowing him to land a sucker punch. Then he kept just beating the living shit out of me. Remiah had tried to help, but I told her to go so she was not hurt anymore. I did not understand why the void monster side of me did not attack and kill my own father.

Maybe there was a way to control this other side so that I could use it at my own disposal. I had tried to bring it out before, but it didn't listen. What was the point of becoming a monster if I couldn't control it? When I reached the small clearing in the trees, I sighed heavily. The relentless ache I had experienced my entire life was unbearable today. I didn't want to feel it anymore.

The sky was a heavenly blue, and the sun warmed my cold soul. It would be a good day to die. I inched closer to the edge of the cliffs. How many times had I thought about throwing myself off, but at the end of the day, I never could? Remiah needed me. I sighed heavily as I ran my hands down my face. I looked up to the sky and begged the stars to stop torturing me with a shitty life.

"Haden?" I turned and glared at Kira. Her red hair flowed around her. Kira was pretty, and she knew it. She used it to her advantage with the noblemen in the village. They all loved her, but for some reason, she was always pestering me. She had always lingered and watched, but I never enjoyed her company. She was too cruel.

"What?" I snapped.

I looked at her, but I didn't look for long. She didn't interest me in the slightest.

"You look upset."

No shit.

"I am."

"Can I help?" She was inching toward me, but I wanted her to keep her distance. She stopped when she was a few feet in front of me. I stared her down as her big, blue eyes filled with hopefulness. Gods, she was unpleasant even to be close to. She smelled terrible, like bitter lemons.

"Help?" I scoffed. "You can help by running back to your little friends and making some more jokes at my expense. And staying far away from me."

Her fake friendliness slipped for a moment, showing me the real her, the stuck-up brat that only wanted me because she could never have me. The sight of her disgusted me.

"I didn't say anything." She glared. "Besides, I much prefer your company." She lifted her hands and grabbed my face before sliding her hands down my neck, then shoulders.

"What are you doing?" I gripped her hands and shoved them away from me. Why did she think I would ever want her touch? There was nothing nice about the way I was looking at her, so why didn't she take the fucking hint?

"I can make you feel good. I can make the sadness go away, and you can make me forget everything that happened to my family."

She leaned in to kiss me, but I turned away from her before her mouth touched mine. Her lips hit my cheek, but then she kissed down my neck, and her hands shoved their way up my shirt. I didn't like it. Before I could shove her, the void began pulsing inside of me violently. Fuck, it did not want her hands on me either.

Get her the fuck off of us. She does not get to touch. Shit. The void had never communicated with me like this.

"Stop," I demanded. "I don't like being touched."

She didn't stop.

"You don't have to pretend you don't like it. I won't tell anyone."

Kill her if you must. He was pissed.

I wasn't going to kill her.

Fine, but Della probably will.

My eyes snapped to the woods behind her when I thought I saw movement. Nothing seemed to be lurking, though, so I tried to focus on the fact that Kira wouldn't take her hands off of me. Her touch did nothing but offend me.

"Get your hands off of me now." I shoved her away so she couldn't reach me.

This made her fake friendliness disappear completely.

"You really are a fucking freak." She sneered. "You should be happy I'm showing you any attention."

"It kills you, doesn't it?" I bared my teeth viciously.

"What?"

"That every man in the village will crawl into bed and share you, but I never will."

She swallowed hard at my insult. I had never stuck up for myself. But the void was buzzing with excitement.

"Do you know why they don't mind sharing you, Kira? Because you don't mean anything to any of them. It doesn't matter how many men you sleep with. They will never love you; they won't marry you."

She gaped at me, and I stopped smiling at her. She opened her mouth to say something but closed it immediately and suddenly looked like she was scared to move. Something made Kira suddenly freeze and turn to look over her shoulder. After a moment, she began looking around frantically, but I didn't know what was wrong with her.

"Haden, did you hear that?" She asked worriedly as she watched the woods.

"I didn't hear anything." But as soon as the words left my mouth, I saw Della. *There she is.* I smiled. Her bronze skin popped against her black clothing. She stood at the tree line, but when Kira looked in that direction, she didn't seem to see her. Della's pretty, star-colored eyes glanced at Kira and then moved to me with a frown.

Way to go, you upset Storm. The void sighed.

"You're still seeing her, aren't you?" Kira looked at my face as I stared at Della and admired her. Every single thing about her caught my attention.

I didn't answer.

I didn't care if she thought I was a freak or told everyone. Remy was the only one who believed I could see a woman anyway. Kira frowned and peered around us. Her blue eyes skipped right past Della, who was watching us—me.

I shook my head like it would get rid of her. It didn't, thankfully.

She was right there. How could no one see her? Della's black hair tumbled in waves over her shoulder when she tilted her head to the side. The dress she wore had small, thin, black straps that showed off her flawless, dark skin. In the shade of the trees, I could see the faint silver light of a glowing tattoo that was wrapped around both of her arms.

"You're scaring me, Haden. No one is standing there." Kira's face looked at me with concern, like I was a freak. My chest was tight with worry that Della would see how others treated me and decide I wasn't worth her time anymore.

She won't think that. The void was confident.

As much as I didn't want to, I looked away from her and focused on Kira. Della had hardly spoken to me. I should not feel this way about someone I barely talked to. But the void inside of me hummed at the sight of her. The memory of how soft her voice had been hit me and made me long to hear it again. Maybe I had lost my fucking mind. But I remembered the feel of her soft hair twisted in my fingers as she stared at me; that was not fake. My hands fisted at my sides. I wanted to be that close to her again.

Kira stepped back up to me, and I stepped out of her reach. Her blue eyes narrowed on me.

"I will snap your fucking fingers if you touch me again." My anger slipped from me.

"I don't understand you, Haden. You don't have any-thing to offer anyone, and I'm here trying to give you company, and you act repulsed by me."

"That is because you fucking repulse me." I sneered at the perfect 'O' her mouth made at my remark. I had never looked at anyone like I looked at Della, especially not this pompous bitch.

Her face was red with indignation. "I'm the only one in this fucking realm that doesn't recoil in disgust when they see you," she yelled.

"What the fuck is your problem?" I snapped at her. "I didn't ask you to follow me."

"You are lying about your feelings for me."

"I'm not," I spoke truthfully. "My gods, woman, how many times have I told you to leave me alone?"

"Maybe something is wrong with you," she muttered. "After all, you see a woman that no one else can." My eyes narrowed on her as she continued her rant. "And you're passing up an opportunity to be with me. I'm of noble birth, and you're lower than shit. You have nothing to offer anyone."

I clenched my jaw angrily. I knew I was nothing. My father made sure to tell me how worthless I was every day. He had told me from a young age how no sensible woman would want to marry a freak. But back then, he had been talking about my elite magic. Now he said it because I saw that woman.

"You are such a bitch." I rolled my eyes. "Do your little friends know that you chase me around, trying to sleep with me? What's wrong, Kira? You already spread your legs for all the noble boys in town, and now they don't want you anymore? They realized you aren't anything special?"

She slapped me, but it was nothing compared to the beating from last night.

"I'm the best you'll ever get," she hissed.

Suddenly, Della was directly behind Kira. Her face was unrecognizable as anger took over her features. Her eyes turned pure white, and it called to the void part of me.

There's my girl. The void was proud of this reaction.

"Why is she speaking to you like that?" Della questioned. "I can kill her if you want."

Yes.

Kira didn't say anything as the woman's angelic voice wrapped around me, making me feel something I had never felt or seen before. Della stared at me with expectant eyes. I subtly shook my head, making her frown. I couldn't take my eyes off her. The way she was watching Kira made me realize that Della had a dark side to her too.

Kira noticed me staring at an empty spot. "Look, the freak is seeing the woman as we speak."

"That's it," Della sighed. She lifted her hands, and the blue sky filled with dark clouds, with lightning cracking above us. Kira glanced up, and when she did, Della moved closer to her. I saw her whisper something to Kira, who froze.

"Who is that?" she asked, hastily looking around. "You can't threaten me; do you know who my family is?" Kira screamed into the woods.

Della watched me closely, smiling like a psycho. Fuck, she was breathtaking when she was mad. Then a bolt of lightning struck the ground at Kira's feet, melting part of her shoes. She stumbled backward. Her big blue eyes widened as she looked around.

"I'm leaving!" she snapped, but she wasn't talking to me. "I didn't want him anyways." Kira turned and ran away. When I looked back at Della, she gave me a look of worry.

"She is unpleasant," she said defensively, like I was looking for an answer to her little outburst. "Honestly, you should have just let me kill her."

She was a bit unhinged, like me.

"Are you possessive, Storm?"

"Only when it comes to you," she whispered like I wouldn't hear her. My heart beat rapidly in my chest at her words for some reason. Her pretty eyes widened. "Shit, I didn't mean to say that out loud."

I smiled as panic filled her eyes.

"I should go," she said, but I could tell she didn't want to leave. She turned to walk away, but I grabbed her wrist and turned her back around. Her eyes stared at where we touched before meeting mine. Something somber filled her features when she looked at my face. She looked... haunted. The void did not like to see this look in her eyes. It began pulsing inside of me, but I didn't let it surface. A sudden noise coming through the woods made us both look away. Remy was walking toward me, and when I looked back at Della, she was gone.

Damn it.

How did she get out of my grip without me noticing?

"Haden, what are you doing out here?" Remiah's blue eyes, which matched my own perfectly, drifted around us, lingering in the woods for a moment. Her eyes softened as she looked at me.

"Just thinking about how shitty our life has been," I sighed as I looked around.

I needed more time with Della.

"I see they threw a tomato at you again." She clenched her jaw. "Maybe you should use your magic to get them to leave you alone."

"And give them another reason to talk more shit about me?"

I shrugged like it didn't matter. But it did. I had never belonged here, and neither did Remiah. Remy looked at me and frowned before looking up into the sky to admire the sunshine. She sighed with contentment before looking back at me. Her smile disappeared as her eyes traced over the bruises our father left on my face last night.

"Do you think our lives will ever get better?" I asked.

I expected her to scoff or roll her eyes at my question. We never let ourselves dream of a life better than what we had. Our parents were worthless drunks. Their parents before them were the same. I did not know how to change my fate so that I would not end up miserable like my father.

"Yes, it's actually part of the reason why I came out here to find you. I wanted to talk to you about something." She nibbled her bottom lip nervously.

"Whatever it is, you don't have to be worried about telling me," I assured her. Her eyes roamed over my face as she moved forward and hugged me tightly. When she pulled back, I saw worry still clinging to her features.

"You remember when you said you saw the woman in town that day?" I nodded. "I believed you right away."

"I know."

"There was a reason why I believed you so quickly, but I was too worried to tell you that day." She paused. "I'm sorry I didn't say anything sooner, but I also started seeing a man that no one else can. I saw him the day you saw the woman. I was in the yard doing chores, and he was suddenly there, watching me. He looked terrified when I asked him what he was staring at," Remy laughed.

I stood still at her confession.

"What do you mean?"

"The day you told me about the woman, I started seeing a man with star-colored eyes. I realized quickly that I was the only one who seemed to see him." Her eyes shifted to the woods. "He's here now. I've been spending time with him. His name is Mikel. I like him; he makes me believe that my life can be better." She squeezed my hand tightly and smiled. "Have you talked to the woman?"

"She was talking to me, kind of, before you got here. Honestly, she seems terrified of me."

Remy chuckled softly.

"He used to be scared of me, too. It takes them a bit to warm up to us."

"Why do we see them, Rem?"

"Maybe it's because we are twins. I'm glad I met him. He is kind." She peered toward the woods like she was reliving fond memories. But then I realized that she was staring at the man, even though I did not see him.

What was wrong with us? Had our father beaten us so hard when we were younger that it fucked up our minds?

My sister looked happy as she stared at the invisible man. It wasn't a look I was used to seeing from her. We were both barely holding on to the will to live. Life had not been kind to us. We were bitter and filled with hatred, but something about seeing my sister look engrossed with this man she saw made me happy too.

However, jealousy also bloomed in my chest at my sister's happiness. Why did Della keep running from me and not stay?

"How did you get him to spend time with you?" I asked.

"I told him he better start staying longer or I would never look at him again. He didn't like that much, so he started talking to me, just very slowly at first. Now he doesn't shut up." She laughed, and I smiled at her. "I'm going to go say hi. Are you going to get away from the ledge?"

"Yes," I promised. She gave me a big hug before hurrying over to the tree line. I watched my sister smiling, cheeks flushed and her eyes wild with some emotion I had never felt.

Feeling as if I was interrupting something special, I turned to head away from them. My mind raced with what Remiah had told me. Why could the two of us see them when no one else could? Were they even real, or were my twin and I equally as fucked in the head? Slowly, I walked through the woods. Nothing in particular caught my attention, but I knew I was being watched. My gaze flickered around the tall, leafy trees.

"I know you're watching me," I called out. She didn't say anything, but she also didn't show herself. "You know you can stay longer next time. You don't have to hide from me, Della. You've already seen my monster, and I'm just starting to catch a glimpse of yours."

I waited, and for some reason, my heart pounded wildly with anticipation. She was watching me from somewhere; I could sense her close by. She stayed hidden, though.

"The next time I see you, I expect you to stay for longer than a minute. If you don't, then I will stop acknowledging you altogether." It was an empty threat. I could not stop thinking about her. There was no way I could walk away.

Maybe I had lost my fucking mind. Everyone in town already called me a freak. They might be right. Sighing heavily, I headed toward my house. As I passed through town, it felt like everyone was staring at me more than normal. I kept my face down because I didn't want to see their disgust toward me.

"Haden." I froze at Kira's voice. When I turned, she was standing with a few fae I didn't know well, mostly guys.

"Kira." I looked over her face, confused. She glared at me with a burning hatred that I had not expected. I realized she was more pissed off about me not reciprocating her feelings than I thought.

"Is it true?" One of the guys chuckled. "That you're still seeing things that others don't?"

My eyes drifted to Kira, and I glared at her because she had told them. I ignored their jabs and started walking toward my house again.

"Stay away from Kira, you freak!" the same guy yelled. Anger filled me because she was the one always chasing after me. So, I turned around and glared at Kira.

"Oh, Kira, did you not tell your friends that you were trying to sleep with me in the woods today?" I spat at her. Kira's pretty face turned bright red. "Stay the fuck away from me, Kira." I tossed that out there just to be a dick. They all shut the fuck up and turned toward her.

"You have a thing for the town freak?" The guy laughed.

"Fuck you, Haden!"

I glared. Then I turned back to my trek as her friends laughed and made fun of her for slumming it with me.

When I got to the front door, I took a deep breath, knowing what would happen when I walked in. I had snuck out of the house this morning to avoid my father; now I was going to have to pay for it. I opened the door and was met with a gut punch that had me crumpled to the floor instantly. My father didn't stop there.

He spewed nasty names at me and told me how worthless I was. He just kept hitting and kicking me until he got tired.

"Get your useless ass away from me." He spat on me as I crawled to my room. My mother sat in her fucking chair watching as always but never sticking up for me. It was hard to think that life would get better than this, but I was happy that my sister was able to feel something other than this all-consuming sadness I felt.

CHAPTER 17

DELLA

I was stalking my mate. Part of me wanted to laugh at the realization, but another part of me knew this was ridiculous. I was sitting out in front of his family home just staring at how terrible it looked. My throat became tight when I saw the missing parts of the roof and the holes in the wood siding. It looked like the wood had been rotting away for a long time, and at some point, this home would cave in on itself.

I had looked around the village today to see if this was the condition of all the homes. It wasn't. Haden's family home was the worst. All I could think about was Penelope and Henry's beautiful home. Haden deserved that life again, not this.

Haden's life this time was nowhere near what he had in his last life. It made me want to curse the stars for their cruelty toward him. He deserves the best of everything. I guess I would need to be the one that did that for him. I perked up when I heard his voice. Gods, I loved his voice. The deep humming of it was coming from behind the house but fading away. I had been waiting for hours to see him so I could follow him without being seen.

I scrambled up quickly and went around the house to see Haden and a petite blonde working on a dead patch of land. Haden smiled brightly at whatever she said. Fuck, he was so handsome. My stomach clenched tightly at how I missed him, even though I saw him yesterday. Technically, I had seen him every day since the incident in the woods with Kira. I stepped closer to them as they laughed together, taking in everything about the way he moved with ease, glancing around as if he knew I was here.

"Do you think Father will be gone all day?" the girl's timid voice asked.

A sister.

"Let's pray to the gods that he is."

I smiled because we had nothing to do with answering prayers like that. The woman turned toward where I stood, and I stopped moving even though I knew she couldn't see me. My mouth fell open as I glanced over her features. She was beautiful with her dark blonde hair and the same stormy eyes as Haden.

He had a twin again.

She was still staring at where I was. Haden stopped hoeing the ground and glanced to where she was staring. He smirked slightly.

"She's here, isn't she?" She looked at Haden. "I can feel it like I do with Mikel."

Mikel.

What were the odds that it was my Mikel—my brother?

"She's here, but she's going to keep hiding like she has been all week." Haden's expression dimmed. His sister looked toward him with her brows pinched together.

"Why?"

"I don't know."

Because I was terrified. I was terrified that Haden would be exactly the same as he was, and I was terrified he would be completely different. I was terrified he wouldn't love me like he did before. I was terrified that he would be taken from me again. Part of me wanted not to get too attached just in case the heavens took him away from me. But I was already attached, and now I was terrified. I could not stop the fear that swarmed inside of me. I was scared that I would hurt him in some way.

"This would be much easier to dig up if the ground were wet." His sister sighed as she rubbed her sweaty forehead. Haden nodded and struggled for a moment before I lifted my hands to the side. Dark clouds moved over the sun, and I heard them sigh with relief.

Then I focused on the large patch of ground they were working on and made it pour over it and it alone.

"What the hell?" She gawked.

"That would be Storm." His face softened. "Thank you."

I let a single crack of lightning skid across the sky. After a moment, the rain let up, and I began moving the clouds away.

"Wait!" she called. "Please, leave the clouds; it feels so nice."

A small chuckle escaped me as I moved the clouds back.

"Holy shit, that is impressive. I will have to ask Mikel what magic he can do."

"Remiah, don't just stand there gawking. Help me," Haden said as he watched her staring into the sky. Remiah.

I walked closer to her and examined her. If Mikel was talking to her, then she was his mate. But he hadn't told me. I guess I hadn't told him either. Maybe he didn't realize what she was to him. I disregarded that thought immediately. Mikel was smart; he would know. Somehow I knew that she was a good match for him. Her purple soul matched Mikel's.

The stars gave us mates at the same time—twins. Somehow, it felt... right. I glanced at Haden and wondered if I had set that in motion when I gave him my bond. I heard Remiah groan, and her stomach growled. Haden sighed.

"We can try and bargain for food," he said.

"It's fine." But I could see how tired she was. When I looked at Haden and saw it within him too. They were not well taken care of. Did Mikel know how badly our mates were being cared for? Did it set off a rage inside of him, too?

This wouldn't do. I swiped my hand out, and a small table, fully laden, appeared. Haden and Remiah stopped what they were doing and gawked at the array of food and drinks. Haden's head turned around as he looked for me. His eyes filled with unshed tears.

"Storm?" He looked right to where I was standing.

Eat.

Remiah didn't need any encouragement. She was at the table looking over everything and then stuffing everything she could in her mouth. Haden walked over to the table slowly and started eating. Seeing them smile made my chest ache less. Remiah picked up some broccoli and handed it to Haden. He scrunched up his nose. I chuckled softly. He still hated broccoli. Something about that made me happy.

"You're such a weirdo." She rolled her eyes and ate it. Remiah looked up. "Thanks," she said to the air, not knowing exactly where I was.

I glanced over at them and smiled. After they were done eating, they got back to digging. Frowning at how long it was taking them, I was trying to figure out what they were actually doing so I could help.

I stood at the edge of the dirt pile and sighed heavily, knowing that I was going to have to talk to him to figure it out. After all, they looked exhausted. I smiled slightly as I finally made myself appear, giggling at the way that it made Haden jump.

"Storm."

Remiah glanced over her shoulder and looked at me. I wondered if she could tell Mikel was my brother. Her mouth fell open, and she looked at Haden.

"What are you trying to do?" I asked softly as I pointed to the ground.

Haden and Remiah stared at me for a moment like they had seen a ghost, then Remiah smiled and started explaining.

"Father told us to dig up this patch of land and pile the dirt for a garden. The dirt we are using is not growing things well."

"That's a lot of work." I frowned. "Here, watch out."

Haden and Remiah stepped away from the ground, and I lifted my hand, letting my starlight shoot out and complete their task in mere seconds.

"Like that?" I asked.

"Yes." Remiah smiled. "Thank the heavens because I was going to die of boredom."

I chuckled softly.

Haden stared at me without saying anything. Slowly, doubt trickled into my mind. Maybe I shouldn't have shown myself. Remiah looked at him and smacked the back of his head softly.

He seemed to snap out of whatever was happening and glared at her.

"You're being rude." She bugged her eyes out. "Tell your lady thank you."

Oh, yeah, she would be perfect for Mikel.

"Thank you, my lady," he said sarcastically. I chuckled softly and nodded.

"You're welcome, Haden."

He swallowed hard and glanced at the house before something flickered in his eyes—embarrassment. His face turned red as he looked away from me, his hand rubbing the back of his neck. My chest tightened at how uncomfortable he was.

"Do you need help with anything else?" I asked because he still wasn't talking. I knew I was awkward, but so was he, and it wasn't great for keeping the conversations going. Remiah sighed at Haden when he shook his head without looking at me. I frowned, disappointment coursing through me. I was hoping he would ask me to stay.

"Okay," I whispered. Remiah's face fell when I glanced at her before waiting for Haden to say something...anything. She watched me stare at Haden, begging silently that he would ask me to stay. He didn't. Gods, I should have just stayed hidden. Instantly, I made myself disappear.

"What the fuck, Haden?" Remiah scolded him immediately. "She wanted you to talk to her, and you wouldn't even look up at her. What is your problem?"

Haden looked up at his sister before dropping his eyes to the ground.

"You know what the problem is," he said. "A man in my social class does not get a woman like her. I have nothing to offer her. She fed us, for fuck's sake, because we can't even afford to eat most days. What am I supposed to say or do? Oh hey, I think you're really pretty. I'm poor, my father is a drunk, my mother is a spineless enabler, my house is falling apart, and I'm wearing clothes that are stained and old. My fucking boots are literally falling apart and too small."

His chest was heaving with anger and sadness. I saw the flash of that other side of him, the void as he called it, in his eyes. "What woman, let alone a woman like her, would look at me and see anything worth loving?"

Tears fell from my eyes as I saw all the self-hatred and devastation on his face. This was different from who he was before.

"I don't think she cares about that," Remiah argued.

"Yeah, well, I do." He stared her down. "Has Mikel seen our home? Have you shown him what kind of life we have?"

She frowned, and I knew she hadn't. Mikel and I did not care. We had everything. The only thing missing was our mate—the most important thing.

"Exactly." Haden closed his eyes tightly. "I'm sorry for bringing you into this. I know that Mikel will love you no matter what."

"And maybe Della will be the same for you."

Haden didn't seem convinced.

"She should find someone better than me. A man should be able to provide for the woman he is with, and I can't do that. I won't ever be able to."

Lightning scattered across the sky as my emotions seeped from me. I did not like that he thought this way.

I loved him before, and I love him just the same way now. Haden was everything to me.

A moment later the door to the house burst open and ricocheted off the wall, making us all flinch. A man who resembled Haden slightly swayed in the doorway. Gods, a whiff of liquor floated through the air and attacked my senses.

"What are you two doing standing around?" he slurred. I watched both of them tense up with fear. My chest was heavy as I watched Haden step in front of his sister, protecting her from whatever he knew was coming. I could see that he trembled slightly, but he did not show it to his father.

The man stumbled off the step, falling into the side of the house. Their mother popped out of the house and tried to help her drunk husband. But he shoved her away, causing her to fall into the woodpile. My anger surfaced immediately.

"We finished," Haden said.

"There's no way you did all of that." His father moved toward them and looked at their work. He nodded like he was impressed, and I relaxed for a moment. I was wrong to let my guard down, though. His father spun toward Haden, backhanding him so hard he fell to the ground.

He kicked him, and Haden groaned in pain. It happened so quickly that I didn't have time to stop it.

"You are a lying little shit. You aren't capable of doing anything that well."

Haden didn't fight back. He didn't move at all.

Fight back.

Why was the void not saving him? His dad yanked him up by the hair, and Haden stared at him with blood running down his chin. It triggered flashes of the night he died. I shook my head as I tried to stop the images. His father raised his hand, but I was not letting him hurt him again. I stepped forward, my rage making me visible.

Haden's eyes widened as my eyes pulsed pure white. His father hadn't noticed me yet, but his mother did.

"Galen!" she warned him. He turned to me and sneered.

"Let him go."

His blue eyes traveled over me, confused, like maybe he was so drunk that I wasn't real. But he was about to know how real I was when I cut his fucking hands off.

"Mind your own business, whore," he warned.

I tilted my head to the side and stared him down. "Drop Haden now," I said in a menacing voice, making him shrink back slightly at my tone. He was a fucking coward.

Galen turned toward me, still gripping Haden's hair tightly.

"Get off my property before I kill you for trespassing." He smiled like I would be scared of him. "This is my boy; I can punish him however I see fit."

Haden's pretty eyes stared at me, begging me to leave before his father hurt me.

"This is the last warning I am giving you. Release Haden, or I will break every fucking bone in your hands so that you aren't able to touch him again."

Galen laughed loudly.

"How'd you trick this whore into thinking you were anything special?" he asked Haden. "You have a thing for weak, pathetic, and incapable men?"

He smiled like he did something with his stupid insult. But men like him were easy to hurt. All they needed to hear was how undesirable and cowardly they were.

"I'm not interested in you, if that is what you are asking." I huffed.

Galen dropped Haden and swung at me in a fit of rage.

"Storm!" Haden tried to step in front of me, but my magic held him back. Meeting his fist with my open hand, I gripped his father's hand in my own. I saw the terror fill his eyes when he realized his strength was nothing against mine. I looked at Haden and Remiah and smiled, trying to reassure them that I could handle this.

"I gave you plenty of warnings, Galen, but I must admit that I was always going to do this." I grabbed one of his fingers, and as if I were holding a twig, I snapped it. He yelled out, and I smiled in his face as I moved to the next finger and broke it as well.

He looked at his wife. "Don't just stand there, bitch, do something!"

She jumped and came for me, but I lifted my hand, and a gust of wind slammed her back into the house. I turned back to him and broke another finger. Then I gripped the last two and squeezed so hard that his bones shattered. I released him, and he fell to his knees, holding his broken fingers and crying. I circled around him, still not done with his punishment.

I looked up at Remiah, who was gawking at me. Then my gaze flickered to Haden. His eyes traveled down the length of me and then back up to my eyes.

"Please," Galen begged, bringing my attention back to him.

"You can beg me all you want, but I keep my word, Galen." I used my magic to force his hands down to the ground. He cried out when the broken hand hit the hard surface. "This is for hurting Remiah." I lifted my heel and slammed it into his broken fingers, crushing his hand into the ground and twisting.

He begged the gods for mercy, and I smiled.

"The gods don't listen to shitty men, Galen." I looked around and smiled when I spotted a boulder. I wrapped it up with my magic and brought it over to hover above his hand. "And this is for thinking you can lay a hand on Haden."

"No, no, n—" he yelled loudly when I slammed the boulder onto his other hand. The sound of his bones breaking echoed around us. No one moved as I squatted down. He was crying like a baby. "Please, take it off."

I looked at the boulder and lifted it with my magic only to slam it down on it again.

"You fucking cunt!"

I could feel Remiah and Haden staring at me, but I was too far gone in my rage to let up. I did not lose Haden for almost 300 years just for his piece-of-shit father to take him from me again. Has he always been this way? Did Haden and Remiah have to grow up with this their entire lives? The thought had lightning scattering above us, striking the ground. Thunder raged loudly in the sky as I thought of how scared they must have been their whole lives.

They had never known love or safety. No wonder Haden thought I wouldn't want him. His parents had made him believe he was unworthy. For fuck's sake, I was beyond reasoning with.

"Here is how things will be going from now on, Galen. If you lay a single finger on either of your children, I will break every single one of the bones in your body." He glared up at me. "And just as your body begins to give out and you start dying, I will heal you, and I will do it all over again."

I could see the hatred in his eyes as he stared at me. Galen was a stupid man, but excitement coiled in my chest as he opened his mouth to argue with me, just as I was hoping he would.

"Fuck you. You could only overpower me because I was caught off guard and drunk. Those little shits are mine, and I will do whatever I please to them."

I clucked my tongue at him.

"That is where you are wrong, asshole." I stood up, moving the boulder and forcing him to rise as well. I healed his hands, and he swung at me immediately. I dodged his weak swing, though, and laughed.

"Storm." Haden moved forward to protect me, but it only distracted me. Galen took advantage of that and punched me in the face. I felt the blood in my mouth as I shot my magic out to block Haden from coming at me again. Galen smiled smugly.

Instantly enraged, I pulled my fist back and punched him in the face so hard I knew I broke my own hand in the process. But I healed it just as quickly as I broke it and grabbed Galen by the hair, dragging his ass in front of his children.

I kicked the back of his legs and forced him to kneel. My chest was heaving so quickly that I thought I would pass out. This fucking bastard. This motherfucking piece of shit. I was out of control. As I held him in place with my magic and gripped his hair in my hand, yanking it back so painfully, I knew I was on the verge of snapping his neck. Fuck, I might anyway.

"Take a good hard look, Galen. You said they belong to you, but they do not. Haden is mine, and if you ever lay a godsdamn finger on him again, I will slit your throat. Then I will make sure there is not a shred of you left before I send you straight to the depths of hell."

I grabbed his hands with my starlight and squeezed, breaking them all over again. Galen screamed in pain. I summoned a blade and held it against his throat, causing him to shut his mouth immediately.

"I want to hear you say it. Tell me that you will never touch them again."

This time, there was no hesitation in his voice. "I won't touch them again," he cried.

I shoved him to the ground, forcing him to instinctively try and catch himself. I smiled when he yelled in agony as his hands hit the ground. I turned to their mother.

"And if you ever try and help him hurt your children, I will send your soul straight to fucking hell with your husband."

Her face paled, and she nodded frantically. Fuck, I needed to calm the hell down. I was angry enough to start destroying shit. I took a few deep breaths before turning to Haden and Remiah. They were gaping at me.

Haden was still bleeding, and I took a hesitant step forward, hoping to not scare him. But he didn't move at all. I lifted my fingers and touched his face softly. He stared at me as I healed his wounds.

"Are you alright?" I asked.

"Yes."

"I lost my cool," I sighed, and Remiah laughed. Haden's lips twitched slightly. "Has he always put his hands on you?"

Haden swallowed hard and nodded.

I turned to his father and, without hesitation, used my magic to snap his arm. He screamed as the crack of bone was heard, and it only made me want to kill him, slowly. Haden grabbed me and turned me. He yanked me to him and hugged me. Instantly my anger subsided. I buried my face into his chest and inhaled deeply. Home. Tears filled my eyes as I held him tighter, like I would wake up and this would just be a dream. I pulled back and looked at him.

"If you need me, just yell for me, and I will come running. If he hurts you, I will kill him next time."

Haden nodded.

His pretty eyes traced over me, and I worried that at any moment he would be repulsed by me and my wrath.

"Does this side of me scare you?" I asked the same question he asked me. I saw a small smirk dance on his lips.

"No."

I made myself invisible to everyone but him and leaned forward, giving him a kiss on the cheek. Haden's eyes closed softly. The scent of his frost filled my lungs, and I felt more relaxed than I had in 300 years. Home. My home was back.

I pulled away.

"Will you be alright staying here?" I looked at his parents.

"Yes, we will be alright, and if we aren't, I'll call for you."

I didn't want to leave him, but he did not ask me to stay. I gave him an awkward wave before disappearing.

CHAPTER 18

DELLA

My eyes drifted to Ivy, the Goddess of Nature. She had shown up at our home unannounced, which she had not done before, because she was convinced the God of the Sea was missing. Ivy was erratic as she tried to explain that she thought someone was stealing gods. Honestly, she had always been a bit eccentric, but this morning was a new level for her.

Her green dress wrapped around her like vines, covering just enough to not be too revealing. Her red hair was up, in a messy bun that had strands falling out.

"Are you sure he is even missing?" Mikel asked.

"No, but he has been gone for months." Ivy was becoming more frantic. "He has never left for this long. Haven't you noticed how uncontrollable the sea has been? It acts as if it is angry because it knows he is missing."

"Admes warned us before that Kaios might be missing." I reminded Mikel.

I glanced out of the window at the stars. It was odd for a god to disappear for months with no one else seeing him. Ivy had visited everyone she could think of, but no one had seen him.

"Did he call to you?" Ivy asked me, drawing my attention back to her. "Maybe he was badly wounded."

"Even if he was, he wouldn't need me to save him. Gods can't die. I promise, he hasn't tried to reach out to me." There was something odd about all of this. I looked at Mikel, who was watching me closely. I could see something was concerning him too.

Ivy paced back and forth, her hand running over her face. "I know it sounds crazy, but I know Kaios; he wouldn't leave the sea for so long."

"It is odd," I agreed. "I thought it was odd when Admes brought it up, but I hoped he was wrong. We never heard anything else, so I figured he returned."

"We will ask around and see if any new information can come from it. Kaios had to be seen by someone," Mikel said.

Ivy relaxed slightly.

"Thank you; everyone else thinks I've lost my mind, but I can feel that this is... strange." Ivy tugged at her dress wrapped around her curvy body, barely covering anything. Her beauty always surprised me every time she visited. "There was a red lily on his doorstep."

I looked up at her gaze.

"Does that mean something?" I asked.

"They are highly poisonous and very rare. Stories tell of red lilies being left on the doorsteps of those marked for bad things. It is a bad omen and warns the victim for weeks that their time is coming. That is odd, is it not? I don't even know where to find them, and I control nature."

I glanced at Mikel, who looked petrified.

"It could mean a million different things," he said angrily. "You are jumping to conclusions."

What an odd reaction. Ivy frowned at Mikel.

"Well, tell that to the God of Superstition. When I told him of the red lily, he told me the same thing. Kaios was marked by someone, and now he is fucking missing, Mikel. That seems pretty credible to me. It isn't just Kaios that is missing either. His mate is gone."

"His mate?" I asked. "When did he find them?"

"He found *him* right before they disappeared. I asked around, and his mate disappeared the same day as him and has not been seen since. How do we explain that? This is not a coincidence."

Mikel's face paled even further, and I knew something was wrong, but I would ask him about it later. Mikel's mind seemed to be far from here now. I could see the worry, the anger, and the confusion in his eyes. My own chest tightened at the sight of it.

"That can't be a coincidence," I agreed. "But what does it mean, and who is powerful enough to take a god and, not only that, keep him for months?"

"I don't know, but I can feel it. Something terrible is happening in the realm. I can sense it in the trees and the flowers. There is evil taking over, and it will consume everything in its path. I've already talked with Brim, and he is looking into it."

Mikel pinched his nose with irritation. What the hell was his problem?

"Very good. We will ask around and see if anyone else is missing. If we come up with anything, I will come to find you. Please, let me know if Brim finds anything out."

"I will." She nodded before her green mist wrapped around her, and she disappeared. Mikel was losing his mind but trying not to let me see.

I watched him begin pacing around the room, rubbing his neck and mumbling. He seemed to forget that I was still there, so I just waited for him to stop with his internal struggle. Finally, he glanced up at me.

"She has to be wrong," he said desperately. "A godsdamn flower is supposed to mean something that terrible?"

Oh, my fucking stars. My whole body went numb.

"You got one, didn't you?" I stood up. "That is why you became angry at her. Mikel, what the fuck?"

"I didn't know." He frowned. "I just thought it was a stupid fucking flower."

Panic gripped me. My brother had been marked by whatever this was. I swallowed hard and began pacing too.

"You are making my fear worse by wandering around like that." His voice made me stop.

"How many times have you received one?"

"Twice. The first one was about five days ago, and there was another one this morning."

"Someone knows you found your mate," I said.

Mikel stilled immediately. His eyes snapped up to mine. I could see the millions of questions lingering in his eyes.

He sighed heavily. "You know Remiah?"

"Yes. I've met her, and she is perfect for you," I said softly. He smiled fondly before his face fell again.

"Are you upset?" he asked, but I didn't understand what he meant. "The heavens gave me a mate, and you don't have one."

I swallowed hard.

"Maybe they will give me a new one."

He shook his head no. "No, they won't. I asked around after what happened. Everyone and everything said the same thing. We only get one mate, no matter what. I even asked Brim."

I stood still at his confession. What would he say if I told him that I had a mate again? He would know that I did something terrible. He would know I broke god laws for Haden. As the God of Judgement, he would have to punish me. But what would it be? Would he take Haden from me?

I wouldn't risk it.

"Well then, maybe I will fall in love again."

Mikel frowned as tears filled his eyes.

"I did not want to upset you; that is why I didn't tell you before. And I didn't want my happiness with Remiah to hurt you."

"It's alright, Mikel, I am happy for you." I walked over and hugged him. At some point I would have to come clean to Mikel about what I had done because I would be claiming Haden this time. But I would keep my secrets until I knew we were safe. Mikel squeezed me tightly. "Now, we need to figure out who the fuck is sending those lilies to you."

Silently, I stared at Haden from next to his bed. He was dreaming again, but it was clear he was distraught. What did he dream of that made him scared enough that he called to me in his sleep? I hadn't heard from him for two days, since I snapped his father's bones. I thought maybe he realized he didn't like me or that I had scared him off.

"Storm. It's alright. You need to let me go," he pleaded as his limbs jerked and twitched under his thin blanket. My blood went cold at his words, and flashes of the night he died hit me all at once. I squeezed my eyes tightly and tried to get them to go away. Please, I did not want to think about that.

I rubbed my eyes roughly. Why did he seem to remember things from his past life? That was impossible. Haden's thrashing around drew my attention away from the flashbacks.

"Haden," I whispered. He immediately stopped his pleading and stilled. His stormy eyes opened and looked at me in a sleep-filled haze, but they closed immediately. Thank the heavens. I exhaled the breath I was holding. I did not need to explain to him why I was watching him sleep. I turned and looked around his bedroom, realizing how different it was from his last.

There was a small sheet of paper sticking out from under a pair of trousers on the floor. Slowly, I went over to it and pulled it out. My heart beat rapidly as I stared at a drawing of me. I was smiling as I stood in the woods. He still likes to draw. I traced the lines of the picture before putting it back. When I turned, Haden was sitting up in bed watching me.

"Fuck, sorry," I said in a panic.

"This is a pleasant surprise," he whispered. My gaze drifted down his bare chest before looking back at his eyes. "What did you think of the picture?"

"You have a knack for drawing." I smiled.

"I didn't know that I could draw until I drew that picture," he confessed as I stepped closer. "Isn't that odd? I had never tried to draw someone before, but when I saw you, my first thought was how your beauty should be admired like a piece of art."

I stopped moving as his words soaked into me. Fuck, why was he not being so timid this time? When I stepped closer, he turned to watch me, his face moving into the moonlight. I smiled when I saw his dark, black eyes staring at me.

"Void."

He smiled softly and nodded. "It happens when I have nightmares. Why are you here?"

"You called for me." I stepped closer so I could sit at the foot of his bed.

"And you came running." He grinned. Always.

I nodded as his dark eyes traced over my face and down the length of my body. Gods, I had forgotten how he could make me feel with just a look.

"I make you nervous."

"Yes."

"Why?" He sat up more so he could shift closer.

"I think you know why." I smiled.

"I'd like to hear you say it, Storm," he challenged.

"Because I like you."

He nodded and moved an inch closer.

"You don't know me."

I smiled as Haden's words from all those years ago flooded my mind.

"I don't know why, but the phrase seems wrong. I feel like I've known you for my entire existence."

Haden moved so he was sitting on the edge of the bed. His eyes pinned me to their spot, and he stared at me oddly. I wanted him to say he liked me back, but the truth was, we didn't know each other. I knew him, but he didn't actually know me.

How many nights had I begged the stars to do this with him—just be near him? It was everything I remembered and more. My gaze traveled down his body, pausing on a scar in the middle of his chest. It was in the shape of a lightning bolt. I reached out instinctively and traced the mark, knowing that is where I had slammed the mating bond into him.

"I was going to ask if you wanted to touch, but I like a woman who takes the lead." His voice was teasing.

But I yanked my hand away when I realized what I was doing. I stood up. I needed to remember that he did not know me well.

"Where are you going?" He stood up.

"I should leave."

"Why?" He stared down at me.

"Because I feel like I will mess this up by saying or doing the wrong thing."

He didn't say anything, so I turned around to leave, but his hand gripped me, pulling me so my back was pressed against his warm, bare chest. His hand sprawled over my stomach and pulled me into him, his mouth brushing my ear and making my eyes flutter closed.

"You can't mess up something that feels like it was written in the stars," he whispered. "You can't run from me. I've seen the monster that lurks inside of you, Della, and my monster has already laid claim to it."

I sighed heavily. He really was a confident bastard when he was like this, and I liked it a lot. He chuckled softly in my ear.

"You like that, don't you?"

"Yes."

His hand ran up my body, between my breasts and up to my throat, gripping it enough that I couldn't move.

"I'm sick of you hiding from me," he confessed. "I'm not letting you leave until you promise to start showing me this pretty face every day."

Gods, he was going to make me do something unlady-like.

"I promise to visit you every day."

He squeezed slightly.

"No, that wording leaves it up for interpretation. Tell me, I will *see* you every day."

"Gods, Haden," I sighed. "I promise to show you my face every day."

"That's my girl," he purred and kissed my neck below my ear. I felt his smile against my skin before he pulled away.

"You're a tease," I accused him as I turned toward him.

"You like it," he said confidently. I did like it.

I swallowed hard as I debated jumping him right this second or teasing him back. A slow smile spread across my lips as I stepped toward him. Haden's void eyes tracked me like prey, but he was my prey now. I traced my finger down his chest as I stared at him in the eyes.

"Do you want to kiss me?"

"I think you know the answer to that," he whispered softly.

I leaned forward, and Haden instinctively moved toward me.

"I want to hear you say it."

Haden gave me a sexy smile. "Yes, I want to kiss you."

I moved forward slightly. Right as his lips barely brushed mine, I summoned my magic.

"I'll see you tomorrow."

"Storm," he warned, but I was already gone.

CHAPTER 19

HADEN

"I thought we could spend the day together," Remiah said, barging into my bedroom. Quickly, I hid the drawing I was working on. Remy raised her eyebrow at me.

"What?"

"Let me see." She walked closer. I shook my head, no, and her blue eyes narrowed on me. I sighed heavily and pulled the drawing of Della out. Remiah's eyes glanced over the page, looking impressed by my talent. She smiled fondly. "You captured her beauty really well."

"Thanks."

"So, are you going to tell her you like her or what?"

"Gods, you are so nosy." I rolled my eyes and stood up. "I'm sure she knows." I tightened my fist as the memory of last night flooded me. I could only remember pieces, but I kept seeing my hand holding her against me by her neck.

Fuck, I hope my void did not scare her away. "What did you want to do?"

"Let's go to our favorite spot. I can pack us food."

I nodded as she clapped excitedly and went to get food ready. I stood up and got dressed as Remy rummaged around in the kitchen. I walked out and couldn't help noticing how different we both were now that our parents weren't beating us daily. Is this what others felt all the time?

"Ready?" Remy turned toward me.

"Let's get going." I smiled and took the basket of food from her. We headed toward the clearing behind the house. We hadn't been here in years. Remiah seemed to have a permanent smile on her face as she closed her eyes and lifted her face toward the sun.

"Gods, it's such a perfect day," she sighed. "Do you think the water will be too cold to swim?"

"Yes," I chuckled.

Remiah frowned slightly before she bent down as we walked, plucking wildflowers and making a bundle of them. She lifted them to her nose, her blonde hair tumbling around her face.

"I love flowers. If I ever get married and move away, I will demand a field of just wildflowers that I can see from the home." She turned to me. "Will you tell Della thank you for me?"

I hesitated for a moment, and she continued.

"There were so many times over the years that I thought of hurting our father, but I was never brave enough to actually do it. I really thought that we would die miserable and pathetic like our parents. She saved us."

Pride filled my chest because the woman I was falling for *had* saved us. I still did not think that Della realized how much she gave to Remy and I by standing up to our father.

"I'll tell her," I promised.

Remy stopped and looked at me with an expression that I couldn't read. She looked like such a proud older sister, even if she was older by only a few minutes.

"I want you to meet Mikel." Remiah glanced away from me for a moment before staring at me intensely. "I think he is going to ask me to marry him," she blurted out.

My mouth fell open, but I could not think of any words. Remiah began laughing as I struggled to form any thought.

"You always said you didn't want to marry," I finally said.

Remiah shrugged and began walking again. The features of her face were softer than they were growing up.

Mikel had done that for her—made her believe that life could be kind.

"That was before I met Mikel. I cannot picture a life without him, Haden. He consumes my thoughts. But it is more than that. I keep thinking that I would do everything over again—the abuse, the shitty parents, being poor—if I knew that he is where it all led to. I truly thought that I was not worthy of love or happiness until Mikel found me."

She glanced at me as we continued to walk forward. I mulled her words over in my mind.

"I never thought you'd be the sappy romantic." I smiled at her, and she swatted my shoulder.

"I know; it's honestly disturbing how much I love him." Remiah's soft laugh filled the warm air around us.

I knew what she meant because I had been trying to convince myself that it was crazy to feel the way I did about Della already. I hardly knew her, but it felt like I had known her for my entire existence.

"For the first time in my entire life, I feel like I can be excited about my future."

"Della makes me feel that way too." I smiled softly.

We walked in silence for a few more minutes before a large pond came into view. Remiah and I had stumbled upon it when we were young. I had used my frost magic to freeze it over, and we would slide around on it. Until

Remiah had fallen through the ice one time. I had barely saved her, and when we arrived home, we were beaten for being soaking wet. Our parents never knew that Remy had almost died that day, but I would never forget it. It was the first time the void had taken over me because I was frozen in fear. The void saved my sister, and I still thank the stars for that because I would've ended myself if she was taken from me.

"Well, what are you waiting for? Freeze it, snow boy," Remiah taunted me as I laughed. I lifted my hands, and my magic seeped from my palms, blowing like a cold wind. It covered the edges of the pond, and the ice slowly formed inward until it reached the center. I made sure the ice was beyond thick enough to hold us. When I stopped, Remiah was just watching me curiously.

"What?" I smiled.

"Do you think it's odd that I didn't get magic?" Remiah had never mentioned the fact that she had no magic, and I did. But it was odd that as my twin she had none, and I had elite magic.

"A little." I nodded.

"Do you think it's strange that no one in our family has ever had magic, but you somehow ended up with it?"

"I haven't really thought about it. I suppose it is a bit strange."

Our parents did not have magic, and no one before them did either. I always thought that magic was inherited, but maybe it was just random luck. Remiah began running toward the frozen pond and slid across the smooth ice. Her smile was bright, and her laugh was contagious. I dropped the basket of food and ran toward the pond to join her.

My boots slid across the ice effortlessly. The wind blew around my face, and I smiled as Remiah followed me. I lifted my hands and let my magic explode from me. The thick forest around us turned into a winter wonderland. Frost and ice clung to the tree branches, and snow flitted through the air and mixed with the sun shining. It was stunning.

Remiah stopped sliding around and stared in awe. I don't know if she had ever seen me use my magic so much or carelessly. Her stormy blue eyes widened as she took in the change of scenery. She blew out a long breath that could be seen in the cold air. Her eyes found mine, and she gave me a smile I had never seen from her before. It was full of pride and happiness.

"Haden, fucking hell, I didn't know you could do this. Why have you never shown me before?"

I shrugged.

"I didn't really think my magic was that impressive until recently. I've never explored all of what I can do."

"This is impressive." She smiled and began sliding around again, letting the snow fall onto her face. "When I prayed to the heavens for you and me to be happy, I never thought that they would answer."

Her words made my chest tight. Remiah had always been the more realistic of the two of us. She never let herself dream of a life beyond what we had. I knew she didn't want to get married before because she was terrified she would end up with someone like our father. I was worried I would turn into him. Maybe that is why I never had any interest in anyone before, because I was terrified I would end up being a piece of shit.

But now I could see that I would never be like him. When you grow up in an environment like we did, it is hard to see past the trauma and hurt to the possibilities. Remiah and I had every opportunity to make our lives exactly what we wanted.

Maybe that was all we needed growing up—someone, anyone, to think we were worthy of loving. I watched Remiah giggling as she moved around the ice. I couldn't wait to see where life took us now. I couldn't wait to see my sister get everything she deserved because she was the only reason for living that I had growing up. Remy saved me countless times.

We stepped off the pond and headed for our food, which was not much. I kept glancing around to see if Della would come.

"Is there a reason you keep looking around frantically?" Remy asked.

"Della promised she would come see me every day, and the sun is starting to set." I frowned.

"Well, the day isn't done yet. She'll come." Remy smiled, but I was worried I scared the shit out of her being void last night. I could not control myself in that state, but the void also acted on the impulses I tried to bury. And it knew how badly I wanted Della.

I glanced around the clearing and sighed.

"Hi." Della's voice came from behind me, and I turned quickly.

"You came."

"I promised I would. I keep my promises, Haden." She turned to Remiah and smiled. "Hi, Remiah."

"Della." Remy's eyes looked at me like she was trying to communicate something without talking out loud.

"Well, you've seen my face. I have to go."

I stepped toward her desperately.

"You just got here."

She smiled at me.

"Did you miss me, Haden?" Gods, she was still being a tease. I gave her a knowing look. "I know, but I had a busy day with work, and time slipped from me. I would stay, but it's family dinner night."

Family dinner night? Della looked over my face for a second.

"I go to my family's house once a week and have a big meal with them. I never miss it. So, I'm sorry, but I can't stay."

"Okay." I said, disappointed.

Della turned like she was going to leave but stopped and turned to us. She hesitated for a long moment.

"Would you two like to come?"

"To your family dinner? Wouldn't that be odd?" I asked.

Della smiled brightly at my nervousness. She stepped forward and tilted her head to the side.

"No, I think they would love both of you."

"We didn't bring nice clothes." Remiah chimed in. Della flicked her wrist, and her magic shot out of her. The silvery mist circled around both Remiah and I, so quickly our hair moved in the wind. When the magic pulled away, our outfits were different. I glanced up at her.

"You don't have to, but you haven't tasted good food until you've had my family's food." She was trying to convince us, and it was working. I wanted to spend more time with her. Shit, I wanted to meet her family. I looked at Remy, and she nodded enthusiastically.

"All right, we'll go."

Della's smile was contagious as her starlight mist wrapped around us. When it faded away, I had to close my eyes tightly to keep from throwing up. After a moment, I opened my eyes, expecting to see a grand castle or mansion based on Della's pretty dresses she wore. But the home looked...homey and welcoming.

Della's eyes did not leave my face, like she was waiting for a reaction.

"Are you sure this will be alright?" I asked.

"Yes, Penelope always makes too much food." She smiled. "I should warn you guys first. They are the nicest fae you will ever meet, but they are nosy and will ask you a million questions. They are a hugging family, too."

"What the hell does that mean?" Remiah asked.

"Every single one of them will come and hug you, even if you try to shake their hands. They are very loving." Della turned and took a few steps before stopping. "One more thing. Penelope has been working on her desserts for hundreds of years, and she is still terrible at it. We do not tell her, and we always eat all of it."

I smiled at the odd bits of information she shared. Remiah and I nodded. Della returned the nod before heading up the steps and walking inside. Immediately, I could feel the difference this home had compared to mine. It was bright and littered with artwork, but it also gripped me like a hug. Something about the welcoming scent of dinner and laughter coming from in front of us made my brain itch.

What would it have been like to grow up in a place that felt so safe, like this? What kind of man would I have become if I lived feeling like this? Della walked around the corner, and the chatter stopped.

"Ardella!" A woman screeched. But as Remiah and I rounded the corner, everyone became silent. My heart pounded in my throat.

"I brought guests." Della gave the woman an odd look, and the woman glanced at Remiah but seemed emotional when she saw me.

"This is so wonderful." The woman walked up to Remiah and squeezed her tightly. "I am Penelope. You must be Remiah."

Remiah nodded at the short woman with dark hair. When the woman looked at me, I had to pause. Her eyes matched mine almost exactly. The void hummed with happiness inside of me, and it was not an emotion he usually shared.

"Haden," she said softly. Then she gripped me in a hug that felt like it should be reserved for family. I hugged her back, unable to help myself. Gods, she was nice. She pulled back and stared at my face. "You were right, Della; he is very handsome."

"Penelope," Della groaned and covered her face as it turned bright red. I chuckled softly at her reaction.

"How's it going, sweetheart?" A tall man stepped forward, and gods, he looked more like my father than my own father did.

"It's going good, Henry." Della wrapped him up in a hug.

"It's been too long since we've seen you." He laughed when Della made a noise.

"Henry, it's been a week." She rolled her eyes, but I saw how much his words meant to her. "Not even a week actually, because I stopped by to give Penelope that recipe I found for dessert."

Henry's eyes widened as he looked at Della before winking. She bugged her eyes out at him. Henry gave Remiah a big hug before he paused to look over me.

"Haden," he said, strained with emotion. He gripped me tightly and didn't let me go for a long moment.

"Oh, I've got to check the vegetables." Penelope ran into the kitchen.

Another man stood up. He had the same stormy eyes as me. He looked at Della.

"Good thinking with the recipe. Did you warn our guests about Mother's desserts?"

Della's shoulders shook in silent laughter.

"Yes." She looked at me with some deep emotion swimming in her pretty eyes. "Haden and Remiah, this is Holden. He is Henry and Penelope's son. And this wonderful woman is his wife, Sara." Della hugged both of them. Like his parents, Holden hugged Remiah before looking me over and gripping me to him like I had been here a million times before.

"Let's sit." Della smiled. "Remiah, you can sit here. This is your seat, Haden." She pointed to the chair next to hers.

I watched everyone glance from Della to me.

"Don't scare him, or he'll never come back." She smiled at them. Della looked at me. "Henry painted everything you see on the walls."

"Really?" I glanced around. Gods, he was talented. I wished I had his artistic abilities. "They're amazing."

"Thank you. It took me a long time to figure out my muse, but once I found it, I couldn't stop." Henry smiled.

"Are you artistic too?" I asked Holden. He shook his head.

"Not a single artistic bone in this body, unfortunately. My brother had all of the talent."

Had. Past tense.

"Haden just recently started drawing, and it is so good," Remiah gushed. My face heated when everyone looked at me.

"It's not that good."

"It's good." Della smiled as she sipped her drink.

"You showed her your pictures?" Remiah asked. Remiah glanced at Della and gave her a big grin.

"It's not a big deal." I shifted uncomfortably. Remiah glanced at everyone as they watched the exchange.

"Haden found his muse, and it's Della."

"Remy," I groaned, embarrassed.

Della and Remy began chuckling. But Henry's eyes filled with something I would expect from a proud father.

"I'm glad you found your muse. That is the hardest part of becoming an artist."

"Here we go." Penelope started bringing in enough plates to feed a small village. Gods, Della was not kidding. My mouth was watering as we began plating the roast and vegetables, as well as three different breads. Remiah handed me the plate of broccoli, and I immediately passed it to Della.

"You don't care for broccoli?" Penelope asked.

"It's never been my favorite." I smiled. Penelope smiled brightly.

Remiah and I had never had food like this before. Shit, we had never sat down at a table with our parents and shared a meal or a conversation, for that matter. I listened to them laugh and joke. But I could not take my eyes off of Della. She seemed so relaxed and carefree as she laughed at Henry's terrible jokes.

Something tugged in my chest at the sight of her happiness. I really liked her like this. Remiah chimed in to the conversation more than I did. She had always been more talkative than me. But they included me when I went silent for too long. I sat back and couldn't help the jealousy in my chest.

I would've given anything to grow up in a loving home like this. I couldn't imagine having parents like Henry and Penelope. Holden was so kind and loving that I wondered if I would have ended up like him. But I ended up with the shittiest parents in the realm. Della's hand covered mine and squeezed.

"Are you alright?" she whispered.

I held her gaze and nodded. She gave me a small nod back and looked across the table at Penelope. Della still squeezed my hand tightly in hers, and I didn't dare remind her so she wouldn't pull away.

"Not to be rude," Remiah said. Oh gods, I braced myself for whatever shit she would say. She looked at Della. "You said this was your family, but you don't look like them, and you call them by their names."

Everyone became quiet and looked at Della. She removed her hand from mine, and I instantly missed it.

"They are my family, but not by blood." Della frowned. "I knew their son before he passed away; he was my...best friend."

I saw the grief flash in her eyes and wished I could take it away from her.

"You don't think Della and I look similar?" Holden scoffed playfully.

"Sorry," Remiah said to Della when she saw how sad she got.

"It's alright."

Della's eyes fell to the plate in front of her, and she pushed the food around without eating any. Penelope and Henry frowned at her but smiled when they saw me looking.

"I hope you saved room for dessert!" Penelope stood up and went to the kitchen. Henry's eyes widened as he looked at me. I saw a terror flash on Holden's face. Della's shoulders shook with laughter as she met Henry's eyes.

"I think since Della gave you the recipe, she should try it first tonight!" Holden called out. Sara was trying her hardest not to laugh. Della grabbed a piece of broccoli and chucked it at his head.

"Wonderful idea," Penelope called from the kitchen.

"Watch your back," she whispered to Holden. He and Henry started laughing loudly. I waited for her to look at me, but she didn't. She seemed to be avoiding my gaze intentionally.

Penelope brought out a plate of small pastries that had some sort of berry inside of them. They looked and smelled good. How bad could they taste? Penelope plated one for each of us before they all looked at Della. She grabbed it and bit into it, chewing slowly.

"This might be the best one so far," Della said.

I smiled when Holden's eyes bugged out of his head. She said it was good. I grabbed mine and took a big bite. Immediately the tartness hit my mouth. Oh shit, this was not good at all. I tried not to show it on my face. Everyone at the table ate their dessert without complaint, and I wondered if this is what true love was. Holden began choking on the bitterness of the pastry and took a drink of water. Della smirked as she finished hers.

"Excuse me," she said softly. Henry gave her a small smile. I watched her disappear up the stairs. Where was she going? The table fell into conversations, and I waited for Della to come back.

"You can check on her if you are worried," Henry called over to me. "Up the stairs, first door on the left."

I nodded and headed up, feeling all of their eyes on my back as I went. There was something oddly familiar about the walk up the stairs—like I had made the trip before. When I got to the room, Della was standing at a wall of hand-drawn pictures.

CHAPTER 20

HADEN

I pushed the door open and walked in. Della glanced over her shoulder, noticing it was me, and looked back at the wall.

"Are you okay?" I asked.

"Yes, just admiring the artwork." She turned and held out her hand for me. The gesture seemed natural to her, like she had asked me to hold her hand before. I took her hand in mine, and she gripped it tightly. My gaze drifted over the sketches of homes on the wall.

"He was talented."

"Very." She nodded.

Gods, I was feeling jealous over a dead man. She obviously cared for him, but to what extent?

"Was he just a friend?" I asked.

She hesitated and opened her mouth but shut it and nodded. Something sad passed through her eyes.

"Thank you for coming tonight," she whispered.

"Are you kidding? I didn't know families could be like this. It makes me feel even shittier about my parents but also hopeful that maybe I can achieve all of this one day."

I heard a small sniffle from Della.

"This is the ultimate dream." She agreed. "We should get going, though." She turned away.

Suddenly, I could feel the void coming up out of nowhere. Before I had a chance to stop it, it slipped over my consciousness and took control. I closed my eyes as the shiver ran down my spine. When my eyes opened, Della was still walking away.

I could feel the overwhelming emotions I had as I realized she was here. My Storm still came to see my family. She still came to my room and admired my artwork. Something possessive and full of grief slammed into me. I had missed her so damn much that it was taking my breath away.

Gods, I wanted to tell her that I remembered us, that I knew why her eyes had become haunted when I was mentioned downstairs. I wanted to wrap her up in my arms and tell her that I was sorry for what happened. Memories of her curled against my dead body slammed into my mind and made me close my eyes, but I swallowed down the emotions that were strangling me. Della was watching me oddly when I looked up, her pretty eyes filled with grief for a man that was still here; she just didn't know it.

I couldn't tell her that I remembered us when I was void. She would ask too many questions about my previous death, and I couldn't explain to her what happened without her leaving me for good. So, I would pretend that I didn't know how wonderful our short time together was and just be content with what we had now.

"Della, you feel it too, right? These overwhelming feelings between us?"

She stared at me, and I wondered how the other side of me was handling this woman so well. I understood that the nice side of me didn't think we were worthy of her, but I knew better. Della was everything we deserved. Our mating bond was glowing warmly between us, and I felt relief when I saw it. But I also felt dread because I didn't know why the stars would let her be mated to me when they knew who I was. She stepped forward and pulled me down to her mouth, giving me a hard, lingering kiss. Fuck, I had missed this. I had missed her.

She pulled back, looking me in the eyes. "Yes, I feel it too." She slipped her arms around me, hugging me tightly. "You're perfect," she whispered. "The heavens went above and beyond when they created you. Both sides of you are perfect to me."

I gripped her tightly and glanced around the room. Fuck, I did not think she would still come home to my family every week. This made me realize just how much she wanted to still be close to me. After 300 years, she was still missing me. Guilt clawed at my chest. She could have had this with Holden if I hadn't messed with her fate.

I closed my eyes and felt her chest moving with soft breaths. She smelled the same—like night and flowers. I pulled Della back and reached up to hold her face gently. After looking into her eyes for a moment, I leaned down and pressed my lips against hers softly. She hummed against me, and I knew that this was right. Della was mine, and the guilt I had for making sure she wouldn't belong to anyone else dissipated as she deepened the kiss.

Her hands came up and ran through the hair at my neck, pulling me to her so I couldn't leave. Fuck, she felt so good pressed against me.

Suddenly, she pulled back and moved away from me. Her gaze flickered around the room, and I saw the guilt that she had about kissing me here—where we had our first kiss last time.

"I can see that you want to bolt, but don't," I said, holding my hands out toward her.

"I got carried away."

I smiled at her.

"You can get carried away with me any time you please, Della."

She chuckled softly and held out her hand for me. I immediately slid my hand into hers, and we left my bedroom and headed back downstairs. My breath caught as I took in my family and how much they had aged. They were laughing and joking with Remiah. All of them smiled when they saw me. Stars, what was this like for them—to see me and know who I am but not be able to say anything?

I frowned slightly. I guess it was the same as how I felt about remembering Della and not being able to tell her. It was bittersweet. But Della still carried her love and grief for me. I could see it in her eyes when she watched me.

"We should probably get going." Della smiled as they all made noises of rejection.

"You two will come back with Della?" my mother asked quickly.

"Of course," I smiled.

I dropped Della's hand and was the one to move forward for a hug. My mother's familiar warmth and scent wrapped around me as she gripped me tightly. I held on a little longer this time, missing the way she had raised me, loved me. She had tears in her eyes when she pulled back but quickly moved to hide them. I moved to my father next and gripped him. He held on just as long as I did. When I pulled back, he patted my shoulder.

"You're a good man, Haden." His strained voice made tears sting my eyes. I turned, and Holden was already there, hugging me to him. Brother. I held him tightly before pulling back and seeing an aged version of myself.

"It was great to meet you." Holden smiled before Sara practically shoved him out of the way and hugged me.

I could see Penelope and Henry whispering to Della. She nodded softly—sadly. I watched as they seemed to be trying to encourage her or make her happy. She seemed to feel my gaze on her and straightened up.

"Are you ready?" she asked us. We both nodded, and her starlight wrapped around us. When it disappeared, we were outside of our shitty house. Remiah thanked Della before looking between us and turning to leave immediately.

Della looked up at me and opened her mouth to talk but shut it.

"Just ask, Storm."

"You only ever make a move on me when you're void."

"Because you scare me," I answered honestly.

"Will your other side eventually catch up so we can be around each other more?"

I smiled and tucked her dark hair behind her ear.

"You want to see me more?"

"Yes." She didn't hesitate.

Fuck, she was pretty when she was confident. I leaned down and kissed her. This time, Della was the one to yank me flush against her. Her tongue swept across my lips. A deep hum left my throat as it dominated mine. I gripped her hair in my hands and tilted her head to the side to deepen this intoxicating kiss.

Della moaned softly as I pushed her into the side of the house below my bedroom window. My other hand came up and gripped her jaw tightly as I took complete control of her. I pulled away, kissing down her jaw and down her neck. Della sighed softly as my teeth grazed her skin. I kissed over her collarbone and then reached up and gripped the neckline of her dress.

"Do you like this dress?" I asked in a whisper.

"Kind of."

"Good enough." I ripped the fabric so I could see her chest as it rose and fell in heavy, lustful breaths.

"Haden," she whispered.

"Do you want me to stop?" I asked as my finger slowly traced over her, the base of her throat, and down between her breasts.

She shook her head, and I smiled at her and then leaned my head down, licking her nipple before drawing it into my mouth. Della gasped, and I pulled away. I could not stop the desire pumping through me. There would be nothing sweet about what I was about to do to her. We had not seen each other in too long. I would give Della exactly what she wanted because my woman liked it this way—rough and untamed.

"Can you be good and not make any noise? I would hate for someone to hear you."

"Maybe we should go somewhere else," she sighed.

"Oh, Storm, you can be quiet for me, can't you?"

This time her eyes widened with lust, and she nodded.

"That's my girl."

I leaned down and did the same thing to her other breast, and this time she was silent, pulling me to her so I wouldn't leave. It would take divine intervention to pull me off of this woman. I kissed my way up her chest and throat before coming to her pouty lips with mine.

Della's hands ran down my neck and gripped the top of my tunic. I heard the tear before I realized she was ripping it. I glanced down as her hands moved over my bare chest. She shoved the two sides of my tunic to the side before pulling me against her.

"I want to feel your skin against mine," she whispered desperately.

Fuck.

My hand moved between us until I felt the bare skin of her leg and lifted the hem of her dress up with my hand.

"Will you be quiet if I sink my fingers into you?" I asked.

She nodded, but I wasn't so sure.

I didn't hesitate as I pumped two fingers into her. She buried her face into my neck and moaned softly. I waited for her to look up at me, and when she did, I slowly pulled my fingers back out again and then pushed them in deeper than before.

"Haden, I lied. I cannot be quiet." She was panicking, and it made me smile. I squeezed her throat tightly as my fingers moved faster. She was trying to be quiet, but she was failing. My hand stopped moving, and she instantly went to protest.

Della used her magic to take us somewhere else, and I smiled at her. I had no idea where we were. It seemed like an abandoned, secluded house in the woods. Della's back was against the wall as we were still outside.

"Tell me how good this feels."

"So good," she said in a needy tone that made me roll my hips into her. "Please keep going." She tried to move against my fingers.

"So greedy, Storm," I whispered as I barely moved my fingers, and she sighed heavily. "I didn't realize you'd be so greedy to cum on my fingers," I muttered. "Would you be this greedy for my mouth or my cock?"

"Haden, please shut the fuck up and make me cum," she hissed.

This fucking woman.

"Answer me."

"Yes. I would be greedy for any part of you that is willing to make me cum." Her pretty, defiant eyes stared into mine as I smiled. Oh, I almost forgot what she liked. I shifted us so my thumb could rub her clit as my fingers started to move again.

"Fucking hell, that's perfect. Keep doing that," she demanded. Fuck. I kissed her hard and roughly—my tongue moving at the pace of my thumb. She was a whimpering mess. I moved my mouth away and held my hand over her mouth, knowing that it didn't matter if she were quiet or not.

Her eyes flashed pure white and then closed tightly as I moved so I could pump into her in just the way she liked it. She shook her head, trying to warn me what I already knew was happening. Della's hand grabbed the hem of her dress, lifting it so we could watch how fucking perfect my fingers looked sinking into her.

"Good girl, Storm," I sighed. "You're going to keep those pretty eyes on me when you cum."

She nodded her head and looked up at me as her body tensed up. Oh, she was close. Her pussy clenched around me.

"That's it, cum for me. Let me feel this greedy cunt clenching around my fingers." I growled softly as my eyes stared into hers. Her moan was quiet only because of my hand, and she came hard and fast. Fuck, she clenched tightly around me as I pumped into her, wanting her to get every ounce of pleasure she earned. Slowly her body relaxed. I removed my fingers from her and brought them up.

Della watched me as I sucked my fingers into my mouth and cleaned her off of me before pulling them out slowly.

"Taste how good you are," I demanded, and Della leaned forward and drove her tongue against mine. We kissed for a moment before I pulled back.

"Fuck, you are perfect." I could feel the words 'I love you' on the tip of my tongue, but I held them in.

"Haden, that was so fucking good," she said as her head fell back against the house.

We watched each other closely. Della ran her hand down my bare chest before gripping me through my trousers. I groaned, and she smiled.

"Let's see how good you are at being quiet." She teased, and I nearly came at the sound of her words.

"Della," I sighed. But she didn't listen to me as she turned us, so my back was against the house. She kissed my chest as her hands made quick work of my trousers and immediately started pumping down my hard length.

Her hand moved exactly how I liked—hard and fast, just like I taught her. Fuck, I forgot how good we were together. She looked up at me with innocent eyes, but I knew better. She sank to her knees in front of me, and I held my breath as she licked up my cock. My hands immediately went to her hair and tangled them in her silky strands.

She pulled me into her mouth, and I could not stop the moan that escaped me.

She hummed around me, and I couldn't help pushing into her throat deeper. I was thanking the heavens for her fucking mouth.

"That's it, Storm; just like that."

She moved faster at the praise. I had forgotten how much she liked to hear how good she was doing. Gods be damned, I was not going to last long.

"You look so pretty with your mouth wrapped around my cock." I moaned as I pulled her hair back, so I was slowly pulling out of her, and then I pushed forward quickly, making her moan. "You're doing such a good job. I'm almost there," I whispered.

She moved against me in the most perfect torture. I could feel my body tensing as she kept going, not letting up on me. She wanted to please me, and I loved that about her.

"Look at me, Della. I want to see that pretty face when I cum in your mouth."

She obeyed immediately.

"Good girl," I praised her and pumped into her twice more before holding her in place as I found my release, moaning softly as she took it all. After a moment, she pulled back slowly, and I yanked her up. Then I kissed her on the mouth that would be the death of me.

She sighed as my tongue tangled with hers. When I pulled back, she smiled at me.

"Well, that was a good way to end the night." Her smile widened. Her hand flicked out, and our clothing was fixed. "How am I supposed to not jump you every time I see you?"

"Storm, you can jump me any fucking time you want. Believe me, even my nice side can't control his fantasies about you. He is just scared." I gripped her face in my hands. "He will not reject you, but I don't know if he is brave enough to make the first move."

"Are you telling me to make the first move on you?" she asked in a teasing manner.

"Hell yes, I am."

She leaned forward and kissed me softly.

CHAPTER 21

DELLA

I was staring at the knick-knacks that lined up every damn surface in Brim's home. My mind was mulling over his words, but I wasn't sure I was processing anything correctly today. I could not stop thinking about Haden. Gods, I missed him, and it hadn't even been a day.

Brim was staring intently at me when I looked at him. He looked like he was feeling guilty about something. I felt it as soon as I came into the house. He didn't know I was coming. Maybe that was for the best, though, so I could catch him off guard. His guilt was suffocating the space around us.

"Are you sure?" I asked Brim.

"Yes." He nodded. "Kaios and his mate were taken, but so was the God of Seasons and his mate."

"So, someone *is* taking gods who have found their mates?" I asked, confused.

"It seems so, but I do not have any answers. I don't understand the connection between red lilies and the kidnappings. But I am working on it." Brim frowned.

"Mikel has received lilies," I confessed.

Brim looked at me oddly.

"Mikel found his mate?"

"Yes, and soon after, he started getting the lilies. I am terrified that someone is going to take him."

Brim began pacing in front of his fireplace. He was talking to himself as if I could follow his train of thought. He wasn't making any sense to me. Brim stilled and looked at me.

"We need to know of every god that has found their mate. They are the targets, so that is how we intercept these bastards." Brim looked at me. "I will visit the gods and see if there are any who have mates that have not been taken."

"What if it isn't just about mates?" I asked. "What would be the other deciding factor?"

"I have no clue."

Great, so we knew nothing. I sighed heavily and hung my head. I could not concentrate today. All I could think about was kissing Haden and going to see him. I needed to focus because there was a major issue happening here, and I felt like it was bigger than any of us realized. The Goddess of Nature had been right; there was something evil lurking in the air of Elloryon.

It felt suffocating and angry. But what could make an entire realm feel so dark and dreadful? Whoever was doing this was powerful—very powerful. Did they know I had a mate? Would I start getting lilies too?

"What's on your mind, Della?" Brim was next to me when I looked up.

"Did Mikel tell you what happened to my mate?" I asked.

Brim frowned and nodded.

"Do you know why the heavens would make such a mistake?"

"The heavens do not make mistakes. They must have had their reasons for mating you to someone you did not love. There must have been a reason you loved his brother instead."

I scoffed.

"A reason? They made me perfect for the wrong man and then took him from me. For what, punishment? I have always followed the laws, and they turned their backs on me."

"But they gave him back to you." He smiled.

My anger disappeared instantly.

"How did you know that?" I narrowed my eyes at him. I hadn't even told Mikel Haden's name, so he couldn't find anything out. I stared at Brim for a long moment.

His guilt doubled in his eyes, and he frowned as he sat in his chair.

"I have a confession," he said as he started rocking. "I had visions of you and Haden before it ever happened. I saw you fall in love, and I knew he was not your mate." Brim watched the array of emotions cross my face before smiling softly.

"Why didn't you tell me?" I said angrily. "You could have warned me."

Brim swallowed hard as he turned his gaze from me.

"He asked me not to." Brim frowned. "And who am I to ruin such a love?"

I stilled.

"Who told you not to?"

"Haden," Brim sighed.

"Haden knows you? How?"

"It's not often that a fae gets the magic of visions. News of it travels quickly, and I caught wind of it when I heard his name from a friend. So, I went to visit him and his lovely family. It was about a year before you met him."

I sank down in the other chair, staring at Brim. What the fuck was happening?

"I told him who I was, and he said he knew I was coming." Brim chuckled. "He said he called for me to come to him. Do you know how rare that is? Do you know how odd it is not to realize that Haden summoned me to him? I thought it was my own choice."

Yes, I did know how rare that was. But I was more concerned about how Brim did not notice he was being summoned. Brim was more powerful than anyone else I had met. He should have known.

"He told me that I had come up in a vision of his future, and he wanted to know if I knew of it."

"Did he tell you what it was?"

"Yes." Brim frowned when he looked at me. "First, he told me that he had visions of a woman so beautiful that he knew she was some sort of angel."

I stared at him, confused. Haden had visions of me a year before we met in his last life. He had never told me.

"He told me your name, and I could not believe it. I was so happy when I heard him say it was you." Brim smiled fondly. "He told me that he knew you were fated to Holden, but he didn't care because he had visions that you would love him instead."

Tears stung my eyes and fell down my face. He knew before I ever told him. Why did he act so upset?

"He asked me how to change fate." Brim looked up at me. "I can't express to you how important this next part is, Della."

I nodded and listened carefully.

"I told him we couldn't, and he argued with me about it. He said he knew it could be changed because he saw..." Brim looked at me. "Haden saw himself as a god in the future."

I looked at Brim, confused.

"He will be a god when we finish the mating process. That is nothing spectacular."

"You don't understand." Brim stood up. "That was impossible in his last life. He could not become a god unless he mated with you, which was impossible because you were linked to Holden by your bond. And then he told me... You can't get mad, Della. You have to swear that to me."

"I will decide my level of anger after you tell me."

"Haden figured out he was going to die. He knew it was going to happen before it did."

My heart felt like it was falling down a bottomless pit. I didn't want to accept that. How could he have known? How could he have not told me? He knew I could save him.

"That makes no sense."

"He thought if you two loved each other enough, the bond would transfer all by itself over time. But of course, it didn't because that is not how it works. When he came to me, he said he thought he could change fate, but he did not tell me why or how."

"What are you saying?"

"Della, he knew he needed to die."

"Needed? Why would he need to die?"

"He had a vision of you physically breaking your bond to Holden in a moment of rage. He saw you slam it into his chest in an attempt to attach your soul to his. He knew everything that was going to happen."

"No..."

"I begged him to tell you, but he said no, and that it needed to be your own choice to make that attempt."

"Why didn't you tell me any of this?" I asked. "I could have saved him. How long did he know he was going to die?"

Brim's face fell. "The day before he died. He was having visions and called to me. When I got to the house, he was a mess."

My mind immediately went to Haden being so fucking sad when I came home that night. I closed my eyes tightly at the realization that he was sad because he would die the next day.

"Della, you still aren't understanding." He took a step towards me and put his hands on my shoulders, looking into my eyes to stress the importance of what he was going to say next. I did not know if I could handle any more news, though. *"Haden was having visions of his next life."* He gave me a small shake and then stepped back again. "No one, and I mean no one, can do that. Not even a god can see that far into the future. Even me, the best seer in the realm, can only see into the future to an extent. And even then, it is choppy at best. Haden knew the details of his future to such a degree that he could have written a godsdamn book with every major and minor detail that was supposed to happen. That is not normal."

My mind was a whirlwind of thoughts. Haden had known he was going to die and wouldn't let me save him. Because he knew he would be mine in his next life. Anger and confusion pumped through me.

"But he was just a fae," I said, confused. "So why can he do that?"

Brim nodded and smiled like I had finally asked the right question.

"Exactly, he was supposedly just fae, but I am not so sure of that now. He can't be just a fae. I don't know why, but I think the heavens intentionally made him the way he is because he is... important. The heavens intentionally did this. We just don't know why." Brim frowned.

"Did he say anything else?" I asked.

Brim nodded, and I knew it wasn't good.

"Just tell me."

My throat was dry and itchy with stress as Brim sighed heavily.

"He started getting red lilies when he met you, and he had a mating bond with a different female that he did not feel anything toward."

I stood up and stared at him. Confusion coursed through me at a new level. That made no sense; he was not a god, and we were not mates—why did he get lilies? Then I felt the wrath of an army inside of me at the thought of him being mated to another woman. I would fucking kill her.

I yelled so loudly that the wall of his home shook. "What the fuck, Brim!" Anger coursed through me. "How dare you not tell me any of this?"

"He bound my tongue!" Brim threw his hands in the air. My mouth dropped open in surprise. Tongue binding was also a rare ability.

He continued. "Tell me how a *fae* can see so far into his own future that he knows of his next life, can tell you when he dies, can bind *my* tongue, and can summon me to him without detection?"

Oh, my gods.

"A fae can't," I said. Brim nodded. "But what can?"

"That is what I do not know. But he was the first one to get the red lilies as an omen of bad luck, and shortly after, he was murdered. And that got me thinking, Della, fae don't reincarnate to be exactly the same as in their previous lives. I had visions of you and him meeting in Kizar during his present life. So, I went to Kizar and saw him for myself. This Haden is identical to his old self; I'm guessing down to every scar. The heavens do not do that. Creatures can't come back exactly the same. Do you know how confusing that would be to the loved ones still alive? And what are the chances that he ends up being born a village away from his previous family?"

My body froze in realization, and I swallowed hard. Somehow, I knew this. I knew that Haden should have been different when he came back. Some parts of his personality were the same as before, but physically, he was the exact same. And sometimes he did and said things that made me think he remembered me, but it was only when he was void. My heart was pounding. I could not wrap my head around this.

"He calls me Storm. He called me that before, and the first day I saw him, he said it again. And he has nightmares of the night that he died. He should not remember anything if he was reborn. Sometimes he repeats things he said in his first life. What does this all mean?"

"Who the fuck is Haden? More importantly, *what* is Haden, and what does he remember right now?" Brim looked at me.

"Is he dangerous?" I asked. Stars, I did not think I could stay away from him even if he was.

"To you, no. You are his mate; he loves you. And I can't stress how much he loved you before, even when you weren't mates. I don't think he is a danger, but I do think he is hiding something. Honestly though, I have no idea if he even knows these things after coming back."

What the hell are you hiding, Haden?

"You can't tell anyone about this," I begged Brim. "If he is this powerful, then someone will want to know why. I don't want him to be in danger."

"Della, after how long we have known each other, I would hope you know you are my favorite god. I will not say a word, but please, tell me if you find out anything about Haden."

"I will."

"Who was his mate?" I asked, my eyes flashing white. Brim gave me a look, knowing that I wanted to go kill her.

"You won't hurt her." Brim was so sure of himself. I would. I wou— "It was Sara."

What the actual fuck? My anger disappeared. Brim was right; I wouldn't hurt her. Tears stung my eyes.

"I meant what I said earlier. Haden loved you so much, even when you were not mates. He loved you so much that he thought it could change fate itself, and I am wondering if he was right. You felt that you loved him enough to change fate, but did he do something to change fate first?"

Why wouldn't Haden tell me all of this before? I could have saved him... Maybe though, maybe he didn't want to be saved. Maybe he wanted to die because he saw what I would do. He had known he was going to die the morning he proposed to me. Did he only do that because he knew he would die? I was questioning everything now.

"Della," Brim said. "There is something else I wanted to tell you." He walked up to me and held my hands tightly. "Something terrible is going to happen to you."

"If Haden dies, I will lose my mind."

He shook his head.

"I cannot see your future anymore," he whispered. "It almost seems like... you die."

"Gods can't die," I reminded him, but even as I said it, I felt fear. I had believed that gods weren't able to change fate either, but I did.

"What if everything we know is a lie?" he frowned. "I see you and Haden in the future, in love and happy, but then he is alone, and you are nowhere to be seen in the visions."

"Maybe I get taken by the night lily creatures."

He shook his head.

"No, I would see it. I cannot see anything anymore." Brim's eyes filled with tears. "The last vision I have of you is confusing and does not make sense."

"Tell me."

"You are standing in the Crimson Kingdom's garden with Remiah."

"What is so odd about that besides the fact I am in Crimson?" I asked.

I don't know if I had ever seen Brim's eyes lose all of their light like this before.

"Remiah was dead. It was her soul floating in front of you."

I shook my head. No, Mikel's mate can't die.

"No." I ripped my hands from his. "Mikel would never let her die."

"It was confusing. Remember that visions do not always give the correct information. Sometimes it gives images with no context. Maybe you were there to save her. What-ever you do, Della, you *cannot* tell Mikel."

"I have to."

"I forbid it." His friendly tone disappeared. "It is my vision, and I forbid it."

"How dare you?" I snapped at him as the odd sensation of his binding magic twisted around me. It felt like betray-al.

"You are getting too irrational, Della. I did it for your own good."

I stared at him.

"You know more than what you are saying."

"Of course, but I won't tell you, and you cannot force me to. Having too much knowledge of the future will drive you insane. You would go mad trying to change the fates of everyone around you in hopes that it would save Haden, but Haden is not the one who needs saving this time. You are."

I understood, but I also didn't. How could he have done this to me?

"I hate you," I sneered with tears in my eyes.

"I will take your hate if it protects you."

I turned from him and left in my star mist. When my magic disappeared, I was standing on the main pathway of Raynor with Haden and Remiah walking toward me. I watched him closely, but I stayed hidden. He did not seem to sense me yet, and I thought maybe it was my enraged state that was hiding me well.

I walked behind them as they laughed about something. Usually, I would smile at the sound of his laughter. But instead, betrayal pumped through me as I watched him. My eyes took in everything about him, from the familiar tips of his pointed fae ears to the same circular scar on his neck that he had before.

Could he see his future in this life? Someone who was that powerful before their death would probably keep their magic, right? Had he seen me coming in his visions? I shook my head as tears stung my eyes. How long had he known that he was going to die before it happened? Was it only a day or longer? I tried to think back to that morning; he had been so sad the night before, and then we spent most of it talking about our future and getting tangled within each other. He let me plan for a future that wouldn't be ours. I still didn't know what he remembered. What if he remembered everything?

Had he been trying to make our last night special? That wasn't fair. If he knew that he was going to be mine again, he should have told me and spared my heart the pain. I had spent the next 300 years wondering and waiting for him, hoping and praying he would be mine.

He should have told me.

Why hadn't he trusted me enough to tell me what was happening or how he was so damn powerful? My body froze when I realized that I had not ever sensed his magic. As a goddess, I should have felt it, but the only thing I felt from him was his frost magic. I glanced up at Haden and wondered who exactly I was in love with.

He paused in his steps and turned directly toward me. His eyes flickering around as if he could sense me. I sighed heavily because I did not know Haden at all, and it was because he had purposely hidden himself from me. How much does Haden remember now about his past life? Because I was not convinced that he was this shy man that I was seeing. The void knew me, though. I could feel the recognition when he shifted. He was confident because he remembered me. I looked around like someone would pop out and tell me I was on the right track.

I needed answers. Sighing, I headed to see the God of Knowledge. He would point me in the right direction.

☽★★★☽★★★☽

My star mist landed me in front of a tall white building with pillars that seemed to stretch high into the heavens. Gods, I hadn't been here in thousands of years, and when I was here, it was only to accompany Mikel. The beautiful structure floated on its own island above the sky, like mine and Mikel's home.

I was out of damn breath halfway up the ridiculous amount of stairs that led to the entrance when I finally said, fuck it, and used my star mist again just to get myself to the top. When I headed for the door, it was already open, and there was a figure peeking around the door with a large tome in his hands. I stared at a man that looked nothing like a god. He was short and skinny as all hell. I did not remember him looking like this before.

"Ardella." He smiled and closed the giant book in his hand. His dark brown hair fell past his shoulders, and his dark skin was flawless as he stepped forward, his brown eyes watching me curiously.

"Avesh." I smiled.

"I haven't seen you in what, a thousand, two thousand years?"

Stars, I was starting to remember how friendly he was. I nodded, and he waved for me to follow. He wore an all-white outfit that I couldn't believe was so pristine. When we walked into the home, it was so large that our footsteps echoed. The space felt cozy, with dark woods and soft lighting that reminded me of a library. The grand staircase split in two, one on each side of us, before curving together at the next floor.

"Would you like some tea?" he asked.

"No, that's alright."

"We'll grab some tea." He smiled. "I have a feeling our conversation is going to be a long one."

"Why do you think that?"

Avesh stopped and turned to me.

"You have never come to see me. Whatever the reason is for your visit, it must be some serious shit for you to think I may be your only hope."

I smiled softly. Know-it-all.

"Tea it is."

"Wonderful!" He exclaimed so loudly that it echoed and ricocheted around the foyer. He flinched slightly. "Gods be damned, I forget how loud it is in this part of the damn house."

He started walking up the stairs, and I followed. The second floor was decorated in the same manner but was not as grand as the bottom floor. The walls here were covered in simple artwork depicting mostly scholarly-type pictures. He led me down a hallway and stopped for a brief moment at an open door.

"Nina, would you mind bringing tea and a treat to the grand library, please?"

I heard a soft voice murmuring back before we kept going. For the love of all things holy, how far was this damn library? After another few minutes, Avesh and I came to the end of the hallway. He shoved the large wooden doors open, and my mouth fell open. The library had millions of books lining the room. I walked through the doors and saw beautiful mahogany shelves lined all the way to the ceiling filled with books of all colors and sizes. There were ornate wooden ladders on wheels that could move swiftly and gently to whatever shelf you needed. I crossed the thick, blue carpet and walked toward the railing in the center of the room.

As I looked around, there was much more than books here. Maps floated around, globes of the realm were spinning on their own, and there were books flying around. As I reached the railing, I gasped. I looked out and saw that we were visiting only one floor of the library. From here, I could see countless levels stretching both up and down, all packed with the same beautiful shelves of books. I laughed when a book zipped past my head. My gaze watched as it flew down into the depths of a lower level.

"Careful, the books do not care if you are in their way. They will hit you without remorse."

"Shit," I whispered, impressed.

"I know, right?" He laughed. "We will sit over here." We walked to the left, and a large sitting area appeared next to us. The beautiful couches were some sort of leather, with dark wood tables sitting next to them and a large fireplace that roared and instantly warmed me. We sat down across from each other, and Avesh stared at me oddly. What the hell was he staring at like that?

I raised my eyebrow at him, and he chuckled. A moment later an older woman came in and set down a tray with tea and an assortment of desserts on it before leaving without a word. I grabbed a pastry and nearly died at how good it was.

"So, what do you need to know?"

I paused, halfway to reaching for my second pastry, and looked at him. He watched me take another one and sigh.

"This will sound crazy."

"Sometimes, knowledge is crazy." He leaned forward and took a pastry for himself.

"I'm trying to figure out what sort of creature can bind a seer's tongue and see so far into their own future that they can see their next life."

Avesh stared at me oddly.

"Anything else?"

"They can summon even a seer to them without the seer knowing they did."

Avesh looked confused.

"There is no creature that can do that."

"Yes, there is," I challenged.

"Is it elite magic?" he asked.

I gave him a pointed look and ate my pastry.

"We both know that this is not elite magic." I paused. "What about being reborn? After someone dies, have the stars ever brought them back in the exact same form? Everything about their appearance is identical."

"Are you describing a god?" he asked. "And it is the heavens that send them back, not the stars."

"Gods can't die." I raised my eyebrow. Avesh gave me a grim look.

"Yes, they can."

I glanced up at him and wondered if I heard him wrong.

"I have been dying to tell someone about this." Avesh smiled as he sat up straighter. He leaned forward, and the gleam in his eyes made me lean forward too. "A god can die when they no longer possess their soul."

"How does a god lose their soul?"

"Another god takes it." He looked at me. "As of right now, you are the only god I know of that can take a soul from another god. But in the other realms, the God of Death in Valynth can as well."

I looked at him oddly.

"How do you know a god can die, though? I have not ripped any souls from any of my fellow gods, and I don't plan on it."

"Once upon a time, you weren't the only god with such a power over the souls of other beings. Hold on." Avesh lifted his hand and muttered something softly. I heard a whooshing sound as a book flew from somewhere in the library and landed right in his hand. Its cover was made of weathered leather, and it was worn on the spine, like it had been read so many times. Something about seeing the book made me lean forward with curiosity. He opened it to a page with a beautiful picture drawn inside of it, showing what I could only guess was a soul being taken from one god by another god. I had trouble wrapping my head around this fact.

The illustration was that of a goddess kneeling in front of a god. Her left arm was raised toward him in what looked like supplication. I looked closer and frowned at the stars drawn on her arm. They were black with a slight glowing effect around the edges.

The text was not in a language I knew. Avesh pointed to the god who was taking the soul.

"This god is Malamay; he was once the God of Life." I couldn't see his face that much, as he was turned to the side.

I looked up at him, and he nodded.

"Who is the goddess he is taking the soul from?"

"That would be Diath, the Goddess of Mischief.

I sat up and looked over the picture. Something about it was so intriguing.

"Why did he take her soul?"

Avesh sighed as he glanced at me.

"Have you ever noticed how all gods are of a positive nature—life, justice, nature, knowledge?"

I nodded, realizing that he was right.

"Where are chaos, suffering, pain, grief, wrath, envy, and pride?" he asked. "No gods are of an ill nature in this realm. And as the God of Knowledge, I thought that was strange. It does not make sense. There is good and evil in life; it keeps the balance. So, why are there no ill-intended gods?"

"Did you find your answer?" I asked.

"Yes." His eyes shined brightly. "It is because of this picture right here."

He pointed to the image of Malamay and Diath.

"They were in love." He smiled sadly. "The first and only fated mates to both be gods. From what I gathered, they were very happy. But the longer they were together, the more mischievous Diath was with her powers, even be-hind Malamay's back. Then, one day her cleverness caught up to her. Diath had tricked Malamay. See, as gods, their children would likely become gods themselves, but they still needed to *birth* them naturally. However, Diath, did not do that. She combined their stars and *created* their children. She broke laws of the gods to create new gods. A direct violation against the heavens and old gods. What Diath didn't disclose either was that she had been born from a black star and therefore was not physically compatible with her mate. Kind of like you and Holden."

"A black star? I have never heard of such a thing,"

"A dead star." He looked at me. "It is what ill-intended gods are made from. Where you are born from a bright, healthy star."

"But the stars would step in if it was that bad."

He shook his head.

"As gods, we give too much power to the stars. They are more like a middle man between the heavens and gods. The stars have not been a governing entity for a long time and hold no real power. But the old gods were tired of being in control of everything, so they created the stars to help out."

I looked at him, still not understanding.

"The seven sins were born, Della. They aren't just simply an idea from a garbled religion; they are living gods—wrath, envy, sloth, greed, lust, pride, and gluttony."

I scoffed.

"There are more than seven sins."

"Correct, but all sins are derived from one of these desires."

That made sense.

"Well, they aren't here, so where are they?" I asked.

"The stars demanded retribution. Malamay was given an ultimatum by the old gods and heavens. He had to kill either his seven children or their mother in order to keep the balance."

What the actual fuck? Avesh met my gaze, nodding like he agreed on how fucked up that was. I stared at the picture and realized he chose to kill their mother.

"He killed his fated mate, Diath," I whispered.

"He literally reached into her and ripped her soul out," he sighed heavily before continuing. "After it was done, the old gods were still wary of the destruction and chaos they might cause, so the children were sent to hell to live—where they could use their naturally given... negativity to rule the tortured and lost souls. It was a win for them. Diath happened to be the first and only goddess to be born from a dead star, and her actions forbid any more ill-intended gods from being created. The heavens made sure of it and did not allow gods to be mated to other gods."

"Where is Malamay?"

"After he ripped out Diath's soul, the old gods killed her out of both pity and fear. No god should live without their soul. Can you imagine all of that power and no soul to control it? She had to die. Malamay could not live with himself. So, he did to himself what he had been forced to do to her, and he ripped out his own soul before ending himself."

"Shit. That is heavy."

"Yeah, some real fucked-up shit," Avesh sighed. He glanced at me and frowned. "If you have not ripped the souls from any gods lately and killed them, then it is safe to say this man you are talking about is not a god if he was reborn. You would have had to rip his soul out of him completely to kill him and allow the rebirth to happen because gods can't die any other way."

"He was stabbed; that is how he died." I told Avesh. "So, what is he?"

Avesh slammed the book shut.

"No fucking clue."

"What do you mean?" I scoffed.

"What you're describing doesn't exist in the texts I've read, and believe me, I have read a lot." He waved his hand out towards the center of the library. "Therefore, whatever you are dealing with is the first of its kind, maybe." Avesh pursed his lips like he was thinking hard. "Perhaps he is just an elite, elite seer."

"That's a thing?"

"Della, no, that is what I'm saying. Perhaps he is just the first of his kind."

"Sorry, it's been a long day," I sighed and grabbed another pastry. "Hey, since I'm here, have you found your mate yet?"

Avesh raised his brow at me.

"Why?"

"Have you heard that some gods have gone missing? Once they found their mates, they both went missing."

"Well then, thank the heavens that I haven't." He frowned. Avesh stared intently at me. "Have you asked this man what he is?"

"No," I said.

"You're scared of him?"

"I don't know what to think about him."

"Chances are he doesn't even know that his magic is that powerful. Most memories don't usually carry over after death."

He was right. Haden probably didn't even know the extent of his magic. I didn't even know if he still possessed the same magic he once had. Maybe he was just fae with some serious elite magic. I leaned back in the chair, feeling a bit stupid. Brim and I were paranoid fools. Haden wouldn't keep something so monumental from me.

"Well, I appreciate you taking time to help me." I smiled. "Sorry I wasted your time."

"Knowledge and company are never wasted time." He grinned.

"I'll let you know if any new developments come along."

He nodded.

"Please, take the rest of the pastries with you." He gestured to them. He didn't need to offer me twice. I smiled and grabbed the tray before leaving.

CHAPTER 22

HADEN

She hadn't come today. I lay in bed and stared at the ceiling, wondering why she didn't come to see me. Did I do something wrong? I could not remember part of the night after I went upstairs to follow her. Should I call her to me? Maybe she only meant that if I was in distress. Fuck, I hated feeling like this, so insecure. It was obvious that she liked me. Or maybe I was making it up in my head. I closed my eyes and ran my hands down my face.

"You do realize that you don't have to physically call for me. I can hear it if you are thinking my name over and over. Della's voice held a slight amusement in it.

I sat up. "Della."

"Haden."

We stared at each other for a moment, and I felt that doubt creeping up.

"Please, stop doing that." She frowned.

"Doing what?" I asked.

"Shutting down on me." Her eyes flashed with disappointment. "You want me near you, but then you act like I am the last woman you want near you. Why?"

I stared at her, and she frowned. Della sighed as she walked over to the bed and sat down close to my hip. My gaze watched her to see what she was going to do. I could feel the panic that I was going to mess this up bubbling inside of me.

"That, right there, that look. Tell me what you are thinking."

"That I will mess this up by saying something stupid." She smiled.

"You won't. Ask me a question," she suggested. "This will be fun; we'll take turns."

I sat up and rested my back on the headboard as Della slipped her shoes off and sat in the middle of my bed.

"Um, what do you do all day?" I was curious.

"I work a lot." She smiled. "And when I am done, I come here to see you. My turn." She paused and seemed to be thinking. "Do you have any magic besides frost?"

"No." I shook my head, and she seemed surprised by it. "What is your favorite color?" I blurted out.

"Orange." She smiled.

"Earlier, I was standing in a field of flowers and was thinking of picking you some, and I realized I didn't know what color you'd like the best. If I'm being honest, I didn't think orange would be it. I thought maybe purple or green."

Her eyes filled with an emotion I didn't understand before she leaned forward and hugged me tightly to her.

"Orange is the color of your soul," she said softly. "It will always be my favorite."

I swallowed hard at her confession.

"You can see my soul?"

"Yes, it's part of my magic." She pulled back. "Do you like me?"

Instantly the insecure feeling filled my chest. What if she laughed in my face about my feelings?

"I can see I am losing you again." She frowned. "I like you. You know that, right? I don't come here for any other reason. I really like you, but I am starting to worry that maybe you don't feel the same about me unless you are void at the time."

"Has my void side said that he likes you?" I asked. Her face immediately flushed. Gods, I liked that a lot. Her eyes filled with confusion.

"You don't remember what happens when you are void?"

"Not really. I can sometimes, but it is only bits and pieces of the memories. Like last night, I don't remember anything that happened after I went upstairs with you. Well, and when he shares things with me, but he seems to know everything that happens when I am the present personality."

Her face became more red. But then her head cocked to the side with confusion.

"He can keep things from you, but you can't keep things from him?" she asked.

"Yes."

Stop talking about this right now. The void was pissed at either me or Della. *You shouldn't have told her that.*

"Isn't that odd for you?" She stared at me.

"Sometimes, but he usually shares important things." I shrugged.

Shut. The. Fuck. Up. He was pissed at me for telling Della this. But it only made me wonder why.

"You didn't answer if you liked me or not."

I was relieved that she changed the subject.

"Yes," I whispered. "I like you so much that it scares me. But I worry that if you do like me back, I will not know how to treat you well enough, and you will leave me. And I worry that you will stop liking me because I am poor. I do not have anything to offer you, Della. I only have myself, and I have been told my entire life that I am not worth anything. The void said you will never feel that way about me, though."

"He did?" Her eyes narrowed on me.

Fucking hell, now she is suspicious of me. He growled.

"I do not care that you are poor." She had tears in her eyes as she stared at me. "And I know that you think I will at some point, but trust me when I tell you I won't. I have everything—money, power, and anything I could ever desire. But I do not have the one thing I have wanted more than anything. You."

I looked at her, unsure of what to say.

"Is there a reason why it feels like we have known each other for a long time?" I asked.

"Maybe it was written in the stars, and if it was, then I thank the heavens every day that they gave me you. I mean it, Haden. There has never been anyone before you, and there will be no one after. Your soul calls to me, and I cannot stay away. We can go as slow—"

I leaned forward and kissed her. Della hummed against me. I pulled away, and her eyes flashed white, looking at me in surprise before falling back to my mouth. She suddenly moved forward and kissed me again. My hands seemed to have a mind of their own as they reached out and pulled her forward. Della straddled my lap as she deepened the kiss. Gods, she could fucking kiss.

After a minute, she pulled back and smiled at me. She gave me one last lingering kiss before hugging me to her. This felt right. I don't know why she felt like home, but I never wanted it to end. I inhaled her intoxicating scent and held her tightly.

"I'm so glad you like me back," she whispered.

I chuckled softly.

"You didn't come to see me today."

She pulled back and traced her fingers over my cheek.

"I was about to come when you started calling for me." She looked in my eyes. "I don't think I can stay away for a whole day."

"Good," I said.

"Can I take you somewhere tomorrow?" she asked.

"Yes." I nodded.

"I'm exhausted; I need to get some sleep."

She gave me a hard, lingering kiss before sliding off of me. Gods, I wanted her to get her ass back over here. She grabbed her heels off the floor, and I felt panicked about her leaving me.

"Wait," I called out. She stopped and looked at me. "Stay with me for a little bit longer. I know you're tired; you can lie with me."

"Haden, are you asking me to stay the night?" She smirked.

My face instantly turned red, and she dropped her shoes.

"I was teasing." She looked around and smiled as she picked up my tunic I had tossed off. She turned around and slipped off her dress. I turned quickly, but not before I saw her pretty bronze skin covered in glowing silver tattoos. She chuckled as she crawled into bed, now wearing only my tunic.

I shifted so I was lying on my back, and Della snuggled right up to me, resting her head on my arm. Gods, she was so natural about this, like we had done this a million times before. Her hand rested on my chest, and I felt a warmth spreading through me. Gods, I really fucking liked this.

"Storm?"

She didn't answer, and I peered down to see her already passed out. So, I wrapped my arm around her and closed my eyes, excited that tomorrow she was spending the day with me.

☽★★☽★★☽

"What is this place?" I asked as the small waterfall fell into a large pond.

"This is our new favorite place." She smiled like she had a secret. She glanced around and laid out the blanket she brought with us.

I admired the beauty of the scenery, not having seen anything quite like it before. The thousands of wildflowers surrounding us as the waterfall created mist in the air that made rainbows seemed magical. But it was Della's big, excited smile that was my favorite thing to see. A willow tree stood by itself off to the left, and something about it made me walk toward it.

As I got closer, I noticed there were letters carved in the tree. I traced them in confusion as Della appeared next to me and looked at it. Her face turned toward me.

"H loves A." She smiled. I could see that something about this carving made her happy. "Haden loves Ardella," she whispered. Her face flushed. "Gods, I'm not saying you love me. I just think it's quite the coincidence."

I smiled as she blushed and nervously tucked her hair behind her ear.

"My gods, I talk a lot when I am nervous, and if I'm being honest, I know I should stop talking. But it's like my mind thinks I can make this awkwardness better if I just fill the silence."

She was spiraling as she kept going on, but fuck, I could listen to her ramble on for hours, and at this rate she would probably tell me her whole life story and everything she ever thought about me.

"But I know this is probably making everything worse. You don't even know me. But I feel like I've known you my whole life." Her eyes glanced up at me as I smiled at her, and her talking faded off. She turned quickly, and I followed her, smiling at her even though she was embarrassed.

"Where are you going?" I chuckled.

She stopped and looked at me with a longing in her eyes. Her awkwardness made me relax. Della was just as terrible at this as I was.

"To swim."

She turned away again.

"Swim? It is freezing."

She turned and smiled at me, relaxing a bit more.

"Come feel the water with me." She held out her hand, and I took it quickly, desperate to touch her. Della led me to the water's edge and leaned down, running her hand through it. I did the same, and my gaze snapped up to her in surprise.

"Holy fuck, it's warm."

"I know. Now get undressed and come in with me."

I swallowed hard, and she smiled.

"Don't be embarrassed." She started stripping off her clothing, and I turned from her. I only turned back when I heard her splash into the water. When I looked, Della was smiling at me, her head the only thing I could see. I started taking off my clothes and noticed she looked away to give me privacy. Something about that seemed wrong.

I walked out into the water next to her and smiled when she looked at me. Her eyes shined brightly as we started swimming around. I watched her but felt an odd tugging in my chest while I looked at her.

"What's wrong?" she asked.

"Sometimes, I get weird chest pains." I rubbed my chest, and Della looked down at my hand rubbing and smirked. She swam over to me, and her hand slowly lifted, resting over my heart. The aching stopped immediately.

"Is that better?"

"Yes."

I leaned down and kissed her. Della pulled back and glanced at my face with questions in her eyes. She looked away for a moment before turning back and looking me in the eyes.

"Are you sure you are fae?"

I chuckled.

"Yes?" I stopped smiling when she didn't smile back. "Why?"

"I don't know. Sometimes it seems like you aren't fae." She shrugged. As she said it, I could feel the void wanting to come up, but I held it in with everything I could. This was my day with Della. I did not need him swooping in and taking over.

"My parents are fae. Unless maybe they are mixed with something else." She looked me over slowly before reaching up and touching my pointed ear. Gods, she really didn't think I was fae. What did I do to make her think that?

"You don't have pointed ears, so what are you?" I asked.

"I'm not fae."

"Witch?"

She smiled and shook her head no.

"Are you a god?" she asked and tilted her head to the side.

"You think if I were a god, I would live where I do?" I raised my brow at her. "I'm flattered that you think I'm good-looking enough to be a god." I laughed.

"So, you are just a fae with elite magic."

"I guess."

Her pretty eyes studied me for a long moment, not seeming convinced.

"You don't have visions?" she blurted out.

"Visions?" How did she know I had visions?

"Yeah, like did you have dreams or something about me before we met?"

I opened my mouth to answer her when I could feel the void being very fucking persistent.

Lie to her. Do not tell her that you knew you'd see her that day in the village. Fuck, he was pissed. I stared at Della, and she waited for me to answer. *Lie to her, damn it.*

"No, I've never had any visions. Should I have?" I smiled to throw her off because the void was raging inside of me. He was upset with her, and I didn't understand why, but I knew that he had never led me astray.

Is she dangerous? I asked my other side.

To my incredible surprise, he answered me back. *She won't harm you. She is just very fucking nosy and observant.*

Am I not fae?

He didn't answer, asshole.

Della frowned slightly before replacing it with a smile that didn't reach her eyes.

"No, I was just curious. Sorry."

She began swimming around, and I watched her intently.

Is there a reason her questions upset you so much? I asked.

He was silent.

Fine, I'll just tell her—

If you do that, you will put her in danger, he seethed. *You do not tell her a single fucking thing I share with you. Got it?*

Fine.

You need to wrap it up. I need to go somewhere and talk to someone. He demanded.

You'll be fine. I want to be with her.

He groaned like a child not getting their way. I couldn't help but wonder what she was trying to figure out. Della smiled brightly at me, and that tugging in my chest made me get closer to her. I would keep the void's secrets if it protected her.

CHAPTER 23

DELLA

Mikel was pacing around like a crazy man. I watched him as he looked up at me and then away again. I opened my mouth to say something but shut it when Pia walked in and saw him losing his mind.

"For the love of the stars, will you calm down?" she sighed. "All you are doing is working yourself up."

"Someone sent Remiah an entire bouquet of red lilies." He stared at her.

"Yes, we know, but you are about to combust." She looked at me as if asking for backup.

I wasn't sure what to say. He had every right to lose his shit, but Pia was right; he was working himself up more.

"She thinks I sent them, and I didn't have the heart to tell her that only a sick fuck would do that." Mikel sighed heavily and began pacing around. "Why an entire bouquet?" He looked at me.

"I have no idea, Mikel."

"It's not good," he said confidently. "Maybe someone is going to take us as soon as I tell her she is my mate and claim her."

I looked up at him.

"That's why you haven't marked her yet?"

That made sense. I was wondering why he hadn't. I was still trying to get both sides of Haden on the same page before I told him. Well, and the knowledge that I had changed fate was making me worried that I would be punished if I claimed him. Gods, and the void was keeping shit from me.

"Yes."

"Maybe you should talk to Avesh and see if he knows anything special about red lilies?"

Mikel stared at me, and I saw a flicker of relief in his eyes that I had any sort of suggestion. I should have asked him while I was there, but the thought didn't cross my mind.

"Thank you; that's a great idea." Mikel came over and gave me a hug. I hugged him back, feeling like a piece of shit because I couldn't tell him that Brim had seen Remiah dead. Maybe her fate would change if Mikel could figure out who this was. "I will go now."

"Alright. I hope he can help."

Mikel gave me a sad smile before disappearing. I looked at Pia, and she frowned.

"This is really fucking bad, isn't it?"

"Yes."

I didn't know how to help Remiah or Mikel. Who would want to kill her? She was so kind, and I had never seen her be treated as poorly as Haden. Why kill Remiah when they were taking the other mates? I closed my eyes tightly. And why was I standing in the Crimson Kingdom with her?

I willed the heavens to tell me how to save her. Mikel needed to mark her so that she wouldn't die; that was the only answer I could come up with, but he was too scared. There was no way I could convince him that he would actually be saving her.

Haden will be destroyed when this happens. How am I supposed to make him feel better when the only family he knows leaves him for good? Images of Haden's funeral in his past life and watching his family grieve started taking over my mind. I needed to get out of here. I could feel my anger and grief taking over my already shitty mood.

"I'll be back."

I used my magic to go see Haden. He was about the only thing that would make my day better. When my star mist disappeared, I was standing on the pathway of his village again.

Confused, I turned around, and my rage doubled at what I saw. Kira, whose presence instantly pissed me off, and a group of men were surrounding Haden. He was looking at the ground as they spoke, not able to meet their eyes. Dark clouds rolled in at my already bad mood. They couldn't see me, but I wouldn't stand by and let them be cruel to Haden.

"The town freak has come out of his shitty home," the ugliest one of the bunch laughed. My chest tightened at the sight. I moved toward him, my heart breaking at how he just took their cruel words.

"Haden, don't take shit from them. Fight back," I demanded. He looked up and noticed me for the first time, but he instantly looked back down.

He still didn't say anything. His damn parents had destroyed any worth he might have had for himself.

"Haden, you are so much better than them. This ugly one, for example, is sleeping with his father's fiancé. And this blonde one with the crooked nose, his family is stealing money from other noble families; they are broke. And her... I can't even tell you how many men she is crawling into bed with to get social status. All because no one wants to marry her."

When I looked back at Haden, he was watching me as I circled around the group.

"Would you like me to kill them for you?" I half-joked. "You are so much better than them."

His eyes filled with sudden emotion. He wasn't used to someone thinking highly of him, but I would spend our life making sure he always knew how worthy he was. He was worth all the stars in the sky.

He took a deep breath.

"Shut the fuck up," Haden snapped at them when they kept talking. I smiled proudly at him.

"What did you say, freak?"

"Shut the fuck up. I didn't stutter."

"Oh, someone thinks they can fight back." The ugly one took a step toward Haden.

I moved so I could kill them if they touched him, but I needn't have worried. His eyes filled with cold frost. "That's it, Haden; use that magic pulsing inside of you." Haden looked at me, and I saw the boys noticed him looking too. I was sure that this side of Haden was unaware of how much power his magic had.

"Look, the freak is staring at his invisible girlfriend."

After a second, I saw the change for myself. Haden looked at me as he cracked his neck, and a shiver seemed to run through him. He closed his eyes tightly, and when he opened them, they immediately found me.

The stormy color of his eyes now almost seemed endlessly black. The void was here, and it made me swallow hard. Haden's soft, friendly features had disappeared and were replaced by hard, unforgiving lines. Fuck me, I really liked the way he smiled at me when he was like this. Like he would make every dirty thought I ever had about him come true. His eyes drifted slowly from my feet all the way up my body, admiring, savoring. I swallowed hard as his gaze set my skin on fire with desire.

"Della, baby, you're drooling," he teased. I snapped my mouth shut as the term of endearment shot lust through me. I could feel my magic pulsing out of control, my eyes flashing white.

"The freak is talking to her."

"Actually, Della, I think I do want to hurt them."

I smiled from behind them. My magic was already causing more clouds to move over us, darkening the sky. Haden's emotionless eyes watched me without a care that these bastards were witness to it.

"But first, Haden, let's put these accusations to rest." He watched me, confused. I smiled as I took a step toward him. The air shifted immediately as I let myself be seen. My eyes stared deeply into Haden's as I continued to walk toward him. The group surrounding him gasped as I made my way past them, not breaking eye contact with Haden for a second. A big grin took over his face as I reached him. I could not stop my mating bond from overwhelming me as I reached out, my hands resting on his chest before they moved up to his shoulders.

"Touch me, Haden," I whispered.

He didn't need any more encouragement as his big hands grabbed me by the hips, tugging me closer to him and wrapping his arms around my back. Stars, he was warm as I pulled him to me for a hug. I inhaled his scent.

"You feel good, Storm," he purred in my ear. His hands slid down the length of my body before coming back up and gripping my hair in his hands. He yanked me back enough so that he could see my face. Gods, we had an audience, and I couldn't care less. His eyes traced over my face before dropping to my mouth.

Would he kiss me if I begged? He gave me a sly smirk like he could read my mind. Haden pulled me against him, hugging me so his mouth was against my ear.

"I haven't stopped thinking about your pretty mouth, Storm. Tell me you've been thinking about kissing me again."

"Yes."

He hummed softly as his mouth kissed below my ear.

"Spill their blood," he commanded. "And I'll give you a reward."

I sucked my bottom lip in and bit down on it, drawing it back out slowly in pleasure as his words turned me on in such a delicious way.

"Who the fuck is that?" one of the men asked, interrupting Haden and me.

I pulled back and smiled at the gaping faces of the mean men and Kira. I held Haden's arm and rested my head on his shoulder.

"Who is that?" Kira hissed, demanding an answer imperiously.

Stars, Haden was like a statue, unmoving and unbreathing. I could feel his power rolling off of him in confident waves. I did not know what side of him I liked more, the shy, quiet one or this one that didn't give a shit about anything— anything but me, that is. Both—I loved both sides.

"Him?" The ugliest man laughed humorlessly. "Sweetheart, I can give you anything you want. Haden can't give you anything. Whatever he said to you was likely a lie. Did he tell you his family is one of the poorest in the village? His father is the town drunk, and his mother is a spineless whore. I can treat you better than he ever could."

I released Haden and took a step forward, my power pulsing from me. The man thought I liked what he said, but in reality, I wanted to rip his ugly face from his body. He reached out and gripped my shoulder like I was his to touch.

Haden reacted instantaneously. Before anybody could move, he had formed a dagger of ice in his hand and immediately stabbed the forearm of the man who was still touching me.

The man grabbed his arm and screamed.

"Do not touch what does not belong to you," Haden warned. "She's mine."

I didn't move a muscle. I could not look away from Haden. I was utterly transfixed by his handsome face. He turned his gaze at me and smirked. My heart was going to explode. Haden was watching me closely, taking in the flush of my cheeks and the white flash of my eyes. I turned to the man who was now threatening to kill Haden and his family, screaming curses and obscenities while tears streamed down his face.

"I think you will be the one I make an example of first." I smiled as my starlight mist circled around him and gripped him tightly.

"Do you know why Haden could see me when no one else could?" I asked. "Did it ever occur to you that Haden's eyes are the only ones I want on me? He is the only man worthy enough to see me; in fact, I kind of want to rip the eyes from your sockets because you are disgusting, and I feel nauseated knowing I allowed you to see what belongs to Haden."

The man was struggling against my magic, but he could never overpower me. I looked at Haden, who was watching me with great curiosity. His void eyes taking in every move I made. He looked so unbothered by the way they treated him, but it pissed me off beyond reason.

Without a second thought, I twisted my magic and snapped his neck.

Everybody gasped as his dead body hit the ground. I turned to the rest of them. They all looked terrified of me.

Good.

"You will leave him alone. You will not throw things at him; you will not look at him. And you," I turned to Kira, "if you ever touch what belongs to me again, I'll rip your hands off. You are unworthy of touching him."

"Who is this, Haden?" Kira demanded.

"I'm his, that's all you need to know. He owes you no explanation for anything."

My hands fisted at my sides. When had I become this possessive and angry woman? I wanted Kira to fight me so I had a good reason to rip her soul from her body.

"Well, I'm the girl he comes to when he wants to feel good; he owes me an explanation," Kira sneered like a bitch.

I didn't flinch at the cruelty of her words. But the thought of Haden with another female made me jealous beyond belief. I turned to look at him, and I swore I saw a flash of disappointment in his eyes at whatever he saw on my face.

My bond demanded that I make sure all these fucks knew he was mine. He would never belong to anyone but me. Ignoring her, I walked up to him as confidently as I could. His pretty, void eyes tracked me like prey. He smirked when I grabbed him and pulled him to me. Haden's hands immediately drew me to him, and my lips slammed into his.

He groaned as he twisted my hair into his hands, leaning in and deepening the kiss. His tongue dominated mine. Fuck, I wanted more. He tried to pull back slightly, but I refused to let him go and just pulled him back against me, kissing him with all the emotions swirling inside of me.

My body was on fire. I was overwhelmed by my lust and smiled as my magic exploded from me, causing lightning to illuminate the sky and thunder to boom so loudly that it startled even me. Haden suddenly broke away from me, his eyes full of something beside the void.

I looked away from him quickly.

Gods, I was never going to get enough of that. Fuck, I had missed the way he kissed me like this. I didn't need to look at him to see he was staring at me with intensity.

I turned my focus back to the assholes gaping at us. Kira's face was bright red with her anger, and I gave her a smug smile. Haden was staring at me. I could feel his eyes, but I couldn't return his gaze right then because Kira had stepped forward. This caused Haden to look at her in such a way that told her if she touched me, hers would be the next body to hit the ground.

"You touch her, and you'll join your father in hell," he warned.

Kira gaped at the threat.

"I always knew you were a fucking freak—" Kira's words ended immediately as I shot my star mist through her chest, ripping her heart out of her chest and bringing it back to be held in my hand as it slowly stopped beating. Her mouth fell open, and her eyes blinked one last time as her brain comprehended that I had killed her. I watched her eyes roll back before her body fell to the ground, dead. The men were watching me as they tried to process what just happened. I tossed her heart at their feet.

"I suggest you get fucking moving before I lose my composure."

CHAPTER 24

HADEN

I don't know how she did it, but I was feeling things while void. And all of them had to do with that fucking kiss. I didn't speak as I watched her stare at Kira's dead body lying at her feet. The men scattered at Della's threat. I watched her back as her shoulders rose and fell in angry breaths. She had been angry as soon as she got here, and I wondered what was wrong.

"Was that you *with* composure, Storm?" My lips twitched. She turned to me, and her eyes were pure white. Fuck, she was hauntingly beautiful when she showed her wrath. "I'd love to see you lose your composure."

Thunder shook the ground beneath us as my words had their intended impact. *Come on, Storm. You've been holding back, and I want to see you take these walls down.* I could see her struggling with something as she watched me. So, I took her hesitation as a chance to admire her more thoroughly. My eyes drifted down the black dress she had on. It was different from what she normally wore. It was casual and stopped above her knees.

I dragged my eyes up, past her chest that was heaving, and focused on those perfect lips. Her mouth parted, and images of her losing herself while using me to find pleasure flashed in my mind. As much as I wanted to close my eyes and savor those thoughts, I knew that now was not the time. I finally glanced up at her eyes.

I needed to know what she knew about me. She seemed suspicious, and I didn't know why.

All I could think about, though, was Della's lips against mine. I couldn't control myself. My thoughts wandered to everything I wanted to do to her. I fisted my hands at my sides so I wouldn't reach out and grab her. Fuck, I would beg her if I needed to, just to feel her mouth against mine again. My eyes were changing colors, and I closed them to try and control myself. But all that did was make the longing worse because images of Della and me together were running through my mind like a wildfire.

"What are you waiting for, Storm?"

She let out a long, worried breath before walking toward my house, leaving the bodies behind without a backward glance. Damn it. Della refused to look at me as she hurried away.

"Della?"

She ignored me all the way to my home. Once we were back in my yard, she turned to me with a pained expression on her face. Her eyes finally met mine, and I felt like I could breathe for the first time since she looked away from me.

Fuck.

"Why are you so upset?" I asked.

I could see her mind warring with itself as she opened her mouth and shut it several times. A moment later she blushed brightly. Fuck, she was going to be the death of me. The thought had my frost creeping from me, freezing the ground where my feet stepped.

"Is what she said true?" she asked.

"What? Who?"

"Kira." Her voice was filled with rage. "About going to her to feel good."

Oh.

This wasn't just rage. She was fucking jealous. My mate didn't want me with anyone else.

"You really think I would touch her?"

She frowned, and I realized she did think that I might, which kind of pissed me off. I took a step toward her.

"Wait, don't answer that. I would go mad if you told me that you actually touched that terrible woman." She stared at me, and I realized that I liked seeing her like this. Possessive. Jealous. Mine. "Actually, fuck that. Tell me right now everyone that you have been intimate with."

I laughed, and her eyes turned white. I stopped laughing. She was pissed.

"Storm."

"Tell me."

"I just did."

Confusion made her eyes slowly lose their white color before her face turned bright red.

"Oh." She cleared her throat. Della took a deep breath and looked anywhere but at me. I could feel her embarrassment through our bond. "I might have lost my composure," she whispered as her eyes found mine.

"Just a bit." I smiled. "But to be honest, I kind of liked it."

She swallowed hard as her eyes traveled over my face. I moved toward her again and pulled her to me. Her body melted against mine as soon as I touched her, and I didn't think I would ever get enough of that.

Her eyes flashed pure white for a moment before she leaned forward and pressed her full lips against mine. I tilted her head so I could deepen the kiss, my tongue tangling with hers. Della moaned into my mouth, and the sound sent a jolt of life through me. It pumped into my veins and made me feel... feral. I kept her against me tightly as

I walked her backward until her back hit the side of my home.

Della wrapped her arms around my shoulders before running her hands through my hair, tugging as she went.

"Fuck," I muttered as I pulled back to see her. Her eyes were filled with desire as her chest rose and fell quickly.

"Don't stop," she whispered.

So, I didn't. I slammed my mouth against hers and rolled my hard length against her, making her gasp. Her hands snaked up my shirt as she ran her fingernails over my bare back. Fuck. My hand ran up her body and cupped her full breast as my hips rolled into hers.

"Haden," she pleaded as I kissed down her neck.

"Della," I breathed as I pulled back so I could see her face. This felt like a dream. It almost didn't feel real. "Did you mean it when you said you were mine?"

"Fuck," she whispered as her eyes glazed over. "Yes."

"Good, because I meant it when I said I was yours, but you already knew that, didn't you?" My hand snaked down her body and rubbed her through her thin dress.

"Yes."

Her needy moan had me rubbing against her harder. Della grabbed me by the collar and dominated my lips with hers as she rolled her hips into me.

I glanced around, not caring if we were caught, but she might. My parents were gone until tomorrow, and Remy had been gone since this morning with Mikel.

"Do you want to go inside?" I asked.

She shook her head.

"No."

"Fuck, you're perfect." I moaned as I slipped my hand up her dress and slowly rubbed it up her thigh, hesitating for only a moment before I gently stroked her most sensitive spot. "Gods, Della, you're so fucking wet."

My fingers slid across her, making her hips surge forward. I smiled at her when she made one of those soft whimpers that I liked so much. That noise would be on repeat in my mind until the day I died. I slowly rubbed her clit, making her eyes close tightly, her fingers digging into my shoulders. The feeling of her all hot and ready for me had me shaking with desire and harder than I had ever been before.

"Let me see those pretty eyes, Storm."

She opened her eyes immediately, and I breathed heavily as she looked into my eyes as my fingers slid into her. Fuck, this might be the most perfect moment to ever exist. I sank them into her as far as they could go, then pulled them out and did it over again and again, each time her eyes going delirious with pleasure.

"Haden," she whispered. "More, please don't stop."

I glanced down and growled when I couldn't see her. I used my free hand to yank her dress up so I could see my fingers disappearing into her tight, wet pussy.

My mouth fell open at the sight. I pulled my fingers out and across her clit, making her whimper loudly.

"Open." I grabbed her jaw. She opened her mouth, and I shoved my fingers against her tongue. "Suck."

She moaned around my fingers as she did exactly what I demanded from her. My eyes watched her plump lips circle around my fingers as her greedy tongue swirled around them. I couldn't take it anymore. My lips crashed into hers, and I swirled my tongue around in her mouth, tasting her arousal.

My fingers sank into her again without warning as my tongue circled in tandem with them, making Della clench tightly around me.

Her noises were driving me fucking mad. I needed to hear more of what I did to her. I pulled back and watched her greedy hips roll into my fingers.

"Look at you, so fucking greedy, taking what you want from me."

Della's eyes glanced down to where my fingers fucked her, and she moaned loudly.

"Haden..."

"Tell me what you want," I said.

"I want you inside of me." Her voice was confident.

"Fuck."

I undid my trousers with frantic hands and pulled them down just enough so that I could lift her by the back of the legs and slam her into the side of the empty house. Della gripped me tightly with her thighs as I tugged her down on me.

Della cried loudly into the darkening sky as I entered her completely.

Her hands gripped my hair as her hips rolled against me. It should be a crime that I had not buried myself inside of her in hundreds of years. She was the closest to heaven I was ever going to feel. I slammed up into her as I watched her mouth fall open.

Then Della took control. She gripped my shoulders, lifting herself up and slamming harder down on my cock.

"That's my girl, Storm. Fucking use me."

"Haden." She was watching my face closely, like she knew that this was always meant to happen between us. "You feel so good."

Thunder echoed in the sky, and I wondered if she did that so no one would hear her coming apart on me. Her pussy clenched tightly as I gripped her jaw tightly before moving my hand to her throat, squeezing tightly as I watched where I pushed inside of her.

"Fucking hell." I was going to fucking cum if I watched that perfect sight for too long.

"Look at me," she demanded.

And I did because we both knew who was in control here, and it wasn't me.

"You might need to create more thunder, Storm, so the realm does not hear you calling my name to the heavens as you cum." She nodded, and I slammed into her as my name fell from her perfect mouth. "Actually, fuck it, let them hear."

"You want them to know who I belong to." She smiled as I drove into her. I leaned forward and kissed her, my hand snaking back up to her jaw before running my thumb along her lips. Della kissed my thumb before opening her mouth and sucking it.

"Della," I warned. My gaze could not look away from the sight.

"Kiss me." I went to kiss her mouth, and she turned so her neck was exposed to me. My lips traveled over her flawless skin. "I'm close, Haden."

I could see the flush creeping up. I pulled back.

"Tell the stars who you belong to." Then I slammed into her as I bit into her shoulder.

A moment later, Della called my name into the heavens, and I swore the ground shook beneath us. Her heavy breathing turned into a moan as I chased my own release. I stared at her, fucking delirious with desire. I had done that to her, and it made me feel fucking possessive now that I had seen it again. No other man would get to see her pleasure. It was mine and mine alone.

"Della," I breathed as her eyes locked onto mine like I was her prey.

"Cum for me, Haden," she purred, and I groaned at how husky her voice sounded. "I will be the only woman who gets you like this."

Fuck, she was possessive, and it only turned me on more.

My hips surged forward, making her moan as I forced my way deeper inside her. Della was heaven and hell wrapped up in one phenomenal woman.

"Della…" I moaned her name as her mouth kissed up my neck. My hands twisted in her hair as my hips moved quicker, desperate for a release. Della knew exactly what I needed.

"Fuck, I will have to start thanking the heavens that they created you and this perfect fucking mouth. It was made to both torture me and give me salvation at the same time."

Della moaned loudly at my words.

"Keep your mouth on me until I cum," I demanded. She listened to me as I shoved my cock deep into her until I felt my orgasm teetering. I held her tightly as I called her name to the stars. My orgasm paralyzed me with pleasure.

After a moment, my hands released her, and we slipped onto the ground, spent and out of breath. Della crawled up my body, straddling my hips before leaning over me. Her lips were swollen and pink as I leaned up and kissed her softly.

"I might die," I breathed. Emotions slammed into me as I looked at her.

Della chuckled softly as she moved her fingers to trace my face.

"You feel like the stars and heavens," she whispered softly.

There was a strong tugging in my chest when I looked at her. I brushed the hair from her face and pulled her to me for a kiss.

"Stay with me?" I asked.

She nodded as we both stood up and fixed our clothing. I grabbed her hand in mine as we went inside my home and headed to the bedroom. I closed the door, locked it, and pushed the dresser in front of it, even though my parents were not supposed to be back until tomorrow. Della sat on the edge of the bed, watching me with a look I could not decipher.

"What are you thinking about so hard over there?" I smiled.

Her cheeks reddened.

"All of the years I waited to meet you were worth it. I would have waited hundreds more if you were who I would get at the end of it."

I walked to her and sank to my knees between her legs. My hands traced over her face. I understood the deeper meaning of her words.

"I feel as though I've known you my whole life," I confessed.

Something about my words made tears fill her eyes. Her hand lifted and brushed through my hair.

"I like you."

I smiled brightly.

"I like you, too."

"Do you believe in fate?" she asked. When she saw the confusion in my eyes, she continued. "That something greater than us decided who we would belong to—who we would love."

"Maybe." What Della and I had felt like it was written by the stars, but I knew better. We had both changed fate for one another. From the moment I saw Della, she had consumed me. My thoughts were hers; every breath I took was for her; my life was hers. She made me daydream of things that I once thought were impossible: love and happiness.

"Well, I believe in it, and I can't imagine the heavens picking someone other than you for me." Her eyes held mine as she said it. "But, I am scared that I will get attached, and then you will be taken from me," she whispered.

Guilt filled me when I saw the hurt I had caused her. I grabbed her face in my hands and looked at her. Images of her smiling at me flashed through my mind. Memories of our first life together made me smile. I needed to get out of here. I was making this too complicated, like last time. I needed to remember that she was part of the plan, not someone I could keep.

I forced myself back, deep in the depths of our mind, and forced the other side of me out. As the change took hold, I closed my eyes and felt their color shift back to normal as the void faded back into the darkness. I was confused for just a moment before the images of what Della and I just did hit me like an arrow.

I instantly felt unworthy of her attention. "If you want me, I am yours. But I would not blame you if you wanted someone more worthy." Even as I said it, I knew I would get rid of any man that tried to take her. If I were her last choice for a male, I would kill every male in the realm so that I was her only choice.

"Actually, that's not true." I was feeling a surge of confidence. "I will never let another man have you. I'll spend my entire life making sure I am worthy of you. You're mine."

Della's mouth parted with surprise.

I leaned forward and kissed her. She hummed against me as she pulled me closer. I deepened the kiss only for a pounding on my door to startle me and cause me to jump back, fear in my eyes.

"Haden?" It was Remy.

Della stood up, eyes wide and filled with fear.

"I should go," she said quickly, but before I could tell her to stay, she was gone.

I moved the dresser from in front of my door and opened it. Remy was smiling brightly at me. Her blue eyes looked into the room and frowned.

"I thought you were talking to someone?"

"She left." I smiled.

"Are you smiling?" she asked.

I rolled my eyes as she let herself into my room.

"Sorry I interrupted."

"It's fine. How was your day?"

"How is Della today?" she asked, ignoring my question completely.

"Fine," I replied sheepishly. Remy gasped dramatically and sat on my bed with me, her legs crossed as she looked at me like I was going to keep talking.

"Well?" She waved her hands to urge me to speak.

"What?"

"Have you told her you love her yet?" Her face broke into a contagious smile. Gods, I loved seeing my sister happy. Remy clapped quietly as I rolled my eyes to avoid the question. "I remember when Mikel started talking to me. It was like we had known each other forever." She smiled. "You feel the same way too?"

"Yes."

"Gods, this makes me so happy, Haden. We deserve to be happy."

I couldn't help smiling at her excitement.

Remy fidgeted for a moment before holding up her finger to get me to hold on for a second as she disappeared out of the room. When she came back, she had a small black box. She carried it as if it was the most important thing she had ever touched. Her blue eyes met mine, and something on her face made me keep my mouth shut.

Slowly she opened it and pulled out a necklace with the most beautiful stone hanging from it. It glowed brightly like a star, but something dark purple swirled in the center. Her eyes filled with tears as she gazed at it.

"Mikel gave it to me," she whispered. "He loves me."

My eyes glanced up at her.

"I love him so much, Haden. It is like we are destined for each other."

My sister was in love. She waited for me to say something. I opened my mouth and then shut it several times, not knowing how to reply.

I smiled. "What's the pendant on the necklace made of?"

"He said he would tell me in a few days, when he comes back, and then it would all make sense why I can see him and why I feel so complete when he's near me."

She touched the stone gently before putting it back carefully. I leaned forward and hugged her.

"I'm happy for you, Rem."

"Thank you." She smiled as she pulled back. "Do you love her?"

My face heated at my sister's nosy questions.

"I hardly know her." Yes, I did.

Remy waved her hand and gave me a pointed look.

"That doesn't matter. You're just scared."

"I feel like I loved her before I ever saw her; how does that make any sense?" I looked at Remiah. I didn't mean that figuratively; I literally felt like I had known and loved Della for years.

"I loved Mikel after talking to him only once. He was so scared and kept saying the wrong things and tripping over his words. Love does not know time, Haden. If you love her, you love her. It's as simple as that. Maybe this is what we get for enduring a life of pain and suffering... happiness and true love."

Her words ran through my mind. Did the gods think our pain and suffering should be rewarded with true happiness? I had already seen a life I wanted with Della—married, maybe with some children, and a house nestled deep in the woods where no one would hear her screaming my name every night.

"I'm exhausted. I'm going to bed. I'll see you tomorrow." Remy gave me a quick hug and headed out of the room. I laid down and stared at the ceiling. Maybe Della was my fate, and if she was, I would spend our existence loving the fuck out of her. I would make myself worthy of her because the heavens knew I would never be able to stay away.

Just as I went to lie down, I felt the cold shiver of the void crawling up my spine even though I had only been present for a short amount of time. I closed my eyes when the shift happened and then glanced around confused for a moment, wondering why I wasn't in my bedroom.

After a moment, I remembered that this was my home in this life, not my last one. What a shithole. I looked around and sighed heavily before making sure no one could get in my bedroom. Then I summoned my black starlight and went to see an old friend.

CHAPTER 25

HADEN

When my magic disappeared, I was in front of an inconspicuous shed in the middle of nowhere, Cerithia. I stepped inside and watched the rotting wood transform into walls decorated with artwork and trinkets from centuries of collecting. I heard him rocking in his chair, but it would have been the first place I looked anyway.

Brim was always in his damn chair, rocking away, having visions, and being a total pain in my ass. I stepped forward, and Brim stopped rocking immediately.

"What?" he said with a bite of anger.

Smiling at his newfound attitude, I stepped forward and looked over his aged face. His white hair stuck out every which way, and his angry eyes pinned me to my spot. He sighed heavily when he saw the black void in my eyes.

"Great, you're back," Brim said with an annoyance that made me smile wider.

"What's wrong, Brim?"

"Ardella told me she hates me." He frowned. "My feelings are hurt."

I sighed heavily and rolled my eyes before sitting in the chair next to him.

"So, she did come here."

"You knew she would," Brim snapped. "You told me to expect her."

"I was hoping my visions were wrong, but I should know better when it comes to her."

I released a long breath as I stared at the flames roaring in the fireplace.

"I would like Haden to come out. I do not like you."

"Careful." I warned him. "I told you that Haden and I are the same."

Brim folded his arms over his chest like a wrinkly old child. I leaned forward and rested my arms on my thighs. I needed to be cautious about what I told this old man because he was a sneaky little shit.

"What did you tell her?"

"Exactly what you told me to."

I nodded and turned to him, my gaze drifting over him to see if he was lying. Relief filtered in slightly as I saw the truth in his eyes.

"Good." I nodded.

"She was devastated," Brim hissed at me. "You realize that, right? You destroyed her with what you did in your past, leaving her in such a manner."

"Della will be alright. I did what I needed to."

"I know you changed fate before she did." Brim stared at me with hurt and confusion. "Are you trying to get the stars involved; is that it?"

Brim was fishing for details that I would not be giving him. I gave him a look that made him huff.

"Then at least tell me what you are," he sighed.

I turned and narrowed my eyes on him, but he just stared at me with his defiant eyes. Brim wasn't going to back down. I shook my head because he gave himself away. I knew he couldn't keep his mouth shut.

"She suspects that I am not fae."

Brim's eyes widened, letting me know that he already knew this.

"Why does she think that, Brim?"

"Because Ardella is smarter than you think, asshole, and you think she will fall for whatever you are doing."

My jaw tightened.

"I know she is smart; I am counting on that."

He looked at me in confusion. I glanced at the fire again, knowing I had said a little too much, but he wouldn't know it.

"Have the visions of her changed?" I asked the question I actually came for. Even in this state, I could feel my heart pound. I hoped that Della coming to speak with Brim would allow him to see her future more clearly.

"Yes."

I turned to him, feeling relief.

"It did?"

"Yes, now I can't see her future at all. Well, I can, up until I see her with your dead sister. But you already know about that part."

Remiah. Sadness made my chest ache.

"How long do I have before Della changes?" I asked.

"For fuck's sake, Haden, you know I do not know that." Brim glared. "It could be one year or two hundred. Visions don't work that way."

"Mine do." I narrowed my eyes.

"Yeah? Well, then use that brain of yours to answer that question yourself."

I exhaled as I pinched the bridge of my nose. This old man was testing my patience, but I could not help enjoying his company.

"You know I can't see her future either."

"Well, I am a mere seer; I can't control this vision shit. Maybe whatever you are…" He stared at me like I would answer him before continuing, "It isn't as impressive as you make it seem."

This man. I chuckled softly.

"I could see everything until she kissed me the first time since I've been back, and now I can't."

"Maybe you should keep your lying lips off of her. It is probably a curse from the heavens."

Gods, he was always so damn defensive of her and assuming the worst from me. I glared at him, and he hissed like a wild animal.

"She loves you." His voice was strained.

"I know."

I knew she loved me. A small smile tilted my lips. I sighed heavily at the realization that neither one of us could see her future now. How was I supposed to know what to do if she was blocking me somehow?

"Why her?" Brim asked. I knew what he was asking, but I still played stupid.

"What do you mean?"

"Why did you have to use her out of all the gods?"

I sighed heavily. Part of the truth was, I wanted her the moment I saw her in Akecia 500 years ago. But there was a worse reason for it too. Della didn't remember our first meeting, and I couldn't let Brim know either. He would know that is when I fucked with fate.

"Because, Brim, I need to make a point to the stars, heavens, and old gods, and what better way to do that than corrupt their *favorite* goddess?"

Brim frowned.

"So, you don't love her." He looked away from me as if I confessed that I wasn't in love with him. "You are using her kindness as a weapon."

"That is part of the point, Brim."

"Will you be able to live with yourself when you destroy her?"

My jaw clenched tightly. He was starting to piss me off.

"I'll be very fucking happy at the end of this." I glared at him. "You all have this warped perception of the realm, and it's time you see everything for what it is. Not everything can have a happy ending."

"You are such a bastard," Brim snapped. "You put her through losing you, for falling in love with you when she knew it wasn't fate, and for what? To prove a fucking point to whom—the stars, the heavens, or what? Is Ardella worth so little to you?"

"Sacrifices have to be made."

"Fuck you." He stood up as if he were towering over me. "Do you think it is wise to corrupt someone with so much power? Della is the balance in the realm."

"I know what she is." I knew everything about her—out of duty, out of obsession. Brim began pacing in front of me like he would magically find the right words to say to save Della from a broken heart.

"Are you going to kill her?"

"No, gods can't die." I smiled.

"Oh, cut the fucking shit, Haden. You and I both know that is not true."

I nodded and sat back in the chair, staring at the frail old man who loved Della like his own child.

"I am not going to kill her."

"Will she survive whatever this plan of yours is?"

"I don't know. That is what I am trying to figure out, and neither of us can use this stupid fucking magic to see what happens to her."

"I know you know more about what she is going to do than you are telling me."

"Of course I do, Brim. But even I do not know the extent of Della's treasons. She has sinned against fate by trying to make me hers, but your precious Della is not done with her trespasses. Della is not innocent in all of this."

Shit.

Brim's eyes widened as he looked at me.

"Treasons against the heavens? I know of one, and that was ripping her damn bond out for you, so what do you know?"

"I'm not telling you anything else."

"You know you really are good at deception." His friendly eyes were long gone and replaced by a hateful man. "I had no idea all those years ago that you were a fucking snake hiding under the nice persona of Haden. And just to make it very clear to you, I do not believe that you only ever had visions of Della one year before you met her."

Gods, he was a nosy little shit.

"I met her 500 years ago. Are you happy?" I snapped and immediately regretted saying it. "I did have a very specific vision of her a year before she saw me in front of my family home."

"Della didn't say she met you 500 years ago," he said as his beady eyes stared at me.

"She doesn't remember."

"Why not?"

"None of your damn business," I snapped.

Brim stared at me for a long moment, seemingly contemplating how much he would argue with me. I would not tell him of my other magic. After a moment, he gave up and sat down, rocking back and forth angrily.

"Where is Abram?" I asked. Brim turned to me and narrowed his eyes.

"I don't know, and even if I did, I would never tell you where he is." There was a new anger in his eyes. "What could you possibly need with one of the old gods?"

"That is not for you to know." I glared. "Did Della go anywhere else looking for answers?"

"I don't know, and if I did, I wouldn't tell you, prick. So your issues are with the old gods then? Since you are looking for Abram."

I closed my eyes and sighed heavily. He was too gods-damn observant. There was no way in hell that I was answering him. Brim and I rocked silently for a long time before he caved and started yapping.

"Red lily," he whispered.

I looked over at him, and he was already staring at me. "Hell's flower." He watched for a reaction. I don't know what he thought I knew about it.

"I already knew that."

"I bet you did," he scoffed.

"Is there something you want to say?" I asked.

"No, you wouldn't tell me anything anyways." He huffed.

I stood up. It was time to get out of here because Brim was getting too grumpy for me. I went to leave, and he sighed, making me pause.

"How did you know it was hell's flower?"

I stilled.

"Because I looked into it after I started getting them in my last life."

"Hmm." Brim had to be taunting me at this point. "Strange." He tried again.

I turned toward him.

"What?"

"Oh, nothing. I just had a *very* difficult time finding out that information."

Shit.

I didn't know what to say.

"If you hurt Della, I will fucking gut you myself." He turned to me, and his eyes flashed red. Well, that didn't seem normal.

"I never said I *wanted* to hurt her."

"But you never said you were doing all of this to save her either."

Brim and I stared at each other before I used my magic and headed back to the biggest shithole I could have received for my family home. When I got there, I could hear my drunk father yelling at my spineless mother. I looked around the small room and pulled out the dozens of pictures that I drew of Della. I traced the lines of her face slowly, remembering every fucking detail of our first life together.

She loves you.

I was counting on it.

I sat down on my tiny-ass bed and knew I should get rest. Tomorrow was going to be a big day. I smiled. Della was finally going to murder my parents.

☽★★★☽★★★☽

"Someone said that you and that whore killed a woman in town."

My father's words slurred as he snuck up behind me. Fear and hatred swarmed inside of me at the sound of his voice. I thought of not answering but knew better than that.

"I didn't kill anybody."

I tried to ignore him, but it was difficult when I felt him staring at me. When I looked at him, his eyes dragged over me like he was trying to figure something out.

"Your little friend did."

"Yes." I smiled.

"Why are you smiling so much, boy?"

"Because I saw what Della will do to you if you lay a finger on me." I stepped forward one step and stared this piece of shit in the eyes. "She ripped that fucking bitch's heart out, and she hardly put any effort into it."

My father swallowed hard but said nothing else. His eyes narrowed on me like he thought I was a fucking liar. My father swayed slightly as he watched me. He was so far gone; I was not even sure how he was walking around. He didn't say anything else, so I turned, continuing my work he interrupted. Apparently, this pissed him off because he suddenly grabbed me by the hair and yanked me flat on my back.

He was able to kick me once before I swiped his feet out from under him. I had never fought back, not really. This time, though, I punched my father in the face before he could punch me. He looked at me in disbelief for only a moment before we both tumbled, but I was quicker than he was. I stood and shoved him, knocking him back to the ground. Then, before I could stop myself, I began to let years of pent-up hatred out on him. It felt so good to finally fight back. I couldn't stop myself. My fists kept punching and punching, connecting with his face and emitting a sickening, wet crunching sound.

I was ending this today. Remiah and I deserved better.

"I'm going to fucking kill you!" I yelled at my father. There was a wrath that burned with the fury of a million stars inside of me, and it wanted out. It did not want to be locked deep inside of me anymore.

He was trying to say something, but I wouldn't let him talk. His blood poured from him as I kept going. I didn't want to be my father when I was older. I didn't want this vicious cycle of family trauma to continue. I was going to break it for me, for Remiah, and for Della.

I didn't feel it at first. The sharp pain in my back started out so small— almost nonexistent—then became more noticeable. It started off like an itch, but then it burned something fierce and wicked. When I looked behind me, my mother was standing there with a dagger, the blade covered in blood, my blood.

Pain paralyzed me. My own mother had stabbed me. Again, she had sided with this fucking monster. It was enough of a distraction that my father was able to gain the upper hand. Before I could stop it, his fist connected with my face. Now he was the one who kept punching me over and over. My head pounded from the beating, and my body ached from the stab wound. The only thought I could think was to thank the gods that Rem had gone to town so she would not witness my death.

"Della!" I yelled into the heavens without thinking.

Suddenly, the bright blue sky swirled with dark clouds, and lightning crackled through the air. What had started off as a beautiful day suddenly reflected what was inside of me. What would Della do when she came to see me and found out that I was dead?

Then I heard her.

"You really should have kept your hands to yourself." Della's voice was wicked as she drew our attention to her. My father fell off me and stared in disbelief. "I already warned you what would happen if you touched him again."

"Mind your own business, whore." He spat at her.

The plain disrespect he showed for her caused me to see red. I used all the strength left in my beaten body to sit up and punch my father in the jaw.

"Don't you ever call her that again." I stood up on my shaky legs, using the house to steady myself. Della's pretty, star-colored eyes were gone and replaced by pure, white, rage-filled ones. Gods, I did not feel good. I held my head as my vision blurred from the pain.

"Stupid bitch, I told you I would kill you if you didn't leave us alone."

"Now, now, Galen, you shouldn't talk to me like that."

Her head tilted to the side as she took a menacing step forward. Her star-like mist swirled around her, but part of it was now black. Gods be damned, she was a fucking sight to see.

"Who the fuck are you?" my father demanded as he stood. My mother looked at Della in silent shock as she held his weight against her, supporting his beaten body.

I blinked, and in that short time, Della had moved to my father. She leaned forward and whispered something to him, and whatever it was had him gawking at me. His eyes flickered from Della to me and back. She stepped backward slowly. Her full lips pulled into a wicked smile. Something told me she had threatened more than just his life; she had threatened his very soul if he ever tried to hurt me again, and seeing her now, I had no doubt that she could take him on.

What kind of elite magic was this? I could feel her magic taking energy from all around us, twisting it back, and pulling everything toward her. Della's eyes found mine, and it made the sky fill with lightning.

My father trembled in fear from whatever she had said to him. Della's power pulsed around her. She did not look scared; she looked excited. Her eyes stayed on me, but all I could do was just stare at her in awe as she came to me.

"Are you alright?" Her hands frantically inspected all of my wounds.

"My back," I groaned. The pain was becoming unbearable. I fell to my knees, and Della quickly fell to hers. Her eyes filled with worry as she looked for injuries. Then her whole body stiffened when she saw my wound. A moment later, the pain disappeared. I knew she had healed my injury, but when she pulled back, her eyes flashed back to being completely white.

"Haden, do you want to say anything to your father before I kill him?"

Her words pulled me from my trance. My mother began sobbing, but I did not feel sorry for her. My father was an evil man, but she was heartless to let him beat me for years. All I could think about was a life without my father in it, and it sounded fucking great. I turned to him, and he looked over at me with terror. There was a pleading in his eyes.

"I hope the gods show no mercy on your soul," I hissed.

This made Della smile.

"Don't worry, I won't," she answered back as she walked menacingly toward my father again. He backed himself against the wall of the house, not even trying to fight her. Della's words rang in my ears: *Don't worry, I won't.*

Suddenly, her silver tattoos blazed to life, and her star mist shot out from her hand as she reached forward, sinking her now-incandescent fingers into my father's chest, smiling wickedly and staring into his eyes. When she pulled it back out, she was holding a fuzzy-looking light in her fist. It seemed to struggle in her grasp for a moment before she squeezed her fist shut, crushing the light until it sparked out. When she opened her hand, a few wisps of gray smoke and dust escaped, floating away on the wind. I could not believe it; she had literally ripped his soul from his body.

I watched his eyes turn vacant as Della stared at him until his body fell to the ground. My mother began wailing, but Della turned to me, her eyes back to the color of stars. She approached me cautiously, like I would spook from her.

She whipped around and faced my mother, who was too busy crying over my father's dead body to care if I was alright. Della stood without blinking. Her steps were quick, and before my mother realized it, Della was standing over her. My mother was pleading for her to bring my father back.

"Don't worry, you'll be joining him in hell," she promised, then she leaned down and said something to her that I couldn't hear. It had to have been the same thing she told my father because my mother's eyes instantly jumped to my face and bored into my own.

Before she could react, Della reached forward, just as she had done to my father. With the same star mist shooting from her hand, she slowly reached in and ripped the soul of my mother from her chest. Once again, she squeezed the pulsing, fuzzy light in her hand until nothing remained but gray smoke and dust that blew away as my mother's body fell at her feet. Della was very still. Her gaze didn't move from my dead parents at her feet, breathing heavily and trying to calm herself down. A moment later, she turned slightly toward me, her eyes full of caution. She took a hesitant step but stopped when I stepped backward. Who the fuck was she?

Her eyes took in my movement, and she didn't try to come closer.

"Do you think I'm a monster?" she asked, her face filled with regret.

All I could do was stare at her, blinking with confusion. Who the fuck was she, and how had she done that to them with such little effort? Della opened her mouth to say something, her hand slowly reaching toward me, but I flinched like she was about to rip the soul from me too. It was just a reflex, but I could see that my reaction devastated her. Tears filled her eyes as she frowned at me.

"I'm sorry," she whispered before turning and running from me. Before I could follow her, she disappeared into her star mist.

I sat on the ground for quite some time, trying to comprehend everything that had just happened. After the shock of it all started to wear off, I realized I shouldn't have reacted the way I did. But by then, Della was long gone. My eyes drifted to my parents, and relief filled me because we wouldn't have to suffer from their abusive hands ever again.

I walked to the shed, grabbed a shovel, and started digging a hole to hide their bodies. I couldn't have Remiah seeing this. It took hours, and when I was done, I walked to the edge of the nearby lake and cleaned myself up, still unable to get Della's broken-hearted face out of my mind.

CHAPTER 26

HADEN

Della didn't come back. It had been weeks since she saved me, and I felt... odd, like something was wrong with me. I felt her loss more than I did for my parents. My chest felt as if there were a hole in it where my heart should be. Rem had been shocked but relieved when I told her what had happened. We hadn't spoken of our parents since.

I lay in my room as Rem left to go meet Mikel somewhere. I had been out in the woods every day and night, trying to get Della to come back, calling for her. But she ignored my begging.

I prayed to the stars, the heavens, the hells, and whatever gods would listen to make her come back to me. What if she never came back? I shook my head. I could not even fathom a life that she was not in. That sounded so terrible that I felt ill at the thought. I rubbed my chest where the insistent tugging wouldn't stop.

My eyes fluttered shut, but a small noise made me sit up slightly in my bed. A moment later, I felt her. Della was close by, but she was lurking somewhere. She sounded like she was crying. I stood and looked out of the window and was surprised to see her standing in my yard.

Relief filled me, and I hurried outside, hoping I didn't miss the chance to speak to her. As I stepped out, Della watched me sadly. I started taking a step toward her, but she stepped back.

"Where have you been?" I demanded. "You disappeared."

My anger confused her.

"I was giving you time."

"I called for you, and you ignored me."

This made guilt fill her pretty eyes. She had heard me and still hadn't come.

"I was busy."

I took another hesitant step toward her but stopped when she looked like she might disappear again. Her eyes shifted to the spot where I buried my parents.

"Why did you leave?" I asked.

"You thought I was going to hurt you." She looked away from me. "I couldn't bear the look you gave me—like I was a monster."

I'd had time to reflect on that night, and the only thing I could conclude was that I didn't want her to leave again. She was not a monster. Della had saved me like she had promised, and I was indebted to her for it. Her power and bravery only made my connection to her grow more deeply.

"I wasn't thinking you were a monster."

Her eyes stayed on me, but she still looked worried. Something else seemed to be weighing down on her.

"I would never hurt you," she said softly.

"I was in shock. I didn't know what was happening." I felt bad for my reaction. "Can I come closer to you, or are you going to leave again?"

Her gaze looked unsure as I took a few steps toward her. An overwhelming sense of need consumed me the closer I got. When I was near enough, I reached out timidly and brushed her dark hair behind her ear. My finger tilted her face toward me, and I leaned down, pressing my lips to hers gently. Della didn't move. Her body had gone rigid, so I pulled away, worried I had just fucked up.

I said nothing because her eyes were shining brightly, and I wasn't entirely sure what that meant.

When I opened my mouth to apologize, Della lunged at me. Her mouth crushed against mine as our arms wrapped around each other, and I lifted her off her feet in a passionate embrace. Della let out a soft moan, and it was my undoing. I headed inside with her wrapped around me. I carried her to my room and sat on the edge of the bed with her straddling me. Della's hands ran through my hair as she kissed me like it was as natural as breathing.

Della pulled away, and I admired her beauty close-up. Her nose had faded freckles sprinkled across it, and her skin was soft and warm. My hands gripped her hips tightly and tugged her against my now-hard length. Her eyes fluttered shut as her mouth fell open. Her noises were driving me wild.

"You're so pretty, Storm."

"Haden," she moaned as she broke my grip on her and stood back up. "We need to talk." Della kept her face hidden from me, but I could practically feel the worry radiating from her.

"Alright," I said, trying to sound like I wasn't fucking terrified of whatever she was about to say. She began pacing around, an unsure look on her pretty face.

My eyes flickered over her tattoos, and I traced the glowing silver on her skin with my eyes. I had never seen anything like them. They were beautiful. One in particular caught my attention: snowflakes that swirled over her chest and down her left arm. She was truly breathtaking.

Her normally bright eyes were white, and full of worry. I could tell she was upset.

"Please, say something because I am terrified." I looked up at her. "Fuck, if you are leaving me, please let me turn void so it doesn't kill me."

Her eyes stared at me.

"Haden, please, I told you I will not leave you."

Della took a deep breath and slowly traced her gaze over my face, her hands fiddling with a part of her dress. Her eyes never met mine as she finally started talking.

"You asked me who I was," she whispered. "I want to tell you, but I don't want you to act differently. I like that you look at me like I'm normal."

Finally, she glanced up at me, her tongue wetting her lips as she took another deep breath. My body and mind braced themselves like she was about to tell me something awful.

"My name is Ardella, and I am the Goddess of Life."

I chuckled because I thought she was kidding. But her face looked confused, then hurt by my reaction.

"A goddess?" I questioned. "You're telling me that a goddess is interested in me?"

"Why is that so hard to believe?" She glared.

"Look around, Della. I live in squalor. How am I supposed to believe that a goddess would show herself to me, let alone be falling in love with me?"

Her star-colored eyes glanced around the dingy room as if she was noticing it for the first time, then they found mine. A silvery haze appeared around her head for a moment, and when it cleared, there was a tall, magnificent tiara sitting on her dark hair. It was black with shimmering jewels that reminded me of the night sky.

"Your soul, it calls to me," she said quietly. "I do not care about your shitty parents or your living arrangements. All I know is that when you are around, all I can see is you, and you are enough for me."

Her words shot through my heart. All of the incredible magical feats she had accomplished, they all made sense now. My mind reeled for a moment at the thought of somebody so... amazingly powerful choosing me as their companion. I thought of the life that I had lived and of the life that I was going to live and knew that she did not deserve suffering. Gods, I had just accepted the idea of her being possibly a noble woman that was interested in me, but not a goddess.

"Then you have low standards for yourself." I stood and shook my head. "I am not even worthy of a woman from a noble bloodline, and you think I am worthy of you?" I scoffed.

All my life I had been told I was not worthy. I was not good enough. I knew that I didn't have anything to give Della. If she was actually a goddess, then she was really scraping the bottom of the barrel with me. The thought hurt. I wished I was enough for her because she had taken up every thought I had. She consumed me.

"Please. I wanted to be honest with you. How can you say such cruel words about yourself?"

"Because it is the truth," I hissed. My eyes found hers and saw that they had dimmed to a light glow.

"Do you want me to leave?" She asked with so much hurt in her voice that I frowned. "Please, don't ask me to leave."

"I need to process what the fuck is happening." I stilled. "Oh, my gods, I've gone mad, right? This is all in my mind?"

"No, you haven't gone mad." She watched me as a million emotions spiraled out of control inside of me. "I am a goddess, and Mikel is a god."

"But—"

"No." She shook her head with anger. "I'm not leaving because you think you are unworthy. I get to make that choice. It's mine to make, not yours. You are worthy. Stop thinking like that. Have I ever made you feel that way?"

"No," I said truthfully.

"You do not get to tell me I can't love you." Her eyes filled with defiance.

She loves me.

Della's eyes frantically looked around the room as she tried to change my mind. She took a step forward, stopping only inches from me. My heart pounded as she fell to her knees in front of me. Her head bowed to the ground as the points of her crown rested on my leg.

"I cannot lose you," she whispered. "I just found you. It will kill me."

A soft sob released from her. Her shoulders shook with her silent cries. When she looked up at me again, I gasped in surprise. The tears that fell from her eyes were glowing like the stars. Something about seeing a goddess crying at my feet twisted my heart. Immediately, I knelt in front of her.

"I'm not leaving. I am a selfish man, Della. I meant it when I said you were mine."

Then I kissed her. Something about our frantic kiss seared something into my chest. Della was branded into me, and I was not willing to give her up. I scooped her up and set her on my bed. I grabbed her crown and slipped it off of her, setting it gently on my side table. Then I slipped her under the covers and held her as she buried her face into my chest.

I felt the insistent demand of the void wanting to come out. He wasn't taking no for an answer this time. I closed my eyes, and the shiver ran through me, taking deep root in every fiber of my body. I opened my eyes and peered down to see Della sleeping soundly against me.

Gently, I pushed her hair from her face, and she didn't move. I would recognize that heavy, calm breathing any-where. She was sleeping, gripping onto me like I would be ripped away from her.

I needed to test something. Slowly, I shifted so I was lying on my side looking at her pretty face. I rested my hand on the side of her cheek and closed my eyes. *Show me her future.* Flashes of what was coming in the next few days flashed in my mind, but I had seen this a dozen times before. *Show me farther into the future.* I demanded desperately.

At first, I thought nothing would happen—like always. But just as I was about to open my eyes, I saw a flicker of light in the darkness that clung to her future. I approached it slowly, cautiously.

What. The. Fuck.

Della was now standing in front of a castle I had never seen before. I tried to step forward, but her magic shielded me from reaching her.

"Storm, what are you doing?"

I froze when I saw Remiah's transparent body floating in front of her. Della looked at me like she was sorry before she lifted a dagger in her hand.

"No!"

Then a flash of Della with black, soulless eyes appeared in front of me, startling me.

I sat up in the bed, gasping for air. What the fuck was happening? I looked at Della, and she was now awake, staring deep into my eyes with a concerned look on her face.

"What's wrong?"

My gaze stared into her pretty, star-colored eyes, and I sighed in relief that they were not pure black, with evil lurking within them.

"Nothing, just a bad dream," I lied.

She frowned at me as I lay down facing her but scooted closer so she could snuggle back into me. I wrapped my hands around her as Brim's words swarmed through me.

Will you be able to live with yourself when you completely destroy her?

I had to be. I didn't have a choice; the fates were already broken. I had already fitted them back together in such a way that Della would not escape the coming destruction. I never said I was a good man. Della just wanted to believe that I was, and that was the start of her downfall.

I closed my eyes, and Della's black, soulless eyes haunted me like they knew everything I had done. My mating bond burned at the thought of my betrayal that hadn't even happened yet. But I would not let something silly like a mating bond ruin the plans that had been set in place long before Della ever met me.

We all make sacrifices, and Della would be mine. Because there wasn't a doubt in my mind that she would leave me as soon as she fit the pieces together. She would never forgive me.

But the heavens, stars, and gods needed to be punished.

And their penance was going to be giving up their favorite goddess to me.

This was the only way. This was not only about me. Others were depending on me. I opened my eyes and watched Della sleeping. Maybe she would understand. Maybe she wouldn't leave me when she understood what the stars and gods did to me—to us. Even if I wanted to stop this, the others would never allow it. They would go after Della if they found out I was mated to her.

And even though I was a heartless prick, I did not want her to be harmed in that way. Damn it. This love for her was turning into a fucking weakness. I rubbed my hand down my face before feeling the other's lurking close by. Fuck. I slid out of bed as gently as I could so Della did not wake up. I slipped on my clothes and used my magic to take me outside.

They were all standing in the woods outside of my home. All of them slipped their hoods off, and I glared at them.

"What?" I snapped.

Mateo stepped forward and sneered at me, his eyes flashing red.

"We thought we should check in with you, since you haven't tried to reach out to us. Are we still on track?"

My eyes narrowed on Mateo because he was my least favorite of them.

"Yes."

"Are you sure? You seem to be very cozy with Della—again. Do we need to make a point to you like we did last time?"

I didn't answer him.

"This time when we kill you, we will make sure that Remiah dies with you. Della will not save her like she did with Holden."

I stepped forward, pissed beyond reason.

"You had no right to hurt Holden."

Mateo lifted his hands up in defense.

"I thought it was you. You were twins, after all. It was an honest mistake."

"You're a fucking liar." I hissed at him. "I would think that you can tell who your *brother* is."

Mateo rolled his eyes.

"Who gives a shit, Haden? If everything goes to plan, then what is the death of one fae?"

"He is off limits, and so is every one of them in that family," I warned.

Elra stepped forward.

"They aren't your family. We are." She reminded me. "You need to be more worried about us—not that fake family and definitely not that bitch goddess, Ardella."

Her green eyes gleamed when I clenched my jaw with irritation.

"I am on track. Della has no idea what is happening."

Elra sighed heavily when I didn't give her more of a reaction. Her gaze didn't leave me, though.

"Did you have any more visions of Thea?"

"No, like I told you before, she might not be inherently bad. She may want nothing to do with this."

"She will want to," Elra said confidently.

"Did you find Abram?" Daya asked.

"No." I had hardly tried. "No one has seen him; it is like he disappeared. Besides, the old gods aren't going to make their whereabouts easy to find."

"Well, him and his siblings must be punished for what they did to us. We will make their deaths a spectacle."

"If you can find them, be my guest."

Elra's eyes flickered to the house over my shoulder before meeting my gaze again.

"Ardella is a problem."

"No, she isn't. She loves me, and she will do whatever I say. She will believe any lie that comes from my mouth."

Elra nodded slowly before stepping forward.

"You better have control over her when we need her." She took another step forward. "You better be ready to let her go when she learns what you did. We don't need you being weak over stupid feelings."

"I have not lost sight of our end goal. Della is not a problem and will not stop me from doing what I need to."

My mating bond burned with my betrayal.

"If she does resist, then you will use whatever force is necessary to make her do what she needs to."

"I'm not an idiot, Elra; I know what I am doing."

"Everything is about to fall into place." Mateo smiled, but it brought me no comfort. They said nothing else as they left. Godsdamn it.

I stood in the woods; my breathing was labored as the visions of Della's future plagued me again. I fell to my knees and grabbed my head as a new image came forward. Pain seared into me as I groaned and fell to the ground. My eyes began fluttering as the landscape around me shifted to the woods I had not been in before.

"Storm!" I yelled, panicked.

"No need to shout," she purred from behind me.

She flicked her wrist, slamming the door to the house shut and blocking it so Thea, Cassius, and Ezra could not come to me.

"Storm."

"Haden."

I let out a shaky breath as she lifted her hand up. Her fingers traced down my face slowly, appreciating the feel of me. My eyes gazed into hers, and there was a small glint of something in them that made me feel better. They weren't completely void anymore.

"Please don't leave again," I said.

Della smiled as she gripped the back of my neck, yanking me down to her mouth. I hummed as her mouth dominated mine. She yanked me flush against her and shoved her tongue into my mouth. Her hands dragged through my hair as my hands gripped her hips, tugging her to me harder.

I didn't feel it at first. The sharp, stinging pain that started in my stomach and radiated through me. Pulling away from Della, I looked down to see a small knife sticking out of me. I glanced at Della, and she smiled.

"That was too easy."

I pulled the knife from my stomach and stared at her. Blood began pouring out of the wound. Fuck, the pain was becoming worse. I stepped forward and grabbed her by the hair, yanking her to me. I held the knife to her throat.

"Go ahead." She smiled.

"Storm, what the fuck was that for?"

She grinned.

"That is my secret." Her eyes were gleaming. Gods, she really was a fucking lunatic right now. I closed my eyes as I tried to not find anything about an unhinged Della attractive. When I opened my eyes, she bit her lip as her eyes traveled over my face.

"I wanted you out here when I confronted your father, and he is hiding from me, so I thought if I stabbed you, he would come running." Her gaze landed on me. "I made sure to stab you where it wouldn't hit any major organs."

How damn gracious of her. It still fucking hurt. There was a slight noise letting me know someone else was with us.

"Ardella, you have become quite eccentric with your tactics to summon us here." The man's voice was deep and familiar.

"You've been ignoring me." Her hands dropped to her sides. Della's eyes burned with rage. "You lied to me."

The vision immediately cut off as I turned to see who the voice belonged to. What the fuck was that? I knew who that voice belonged to. I could never forget it, but I didn't understand how it was possible that he was involved in this. There was no fucking way that vision was accurate.

CHAPTER 27

DELLA

Mikel was staring at me, but I refused to look at him. I had not been able to look him in the eyes since I learned that Remiah was going to die. I was determined to change that fate. She was not going anywhere, and my brother would never know what her true fate was. I needed him to claim her but wasn't sure how to bring it up casually.

"So..." I glanced up to meet Mikel's eyes staring intently into mine. Why the hell was he looking at me like that?

"I was getting worried because you haven't looked at me the past few days." Mikel raised his dark brow at me.

I rolled my eyes to throw him off my tracks.

"So, when are you going to claim Remiah?"

Mikel startled back like I had slapped the shit out of him.

"Where did that come from?"

"My brain." I smirked when his cheeks turned bright red.

He began pacing back and forth, rubbing his neck like he was stressed the fuck out. Gods, he was stressing me out.

"What is wrong?" I asked.

"I am terrified." He frowned at me. "I am too terrified to tell her that she is my mate. What if she doesn't love me?"

Realization filled me.

"You are worried that what happened to me will happen to you." I looked away from him.

I heard him sigh heavily before walking over to me and sitting next to me on the couch. Mikel grabbed my hands in his.

"You are the strongest woman I have ever met," he whispered, and it made me look at him. "I am not just saying that because you are my sister. I have told Remiah how brave and smart and kind you are. I truly admire you, Ardella. And sometimes I hate the stars and heavens for what they did to you."

I stood still at his confession. As gods, we were not supposed to curse the heavens or be angry with them. And Mikel was the last god I would expect to say that.

"I am angry *for* you. Out of all of us, are you the one that the heavens fuck up the bond for? It's not fair. How could Abram let this happen?"

"The heavens do not make mistakes, Mikel. Maybe there is a purpose to all of this. You and I both know that Abram would never let this happen if he could."

"See, that is what I am talking about. You are more understanding than I will ever hope to be. If I tell Remiah that I am a god and her mate and she turns me away, I will find a way to end myself. I cannot survive it. I am not brave like you. I would turn into a villain. I would fall from the grace of the stars."

I rested my hand on his cheek and frowned at him.

"You are brave, Mikel, and you don't need to be scared. She will love you. She does love you. Why haven't you told her you are a god?"

"She thinks I am a nobleman, and I can see it in her eyes that she does not think she is worthy of me. What will she do if she finds out I am a god, and she will be a goddess?"

"You will spend your life making sure she knows that she is the most worthy and deserving woman, Mikel, by loving her so fiercely that she cannot doubt it."

Mikel nodded and brought his hand up to cover mine.

"I gave her my star."

I sat up a bit more.

"You did?"

"Yes, but she does not know its significance. I told her I would talk to her about it soon, but I keep putting it off."

"Well, stop," I encouraged him. "Tell her and claim her."

"I'm also worried about her safety because of the red lilies. What if whoever sent them is waiting for me to claim her to take us?"

Shit, that slipped my mind.

"You don't know that. Besides, we can move her here to protect her."

"She would never leave her twin brother."

I smiled softly to myself.

"Then he can come too, if he wants."

Mikel seemed to be thinking over my words. He knew I was right. It was safer for him to claim her. Once he did that, then she couldn't die because she would become a goddess.

"I love you." He smiled. "I thank the heavens that I was created with you."

"I love you, too."

Mikel stood up and sighed. "I'll claim her within a few days. I want to make it perfect, though."

"She will love whatever you decide."

"I'm going to go see her. I will probably be home late."

I nodded. "Have fun."

Mikel disappeared, and I glanced around the big, empty house. My visit with Brim weighed heavily on me today. Haden didn't seem like he was keeping things from me, but maybe he was very good at lying. There was no reason for it, though. I was not convinced that he was a fae with elite magic. Something about it didn't seem right.

I sat up quickly. Without giving myself time to think, I summoned my star mist and went to his first parents' home. I didn't bother knocking and barged in. Penelope and Henry looked up at me, staring like I had lost my mind.

"Della," they chimed. "What a pleasant surprise."

"Sorry to barge in, but I wanted to ask you some questions about Haden."

Their eyes lit up; they loved talking about their children. They nodded as I sat down on the couch across from them, waiting patiently for me to begin.

I took a deep breath. "I'm going to ask a lot of strange questions, and I don't really have an answer as to why."

"Oh, that's fine; ask away." Penelope smiled.

"Alright, Haden and Holden are your children, right? You didn't adopt them or find them or something."

"I gave birth to both of them," Penelope chuckled. "Although it was so odd because we had magic spells done three times to check on the baby, and each time they said a healthy baby boy."

"You didn't know it was going to be twins?"

"No, Haden came after Holden, and it was such a surprise."

"Aren't those spells always accurate?"

"Yes." Henry frowned. "When we went back and told them they had been wrong, they said they weren't. There was one boy, and he was healthy."

I didn't know what that meant, but it felt important.

"Was Haden an odd child?" I asked.

I was desperate to know anything more about him. There had to be more clues as to what he was.

Penelope answered. "Not really. Besides the visions that we told you about before. But, I mean, he was always exceptional at everything he did, was very well-mannered, and did everything we ever asked."

Hmm. That told me nothing.

"His magic was odd," Henry said. "Don't you think?" That made me perk up. I had always thought it was odd that Remiah and Holden didn't get any magic because they were twins with Haden. They should have received something.

"Does anyone in your family have frost or vision magic?"

"No, but I'm not talking about that magic." Henry sighed. He looked up at me, and Penelope frowned at him as if she didn't want him to say anything. "Have you ever heard of mind jumping?"

My stomach tightened at this new information. He had more magic than I knew of.

"No."

"We haven't either, but that is what he called it when he was younger. Have you ever noticed this new version of him changing personalities?"

The void. My heart began racing at this.

"He calls it the void," I whispered.

Henry nodded. "That's what he called it before as well. It was like a more confident...dangerous version of himself."

"Yes. Can he control it?" I asked.

"Yes," Penelope chimed in. "But he hadn't been using the magic very often before he died."

"Is that mind jumping?"

"That is a part of it. But Haden can jump into others' minds and manipulate them," Penelope admitted. "We don't like to talk about it and don't usually bring it up in conversation."

What the actual fuck? Mind jumping? That was not a known magic. None of his magic was, except his frost. I sat up straight when I realized he could have been using it on me.

"I wish you had told me this before. Will I know if he uses it on me?"

"No, well, maybe because you are a goddess. But his magic doesn't work the same with each creature. He can see memories sometimes. He can manipulate the mind sometimes. He said, it isn't guaranteed."

"He can see memories?"

"Yes." Henry ran his hand through his hair. "Did he explain to you how he saw his visions?"

I shook my head.

"He would jump into others' minds and then look into their future and see things through their eyes. It was like he defied time. He could see events that have not happened yet. We knew this wasn't common magic, but by the look on your face, I'm wondering if it is more serious."

"I am pretty sure that he has inherited the same powers as his past self. Haden's magic should not be able to exist," I said. "Especially if he is just a fae."

"If?" Penelope asked.

"Fae can't do these things. Maybe gods, but even that is a stretch. I have never met a god with powers like that."

"What are you saying?" Henry asked, confused.

"I'm saying that Haden can't be a fae, but I do not know what he is."

Penelope glanced at Henry before looking back at me.

"When we went to the witch that did the magic spell while I was pregnant and told her she was wrong, she called Haden a demon."

I exhaled.

"He is not a demon."

They sighed, relieved, but I knew that just meant that he could be something worse. They stared at me, hoping I had answers, but I didn't. I didn't even know what else to ask because I was more confused than I was when I first got there.

He can see memories. He can jump into minds and manipulate them. He sees visions of others in the future. Haden was dangerous just for this magic alone. He was more powerful than any god or all the gods lumped together. I swallowed hard. Haden was keeping his secrets locked away within the void. I was sure of it. That was when he acted and said things he used to. Gods, when we slept together, he knew everything I liked.

He remembered.

But how much?

Did he remember all of the time or only while void?

"I don't have answers, but I will let you know if I find them," I promised as I stood.

"You won't tell anyone, right?" Penelope asked with tears in her eyes. "He told us that if anyone ever found out, the stars or heavens would be sent to find him for breaking the laws of the gods."

"I won't say a word." I reassured her and hugged them so I could leave before they saw my fear. I summoned my star mist instantly and went home. I gripped my chest tightly as I sat on the bed. No, this couldn't be happening.

Haden knew of the god laws.

He knew that the stars were not merely a figment of imagination; they were a real, governing entity. He shouldn't know that. Only gods know god laws. I was losing my fucking mind. I began pacing around my bedroom. Haden didn't seem like a god. Avesh said he wasn't. But what if we were wrong?

There was no fucking way he was a god. Gods do not mate with other fucking gods—not since Malamay and Diath. He couldn't be a god.

I stopped pacing and cocked my head, a faint sound reaching my ears. I had been too busy losing my shit to realize that Haden's voice was in my mind, calling my name. Did he know I was onto him?

I took a deep breath and pulled myself together. I needed to keep myself in check if I was going to get to the bottom of this. I summoned my star mist and went to him. When I got to his bedroom, he was sitting on his bed, shirtless. I swallowed hard as my eyes traveled over him.

No. No. I needed to rein in my desire. I needed answers, and he was going to give them to me.

"I missed you, Storm." He smiled softly. He wasn't void. I needed him to be void because I was convinced that was his true self.

"I missed you, too."

I smiled when I thought of a way that I could trick him into going void. Immediately, I started stripping my clothes off as I walked toward the bed.

CHAPTER 28

HADEN

Excitement immediately pumped through me.

"Della?" I started to ask, but she said nothing, just stripped her clothing off on the way to my bed. I went to sit up, but she shot her star mist out and pinned me to the bed by my wrists.

"I couldn't focus properly on work today because all I thought of was you below me, begging me to cum." Her voice was seductive as she ripped the sheets from me.

"Fuck." I swallowed hard as she smiled at me. She must have heard me calling for her. I didn't know if she would actually come, but fuck, I was glad she did.

Della watched me closely as her fingers traced down my bare chest and to the waistband of my only piece of clothing.

"I want to hear how much you want me," she demanded.

Fuck, I didn't know if I could fucking talk right now.

"There is nothing I want more in the realm than for you to use me however you want, Storm. My body is yours."

Her eyes glowed brightly as she ripped the clothing from my body. Eyeing me like a piece of meat, she reached out and grabbed me, stroking and teasing me.

"Della...."

"I like seeing you like this, Haden, at my mercy." She leaned over me, pulling my hard length into her mouth. My head fell back on the pillow as my mouth fell open. Della was teasing me, but I was fucking loving every second of it.

"Please."

"Tell me what you want, Haden." She watched me, her eyes staring straight into mine, her hand stroking me.

"I want to taste you."

The void was demanding to come forward with such ferocity that I was not able to stop the change from taking over. I closed my eyes; the shiver ran down my spine as the void pumped through me with excitement. I closed my eyes tightly as it clawed from the dark depths of my mind and took over.

When I opened my eyes, Della's perfect face was watching me intently. When her eyes met mine, she stroked me.

"Fuck, Storm." I pulled my hands forward only to be stopped by her magic.

She released my cock and leaned over me, her naked chest rubbing against mine. Fuck, she was a tease. Her hand slid up my chest and gripped my face, squeezing my jaw tightly.

"You came out to play." She smiled. "Such a good boy."

Fuck me. Della was trying to kill me with her dirty mouth.

"I will always come out to play with you, Della." I tried to lean forward and kiss her, but she pulled away, straddling me with her legs and keeping me from reaching up. Need for her pumped through me violently. She seemed to be thinking about something as she watched me silently begging her to touch me.

"Kiss me, Storm."

Her jaw clenched, and her eyes became defiant. Oh, she was in a mood. After a moment she relaxed on top of me.

She leaned forward and kissed me, hard. Her hand squeezed my jaw as her mouth dominated mine, her tongue forcing its way past my lips. I groaned as I tried to reach for her again, but she didn't let me. Once again, she pulled back.

"Are you ready to play?" she asked coyly.

"Yes," I exhaled.

She seemed to be thinking about it for a second. Then Della's lips pulled into a seductive smile, and she slowly climbed up me, straddling my chest so that I could see her perfect pussy. But she did not move to my mouth. Instead, I had a perfect view of her fingers playing with herself. She rubbed her clit before sinking two fingers inside of herself. My breathing was ragged as I tried to reach for her, but her magic did not let go of me.

"Della," I breathed.

Her eyes stared down at me as her mouth fell open with pleasure. This fucking woman. She looked down at me before grabbing my jaw.

"Open for me."

My mouth fell open immediately, and she shoved her fingers inside, her arousal taking over my senses. I sucked on them desperately, my tongue swirling to take in every last drop of her.

"Fuck, look how desperate you are for me," she whispered. I watched her pull her fingers from my mouth, and she replaced them with her pussy. Della put all of her weight on me as I sucked her into my mouth, my tongue dragging through her wetness like I was a man starving.

"Open your eyes. I want you to see what only you can do to me," she muttered, and I obeyed. Her eyes stared into mine. Della was in complete control of the pace as she rolled her hips against my face slowly. But I could see the red flush creeping up her chest. Her orgasm was building up quickly. Her hips began moving faster, and I moaned against her.

Her hand ran through my hair and tugged it roughly as her hips moved frantically. Shit, I might cum from watching her.

"Haden..." she said in a breathless plea. She was so close, so I doubled down on her, my mouth devouring her completely. "Yes, yes, yes," she chanted as her orgasm slammed into her. She was a pleading mess above me, her body shivering with pure pleasure. I watched everything about her, mesmerized.

"Fuck, you are so fucking perfect." She moved away from me, her hand gripping my jaw again as her mouth devoured mine, our tongues tangling as she rolled her hips against mine, teasing me.

"Della, please, I need you," I begged.

She smiled as her hips pushed down, and in one quick movement, I slammed into her. My eyes closed tightly, and she didn't move. She kissed my jaw and down my neck before sitting up. Della watched me closely as she started to move against me at a pace that I felt would kill me with pleasure and send me straight to hell.

"Stop teasing me, Della," I demanded. I pulled against her magic as I tried to reach for her. "Please, let me touch you; this is the worst torture you could give me."

"You like when I tease you," she said with confidence. I groaned. "Tell me that you do."

"I love it when you tease me," I said through clenched teeth.

"Good boy. If I let you go, are you going to give me what I like?"

"I will give you anything if you let me touch you." She smirked.

Della rolled her hips against me a few more times before releasing my wrists from their hold. As soon as she let my hands go, I yanked her down to me. I pulled her by the back of the neck so her lips were an inch from mine. She tried to close the distance, but I twisted her hair in my hands and refused to let her as I slammed my hips into her harshly.

"Haden...fuck." Her moan was desperate. "Kiss me."

"You liked teasing me, Storm; now it's my turn."

She tried to push closer, but my grip on her hair tightened. My other hand moved up and gripped her throat as I slowly pushed deep inside her. She was begging me now, but I wanted more. I rolled us over and refused to let her touch me. My one hand pinned both of her wrists above her head. My other hand snaked down between us and rubbed her clit as I pounded into her.

"Haden."

"Listen to how fucking desperate you are," I breathed. "I like how shamelessly you beg for me."

I waited until I saw the red flush creeping up her chest and her mouth fall open before I pulled my hand away and stopped moving.

"What are you doing?" She cried out as her orgasm teetered on the edge.

"You think I'm going to let you cum before I'm ready to be done with you?"

Her eyes widened at my words, but I just gave her a smile.

"You'll cum when I want you to, and not a second before," I growled out as my hips moved forward again. I couldn't help myself. I leaned down and kissed her, controlling every part of her body with mine. She moaned loudly. I could feel her pussy tightening on me, so I stopped moving again. Again, she tried to move against me.

"You're fucking greedy for me, aren't you?" I asked as I gripped her jaw.

"Yes," she whispered. "Please, I need to cum."

"You'll take what I give you, Storm." My hips surged forward again.

Her eyes burned pure white, and I could feel her power pulsing around us.

"Beg me to cum, and I might let you." Fuck, I could feel the need to tell her how much I loved her bubbling up. How did she make these emotions happen inside of me?

"Please, Haden, I want to cum around your cock until you lose yourself inside me."

Fuck me.

Della's eyes widened as my own seemed to get darker. Then she smiled when I sat up, roughly pulling her hips closer to me. She went to touch me, but I shot my frost out, making cuffs around her wrists and causing her mouth to fall open in surprise. My hand pushed down onto her stomach as I slowly slid into her.

"I love it when you do as you're told, Della—when you submit to me." My praise had her clenching tightly around me. My hand slid up her body between her breasts and gripped her throat. She let out a loud moan. I pulled out of her, flipping her over.

"I wish you could see how pretty you look like this." I ran my hands over her ass before squeezing my fingers into her flesh. Della pushed herself back into my touch, and I smiled. I glanced around the room and paused when my eyes landed on the mirror against the far wall. I got off the bed, making her turn her body to see what I was doing. Bringing the mirror closer to where we were, I crawled back into the bed and grabbed her, making her wrap her legs around me. She kissed down my jaw and neck.

I gripped her hair and pulled her back so I could kiss her, then I stood and brought her to her feet, turning her so her back was to me.

"Kneel," I demanded.

She sank to her knees slowly, smiling at me as she kept her eyes on mine in the mirror in front of her.

"Now you'll be able to see how pretty you look as I fill this greedy pussy and make you cum."

"Yes." She moaned.

I knelt behind her, forcing her down on all fours, and filled her without warning. Her eyes closed tightly. I gripped her soft hair in my hand, tugging until she was looking at me, as my other hand gripped her hip. Her hands were still bound in front of her.

"I want to hear that you're mine."

"I am yours, Haden—only yours." She moaned loudly as my tempo picked up. "You own me."

"Yes, I do." I groaned. "I have only ever belonged to you." Fuck, I wanted to claim her. I wanted to tell her just how much I loved her.

I could feel my own pleasure increasing. I would not be lasting long.

"Haden, please, I'm going to cum."

I watched her face in the mirror, her teeth sinking into her plump bottom lip, her eyes pure white. Her starlight was seeping out from her, illuminating the room. The sudden lightning outside made me smile at her. I looked like a monster behind her, with my eyes black, my chest sweaty, and my face in hard lines as I focused on making her cum harder than she ever had before.

"Haden..."

"I know, Della. Let's cum together."

I sank deep into her before pulling out and surging forward at a pace that would have me releasing in no time. Della was making noises that only pushed me closer. Her hips shoved back into every thrust.

"Cum for me, Della."

The red flush crept up her chest as her eyes tightened. Her fingers dug into the floor. The lights in the house flickered. The ground below us shook, and her body fucking glowed like a damn star. Her orgasm had me sinking deep into her to find my own release as she clenched around me. She called my name out to the heavens as I buried myself inside of her and came so hard that my frost magic exploded around us, sprinkling us with snow that instantly melted on our hot skin.

I fell to the floor on my back, and Della smiled as she broke her ice cuffs and stared down at me. Her eyes traced over my face slowly.

"For fuck's sake, Haden, I do not know how I will ever get tired of having you."

"I hope you never get tired of me, Della, because I can do this for the rest of my existence."

She gave me a look that I wasn't sure how to decipher.

"You are so handsome," she whispered softly. Her fingers pushed my hair back before she kissed me gently. When she pulled back, her eyes stared into mine with curiosity.

"You're beautiful, Storm. You remind me of the most perfect piece of art."

Her eyes flashed with something.

"The void is magic, isn't it?" she asked innocently. "You said it wasn't, but it is."

Oh, my clever fucking girl.

She was probing for answers without being obvious. She was trying to seduce answers from me. Gods, that made me proud. I watched her look over me like she missed me. I swallowed hard because I knew how hard it was for her to have me leave for 300 years. She thought I didn't remember her, or us, or how fucking beautiful we were together.

"I don't know," I lied.

My answer made a look of hurt flash in her pretty eyes. She looked away from me, then stood up and slipped her clothes back on.

"What's wrong?" I already knew what was wrong. Me. I was breaking her heart.

"Why are you not being truthful with me?" Her gaze finally found mine, and I saw the tears in her eyes.

"I'm not lying to you." I fucking lied through my teeth and hated myself for it.

"Do you not trust me?" She frowned when I didn't answer her. "Do you think of me like I think of you?"

She was using my own damn words against me and thought I wouldn't remember. *Please, don't do this, Storm.* Della frowned and stared at her hand, fiddling with something. I stood up and slipped on my clothes.

I stilled when I saw what it was. My ring. She was still wearing it, and something about knowing that made my chest tighten. I watched her face go through so many emotions before she looked at the ground.

"That was your whole plan when you lured me out to play with you. You thought you'd fuck answers out of me?" I was irritated that she was suspicious of me. She was too damn observant for her own good. Della looked up at me, and the hurt in her eyes would stay with me forever.

"So, you don't trust me," she whispered.

I just stared at her, wishing she would drop it.

"Answer me!" Tears were falling down her pretty face.

"I have nothing to say," was all I could come up with.

"If you do not want to tell me the truth right now, then I will leave, and I will not come back," she threatened.

"You're being irrational," I said angrily. "Drop it."

"Last chance." She swiped the tears from her cheeks and swallowed hard as her anger turned into confusion. "Why won't you tell me? You love me, so please, stop lying to me. I won't be angry with you."

This questioning needed to stop.

"I don't fucking love you." I bit out and the moment the words left my mouth, I wished I could pull them back to me. Della stumbled back as if I had struck her with my hand. Gods, her devastation slammed into the mating bond and sucked all the anger from me. When I stepped toward her, she stepped away. I had broken her heart.

"Storm..." I pleaded.

"Fine, then I will stop wasting my time coming here." She tried to sound angry, but it came out broken-hearted.

"Please, I didn't mean to say that."

When she looked at me, I knew I had fucked up big time. She had loved me for hundreds of years, and I just took the one thing she held onto—the fact that we loved each other.

"Well, you did say it. And it must have come from some-where."

"Just stay with me, and we can talk." I asked, reaching out to her. My mating bond was desperate for me to fix the injury I had caused her.

"You mean you will just keep telling me lies and think I am too stupid to know?" I closed my eyes tightly and tried to control my emotions. When I opened them, Della looked like she was going to bolt. The longer I stood here silently, the more I could see the hope fade from her eyes.

She looked away from me, turning to wipe her eyes. I could hear the soft sniffles she was trying to keep in, but her shoulders shook silently with her silent sobs.

"I was still all in," she whispered without looking at me.

Tears immediately stung the back of my eyes as her words hit me exactly like she intended them to. I thought she would keep pushing it, but she summoned her star mist and left without another word, making me feel like complete shit. I ran my hands down my face. I knew I should stay away, but the heavens and hell knew I couldn't.

CHAPTER 29

HADEN

Della hadn't been back in ten days. I was starting to get worried. I had called for her. I had begged for her to come back, but she had not returned to me. I refused to leave and take the void with me. This was just complicating everything when I needed to focus on my purpose for being here.

Ardella, the Goddess of Life, was going to destroy everything the old gods and heavens had set into place. Her actions were going to defy the laws of existence, and I needed to make sure she did that. But I couldn't focus on that. All I could think of was her heartbroken face. The longer she was away from me, the more I felt like shit. If ten days felt this bad, what would forever feel like? Then again, what had 300 years felt like for Della?

I hadn't left my bedroom all morning, but when I heard Remiah humming, I decided to get up. I slipped on my clothes and walked into the living space.

Remiah was dancing and humming in the kitchen. I froze when star mist appeared. *Della.* I stepped forward but stopped when a tall man with black and bronze hair stepped from the mist and stared at me. He had the same eyes my Storm did.

His gaze flickered over me and then to Remiah before coming back to me. He looked terrified of me. He shifted his body slightly, the flowers in his hand making a noise that alerted Remy.

"Mikel!" she said excitedly. "What a nice surprise." Remiah wrapped her arms around him, hugging him with her whole body.

"I'm sorry I showed up uninvited." He smiled at her. "I missed you too much."

His eyes flicked over to me and nervously held my gaze.

"You look like Ardella," I said.

His whole body went rigid. He straightened his back as he looked over at me.

"You've met my sister?"

"Yes. She comes and says hi to us every now and then. She helps us out."

"Yes, Remiah told me." He nodded. "I'm glad my sister has been kind to you."

You have no idea.

Mikel looked confused as he looked over at me. Could he tell something was not quite right with me?

"Dells mentioned she met Remy, but she didn't mention that she met you." Mikel frowned slightly. Obviously, he didn't think Della would keep secrets. "I'm sorry, why is she visiting you both?" he asked.

"Didn't you ask her?" I looked at him.

"She made it sound like she ran into Remiah by chance."

I smiled at him.

"You can ask her."

"Or you can tell me." He glared.

Remiah was watching the exchange between us, confused.

"Why are you upset?" she asked him. "I told you before that your sister seems to like my brother."

Mikel looked at me and frowned as he thought of something. I gave him a small smile. He seemed to snap out of it when he glanced at Remiah.

"Sorry, I didn't realize you meant like as in she had feelings for him," he said, confused. His eyes traced over me again. Did Della tell him about us before I died? He reached down and kissed Remiah. "Sorry, Della and I have been having a hell of a week with work stuff." Mikel turned to me and walked forward. "It's nice to meet you, Haden. Remiah hasn't stopped talking about how great you are."

I reached out and shook his hand, which he squeezed more than necessary.

I smiled at him. "It's nice to meet you, Mikel; unfortunately, Della never mentioned you."

His jaw tightened.

"Haden Vale, why are you being an asshole?" Remy snapped.

"It's alright," Mikel said.

I tried to keep my curiosity to myself, but the bond was demanding to know where she was. Who was she with? Was she alright? Did she feel as terrible as I did?

"Where is your lovely sister? We haven't seen her around."

Mikel's eyes traced over me, and something like concern flickered through his eyes. Well, that didn't make me feel better. He ran his hand through his black hair.

"She is at home feeling a bit down lately. I'm sure she will come back when she is ready."

She misses me. Or rather, I broke her heart. I nodded and looked at Remy.

"I've got some things to do. I'll be back later."

I headed out of the house and made my way deep into the woods so I would not be seen by Mikel. I summoned my starlight magic, and when it disappeared, I was standing outside of Della's home in the sky. The large home was made mostly of glass, making it easy to see everything inside, especially because it was dark up here in the sky. I looked over my shoulder to see the view of the stars from up here.

It felt like the heavens. It felt... odd.

I walked around the house looking for her. After a moment, I came to the window outside of her bedroom. Ardella was in bed, and by the steady rise and fall of her chest, I could tell that she was sleeping. I used my magic to appear in her room. Slowly, I walked up to her bed and stared at her pretty face. As soon as my gaze landed on her, my bond calmed down and the tension left my body.

Her room smelled like her, making my chest ache with longing. Della was wearing a man's tunic, and jealousy instantly reared its ugly head. I wanted to wake her and demand she take it off, but as I leaned down toward her, I could smell my own scent coming from it. I swallowed hard as I realized it was mine from a long time ago. Confusion filled me. How often did she sleep in this?

I glanced around the room and paused when I recognized a drawing on her desk. I walked over to it and traced the lines of the house I had drawn all those years ago. The home I wanted to build for us, back when I was stupid enough to think I could have both Della and retribution on the stars. Now I know better. Sighing, I set it down and opened the top drawer of her desk just to be nosy. It was overflowing with letters. I grabbed one of them before looking over my shoulder at her.

She was still sound asleep, so I opened the letter, not caring about her privacy. Someone was writing her letters that she thought were important enough to keep. I unfolded the sheet of paper and scanned the words, my heart immediately breaking.

> Today proved to me that no matter how much time passes, it will never be enough to get over you. Sara and Holden got married, and I was happy for them. But if I'm honest, all I could think about was how we were supposed to do that too. I couldn't even stay for the whole celebration. I have not stopped crying.

I feel as if I am dying, slowly suffocating without you. And even though I know it is impossible, I sometimes wish gods could die. What am I supposed to do? I have an existence of this heartbreak and longing. I feel as though I am in hell, being punished for loving you.

And even though it is crazy, I still hold out hope that maybe the heavens and the hells will hear my pleading for you and show mercy on me. That maybe they will give you back to me. But each year that passes, that hope slowly shrinks inside of me.

I am all in.

-Always your Storm

I opened another letter and realized they were all for me. My heart raced as I desperately wanted to rip each one open and devour her thoughts. I grabbed one from down at the bottom. Its color was no longer white but yellow and faded from time. Slowly, I opened it, knowing I was a glutton for punishment.

All that I see when I close my eyes is a life I no longer get to have. You have only been gone for 434 days, and I feel like I can't remember the way your voice sounds anymore. Your memory haunts me with everything I do. All I can think is that you will never get to experience anything again.

I will never kiss you. I will never laugh with you. I will never fight with you. I will never marry you. I will never have children that get your artistic abilities or pretty, stormy eyes. I will never get more memories with you.

I have cursed the stars every day since they took you. Why must I be punished for loving you too much? Shouldn't they want me to be happy with whoever I choose? And maybe I will get you back, but how long must I go through this torture?

I spend my days sitting in my room, and when that becomes too much, I go to our home. The one you started building, I still work on it. I rebuilt everything you had up before it collapsed. And I am determined to see that this dream of yours gets completed. Maybe I am hopeful that when you come back to me, I will have something to give to you even though you will not know the significance.

That might be the only thing keeping me go-ing—that damn house. I keep thinking that we will need a home to live in. A home like your parents', where it is filled with your art-work, and you can tell it was a home built with love. It is a way to stay close to you, and I can't wait for you to see it one day.

I'm all in.

-Always your Storm.

I folded the letter carefully as the tears stung my eyes. Turning around, I watched her and felt overwhelming emotions. I was not used to feeling things like this when I was void. She worked on the house for us. I swallowed hard as I tried not to let this affect me. But I knew deep down that this meant more than anything else she may have done.

She stirred in the bed, and I quickly put the papers back and disappeared from her room.

When my magic disappeared, I was in the field where the house I was building used to stand. I remembered it collapsing that night. So, I took a deep breath and turned toward where it stood before. My breath left my lungs as I saw that it stood, completed. It was just as I had drawn it, down to every detail. Fuck, could I really go in there and see what she did for me without getting too emotional?

Part of me had locked this dream away deep in my mind and heart so I did not have to feel the grief. I had been too reckless back then. Della made me think things could be different. I wanted things to be different. I wished there was a way to have Della and complete my duty, but Della was part of the plan, and it was already in motion. But fuck, I did not want to do this to her anymore.

My gaze swept across the land it sat on, and I could see the memories of Della and I playing out in front of me. My chest ached with grief. I lost that life too, and I knew I wouldn't get to have it now, but if I could, I would have done it with her.

I had to see it.

Once.

Slowly, I walked up the stone path she laid out with flowers on either side. As I ascended the stairs, I admired how well she did. The front porch was long and wrapped around the house, and she even carved flowers and vine detailing into the posts. I traced my fingers over it and sighed heavily.

I gripped the handle to the door and pushed it open. Emotions slammed into me as I took in the space. I walked through it, admiring the woodwork and the furnishings she had collected over the years that were a perfect combination of us. I moved through the seating area and into the space I wanted to see the most.

I rounded the corner and let out a shaky breath when I walked into the kitchen. She had saved the cabinets that I made but added a few more to them. I smiled softly when I saw the makeshift stool I had made so she could sit with me. She kept it. Turning, I gazed out of the large window, admiring how the sunset reflected off of the smooth surface of the pond.

Where I asked her to marry me.

"I can't believe she did this," I said to myself. I made my way upstairs. This was the part of the home I had never worked on. I never really had a vision for the rooms or how many to have, so I was excited to see what Della saw for it. When I got to the landing, I could see two doors on each side of the hallway and one at the end.

One by one I opened the doors to see bedrooms that were empty, waiting to be filled by a family that would never happen. I hesitated when I reached the end door, knowing that it was supposed to be our bedroom. I opened the door, and my mouth fell open at the large space. It had hardly any furniture in it, but Della had made the entire wall out of windows so we could see the pond and mountains in the distance.

The room had its own fireplace in the corner with shelves for books lining the wall. I saw a door to the left and figured it was a washroom. But my eyes stung and tears fell when I saw the art table she had set up in the other corner. Love and self-hatred pumped through me. Della had always been too good for me, and this just confirmed it. I did not deserve her. She was here building us a home for a future that would never happen, and I was using her to punish the gods and stars.

I had foolishly let myself believe once before that I could have both her and vengeance, and all that got me was six stab wounds before dying. I closed my eyes, and I could almost picture a life where I was a better man, and Della would never be betrayed by me. We would've been so fucking happy. I could've made her happy if I was born differently.

My throat was tight as I tried to swallow down the emotions. Tears fell down my face as I looked at this bedroom that seemed to mock me. My chest ached as I thought of all the memories we could have made here. I stared out of the window to the pond and thought of that morning I proposed to her. Would fate have changed on its own if we got married? The mating bond between her and Holden could've died and transferred to me. I ran my hand through my hair and sighed. It didn't matter. Even if it would have, Della would kill the bond as soon as she figured out I was a liar.

Maybe I should have left her alone. Holden could've made her happier than I ever could. I could've chosen a different god or goddess to manipulate. That would have made all of this easier. At least then I would be fighting my feelings of loving my enemy and making sure I fulfilled my duty even if it was at the cost of losing her forever.

I needed to get out of here. A woman who was too good for me had built this because she thought this future would happen, but I knew better. I couldn't even let myself admire the perfect home as I left it, slamming the door shut and running—running from my past, from the woman I was destroying, and from the hurt and devastation I felt that I was responsible for.

After a minute, the air around me shifted into something heavy—evil. I stopped running and closed my eyes, almost scared to open them. When I did, I scanned around me, fearing who I would see. I sighed when I saw them. Six cloaked figures were standing in front of me, waiting for answers that I didn't have.

"Haden," the one in the middle said with a bite of annoyance in her voice. "Have you figured out what Della's treason is? What sets this whole fucking thing off?"

"No."

They all stepped forward at once.

"Are you lying to us?"

"Why the fuck would I be lying?" I snapped.

They chuckled softly.

"Because you are protecting *her*." They were silent, wanting me to confess to this, but they could fuck off. "Do we need to remind you of what happened the last time you went off course?"

My jaw clenched tightly.

"In fact, wasn't it this very spot that you bled out and died?"

Memories of Della trying desperately to save my life plagued me, making my whole body tense with my own grief.

"I can't see into her future anymore. I do not know; it could take years to figure out. Maybe try a little fucking patience."

They were dead silent, and I could feel the tension running off of them.

"You better not be using this as an excuse to do what you did last time. She is not yours to keep. This isn't some fucking fairy tale. You get her future to stay on course with your first vision of her, and the old gods will be forced to step in. Which is exactly what we want. You don't get to plan a future with her like you tried last time."

"I'm not protecting her. I am trying to get close to her so I can figure out what she is up to."

The figure in the middle took two steps forward and I knew it was Elra. Her cloaked head tilted to the side as she assessed me.

"You need to keep in mind that once Ardella breaks this law, then it will give us permission to come back to the realm for good. These heavenly gods will not be able to keep us out again. You can *not* interfere in her fate."

"Trust me, I have not forgotten," I snapped. "Are we done with this conversation?"

"No, we have found out from another source that this issue with Della comes after Thea Alzara breaks her curse."

I nodded.

"She isn't even cursed yet, is she?" I asked. I didn't understand what was so important about this Thea in all of this.

"No, but it is coming very soon," she confessed. "This could take years for her to break the curse, and we do not need you getting caught up in your life with Ardella. You will not come back to the surface until after Thea breaks her curse. Nice Haden needs to be in control. And you must not influence him like last time."

"He is going to get attached to her." There was no way any side of me could resist her.

"No, she is about to destroy his heart, remember?" I didn't need to see Elra to know she was smiling. "Do we need to bind you inside?"

"Good fucking luck," I hissed.

"We can kill you again. Would you like to watch her go through her grief for you once more?"

Fuck no. I never wanted her to go through that again.

"Fine. I will go away until Thea breaks her curse."

They disappeared without another word, and I felt so fucking angry that I could kill the entire realm. They were pretty fucking stupid if they thought that keeping me hidden away was going to help anything. No matter what side of me is present in the moment, it will always be attached to her. But they didn't know she was my mate, and that was one secret I would not tell them. The real question was, will Della forgive me when she knows that she broke divine laws for me, and I used it against her?

No, she wouldn't, and I hated myself for it.

CHAPTER 30

HADEN

My bedroom felt empty as I sat here thinking of how my time with Della was running out. I was a desperate man. I grabbed the mating bond that floated in front of me and yanked on it incessantly. She would think the bond was calling her and never suspect that I knew what she was—my mate. In a sick twist of fate, the heavens decided that we should be bound. Maybe it was an attempt to protect her from me. Or me from her?

I tugged and tugged on my mating bond. My time was running out with Storm, and she was ignoring me still. It had been two days since I snuck into her home. I refused to let the void disappear for possibly years until I saw her again. My mating bond would never forgive me if I left her so sad. Not that she would know I was gone. At least she'd have me in a sense.

It didn't take long for her to come. As soon as her star mist disappeared, I jumped up and hugged her tightly. Della's arms wrapped around me and squeezed hard.

"I'm sorry."

Della pulled back and stared at me. Her pretty eyes glancing over my face with confusion.

"What is wrong?"

I should have known that she would pick up on my emotions. I smiled at her and brushed her hair from her face.

"I missed you."

"Did you?" she asked, making me pause. "Or is this some sort of manipulation?"

I froze. How much did she already know?

"I'm not manipulating you." I frowned.

"That means nothing. You could be, and I would not be any wiser, right?"

"Right," I confessed, which caught her off guard.

"You are keeping things from me." Her voice was so hurt.

"Yes, but you are a clever girl; you knew that already."

Her eyes filled with tears as she looked at me. Please, don't cry, Storm. She looked away from me like she would be able to hide the tears from me.

"Why?"

"I cannot tell you." I wouldn't because I didn't know what her intentions were yet. I did not know if she was the villain in this story, but everything pointed to yes. She couldn't find out too much, or she would know who I was and stop me.

"You remember things when you are void."

I didn't answer her.

"Fine, then tell me what you are. I know you aren't a fae." She turned to me, her eyes burning pure white. God, she was fucking beautiful. "Tell me anything, Haden."

"There is nothing to tell." I begged her to drop it.

She let out a long, heartbroken sigh. Her shoulders slumped as her eyes faded to a dim silver. Della looked anywhere but at me. I watched the wheels in her mind spinning, desperate to come up with anything to convince me to change my mind.

"I need to talk to you about something that will make no sense to you until it happens."

She looked at me oddly.

"You had a vision."

"Yes, and it involves you." I frowned. I ushered her to sit on the edge of the bed and stood in front of her. "Something odd is about to happen to a woman you have never met before. Her name is Thea Alzara. When you are called to her, her mate Cassius will beg you to let her stay."

Della's eyes stared at me, full of confusion.

"You will make her stay."

"I don't take her soul?"

"No. You do whatever you need to to make sure she stays alive. Do you understand?"

"Yes, but why?"

"She is important," I sighed. "The stars want you to do this."

"Why does it feel like you are going to disappear?" she said with a frown. "If you are in danger, I will save you."

I reached forward and brushed my hand across her face. It was difficult to picture her as a villain in my story when she loved me like this.

"I don't need saving, Storm."

Her eyes filled with tears.

"I do not want to live without you again. Please. Do not leave me."

Too late for that. I knew what was about to happen to Remiah and I, but I could not change the fate. This is when I stopped being able to really see what happens in Della's future. I do not know what she does to try and save me, but it is important. I cannot interfere with fate.

I knelt and wiped the tears from her cheeks. I leaned forward and kissed her softly.

"I'm sorry I said I didn't love you," I whispered. "I do love you."

Her eyes immediately filled with tears.

"I love you so much, Storm, and I hope deep down inside of you that you knew I really did."

"I love you too, Haden." She leaned forward and kissed me. I pulled back and traced my fingers down her face.

"You will leave here tonight, and you will not remember me anymore." I could give her this little piece of information. It was true, but it was more like she wouldn't remember my void side. "I have loved you in my first life and this one."

"Haden, you do remember," she cried and hugged me. "Please, I love you, don't leave me. I will fix whatever is going on."

I pulled back and gave her face a once-over, knowing that this fate was forged in stone, and by changing it, I did not know what the consequences were. I had to let this happen.

"You did so good on the house, Storm. It was exactly as I pictured it for us."

Her gaze traveled over my face with confusion.

"Haden..." she cried loudly, and it broke my heart.

"Kiss me, Storm."

She leaned forward and kissed me deeply. She pulled me to her, tilting her head to the side and pushing her tongue against mine. Della was desperate because she knew I was not changing my mind. I pulled her to me as I used my magic to jump into her beautiful mind and immediately began digging into her memories, looking for anything to do with me being void.

I groaned as she yanked me backward on the bed. Our mouths were desperate as my magic started scrubbing away the memories I didn't want her to have. I erased her memory with Brim, with her asking my parents about me, all of her suspicions of me.

Tears stung my eyes as the visions of us played like a perfect story in her mind. I gripped her jaw as I hesitated with the last memory I needed to scrub away. For just a moment, I wanted to live a little longer where Della and I were still this—perfect. But in reality, we were never supposed to find one another: enemies, polar opposites, forbidden. Maybe that was why it felt too good. Because I knew this was not written by heaven or hell. We chose to be with each other and changed fate so it would happen. But now I was about to destroy her anyways.

Maybe I should have left her alone 500 years ago when I saw her. If I hadn't messed with her mind back then, maybe this would have ended better for her. Even as the thought crossed my mind, I knew I didn't regret it. I started scrubbing the image of me from her mind as I told her to save Thea. I left enough of the memory that she would follow through, but she would have no idea why.

I pulled back and stared at her. Her tear-filled eyes looked back at me like she loved me more than anything. In another life, maybe we could have been happy together. In another life I would have gotten to marry her; I would have shown her how much I love her. Maybe in another life we wouldn't be ripped apart by what we were. I ran my hand down her pretty face.

"Please," she whispered in one last attempt.

"I am all in," I said just so I could watch her pretty face soak in those important four words one last time.

"I love you more," she whispered.

Tears fell down my cheeks, glowing black. Della gasped when she realized what I was.

"Haden, you're—"

Then I scrubbed the last minute away from her mind permanently as black tears fell on her pretty dress. I wiped it all away as if it never happened. I tried to convince myself that she would be safer this way, but I also knew that I needed her to forget for me. After I scrubbed everything away, I manipulated her mind to go into a deep sleep. Her eyes fluttered closed as she lay under me.

I rested my head on her chest and cried, letting myself grieve her without holding back. This was it, the beginning of the end of us. All the pain and suffering we had already gone through, and it was just the beginning. I didn't want to leave her again, but I had no choice. This was bigger than me, and the plan couldn't be stopped.

And I begged the heavens and the hells to not do this to me. I did not want this to be a permanent goodbye. Her scent filled me, and I feared that I would forget what she smelled like. Leaning forward, I kissed her softly before picking her up in my arms and taking her to her bedroom. I used my magic to put her in my old tunic before tucking her into bed.

I brushed my fingers through her hair before kissing her forehead softly.

"I do not understand where we go wrong, Storm, but it is about to destroy a realm. Our love is the end of everything we know. *You* destroy everything. What are you about to do because of me?"

I wanted to wake her up and tell her not to save me.

I was not worth this.

But Della was the key to everything. I needed her to fall from the grace of the stars to free me and my siblings.

I picked up her hand that had my ring on it. The red jewels glowed brightly when I touched it. I kissed her hand. My greedy eyes traveled over her face once more.

"I love you more."

Then I left her room and the good memories of us with her.

)★★★)★★★)

For fuck's sake, I felt ill. My head pounded as I sat up in my bed. I glanced around, not remembering what happened last night. My mind strained to remember what I was doing last. Gods, I couldn't remember anything from the last few days.

I heard Remiah laughing in the kitchen and stood up and dressed. When I came out, Della was smiling at me.

"Morning, sleepy," she said. "I came earlier, but you looked so tired. So, Remiah is teaching me how to make your favorite dessert."

I looked at her, feeling confused about why she wasn't angry with me but not remembering why I felt that way. Slowly, I approached her, and she leaned in and gave me a soft kiss.

"What's wrong?" she asked, looking me over.

"I don't feel very good," I said truthfully. Della immediately became serious, her magic going frantic around me. After a moment, she frowned.

"You aren't sick, but there is some serious tension in your mind. I can make you some tea."

Before I could say anything, she had a tray of tea in front of her. She picked up the cup and handed it to me.

"Thanks, Storm." I smiled and drank it. Instantly, my shoulders relaxed. I glanced around at the mess she and Remiah were making as I stood at the counter and watched them. My gaze kept going to see how carefree and happy Della looked.

I couldn't stop smiling at her as she set a plate of small pastries down in front of me. She was so pretty.

"Be honest if they taste horrible."

I picked one up and took a big bite from it. Fuck, that was good. I took another bite, and she smiled brightly.

"Good?" she asked.

"So fucking good, Storm."

She grabbed one and took a bite. Her eyes widened.

"Holy shit, this is good."

Remiah picked one up and stuffed it into her mouth. She hummed in approval and shook her head.

"We did good," she said with a mouth full of pastry.

Della and Remiah began laughing. I couldn't help but think how perfect this day was starting. Della glanced at me, her eyes drifting over my face. I smiled at her before grabbing her and pulling her in for a hug.

Remiah smiled brightly at the two of us.

Suddenly, the wood popped in the fireplace, making me jump and turn quickly. My heart pounded with fear, and I wasn't sure why I was having such a reaction to the noise.

"Are you alright?" Della asked as she looked at the fire.

"Yeah, I just feel jumpy for some reason." I frowned. Della looked up at me, and her expression changed.

"Maybe it's because you know what is happening today."

I stilled and stared at Della, confused.

"What?"

"You know what today is, and you don't want it to happen." She tilted her head, her smile now filled with something... evil. I looked at Remiah, but she seemed to be frozen and unaware of whatever the fuck was happening. "You can feel it, can't you?"

"Feel what?" I asked, backing away from Della as she stalked toward me.

"That this is the beginning of the end of us." Her smile widened. "You did this to us. You did not love me enough to save me."

"I will always save you."

"Fucking liar," she sneered, her face contorting into anger. "You will be the reason for my own downfall, and for what? Because I loved you too much?"

"I love you too. I don't know what you are talking about,"
I said, panicking.

Della frowned at me, a real sadness taking over her face.

*"You could have changed my fate, but you didn't, and now
I am damned."*

I shook my head, trying to process her words.

*"I would have moved heaven and hell for you." Her glow-
ing tears fell quickly. "I would have rewritten fate for us."*

"Storm, please, I don't understand!"

*"Then wake up, Haden. Wake up and see why the noise of
the fire scared you. This is the night that you destroyed us."*

*Then she shoved me backward, and I was falling through
the stars and heavens straight for the ground.*

☽★★☽★★☽

I sat up in my bed, gasping for air. What the fuck kind
of fucked-up dream was that? Shit, I was hot. Why was I
sweating so damn much?

"Haden!" Remy yelled from her room.

My gaze immediately went to my door, and I realized I
could see smoke barreling in. The flicker of flames could be
seen under my door, and I could hear the noise of burning
wood popping like it did in my dream. Our home was filled
with flames and smoke. Shit. I got up and ran to Remy's
room only to be met with a collapsed portion of the wall.
She was trapped.

"Haden!" She cried from the other side. "Please, help me!"

"I won't leave you," I promised as I tugged and pulled on the wooden beam, but it would not budge. *Please*, I begged. Tears stung my eyes, and I began to crouch to stay away from the smoke surrounding me. I used my frost magic to try and stop the flames from moving, but it was too much for me to have any effect at all. The heat was too overwhelming for my cold. I hurried to my room and crawled out of the window, then ran around the house to Remy's window.

I jumped up and grabbed the ledge, peering through the haze inside. I saw that she was lying on the floor, unmoving. Her room had no flames like mine did, but it was filled with smoke. Fear ran through me, but the void did not come to save me with his bravery.

"Remy!" I called to her.

I hoisted myself up and through the window, dropping to the floor with a heavy thud. Pain seared through my leg, but I couldn't focus on it now. I limped over to her. As I rolled her onto her back, I could see she was still breathing.

Coughing, I picked her up and carried her to the window. With all of the strength I had left, I pushed her through it. Just as she fell through the opening, part of the roof collapsed, trapping me under a beam. Terror and smoke filled my chest. I didn't want to die. Della's face popped into my mind. I couldn't leave her now; we loved each other.

"Storm!" I yelled, hoping she would hear me. I felt my head begin to swim, though, and before I could call out again, everything faded into blackness.

CHAPTER 31

DELLA

Gods, I had been confused all day. I looked around my room because it felt different somehow, but nothing was out of place. My head ached and pounded as I tried to remember what the hell I was doing last night. But nothing came—no memories. Maybe I had passed out in bed earlier than I realized.

I glanced at my bed and frowned. I didn't even remember coming in here. Last I remember, my mating bond was going crazy. What the hell was wrong with me? I glanced out of my bedroom window and stared at the dark sky illuminated by millions of twinkling stars.

Gods, I missed Haden.

Maybe I should wait to go to Haden's house tomorrow; I'm sure he is sleeping.

But the other part of me couldn't wait. My heart pounded as I thought of him. All day, flashes of him and me together had plagued me. My stomach clenched tightly as I went to my closet. I grabbed the small, black velvet box and opened it.

My star swirled orange and silver, a symbol of our mating bond. The orange represented the color of his soul, and the silver matched mine. Tonight, I was going to tell Haden he was my fated mate. I smiled softly. I had not known if this day would ever come. I loved him so much it was all-consuming. I do not know how I had lived without him for so long.

Suddenly, Haden's voice boomed into my mind, sounding terrified. I dropped the box and left it on the ground, summoning my star mist immediately. I was at his home within seconds. Horror filled me when I saw it engulfed in flames. Fuck. I could feel death lurking closely. Someone was dying here tonight. I could feel their soul tugging me to them so I could collect them and send them on to their next destination, as was my job as the Goddess of Life.

"Haden!" I called out in a terrified voice. Panic raced through my veins as I desperately looked around for him. He had to be alright. He must be outside. He had to be safe.

"Haden, please!" I cried out as I ran toward the flames. A small movement by the side of the house had me running.

Dread filled me when I realized it wasn't Haden. It was Remiah. I dragged her farther from the house.

"Where is Haden?" I asked, panicked.

I could not lose him. Tears streamed down my face as she opened her mouth. Before she could answer me, though, I saw him.

His soul was lingering by the window, almost completely out of his body. He was watching me with sadness that made my heart stop. *Not again. Not again!*

"No!" I screamed and ran to him.

I held my hand out towards the house and then pulled it back with a hard jerk, my magic causing the side of the house to blow out.

Black smoke came billowing out, and I called the wind and rain to help me stop the flames and clear the air. Tears streamed down my face as I desperately looked for his body, his soul form watching me as I fell apart. It was not complete, though, which meant he was still alive.

"Haden!" I called into the smoke.

His nearly lifeless body was lying under a beam. With my magic, I shoved it off of him and dragged him out of the house. Tears ran down my cheeks, and I stared at his handsome face that had smudges of ash on it. I gripped his face in my hands and begged him to open his eyes. I could not lose him.

"Please, do not leave me. I love you!" I cried to the stars. "I will die if I lose you again."

I could feel him slipping away. My eyes shifted to Remy, who was unconscious. She was slipping away too. There was only one soul I was here to collect, though. I knew deep in my heart that it was Haden's, but I could not let him go. I refused to let him leave me. Haden's soul was almost gone from him. His orange form knelt next to me as he watched me sob and hold his physical body.

"Della," he whispered.

"I can only save one of you," I cried to him. I shook my head frantically because I knew what he would say.

"Save Remy," he said without hesitation.

I shook my head no. I couldn't, even if I wanted to. The thought of Haden dying and never having a life with him was soul-crushing. My mate bond would never allow such a thing—just like with Holden. I did not have control over the need to save what was mine. I would sacrifice the entire realm to save only him. But it was *his* fate to die tonight.

"Did you hear me? Save Remiah. It's alright, Storm; maybe we will meet again."

Tears burned my eyes as emotions clogged my throat. I pulled his lifeless body to me and sobbed against his unmoving chest. I could not live in that hell again. What are the chances that the heavens gave him to me again?

A painful sob tore from me as our mating bond severed and faded away. The pain was too much.

He was dead.

"Storm…" he whispered. "You have to let me go."

I didn't know what he meant until I realized I was gripping his soul in my hand.

No, why must I lose him?

Panic wrapped around my heart and squeezed until I could not think properly.

"I'm sorry, Haden, but I can't," I whispered as I held onto his soul with one hand.

I can rip souls from gods.

Avesh's words came to me out of nowhere, and I knew what to do. Lifting my other hand, I demanded that my own soul come forward. My soul ripped away from me as I called out to the heavens at the agony I was feeling. A constant stabbing sensation tore through every fiber of me as I ripped myself apart to save Haden.

"Storm, stop."

My silver soul floated in one hand, and I looked at Haden. He looked so fucking confused. Memories of holding Haden's dead body 300 years ago plagued me. I already buried him once. I already had to live in that fucking hell, and I couldn't survive it again.

"I cannot lose you ever again."

Then I ripped his soul in half, slamming the half of my soul against his before forcing it back into his body.

Then I took the rest of his beautiful orange soul and slammed it into my own chest. Our blended souls seeped into his lifeless body, illuminating it in the dark night. The pain was nearly unbearable for me as the fused souls came together inside of my chest. I knew I had broken god laws to save him, but I did not care. My silver soul intertwined with his orange one immediately, fueling it with enough power to make sure he lived. I put my hand over his chest, and it glowed gold as I seared my mating mark onto his skin, claiming him as mine so he couldn't die.

Then I turned toward Remy and hesitated for a moment. The heavens will forgive me for saving my mate, but not for disrupting the balance so much. Her soft purple soul illuminated as she began dying. Saving Haden was the only thing I could think of. I reached forward and gripped her soul, ripping it forcefully out of her to keep the balance. Immediately, I let go of her soul, and she disappeared before I could even blink.

"No!" Mikel's voice suddenly boomed behind me. His voice snapped me out of my panic. What did I do? "Remiah!" He knelt next to her and grabbed her lifeless body. Her soul had already left. She could choose to move on or stay, but I wouldn't know what her choice would be.

I watched my brother's face contort with devastation and grief—like mine looked when Haden died all those years ago. He was begging and pleading with her to open her eyes.

"I love you, please open your eyes," he cried to her. Confusion about what I did swarmed my mind so much that I did not see Haden was awake again.

"What did you do?" It was Haden's voice as he crawled out of my arms and across the ground to Remy. Our two souls twisted together within his chest. My silver soul coiled tightly around his orange as if it was a shield. Haden looked back at me, heartbreak taking over his face. "Storm?" he asked, confused.

"Haden..." I whispered as I watched the love for me in his eyes shatter when he looked at Remiah and back to me.

"Why?" His voice broke, and I shook my head. Mikel was yelling to the heavens, and the roar of the fire was overwhelming as I tried to find the words to tell Haden.

"No, no, no." Mikel sobbed loudly.

I was paralyzed by the grief in my mating bond with Haden. Then I saw the necklace Remiah wore around her neck and felt my whole world stop. Mikel's star hung on a chain and lay on her pale throat. Panic gripped me tightly. I couldn't breathe. I killed her. I took Mikel's mate.

What have I done?

I glanced up when I saw movement in the tree line, thinking it was Remiah's soul, and maybe I could make this right. I was surprised to instead see tall figures standing in the shadows, all with deep hoods pulled down over their faces. The same ones that had been here the first time Haden died. Were they the stars? They disappeared before I could comprehend what or who they were.

"I told you to save Remy, not me!" Haden glared at me as I sobbed, unable to form any words at the realization that I killed Mikel's mate. This made Mikel turn his murderous eyes to me.

"You could have saved her?" he hissed.

I kept shaking my head no because I couldn't save her. Haden had to be saved. I wasn't going to live without Haden; he was my mate. It was an impossible choice.

"Haden, please," I barely managed to choke out. "Forgive me..."

When he looked at me, I saw no emotion in his eyes, deep blue pools of nothingness. I had done that to him. The realization ripped my heart in two.

"Forgive you? I fucking hate you!" Haden yelled at me. "I wish I never met you. I wish you never talked to me. Do you hear me? I fucking hate you!" He was kneeling next to Mikel and Remiah. "I will never forgive you."

"Please…" I sobbed. Our mating bond floated between us again, but it was partially black now.

Haden turned to me again as he glared, cold hatred radiating from him so much that I could see his and Mikel's breath as they both cried over Remiah's body.

"I will never forgive you for taking my family from me. You're an evil fucking monster. I never want to see your face again. You are dead to me. Do not ever come near me again, or I will kill you."

"Haden…" I tried to breathe, but it felt like I was dying. "Don't leave me."

This pissed him off more.

Haden stood up and came forward. He gripped me hard by the back of my neck and dragged me to Remy's lifeless body, his fingers flexing so hard I thought he would snap it.

"She deserved to live, not me. Unless you can bring her back right now, then I don't care how much you cry. I will never forgive you. Bring her back now." He shoved me close to Remy, and I cried even harder. She looked beautiful, like she was sleeping. But she was dead, and I had killed her. I had killed Mikel's mate. I had taken her from him, and now, I hated myself for it. He would feel like I did for the past 300 years.

"I can't," I cried.

"You mean nothing to me. You'll leave, and I will never waste another thought on you. You fucking disgust me."

He let me go, and I fell on my back and sobbed to the stars above. I begged them for her soul to come to me so I could give it back. I wasn't thinking clearly. A moment later, Mikel's face overtook my view.

"You took her from me," he sobbed quietly. "How could you take her from me?" He cried so violently that his starlight lashed out and gripped me tightly, threatening to snap all of my bones.

"I wish to the stars that you had never been created." His words were like a dagger into my heart. I had lost everyone and everything I loved.

I sat up and saw Haden cradling his dead sister, begging her to open her eyes. He cried about how she was always the stronger one of the two of them, that he was nothing without her. He apologized for ruining their lives and that he had let a monster into their home.

My mate bond was sending waves of pain through it, punishing me because I had hurt him, because I had failed him, and now he was cursed with an existence of suffering alone. My bond was frantic for me to fix it.

"Haden, please," I whispered as I stepped toward him. I found myself begging the heavens to bring her back, and I would take her place. I did not want to see Haden upset. I didn't mean to hurt him or Mikel. I had ruined him. I had taken away everything from him in a desperate moment. My mate hated me.

"Leave!" he yelled. "I never want to see you again. My life will be better when you leave it for good."

"But I did it because I love you. I'm sorry," I sobbed.

"You think this is the act of someone who loves me? I don't want your love, Ardella. I will never love you back. You are not worthy of me. You are the last woman I could ever love in this whole fucking realm," he yelled. His eyes were filled with tears. "You have destroyed me," he whispered.

His words made me stop talking.

He was right.

I didn't deserve him.

I was a monster.

I ruined everything.

All I could do was watch him and Mikel beg Remiah to come back. My mate bond swelled with suffering, and I cried out at the pain it caused. My hand came up to grip my aching chest. I froze at what I saw on my arm, though. There were three black marks in the shape of stars that seemed to be seeping into my veins. The reality of what I had done to save Haden crashed around me. I was now marked by the heavens for treason against the gods. I had broken the divine law by betraying not only my brother, a fellow god, but my fated mate as well. This was the mark of somebody that would never be forgiven.

Haden's hatred was my penance, and I would never be able to work off my sins. The heavens had decided that I was not worthy. Slowly, I was falling from the grace of the stars and into this hell I had built myself. What would happen when I finally hit the ground and shattered?

I glanced at Haden, trying to picture him smiling at me, but every moment I ever had with him was now tainted by what I had done. A breeze swept over us, and when I looked up, a cloaked figure stood at the tree line again. I could feel their eye upon me. They had to be the stars. The heavens sent them to deliver this message.

A sob broke from me because I was now on borrowed time. But what happens to a god when their treason catches up to them? I looked at Haden once more, begging silently for him to look back at me, but he refused to meet my eyes. This was punishment for what I did 300 years ago. The stars gave him back to me to use him as punishment.

He was never going to be mine to keep. I cried to the stars to let me make this right. Whatever the cost, I would pay it.

Please look at me. Please don't hate me. I cannot lose you again, Haden.

He didn't. Haden watched Mikel hold Remiah and sob into her unmoving chest. Mikel's screams and sobs would be burned into my mind for the rest of my life. I closed my eyes, trying to get rid of the heartbreaking, soul-crushing sounds.

"Leave!" Haden's voice forced my eyes to open.

I took a step toward him; my bond was desperate. Haden's hands came up and made a wall of ice so thick and tall that I could not get through it. My heart shattered as I realized I would not get through to him. How could he ever forgive me?

I used my star mist and disappeared, intending to leave his life for good. When I landed on my knees in my bedroom, a violent scream tore from me as our mating bond tried to break. No, no, no. I gripped the mating bond between us and willed it to stay in place. *If you break this, I will find a way to bring it back,* I warned the heavens.

There was a wrath burning so violently inside of me that I could not stop my threat.

"I will turn my back on everything for him, I fucking swear it!" I yelled. "If you take this, I will destroy everything to get it back!"

The bond immediately stopped tearing and calmed down. I was filled with so much rage as I looked around. How fucking dare the heavens do this to me. I had always followed the rules and laws, and now I had lost my mate twice. My magic was swirling inside of me. Wind whipped around the room, and lightning struck the ground outside.

Papers flew from the desk as the wind knocked it on its side. My letters from over the years flew around me, mocking my pain. My head hung low at the realization of how badly I had hurt Haden. Not just him, though. Mikel too. I broke Mikel. I was so fucking angry with myself. I tried to not lose Haden, and I ended up losing him anyway.

I fell to the floor on my side, unsure if I was destroyed beyond repair this time. How could I survive this again? Not only that, but how did I mourn a man who was still alive when I knew I did not get another chance? The stars and heavens fucking hated me, and I didn't understand why. Was I cursed for what I had done 300 years ago?

The heavens did not forgive me for saving Haden.

"Why did you give him back to me if you were angry with me?" I asked the stars and heavens. *We give too much power to the stars.* Avesh's words circled my mind. But I needed someone to blame. The stars had taken Haden from me twice, and now I knew he would hate me for existence because I had claimed him.

Haden wouldn't be able to die ever again. I had cursed him with a lonely, pain-filled existence because I was a selfish woman. Tears fell from me as I lay on my floor, surrounded by the letters of a heartbroken woman who could never make this right.

Haden was not mine.

He hated me.

I hated myself.

I did not deserve to be a goddess.

I broke Mikel.

I destroy everything I try to love.

I did not know what I was supposed to live for now. I had done what I needed to so that I could save my mate.

Something deep inside of me broke. I could feel my insides being tainted with an intense wrath that wanted to climb into the heavens and hurt the stars. I groaned in pain as a shooting pain started on my wrist and climbed up the length of my right arm. When I looked, there were four black stars on my skin now, but each one was cracked and broken.

I instantly recognized them as the same markings on the picture of Diath. She had been marked by the stars for her treasons, and now so was I.

I was falling from the grace of the stars for a man who hated me.

CHAPTER 32

HADEN

My vision was blurred from tears as I stared at the mound of dirt in front of me. I had buried my sister at our favorite spot. I would not survive this grief. How could Ardella do this to me? How could she think I would ever be alright with her decision? My mind raced with thoughts, but none that made sense. I felt as if I was dreaming, and I would wake up to realize this wasn't real.

My mind and heart did not understand how Storm could do this to us. She loved me.

I did it because I love you.

Her words mocked me. This was not an act of love.

What was I supposed to do without Remy? I had no one left. I had no home. I had nothing. I lost the woman I loved, and now I hated her with the heat of a thousand suns. I would make her pay for this one day.

Tears fell from me, and sobs racked through me so violently that I didn't hear that someone else was here. I turned, expecting to see Della or Mikel. But I stared up at the six cloaked figures. They stood in a straight line in front of me. Their cloaks were black but shimmered with a dark red that looked like stars. Dread filled my chest as they hid behind their hoods so I couldn't see who they were.

"What?" I snapped to hide my fear.

It was silent for a moment, but I could feel them staring at me, watching me fall apart, and I swore they were enjoying this.

"We want to speak to the void," a woman's angelic voice said.

I opened my mouth to demand why, but I didn't get a chance. The void was already racing forward. I could feel it clawing up my spine at the request. I couldn't even fight it as it dug its claws into my bones, seeping itself into every fiber of me. I closed my eyes, welcoming the feeling of nothing taking over. I did not want to feel anything. I didn't want to face what Ardella did to me.

The shiver ran through me as my eyes opened. I stood, feeling the devastation of what happened tonight. The grief of losing Remiah was consuming, but losing Della that way was ripping me apart. I missed being able to not feel a thing as void; now emotions were a constant battle.

"What the fuck do you want?" I hissed.

"Can you fucking believe what she did?" Her voice was full of shock. No, I couldn't. "What do you feel like with half of her soul?"

"The same." I lied. I could feel something was different. Part of Della was living inside of me, and I only felt closer to her, which was probably a problem. But that made me wonder what she felt. I had watched her keep the other half of my soul. What would happen when good and evil collided inside of a goddess?

"Hmm, maybe it will change as time passes." I could feel her beady eyes on me. "She didn't even hesitate to commit treason against the heavens."

Because she fucking loved me.

I swallowed hard to keep myself in check. I couldn't let them know that I felt terrible for what I had let her do.

Mikel hated her. She hated herself, and now the other side of me hated her too. There was only me left, and I was not allowed to tell her that I loved her and understood.

"It has started, but she isn't done yet. There is still something else she does that will crumble everything. I'm just trying to wrap my mind around what the hell could be worse than ripping her soul in two and giving away a part of it—especially to you."

That was what I wanted to know too. What was Della going to do that would make her fall from the grace of the stars? It had to be terrible.

I couldn't feel her through the bond, and panic gripped me at the realization. Without being obvious, I glanced down to my chest and sighed in relief when I saw the golden bond still intact and floating. But I could see the edges of it fade into black. That couldn't be good.

"You have one more task before you disappear."

She tossed the cloak to my feet. I exhaled through my nostrils as I slipped it on. I hated this damn itchy thing. Their magic wrapped around us, and when it disappeared, I froze in my spot. We were outside of Della's home, directly in front of her bedroom.

She was lying on the floor, papers scattered around her. I looked around us when I smelled the charred ground—lightning strikes. She was devastated, and I could feel my own emotions bubbling up.

Storm.

Her body shook with sobs. I didn't want to see her like this. But they forced us into her room, and we circled around her where she had collapsed on the floor.

She opened her pure white eyes that were full of devastation. Della didn't flinch or move when she saw us, and the understanding broke me. My mate was shattered. She didn't care what happened to her. I swallowed down the tears that stung the backs of my eyes.

"Ardella, Goddess of Life, you have been marked for your treason of god laws. Your sins will demand a price; consider this a warning for what is to come." One of them spoke. Her hand instinctively rubbed her right forearm, and I stared at the four broken stars marked into her skin. The points of the stars were scattered and had seeped into her arm, making it look infected. It glowed slightly orange around each one. The heavens or old gods had already marked her.

Just like my mother.

Della looked up at me, not realizing who I was because of this stupid cloak. I twisted the red hell flower in between my fingers before tossing it next to her. She looked at the flower and closed her eyes tightly. The flowers were just a reminder to the old gods and heavens that they could not keep us locked away. It was more symbolic than anything.

"You will pay for your sins."

She didn't fight us. She didn't say a word as tears flowed down her face. Della was broken, and I knew that this was not the worst of it. Della was just getting started on her treasons, but I was not sure which one set off her destruction of everything the heavens and old gods created.

She reached forward and gripped the flower in her hand and pulled it to her chest and began sobbing. My mating bond wanted me to crawl to the ground and hold her. I want to tell her that I didn't hate her. I understood that she had no choice but to take Remiah. I hated that fate was being so cruel to her.

I did not want to see her so destroyed. I stared at her as she whispered for me to forgive her, not knowing I already had. The good side of me did not understand that Della didn't have a choice in this, and I worried what kind of damage he would do to her heart before I could come back and fix it.

If I could fix it. If I could save her and us.

This is what your precious heavens had given you, Storm. They did not think you were worth making happy. They were punishing you for loving the wrong man. You were never supposed to *actually* love me. I knew that was all my fault too. Della may be the destruction of Elloryon, but I was the fire that lit the fuse.

We were destined for heartbreak. We were destined for destruction. And we would destroy each other in the name of love. My greedy gaze drifted over her, and I got no pleasure from her sadness like the rest of them did. This damn bond was making me weak.

I needed to remember what I saw in my vision. Della was the key for us to be free. Storm was the answer to everything. And because of that, she would destroy everything the heavens and old gods had put in place. She would be the downfall of the heavenly gods and stars. Because once we escaped our prison, we would never be put back.

The seven of us would rain hell down on the realm that tried to keep us away.

There were footsteps coming from outside of her room, so I used my magic to take us outside of the house. We watched closely, expecting Mikel, but it wasn't him who entered. It was a tall man with black hair and fancy robes that stepped inside. I watched closely as he didn't hesitate to scoop Della up in his arms. She gripped him tightly—like she had done it a million times. Then he laid her in bed. My chest ached with jealousy.

"Looks like your goddess is already cozy with another man," Elra said just to piss me off, but it worked. Who was this man? We couldn't see his face.

My blood ran cold when he leaned down and pressed a kiss to her forehead—like he had done it so many times before. Della shook her head at whatever he said before sitting up and hugging him against her. My wrath was getting to a boiling point. I was going to lose it.

I wasn't sure which one of them used their magic to take us back to the field where I buried Remiah. But as soon as my feet were planted on the ground, I ripped the cloak off and tossed it aside. I wanted to go right back to her. I wanted to pull her out of the dark storm inside of her and remind her she was good, she was kind. That man was too familiar with *my* mate.

"You will scrub this memory from your brain enough that your *nice* side can't remember."

Fuck her and her jab at me, but I was in no mood. My wrath was becoming almost uncontrollable, but I nodded.

"We have found the trifecta." She slipped off her hood, and Elra's blonde hair fell over her shoulders. Her red eyes stared at me with a smile on her pretty face. Nothing but a lurking sense of evil filled her eyes.

"Who is it?"

"A royal couple who have nearly every sin running through them already. They are greedy, full of wrath, and envious of everyone. They are both lustful—leaving their marriage to find pleasure in others. They are gluttonous; you should see the excess of their castle, and it is so fucking ugly, too." Her eyes flickered to me as the rest of them let their hoods down.

I didn't bother looking over them. I watched Elra.

"Way too fucking prideful. But one thing they are not is sloth. However, we found the perfect man to step in and complete their sins. His name is Prince Jesper of Kizar, and he is the laziest royal I have ever witnessed."

"Who is the couple?" I asked again.

"King Luren and his wife Gwyn of Cerithia." She smiled. "Thea's father and stepmother."

That's why they were so obsessed with Thea being star-blessed. Della had created a goddess, not knowing that my siblings thought she would help us. My visions of Thea showed her as a monster, causing destruction as she stood in a colosseum ripping men apart with hardly lifting a finger. Maybe I shouldn't have told my siblings that a goddess was born due to sin—her father strayed from his marriage for greed, for power. A man that evil could not produce a goodhearted woman. And Della had star-blessed her without knowing.

"Thea is the first goddess born of sin, and your little girlfriend made it happen. She will be important to our plan. You will find a way to befriend Thea and manipulate her into being on our side."

"How am I supposed to do that when the other side of me won't remember?" I asked.

"You'll figure it out," Elra said, with her bitchy attitude.

"You do realize Thea may not end up like we did? What happens to your plan when you find out she is *good-hearted and nice?* We don't need them to raise hell in Elloryon. Della is already falling from grace, and when that happens, we will be released from hell for good."

"Then she will fall with the rest of the gods. And it will benefit us to have the fae start hating the gods so we can use them. We still don't know what magic we will have besides our starlight." Elra stared too intently at me. "But with a father as evil as Luren, I do not know how she will ever resist the dark side of her. Unless her mother is a fucking saint or something." Elra rolled her eyes.

"We will give the gods a choice: join us or die. Besides, we still need to find all of the old gods that were there when we were cast into hell for the sins of our fucking parents. Because they are the ones that did this to us. Abram gave us this fate, and we will kill him for it. And the heavenly gods will pay for not standing up for us. Then we will take over everything. We will bring hell to Elloryon so everyone can know the life we were damned with."

I looked at her and didn't say anything. She frowned at me, but I knew it was to mock me.

"Do we need to worry that you will interfere with your whore when you come back?"

Well, that was the last thing I needed for my patience to snap. I pulled my fist back and punched my sister in her smug face. She fell to the ground, laughing at my outburst.

"Watch yourself, Elra," I sneered.

She stood up and laughed as she wiped the blood from her cut lip. I could see that she was pleased to see me lose my shit. Violent bitch. Elra glanced around at our other siblings before looking at me.

"You will not come forward until after Thea breaks her curse. In fact, I think you will not be allowed to come out until you see Della for the first time after the curse breaks."

What an odd request. My gaze flickered over her face to see if I could pick up anything from her.

"Why? You know something and aren't telling me."

"Well, then call it even, Haden, for deviating from the plan the first time around."

"I paid for that already. You fucking killed me; do you not remember?" I glanced around at our siblings. "Each of you stabbed me for my sins, and I had to go through the painful fucking process of being reborn."

Elra smiled, as did our siblings. Sick fucks.

"Well, we don't want to wait so long again, so let's all stick to the plan this time."

"Are we done with this pointless fucking conversation?" I clenched my fists at my sides to stop my wrath from taking over completely.

"Yes, we'll see you when we see you, *Wrath*."

Her greed-filled eyes stared into mine before they disappeared. Fucking heathens. I glanced back to where I buried Remiah and frowned.

He would never forgive Storm for this. I paced back and forth as I tried to figure out what to do. I knew, deep in my tainted soul, that I would destroy her while I was gone. I ran my hands down my face and stared up at the heavens.

I raised my hand and flipped the stars off.

"Fuck you for doing this to her!" For doing this to me. I closed my eyes and hung my head. I couldn't help but recognize that the stars were very fucking clever. They thought that by making me her mate, I would save her. But they were also willing to sacrifice her for the greater good of the gods if I refused.

I sighed heavily as I waited for anything, anyone, to pop out and tell me what the fuck I was supposed to do. After a moment, I gave up. This was supposed to happen. Della was supposed to become the villain, and I would lose her no matter what. I should be happy that when I retreat deep inside of myself, the nice side of me would destroy her.

Maybe she will get the fucking hint to not love me. She needed to hate me because at some point she was going to find out what I did. Storm was going to know that before she changed our fate, I had already done the same thing. But maybe that was my punishment.

I was never supposed to *actually* love her.

The Goddess of Life and the God of Wrath should have never crossed paths—we should have never fallen in love. Now Della had half my soul, and I wondered what would happen to her. What would happen to the realm now that my mate took half my soul and damned herself with it? Would she kill me when she realized I was a God of Hell?

She was in love with a monster, and the day she figured it out would be the end of us. But would I survive the wrath of a goddess who loved and sacrificed everything for the wrong man?

CHAPTER 33

HADEN; 7 YEARS LATER

My body ached as I opened my eyes. I glanced up at the cliff high above me, the one I had just hurled myself off of. Like all the other attempts to end it all, I failed and didn't die. Fucking Ardella had stolen my only way out of this shitty life when she saved me.

I groaned as I stood up like I hadn't just jumped from a cliff. My body ached, but I could not die, no matter how many times I tried. It had been seven years since Ardella took everything away from me.

Images of her crying and begging me not to leave her plagued me, but I shoved them away.

Her words from that night replayed over and over in my head. My chest ached like it did every time I thought about what she did to me. Part of me couldn't believe that I made it seven years without her. Then the logical part of my brain kicked in. I should not miss a woman who was a cruel, heartless monster.

"I fucking hate you," I hissed to the sky, hoping she heard me. "I hope you are fucking miserable wherever you are. You are a coward to never show your face to me!"

She had not shown herself once in the past seven years. I didn't feel her lurking in the shadows, and I hadn't felt her close to me since the night she murdered Remy. I walked through the silent woods toward the small cabin I lived in. It was secluded and away from everyone, far from my old life.

Ardella was probably living a wonderful fucking life. She had probably forgotten about how she murdered Remiah and that she ripped apart my entire fucking heart and lit it on fire. I hated myself for missing her. I hated myself for wondering where life could have been now if she hadn't destroyed us.

I sighed heavily as the tugging in my chest became too much. Gods, it felt like I was going to fucking die. I prayed I would. This life was like living in fucking hell, my own personal one. I had just started walking again when dark clouds suddenly moved over me. For a brief moment I glanced around, wondering if it was her. Was this her storm that moved across the sunny sky? I let myself be hopeful for a moment before wrath like I had never felt before gripped that hope and tore it into tiny shreds.

Ardella did not deserve my hope. She didn't get my happiness. She didn't get to have any part of me ever again. A sudden, sharp pain deep in my chest had me bending over to catch my breath. Fuck, that hurt. When I glanced up toward my cabin, I felt dread. Loneliness was the worst torture on a soul.

The silence was the worst part of it. I woke up each morning to a deafening silence. I went to bed with the same thing. I did not look forward to anything. My life was pointless. I started walking forward again.

A flash of red stopped me immediately as I approached my cabin. A moment later, Nev popped his head around the corner. Relief filled me for a brief moment before irritation. I was not sure I could handle Nev and his crazy fucking plans today. The man was always scheming, and I did not want to be involved in it.

"You look like shit." Nev eyed me.

"Thanks." I glared. "What do I owe the pleasure of your visit to?" I sighed as I walked inside. Nev followed without an invitation, which was nothing new. The guy really fucking annoyed me, but he was the only one that seemed to know I was alive and that checked on me. It was the only time my home was not silent.

"I have a business opportunity for us." His blue eyes shone brightly.

"No thanks." I tossed my boots off and sat on my chair, where I would probably sit until I passed out. Gods, this guy really was fucking persistent. I stared up at him as he watched me curiously.

"You didn't even hear me out." Nev glared as he stole my bread and ate it. "We can make a lot of money."

"I have no use for money." I had no one to spend it on.

Nev rolled his eyes and walked toward the front door like he might leave, but instead, he shut the door and turned toward me with a mischievous smile.

"Everyone has a need for money." He watched me as I ignored him before sighing. "Alright, what about a need for a wish?"

Great, he had completely gone mad since I saw him last. I said nothing. His eyes looked at me carefully as I watched. Nev was completely crazy. I knew this, and I should have told him to get the fuck away from me. *Maybe I will move. Yeah, I could pack up my belongings and move away so he could never find me again.* Gods, that sounded fucking tempting.

"Crimson is doing trials, and the winners get a wish granted," he said.

I stared at him, wondering if I should kick him out or if I should indulge in this madness. Fuck it, I was bored.

"How hard are these trials?" I asked, intrigued.

"Hard, but Prince Jesper asked for me to go help stop one of the other contestants from finishing. He said I could bring a friend." His eyes glanced at my sad cabin before looking back at me. "It's not like you're doing anything else with your time."

Prince Jesper. Why the hell would he care about the Crimson trials? Jesper was not his father in the slightest. He would be a poor ruler when the time came, which seemed to be soon because his father was ill. *Maybe I should leave Kizar before he ruins it.* Crimson sounded nice.

"Who is the contestant we're stopping?"

"Thea Alzara from Cerithia."

Something about the name stuck out to me, but I couldn't place my finger on it. There was an itch in my brain like a memory would surface, but nothing did. Gods, I felt like this was important.

You need to go, the void said. He had gone missing after Remiah died.

Where have you been?

Nothing.

I had no idea who this woman was, and I wasn't sure why I was so fixated on her name like I knew her.

"A woman." I didn't know how I felt about this. What did it even mean, that we needed to kill her? "I don't want to hurt her."

"We don't have to kill her. We just need to fuck with her so that she doesn't finish. Come on, man, I could use a wish, and so could you."

Maybe I could wish to go back to the night of the fire. Then I could prevent it. I wouldn't have to lose Della. I could save Remy, and Della would still be mine. I wouldn't have to fight these overwhelming emotions for her. What would my life look like now if I had never lost Remy and Ardella seven years ago? Better than this hell I had been living in, this very lonely hell. The hell that made me dream of a woman I could never have every single fucking night.

"Fine."

"I fucking knew you'd pull through," he said with a smile. "Pack your bags; we're leaving in the morning." I watched him leave and said nothing else to him. A wish. I would wish to go back to the night of the fire. I would not go to sleep. I would make Remy leave and go see Mikel. I would not have to lose Ardella. I would not have to tell her I hated her even though I loved her. I would not have to live with her betrayal. I would not have to hear her tell me she loved me out of desperation. I would be able to tell her that I loved her back.

When I glanced around the cabin I was living in, reality hit me. I was completely alone. The only fae that knew I even lived here was Nev, and even that was not comforting. Della had ripped everything away from me. Not only Remiah, but the life I had imagined with Della. A life I thought I would be blessed with because of all the pain and suffering I had endured. But I didn't know my life could be so much worse than it was growing up. I didn't know that the woman I loved with every fiber of my body would completely cause havoc.

My eyes closed tightly, and Ardella's face haunted me. I tried to shake it from my mind, but I couldn't.

I hate her. *I hate her. I hate her*, I reminded myself.

☽★★★☽★★★☽

Nev's words played on repeat in my mind as I walked Thea back to her room after dinner. I knew she was uncomfortable with me following her. I was not getting any pleasure from causing her discomfort, but I needed that wish. If that meant that she had to be weirded out by me, then so be it.

"Thanks. Goodnight," she said quickly as she opened her door.

I grabbed her arm before she could leave. Fuck, I didn't like doing this.

"I'm glad you decided to form an alliance with us." I smiled.

"Let go of me," she said, struggling to get her arm free.

"I'm not the enemy here, Thea. You can trust me." I gave her a sinister look. "You do trust me, right?"

"Haden, you're hurting me. Let go." My smile only grew more wicked the more she struggled against me. Frost moved over the sleeve of her cloak. I could feel her fear.

"Is there a problem?" Cassius stood ten feet away in the shadows. I hadn't heard him, and apparently neither did she. I plastered a friendly smile onto my face and summoned my frost magic back.

"Just saying goodnight after hanging out with my girl." The phrase made my insides twist with guilt, like I was betraying Della. Which pissed me off.

"She's not your girl," he snapped back.

"Or yours, apparently." It was clear that he had some odd infatuation with her. I saw the way he watched her closely. The Crimson captain had a crush on her.

Cassius shifted his eyes to Thea before focusing on me again, his mouth in a hard-pressed line. After a moment, I lifted my hands in a sign of defeat and stepped away from her because he looked like he might rip my fucking head off.

"I'll see you tomorrow, *friend*," I said to Thea. I only made it a few steps away before Cassius hissed my name. I stopped, and we stared at each other.

"If you touch Thea like that again, I'll rip the arms from your body."

I glared at Thea over his shoulder. I knew without a doubt that he would rip me to tiny pieces for the woman. "Somebody sure is possessive over something that doesn't belong to them," I taunted him. His fists clenched, but I turned and disappeared.

I did not make it very far before I heard him coming up behind me. When I turned, Cassius' eyes were pure black. I didn't even have time to react as he grabbed me by the neck, lifting my feet off the ground. As he went to slam me onto the ground, his shadows moved us out of the castle and deep into the woods.

My back slammed into the ground, making me groan in pain. Cassius stood up and towered over me.

"Stand up so I can kick your fucking ass," he sneered.

I was looking for a fucking fight. I stood up and shot my frost magic out and tried to freeze him to his spot, but Cassius shot his shadows out to block it, which gave me the perfect opportunity to punch him in the face.

He stumbled, and I tackled his ass to the ground. I punched him again and again before he finally punched me, knocking me off of him.

"Fuck." I grabbed my face as we both struggled to stand. Cassius' chest was heaving as we stared each other down.

"I know you are here to stop her from completing the trials." There was a flash of hurt in his eyes as he said it that made me pause. Misery recognized misery. "You aren't Cerithian, so which kingdom is teaming up with Luren this time?"

I hesitated, confused. Something inside of me told me to tell him.

"Kizar."

His jaw clenched tightly.

"Jesper?" he said.

I nodded.

"That little fucking bastard. What did he offer you?"

"Nothing. Nev approached me and said we got a wish. I need that wish," I confessed.

Cassius shook his head.

"There is no wish." He looked over at me. "These trials are so Thea will break her curse."

Why did this sound familiar? Disappointment coursed through me when I realized my only chance at fixing my shitty life was not real. I stared at him and realized he was possessive of her because he *was* in love with her.

"You do love her."

Cassius sighed heavily. There had been rumors going on with the contestants, but as soon as they started, the Crimson contestants had stopped them.

"Of course I do. She is my wife." He stared at me. "She just doesn't remember; that is why we are doing these trials, so she will break the curse and come home to me."

"But isn't she from Cerithia?"

"Yes, it's a long story." Cassius looked at me with defeat in his eyes. "You have two options. You keep helping your fucking psychotic friend, Nev, and I will skin you both alive. Or you switch sides and help my wife come back to me."

"Why would I do that?"

Cassius looked at me.

"Because you pity me, and I am so tired of doing these trials. I will give you anything you want if you switch sides and help me."

I wasn't sure what to do. Did Nev know that she was his wife? I would have never agreed to help him if I had known that this man was suffering like this. I could feel his desperation—his devastation.

"Or I can kill you right fucking now." His eyes flashed black as I took too long to answer him.

"Nev is not my friend." I smiled and saw a bit of relief flit through his golden eyes. "I will help you if you promise me that I can start over in Crimson. I want a job in the guard and a big piece of property of my choosing."

"That is all you want?" Cassius questioned. His dark brow raised at my odd request.

"No, but it's the only thing you can give me, unless you can bring someone back from the dead and change the fact that the woman I loved destroyed me?"

Cassius stared at me oddly. I could see questions swarming in his eyes, but he wouldn't ask.

"A fresh start in Crimson it is." Cassius looked around us before looking at me. He seemed to hesitate for a long time. "I know a goddess; she's become a friend since Thea's curse. I can ask her to help you if she can."

"I don't know if a goddess would be able to change fate."

"Ardella probably could."

I instantly stilled at her name falling from his mouth. He noticed the shift in my mood. He cocked his head to the side. No one had said her name out loud in front of me in seven years. But I also really fucking hated that this prince of Crimson knew *my* Ardella on such a personal level that he thought she would help him.

I could not stop feelings of jealousy pumping through me. He had seen her. She hid from me, yet she let this guy see her? That really pissed me off. I swallowed down the wrath bubbling up inside of me. Gods, I willed the void to come out and take over so I would not lose my fucking shit, but like the last seven years, he stayed hidden away. Not once had he come out to help me. It was stupid to think, but I truly wondered if he was pissed at me for hating Ardella.

"Are you alright?"

"I don't need help from *her*," I said with so much venom that he immediately narrowed his eyes at my reaction.

"You know her already?"

"Yes, and I don't need anything from her," I hissed.

Cassius threw his hands up and nodded. I sighed heavily as I closed my eyes and ran my hands through my hair, trying to keep myself in fucking control. When I opened them, Cassius was watching me with confusion in his eyes. Could he recognize that we both shared the same misery?

"You lied," he said, confidently. Before I could say anything, he continued. "You said your surname was Winters during check-in, but it is Vale. Isn't it?"

"How—"

He chuckled softly before muttering something toward the sky. His gaze met mine. "I was starting to think Della was wrong all those years ago."

"I don't understand. She told you about me?" I watched him curiously.

He nodded. "Yes. She said you'd come and that you are important."

My chest felt warm at his words. Cassius rubbed a mark I had not noticed on his wrist before—four orange stars in a row on his wrist.

"What is that mark?" I asked.

Cassius looked down before giving me a concerned look.

"I made a star bargain with Della when Thea was cursed." He looked over me oddly. "Della said you and I would become very good friends, so good that we would consider each other family." Cassius seemed to be thinking about something. "She had a message for you when you came to Crimson."

"She did?" I stepped forward.

"That Crimson is your new home. You will be very happy here."

I stared at him. How did she know years ago that I would come here—that I was searching for a new place to call home? My gaze fell to the mark on his wrist, and the void seemed concerned about it.

Ask him what the bargain was for. Gods do not make those unless it is serious. The void almost sounded worried.

"What was the bargain you made?"

Cassius sighed heavily before rubbing the back of his neck. His gaze met mine. "She wouldn't take Thea's soul, and I had to do two things in return. First, I had to give you anything you would need to start over here. And the second one..." His gaze looked away from me. "I had to keep her secrets for her."

What the fuck does that mean? The void was not impressed.

"What does that mean?"

"It means that Della went to great lengths to hide something, even from herself, and when the time is right, I will break the magic binds she put on herself."

Damn it, Storm. What did she do?

"Tell me." I demanded.

He shook his head. "I can't because I do not know what it is. She didn't share. I'm sorry, but that is all I can say."

The void was angry, but he retreated back into the dark depths and disappeared.

"Okay, fine. I don't care. She can stay far away from me."

"Well, you'll end up seeing her if you stay," Cassius warned me.

I could not stop the feeling of excitement that pumped through me, but I stopped it just as quickly as it started.

"Why?"

"She is trying to help as much as she can. I don't know why. I owe her everything for not taking Thea away. But if I am honest, she seems like she is the one that owes me something. It is like she wants to make this right even though it isn't her fault. Maybe because her asshole brother is to blame for my wife being like this."

"Mikel?" I asked. Images of Remiah immediately ran through my mind.

"The one and only asshole." Cassius frowned. "It's not typical for fae to just know gods." It was a question, but one I wasn't sure I knew how to answer.

"No, it's not."

"You don't have to tell me, but Ardella will be around, and you need to be nice to her. She has been through a lot."

I scoffed.

"Did she tell you that?" I asked.

"No. I can see it in her eyes. You will know what I mean when you see her. She is haunted by something, and she is desperate for Thea and me to both survive and live a happy life."

I swallowed down my emotions. She was haunted by what she did to me.

"Fine, I will try my best."

Cassius walked forward and stuck out his hand. I shook it and smiled.

"You are a Crimson Guard from this moment on, and as your prince, I am ordering you to keep your future queen alive."

I smiled as I felt his power pulsing from him.

"We have a deal, Cassius. My only job is to keep your wife alive."

Secrets & Curses Of Gods

Chapter 1
Haden—500 years ago

When I came to Elloryon, I always seemed to surface in Akecia—the only kingdom that had snow. I glanced around, my cloak keeping my face away from the fae in the streets, not that they could see me. I was on a mission today to find the God of Knowledge. Avesh had to have the answers I was looking for, and I could not believe that I hadn't thought of him before. But just as I was about to summon my star mist to leave this place, I stopped. A woman was walking frantically up the pathway.

She seemed to be looking for something in particular. But that wasn't what stopped me. She was a goddess—a fucking beautiful goddess. Her star-colored eyes glanced at me for a moment before she kept going. Her dark hair fell in waves down her back as she weaved through the fae. I abandoned my goal of going to Avesh for the moment.

I had never seen a god or goddess when I came to the realm—maybe that is why I felt compelled to follow her. She walked around the fae, who did not seem to notice her. Just like me, she was invisible. The woman didn't wear a coat in the frigid temperatures, and I wondered how she could stand the cold.

She turned quickly down an alleyway, and I cautiously followed. The alley was not busy, but the buildings were blocking most of the sunlight, so it was gloomy and difficult to see through the blizzard. The goddess seemed to be very determined to get to wherever she was going. Her steps were deliberate and fast-paced before she suddenly stopped.

She turned to the left, and I saw her shoulders slump at whatever she saw. Slowly, she stepped forward, disappearing behind a small stack of wood. I used this opportunity to move closer to her to see what she was doing. When I glanced around the stack of wood, she was kneeling in the snow, holding the hand of a woman who was bleeding from a wound.

"I don't want to die," the woman cried.

"Shhh, you will be alright." The goddess' voice was soft—lovely.

She glanced over her shoulder and stared directly at me, letting me know that she could see me when no one else seemed to be able to. Her head tilted to the side for a moment before focusing back on the woman. I knew she couldn't see anything about me, but would she know I was a God of Hell?

The woman was crying softly as the goddess reached out and rubbed her hand against the side of her face to comfort her. The whole interaction was peaceful and, honestly, made me feel uncomfortable.

"It's time, Fiona; this won't hurt," the goddess whispered.

Fiona was hardly breathing as the goddess lifted her hand, and even though I couldn't see anything, I knew she was helping her transition into death. I watched the woman take one last breath before the goddess stood up and sighed heavily.

She looked at me, but just when I thought she was going to say something, she started running out of the alley. I followed her, jogging to keep up, but she turned a corner and vanished. I couldn't see her anymore and worried that I had lost her as I rushed to where she had disappeared. I stopped in shock when I rounded the corner myself and found a dead-end alley with no way out. I slowly walked on, looking for anywhere she could have gone, but there were no doors or windows to have entered, nothing but brick walls all around. When I got to the end of the alley, she suddenly appeared behind me, gripping my arm and tugging me back before slamming me against the wall of the building by my throat.

"Fuck," I groaned in shock.

I looked down, my eyes widening when the goddess lifted her hand and summoned what looked like a small ball of lightning to it. *Shit.*

"Why are you following me, and how can you see me?" she hissed.

I was caught off guard by how pretty she was. Her eyes were the color of the stars, which may convince me to admire their beauty. Her bronze skin was slightly red, whether from the cold or her anger, I couldn't tell. My gaze traveled over her small nose covered with light freckles before dropping down to her pouty lips. Fucking hell, she was breathtaking.

She moved the lightning closer to my neck, its shape forming instantly to look like a knife.

"I don't know why I can see you, but I was curious where a woman with no coat in negative temperatures was running off to."

"Have you ever thought of minding your own damn business?" she snapped.

Gods below, she was pissy, and it made me smile.

"Did you ever think that I wanted to see where the pretty goddess was going to?" I countered back.

She stilled as her pretty eyes traveled over me, but she couldn't see my face. I lifted my hand and yanked my hood off. It didn't matter if she saw me and recognized who or what I was; I could scrub her mind. I didn't dare take my eyes from her face. I was desperate to see her reaction to me, and she didn't disappoint.

Her eyes widened and her pupils dilated, letting me know that she liked what she saw. Her lips parted, and I barely heard the soft gasp she let out before swallowing hard. I smiled at her, and her cheeks flushed brighter red.

"You like what you see?" I teased.

She scoffed and let me go. "No."

Ouch. I stared at her, and she lowered her hand to her side. "Lying is a sin."

Her eyes met mine, and she smirked. "So is being prideful." She paused for a moment. "I think the stars will forgive me for lying." My smile fell. Gods, she was flirting with me. I don't know why I thought the gods here would be prudes. Her gaze traced over me again like she was trying to burn this moment into her mind. Her eyes burned brightly when she looked into mine.

"So, you *do* like what you see."

She gave me a nonchalant shrug, and I wished she would stop being such a damn tease. I could see it in her eyes that she liked the way I looked, or maybe I was a desperate man. Besides finding my freedom, I did not long for much of anything else. But this goddess made me want to fall to my knees and repent for my sins.

What would she think if she knew who she was talking to right now, and why did I care? My eyes traveled over the glowing silver tattoos on her arms, and I wanted to trace them—either with my fingers or tongue, I didn't care.

"Is this how you always approach women?" She glanced around to see if anyone was able to see us.

"Maybe." I watched her eyes travel over my face again. "Why? Is it working?"

"Maybe," she said with a smirk. She released me slowly before turning and walking away. I quickly followed her, though. Where the hell was she hurrying off to without a damn word? Fuck, I was a glutton for punishment as I eagerly followed her. She glanced over her shoulder to make sure I was behind her. It could be wishful thinking, but I swore she looked pleased that I was behind her.

"Are you not cold?" I asked.

"No, I enjoy the cold."

She was silent as she wove up the street, avoiding running into fae that would not even feel her if she did. I watched her closely, finding her pleasant, and that was probably the first sign that I should stop following her around like a lost dog. But gods be damned, I ignored all reason and continued to follow her. After another few minutes, I finally spoke. I wanted her to talk so I could memorize her pretty voice.

"Where are you going?"

She glanced at me before grinning. Her eyes twinkled with mischievous amusement.

"I was just seeing how long you would follow me for." She stopped and stared at me. "Do you make a habit of stalking others?"

She put her hands on her hips and tilted her head to watch me.

"Let's not pretend that you didn't want me to follow." I stepped toward her, and she didn't back down. Fuck, she smelled like what I would expect heaven to smell like. That scent would forever be ingrained in my memory. "Tell me to leave, and I will."

She paused but didn't tell me to leave. Her eyes stayed on mine, almost like there was a silent challenge in them.

"Tell me your name."

"Haden, what is yours?"

"None of your business." She tried to walk off, but I pulled her back and smiled down at her.

"You playing hard to get is only making me more interested. So, if that is your intention, you are succeeding."

Her face immediately burned red, and her pretty eyes flashed white. Fucking hell, she did like this. What a tease.

"Sorry to break your heart, but I am taken."

Did I hear her correctly? I watched her closely to see if she was full of shit. But she just watched me curiously back.

"By who?" I was irrationally pissed that this stranger had a man already.

"My fated mate." She frowned as her eyes fell to the space between us. "Technically, I haven't met them yet, but I will one day, and they are the only ones we are supposed to want."

Gods get fated mates... Did that mean that me and my siblings did too? Interesting. That would explain why no one ever appealed to me. But she did, so what did that mean?

"Well, maybe you just met him." I smiled. "Since it's clear you like what you see."

Her eyes traveled down the length of me and back up. I swallowed, watching for any hint that she was displeased.

She didn't give me an answer, only raised an eyebrow at me in an adorable way. She held her hands out, as if inviting me to look her body over as well. "Do you like what you see?"

"I think that's pretty obvious, goddess. I am following you around hoping you will talk to me some more."

Her eyes traveled over my face, and she frowned. "You aren't my mate."

I stared at her. How could she be so sure when we had only just met? To me, it felt like my soul... recognized hers. "How do you know?"

"I don't. I'm guessing." She started to leave but turned back to me, as if unsure about something.

"What if you are wrong?" I asked.

She took a deep breath before smiling at me in a way that shot warmth straight through my cold heart. My gaze stayed on her face, and all I could think was that I did not want another man to get this smile from her. This was all for me. I wanted to see this smile every day for the rest of my life. This had to be destiny because I wanted to haul her over my shoulder and drag her to Hell with me so I never had to say goodbye.

"I'm hoping I am."

My chest squeezed at her confidence. Fuck, she was perfect. Gods, this day had quickly become the best in my existence. I stepped forward without thinking. I wanted—no, I needed to be closer to her.

"I'm hoping you are too. How will we know?"

"Fate will tell us."

I glanced around and realized I was running out of time. I really should go talk to Avesh. I ran my hands down my face and stepped toward her again. I did not want to leave her.

"Give me your name."

I lifted my hand, desperate to feel her smooth skin under my fingertips at least once. She didn't move from me, but she hesitated before she spoke, like she might keep it from me.

"I will beg for it if I must," I whispered.

"You would fall to your knees for me and beg for something as simple as my name? Why?"

"So that when I start praying to the stars and heavens, they will know which goddess I am begging for."

I had never prayed a day in my life, and if you would have asked me about it twenty minutes ago, I would have laughed in your face. But then again, perhaps I had never found anything I thought was worthy of a prayer. If praying would help to make her mine, then I would pester the stars all day for her. I would annoy them so much that they had no choice but to either let me keep her or hear me for the rest of their lives.

She raised an eyebrow at my comment and smiled again. "I am Ardella."

The name alone sent a jolt of life coursing through me. My heart and soul buzzed like they had waited our entire existence to hear it. It rose to the surface, like something that had been buried deep within.

"Well, Ardella, maybe the fates will decide that we are supposed to be together." But even as I said it, I knew the stars would never let me have her. She was a heavenly god, and I was a God of Hell. Her eyes stared at me, as if trying to read my thoughts. I knew I couldn't let her remember this day with me, though. At some point in the near future, I would be walking this realm with ill intent, scheming up a plan to break the stars, and I did not need her recognizing me.

But I hesitated because this meeting had been... perfect. I didn't want to become a nobody to her again. Somehow that just seemed wrong. Ardella gave me a bright smile before she slowly reached out and pushed my hair from my forehead. I inhaled sharply at the action, her touch sending a spark of electricity through me. She acted as if this were a normal occurrence between us.

"You look like you're about to bolt," she said coyishly.

"I am supposed to be somewhere, and I am very late." I didn't want to leave, though. She gave me a look like she knew what I was thinking.

"I'm confident that our paths will cross again, Haden, so don't look so disappointed."

"I look forward to it. Maybe by then, fate will catch up to us."

"Let us pray to the heavens above and the hells below that we meet again," she said, but something about the statement made me pause. She knew there were gods of Hell, and she was willing to pray to them for me. Didn't that go against the stars?

"Until the next time, Ardella," I whispered before frowning slightly as I jumped into her mind.

I closed my eyes and started scrubbing away our meeting. But at the last moment, I stopped and opened my eyes. Could I change fate so that she *was* mine? The stars could not keep me from her if we were mates. They would have to let me out of Hell for more than a few hours.

Fuck.

I didn't care if they only let me out for five minutes a day to be with her; I would take any scrap they sent my way when it came to her.

Without giving it much more thought, I scrubbed our conversation, but I left bits and pieces so that she would feel drawn to me if she saw me again. I leaned down and stared into her vacant eyes. Her mind was shut down because I was in it, manipulating her.

I closed my eyes and started thinking of us, projecting images of a fabricated future together. Then I put them deep in her mind, hoping that if we ever crossed paths again, she would see these fake thoughts and feel like we were supposed to be together. I opened my eyes and leaned forward, planting a kiss on her forehead.

"I do not care if fate says you belong to another; they are wrong. You belong to me, Della, and you'll remember that when you see me again. No matter what, I will be who you chose." I gave her a small memory of my face, burying it deeply in her mind.

Even if I must break the threads of fate, I would do it. She was not going to belong to anyone but me. Maybe this was why I belonged in Hell, because I was a selfish man. But the stars should have never let her cross paths with me. I always get what I want, and the only thing I wanted was this flirty goddess in front of me. I hesitated before leaving.

She wouldn't remember me until we saw one another again, but I wondered how long that would be. Hopefully not too long. I traced over her face with my gaze, memorizing it in my mind. Then I pulled my magic from her mind and disappeared.

When I left Ardella, I immediately went to the home of Avesh, the God of Knowledge. The building was too white for my liking, blending in with the cloud that it sat on, hovering over Elloryon. I needed to hide that I was a God of Hell, so I glamoured my face to look more like a regular fae. If anyone had answers about getting my siblings and I out of Hell, it was him.

He was surprised to see me when he opened the door. Avesh was shorter than me by a few feet.

"Can I help you?" His voice was timid.

"I was sent here to look into curses for a king and wondered if you had time to help me."

His dark eyes traced over me, slowly, and I worried that he could see through my glamour. To him, I should appear as a servant with poor clothing and long hair.

"I will never turn down someone wanting to learn." He opened his door, and I walked in. The space was vast, but Avesh quickly walked past me, and I hurried to catch up. We walked up the left side of a split staircase. My gaze swept across the ungodly amount of space in the foyer.

Avesh led me down a hallway that seemed to go on forever. My fucking gods, how long would we be walking for?

"It's quite the workout." Avesh looked at me over his shoulder and smiled.

After a few more minutes we came into a vast room that must have had a million books in it. Books flew past our heads, maps floated around the space, and globes spun around.

"Damn." I sighed as I took in the overwhelming space filled with mahogany shelving and ladders.

"It is incredible," Avesh said, like this was his first time seeing it too. "What kinds of curses did your king wish to learn about?"

I hesitated for a moment, unsure of how to get him to bring up my parents' curse.

"He said he wanted to learn about the oldest curses to exist." I shrugged.

Avesh nodded. "Then we should discuss Malamay and Diath."

Thank fucking gods, that was simpler than I thought. I nodded, nonchalantly, like I wasn't dying of excitement inside.

Avesh held his hand out and muttered something I could not hear before a loud whooshing noise started in one of the lower levels of the library. It only took a few moments before the book landed in his hand. He led me to a cozy sitting area, and I took the chair opposite him.

He flipped open the book, and I stared at the picture of my parents in the book. Disgust filled me about what the heavens and their gods made my father do.

"This curse is the longest-lasting curse in history," he stated.

I sat forward. It was about damn time. I wanted to ask him where he got this book, but I couldn't ask too many questions without being suspicious.

"I heard about this, but I thought it was a rumor," I lied. "Didn't they have a bunch of children that were sent to Hell?"

Avesh smiled like he did every time I asked a question. He was too fucking eager to talk about this, so I knew he would spill something about the curse with hardly any input from me. I wasn't sure how much he was allowed to share about it, but if he knew the answer for how it could be broken, then I would get it. He had to know something; otherwise, I was fucked.

"Seven. The seven cardinal sins, which are now the Gods of Hell."

"So, they are real."

"Of course." He nodded as he looked at the picture of my parents. "Most stories are rooted in truth."

"Why don't they just leave Hell?" Playing dumb was the best way to get him to overshare.

"They can't," he sighed. "When the stars sent them there, they made sure their souls were tied to it, so they cannot leave for long periods of time or sometimes at all. The old gods worried that they would cause havoc after what their mother did—they felt that they couldn't be trusted. But sometimes, I wonder why they are not trying to break their curse."

Praise this little naive heavenly god in front of me.

"Break the curse?" I watched Avesh closely as I asked him about it.

He nodded with a dramatic sigh. "Every curse has a key—a way to break it. Curses are not permanent, and there must always be a solution to end them. Even if the stars, heavens, or gods are the ones to cast it."

"How could they ever break a curse like this, though?"

Avesh smiled, and it made my heart beat faster. He knew how to break it. Behind meeting Ardella, this was becoming the second-best thing to happen to me.

"The answer to the curse must be where the cursed can find it. Call it...universal laws. So, the heavens and old gods gave me the answer, knowing that I would never give it to a God of Hell."

Fuck, I felt bad for him because he was the worst secret keeper I had ever fucking met.

"Smart," I agreed. "So, what do they have to do?"

His gaze met mine, and I saw the suspicion in his eyes. Don't make me force you, prick; just tell me. I leaned back and grabbed one of the pastries his cook brought in. I tried to make myself as unassuming as I could, but I felt like I might explode.

"Why do you want to know?"

"Well, honestly, I came here for the king, but I find this story absolutely intriguing. I always thought the tales we heard growing up were meant to scare us, but now you're saying they are true. I'm curious about what the stars would make them do to break a curse of this magnitude."

Avesh nodded and leaned back. I knew I had him.

"Well, honestly, it wasn't just the stars that decided the punishment; it was the old gods that determined the key to breaking the curse. And they made it practically impossible."

Well, that didn't sound very fucking good. He watched me for a moment before sighing.

"The whole argument was that gods are inherently good, but obviously that was not the case with Diath because she was born from a dead star. Diath argued with the stars that nobody was born a particular way and that anyone could become good or bad, to which they disagreed.

"They believed that gods and goddesses that were born from a normal star would never do what she did. They would never trick their mates into creating life in a forbidden way—like from a dead star. They would never disrupt the balance of the realm for selfish reasons. So that is what her children must do."

Was I stupid because I did not understand what that meant? "Do what?"

"Corrupt a god of good nature."

How the fuck was I supposed to do that?

"Well, how do they do that if they are stuck in Hell?"

"They can leave Hell for a short time, but they must always return before too long. To leave Hell, they can be temporarily reborn as a fae, which gives them one lifetime to complete their try. However, they are mortal in this form and can die. If that happens, they return to Hell, and their turn is done. Then one of the other siblings can try."

"How do they get reborn?"

"Tell the heavens they wish to use their turn."

Simple.

I nodded and ate my pastry; my mind was racing with this news. There was no way in hell I was telling my siblings about this. They had no idea I was here talking to Avesh today. I couldn't believe that there was a way to leave Hell for good.

My mind went to Ardella, and I knew that she could be my ticket out. Dare I ask questions about her?

It would be risky, but I wanted to know everything I could. Was there a way to change the fate of this goddess and make her mine? The idea that she would feel something for another man made me feel sick. I wanted to be what made her happy, and I would do a damn good job at it.

"Can I ask a personal question?"

"Sure." Avesh nodded.

"How do gods know when they meet their mates? I heard the king discussing it, and the whole idea of fated mates is so odd to me."

Avesh looked surprised by my question. I took a bite of my pastry and watched him.

"A bond forms between the two; usually they can see it floating between them."

"How long does that take?"

"Sometimes it is instant, and sometimes it may take a few interactions. No one knows. Gods and goddesses have to wait lifetimes for their mates to come, but the heavens always pick the best mate for us."

I nodded. Well, that was a lie if I did not end up with Ardella. No man would treat her better than I would.

"Do the cursed gods in Hell get mates?"

"No, the heavens did not think that they should be mated to anybody. Maybe that will change if they break their curse, but until then..."

Avesh watched me oddly.

"Do gods bond together?"

"No." Avesh looked at me. "Not since Malamay and Diath."

Well, that answer pissed me off. My eyes burned with my wrath, and I looked down so Avesh couldn't see.

"What goddess is Ardella?"

"You know Ardella?" His tone was suspicious.

"I met her before I came here."

I looked up at him and saw that he was beginning to question my motives for being there.

"The Goddess of Life, the stars' favorite." I raised my eyebrow at him questioningly. "Do you think they would give that title to just anyone after what happened with Malamay? Ardella was created specifically for that title, and she has been exceptional at it."

Hmm, my little crush just happened to be with the woman who took my father's role. What better way to break my curse than to corrupt the stars' favorite goddess?

Della would turn bad, and we would rule together; that would be the only way I could protect her from my siblings. It was the only way I could keep her.

"What king did you say you are doing this for?" Avesh stood up. Shit, he was onto me. I didn't want to waste my energy with another lie, so I smiled at him.

"I didn't say, because I didn't come for a king. But you already pieced that together, didn't you, Avesh?"

He paled as he stared at me. "Who are you?"

I stood, dropping my glamour. "Haden Vale." My eyes flashed red. "God of Wrath."

"I can hurt you without lifting a finger." He glared. But there was fear in his eyes. Avesh was too small to take me on in a physical fight, and I was honestly in no mood to fight him with magic. I stepped toward him, and Avesh let out a shaky breath and backed away. I took pity on him.

"Do you really want to fight, or can we just part ways?" I asked.

His eyes narrowed on me with defiance, but I knew he wouldn't fight me.

"Don't worry, Avesh, I will scrub away the memory of you helping the Gods of Hell escape, since you have been helpful to me today. But I want you to answer one more question."

"Fuck you."

I grinned at his sudden burst of confidence.

"Can a mate bond be changed? Can it be transferred?"

"Why?"

"Because Ardella and I can't be fated, according to you, but I don't like that answer, so how do I change it?"

His eyes widened, and he became a defensive little prick.

"She would never give a God of Hell the time of day," he hissed. "Ardella is too good for you."

I glared at him and took a step forward, but he let out a startled cry and moved backward. It was actually making me extremely uncomfortable to see him crying.

"I didn't say she wasn't. Now tell me."

"Bonds can't be broken or transferred. We get one mate, and that is it. She will never belong to you."

I was instantly pissed off at his snarky-ass comments. My wrath took control as I jumped into his mind and scrubbed away the conversation we just had. In fact, I scrubbed the entire day from him.

Once I was convinced that his memory was scrubbed away of any hints that I came and saw him today, I started to pull out of his mind. I moved Avesh to his chair and manipulated him to go to sleep. Before I could leave, though, a vision suddenly exploded into my mind, causing me to fall to my knees. I closed my eyes as images of Ardella ran rampant through my thoughts.

In the vision, her back was turned toward me, her shoulders rising and falling with angry breaths.

"Storm?" I called out to her. Gods, I felt terrified, but not of her. I felt it for her.

She turned to me, and I lost my ability to breathe when I saw her eyes burning red with wrath. The realm all around her was destroyed. My eyes fell on her forearm. Seven broken stars marked her, one for each of the stars that had made her.

When I looked up at her face, she began crying. Her tears no longer glowed like the stars, as with most gods, but were now as black as the depths of Hell.

She had already fallen from the grace of the stars.

"Della?" I stepped toward her with my hands up.

As soon as she saw my face, she stopped crying. Her head tilted as she studied me with red eyes.

When she began to smile, I stopped moving toward her. My heart squeezed at the sight of her, but there was no recognition in those eyes. Only evil lurked in their depths.

"Storm?"

Her gaze traveled over me.

"You should probably keep your distance from me," she warned, her voice full of nothing but indifference.

I stopped immediately and realized that I was looking at a version of Della that I never wanted to see.

"You won't hurt me," I said to her softly.

"Yes, I will." Her eyes flashed with concern for only a moment before they lost all emotion again. Then she stepped toward me, and everything went black.

ACKNOWLEDGEMENTS

This book would not exist without the support of so many incredible people. To my family—thank you for believing in me, even when I doubted myself. Your encouragement has meant everything.

To my readers, whether you've been with me since the beginning or are just discovering my work—thank you for stepping into this world with me. Your love for stories and the characters within them is what makes this journey worthwhile. I hope to continue to make characters and stories that you will fall in love with.

To my editor, Audrey—your insight, patience, and honesty helped shape this book into something I'm truly proud of. I am endlessly grateful for your time, dedication, and willingness to push me to make this story the best it could be. You always see the beauty in my chaotic words.

To my book cover designer, Nimesh—you take my visions and turn them into reality.

Let's not forget my incredible ARC readers—you all have my heart. Your reviews, support, and love for these stories have meant the world to me. Truly, I wouldn't be writing today without you. You're amazing, and I'm so grateful for each of you!

With gratitude,

Shay Taylor

ALSO BY SHAY TAYLOR

Secrets & Curses Series:

-Secrets & Curses of Exile

-Secrets & Curses of Cerithia

-Secrets & Curses of Crimson

Upcoming Releases:

-Secrets & Curses of Gods

-Fourth Born Series

For updates on upcoming releases, exclusive content, and more, follow Shay Taylor at:

www.authorshaytaylor.com

@shaytaylorauthor on TikTok and Instagram